SONG of the DOVE

SONG of the DOVE

A Novel ~ Kay Murdy

Dedicated to my Auntie Marie,
who first taught me how to see.

SONG OF THE DOVE
A Novel
by Kay Murdy

Edited by L.C. Fiore
Cover art by Mary Southard, CSJ
Inside front cover art by Bigstock
Cover design, interior design and typesetting by Patricia A. Lynch

Copyright © 2013 by Kay Murdy

Published by ACTA Publications, 4848 N. Clark Street, Chicago, IL 60640, (800) 397-2282, www.actapublications.com. All rights reserved. No part of the commentary in this publication may be reproduced or transmitted in any form or by any means, electronic or mechanical, including photocopying and recording, or by any information storage and retrieval system, including the Internet, without permission from the publisher. Permission is hereby given to use short excerpts with proper credit in reviews and marketing copy, church bulletins and handouts, and scholarly papers.

ISBN: 978-0-87946-523-0
Library of Congress Number: 2013955591
Printed in the United States of America by United Graphics, Inc.
Year: 25 24 23 22 21 20 19 18 17 16 15 14 13
Printing: 15 14 13 12 11 10 9 8 7 6 5 4 3 2 First

Contents

Song of the Dove / 1

Map of First-Century Israel / 246

Glossary / 247

A Note from the Author / 255

The Song of the Dove

Get up, my dear friend, fair and beautiful lover—come to me! Look around you. Winter is over; the winter rains are over, gone! Spring flowers are in blossom all over. The whole world's a choir—and singing! Spring warblers are filling the forest with sweet arpeggios. Lilacs are exuberantly purple and perfumed. Come, my shy and modest dove—leave your seclusion, come out in the open. Let me see your face, let me hear your voice. For your voice is soothing and your face is ravishing.

Song of Songs: 2:10-14
(The Message)

1

The hastening twilight made purple gashes in the hillsides of Natzeret, and dark columns of cypress cast their lengthening shadows on the road. Miryam hurried along, hugging the squirming bundle close to her breast. She had taken the sheep to pasture early in the morning, and her mother and father would be worried when she had not returned.

"It is late for a young girl to be out alone," Naftali called from the door of his house, cradling his son in his arms.

"I am not alone. I have my sheep," Miryam nodded to the flock trailing behind her. "Is Yonatan well?" she asked, knowing that the infant had been blind from birth.

"Yonatan is always well." Naftali smiled as children rushed past to get home before dusk. "And you, what have you in your arms?"

Miryam called over her shoulder as she went on her way, "A gift for my mother!"

The setting sun had almost touched the horizon when she saw the golden patch of light in the doorway where her mother stood.

"Eee-maa! I am home at last!"

Hannah came to greet her, looking distressed. "Where have you been? You should have been home long before this."

"Look, Ima." Miryam opened her shawl and revealed a newborn lamb bleating in her arms. "The old ewe dropped him early and the labor was difficult. Its forelimbs were turned back. I tried to help her…."

Hannah gasped. "Miryam, look at your dress. It is covered with blood."

"I am sorry, Ima. There was so much blood. The ewe did not live, and the lamb mourned its mother just like a child." Tears welled up in her soft, brown eyes. "Ima, I did everything you taught me. When the lamb was born I tickled its nose with straw just as you showed me, trying to get it to take a breath."

Hannah slipped her arm around her daughter's slight shoulders. "You did what you could."

Yoachim came outside, hobbling toward them. "Daughter, did you dally on the way? It is long past suppertime. Your mother and I were worried."

"Look, husband, a newborn lamb." Hannah took the creature from Miryam's arms and held it up for him to see. "A good sign, yes? Perhaps better days are coming."

"If it lives to see tomorrow," he said, frowning.

Miryam ignored his dismal forecast. Her father had lost hope when an accident put an end to his prosperous business in Yerushalayim. Unable to pay King Herod's taxes, he lost his land and moved the family to Natzeret.

"Come, come, ladies," she called to the stubborn ewes. Pushing their rumps, she guided them into the sheepfold. When they were safely inside, Hannah helped her pile thorn bushes across the entrance.

Yoachim limped into the house and returned with a basin of water. "The lamb must be bathed before we lose the light." He took it into his gnarled hands, and, squatting with difficulty, he put the small creature into the water. The lamb thrashed about, but soon calmed as Yoachim gently washed away the mucous and blood.

"Watch! When the wool dries, it will spring to life and give him a warm blanket." He rubbed the lamb with a towel, and its dense coat did just as he said. "Look! A pure unblemished lamb. Perfect for the temple sacrifice."

"Abba!" Miryam tried to take the lamb from her father, but Hannah snatched it in her strong hands and dropped it into the enclosure.

"Please, Ima, it is cold," Miryam protested. "The lamb can sleep with me. I will keep it warm."

"The ewes can tend to him," Hannah said, watching as the lamb struggled to stand on its wobbly legs. "Perhaps one of them will give him suckle."

The sheep milled around the orphan, but none of them did. Hannah looked grim. "Miryam, go and take off those filthy clothes."

Miryam went inside to a dark corner of the house. Hidden from view by a single curtain, she slipped off her blood-stained gown and undergarments. At fourteen she was slender and small-breasted, more child than woman. Hannah took the clothes outside, dousing them in the same basin that held the lamb's blood. Miryam shivered as she waited for her mother to bring fresh water.

"There is precious little left," Hannah complained when she returned.

"I will go to the well and fetch more," Miryam offered.

"No daughter, it is too late. You can go in the morning."

Miryam trembled as her mother poured the cold water over her skin. Scrubbing herself clean, she dried with a rough cloth, and slipped a clean garment over her head.

Hannah smiled as she brushed her daughter's long black hair. "Like a flock of goats, moving down the slopes of Gilead," she said with admiration.

Miryam kissed her cheek. She loved the way her mother cared for her.

Hannah went to stir the pot with a long forked stick. "Come eat your dinner. I am afraid it is cold," she grumbled.

The savory smell of the stew made Miryam's mouth water. In her excitement, she had forgotten how hungry she was.

She breathed in the pungent aroma. "Thank you, Ima."

Hannah poured the stew into a bowl and handed her a piece of flat bread. Miryam said a quick prayer, and joined her father on the stone stoop. She crouched on her heels beside him and ate in silence, sopping up the stew with the bread.

"Abba," she said, laying her empty bowl aside, "Tell me about the time you took me to the temple in Yerushalayim when I was a little girl."

"You are still a little girl," he smiled. "And why do you want to hear that old story, eh? You have heard it countless times."

"But I do not remember what happened, and it seems so real when you tell it."

"All right, all right," he sighed. But for a long while he said nothing as he watched the evening star rise in the dark sky.

"Abba?" Miryam asked, looking impatient.

"I was remembering the first time I met your mother—it was at the Golden Gate of the temple. I introduced myself: 'I am Yoachim bar Shmuel, a descendant of the tribe of King David.' And she replied with a proud look, 'And I am a member of the family of Aharon, the brother of the great lawgiver, Moshe!" He chuckled. "It was always that way. Your mother had to have the last word."

He drew in a long breath. "Your mother and I were blessed in many ways, except for one great sorrow. After twenty years of marriage we had no children. Year after year we prayed, but no child came. People said she was childless as punishment for our sins."

Miryam rested her head on her father's shoulder. She could not believe that either of them could sin.

"'Why was I born?' your mother would wail. 'The birds build

nests for their young, yet I have no child of my own. The animals of the earth and the fish of the sea are fruitful, but no fruit comes from my womb.'"

Then a smile lit up his craggy face. "But at long last our prayers were answered. A beautiful little girl was born on the feast of Rosh Hashanah." He pulled Miryam close. "Do you know that the shofar was blown to announce your arrival?"

"Abba, I know that is not true. The shofar is blown to announce the New Year."

"Ah no, my daughter, the shofar told everyone: 'The child's name is Miryam, and she has been blessed from the moment of her birth!'" He scratched his beard. "You know, I often wonder about the meaning of your name. Does it mean 'bitter'—like myrrh?"

"No, no," Miryam objected. "My name means 'strong!' Like the sister of the great prophet Moshe!"

"Who knows?" He patted her face. "Perhaps a new Moshe will find another Miryam at his side to liberate our people."

"Abba, you promised to tell me about the time you took me to the temple."

She leaned against his knee, and he stroked her hair. "Well, when you were born, your mother carried you around so much it seemed your feet never touched the ground. I wanted to bring you to the temple and dedicate you, just as our ancestor Hannah committed her son Shmuel, the prophet. But your mother said that you were too young. We should wait until you were three years old…when you were really grown."

"Abba," she urged, "please tell me more."

"Well, at last the great day arrived. And as we entered the temple, before we could stop you, you ran ahead, right up the fifteen steps to the Court of Yisrael. The kohen looked at you with displeasure. How could a little girl know that she could not enter the men's court? But then the kohen bent down, took you in his arms and kissed you. Can you imagine? The kohen blessed you! A little girl like so many others. And then…and then…."

He paused as though he had forgotten the story. She poked him in the ribs, and he laughed at his little game.

"And then," he raised his hands, "the kohen shouted for all to hear: 'This daughter of Yisrael shall be blessed for all generations. Through her, redemption will come to the sons of Yisrael. The angelic host will nurture her like a dove, feeding her from their own hands!' Then the kohen placed you on the third step of the temple. And you danced and danced, just like Moshe's sister danced when she entered the Promised Land. Everyone watched as you whirled about, and I knew then that all of Yisrael would love you!"

"Abba! Every time you tell that story you add something new. I think you made it all up."

He kissed her brow and smiled. "Well—it is a true story, even if it did not happen that way."

Hannah had been listening from the house. Her thoughts turned to a dream she had when Miryam was born—her tiny child drenched in golden light. In an instant, she was grown. The whole world bowed at her feet calling out, "Mother, Mother." Then her daughter turned into a fierce lioness, protecting a cub lying in her lap. At once the cub became a slaughtered lamb, bloodying its mother's clothing. Hannah often feared what the dream meant, but she never told her daughter. Some other day perhaps, some other time.

Miryam woke with a gnawing ache in the pit of her stomach. She drew up her knees, rocking back and forth. Despite the pain, she sensed that something strange and wonderful was happening inside her. Her breasts had begun to develop, and she knew what would soon follow. When she stood up, a flow of blood confirmed her suspicion.

Hannah was busy preparing the daily bread; she turned to see her wide-eyed daughter staring at her. "Ah, today you are a woman," Hannah said, seeing Miryam's blood-stained tunic.

"Am I unclean now, Ima? The blood…does it make me unclean?"

Her mother drew a long, slow breath. "It is the curse of women. The blood will stop, but while it flows you must not cook or even touch your father's dishes."

Miryam looked downcast. "Am I not to touch Abba?"

"No, my daughter, otherwise he will be unclean too." She looked into her daughter's sad face. "It is the law, and it must be obeyed."

Miryam went behind the curtain and removed her clothing. Hannah slipped a fresh dress over her daughter's head and gave her a cloth to catch the blood.

"Now go and see how the newborn is doing," she said.

Miryam went out to the sheepfold, wondering about the blood she shed and the bloodied lamb she saved. She stopped short, clasping her hands over her mouth, unable to stifle a shriek. The lamb was dead.

Hannah came running. Seeing the lifeless creature, she drew her daughter close.

"Birth and death—that is our lot," Hannah sighed. "You are either a midwife helping a woman give birth, or you are attending someone's death. Life is hard, Miryam. Life is hard!"

2

"You have now reached the age of marriage," Yoachim announced. Most of Miryam's friends had been betrothed at thirteen or fourteen when they reached their third menses. A few were not married until fifteen or sixteen, although by then they had no choice but to be shepherds' wives, often raising their children alone, their husbands gone for long stretches at a time.

"Tomorrow I will go to the marketplace and discuss with the other men who might make a suitable partner for you," he told her.

But Hannah had her own proposal. "Have you considered Yosef, the carpenter?"

Yoachim looked surprised.

"You know him, husband. He is the young man who moved here from Beit Lechem. Everyone speaks well of him. What is more, I have seen our daughter exchanging glances with him in the market."

"Ima," Miryam moaned, embarrassed.

Yoachim stroked his beard. Hannah pressed him. "I have heard that Yosef is an honest worker. They say that if he makes an agreement for a piece of work, you can be sure it will be done properly and on time—his 'yes' means 'yes' and his 'no' means 'no.' He would make a fine husband for our daughter."

Although Miryam knew that she would have no say in the matter, there were times when she observed the handsome young man, tall and angular with a ruddy complexion, his hair black and wavy, his beard forked at the chin. But it was his eyes—deep-set with thick lashes, that attracted her the most.

Before long, Yoachim sent word to Yosef to come to his home, and the next day he arrived. As he entered the house, he nodded to Miryam. She lowered her eyes, wondering if he was aware of what her father's summons meant.

"Is there a piece of furniture you want me to make, or perhaps a stone wall for the sheepfold?" Yosef asked.

Yoachim sat down on a mat on the earthen floor, motioning Yosef to sit beside him. Hannah and Miryam stood by the door.

"I have an important matter to discuss with you," he said, clearing his throat. "I hear that your father lives in Beit Lechem; otherwise, I would have spoken with him first."

"My step-father," Yosef corrected him. "Heli was my mother's second husband, blessed be his memory."

Yoachim nodded and paused for a moment to collect his thoughts. "Yosef, it is said that forty days before a male child is conceived, a voice from heaven announces whose daughter he is going to marry."

Yosef's expression showed that he realized why Yoachim had invited him to his home.

"I am thinking that you would make a good husband for my daughter Miryam," Yoachim blurted out. "It is a match made in heaven."

Hannah cleared her throat, glaring at her husband from the doorway.

"Well, in truth, it was my wife who suggested the match," he added. "She told me that you are a hard-working, honorable man. From the way she talks, I would not be surprised to see lilies sprout from your staff!"

Yosef's face flushed but he said nothing.

Yoachim grew serious. "Tell me about your family."

"I am Yosef ben Yaakov of the House of David," he answered proudly.

"And are you a dreamer like your ancestor Yosef?"

"I am afraid that I am more practical. Still, a man must have his dreams."

"But I have interrupted you. Please, you were saying about your family?"

"My father Yaakov died in my youth, and my mother remarried. When she died, I did not feel I had a home with Heli, but I knew I would always have a home with my older brother, Klofah. And so I moved to Natzeret to work with him in his carpentry shop. My brother's wife is named Miryam—like your daughter," he said, glancing her way. "We call her Miri. She has a son by her first husband Alphaeus. When he died, she married my brother and they had three more sons."

Yoachim smiled. "Your family is very fertile. You can make me grandfather of many children."

"Abba!" Miryam gasped.

There was an awkward silence. Then Yosef continued, "I am a responsible man, skilled in wood and stone work, as was my father and his father before him. I make a modest living but I can support a wife and children."

"So, it is agreed. You will marry my daughter, yes?"

Yosef gazed at Miryam and their eyes held. "Agreed."

"Just think," Yoachim beamed. "My daughter will marry into the House of David. Royal blood, no less."

Yosef shook his head. "I am afraid that in these days it is no great privilege to be a member of the House of David. I am only a humble carpenter."

"Ach! You are a son of David!" Yoachim clapped the young man on the shoulder. "And my grandsons will be sons of David, the most famous family in Yisrael.

Miryam looked down, smiling. Her mother grinned.

The entire neighborhood was soon aware that a betrothal was at hand, and a small crowd gathered at Yoachim's door. A scribe from the village greeted him as he entered the house. "Shalom! Peace and blessings!" Then he set about writing the marriage contract according to the decree of Moshe. The bride price, the compensation for the loss of a daughter's labor, was agreed upon. Yosef and Yoachim signed the document, and Yosef's brother Klofah and Naftali, their neighbor, acted as witnesses.

The scribe studied the young couple. "My children, are you aware that marriage is a sacred duty, a commandment from our Creator to be fruitful and multiply?"

They did not look at one another, but merely nodded.

Yoachim poured a cup of wine and handed it to Yosef, who lifted it and held it out to Miryam. "This cup is a covenant in my blood, which I offer to you. If you will be my wife, I will love you and I will give you my life." Their eyes met and he waited for her to answer.

She received the cup, replying in a whisper, "I belong to my husband, and he is mine."

"Behold, you are made holy according to the Law of Moshe and of Yisrael," the scribe said. Then Yosef gave Miryam a gold coin to seal their betrothal.

"Shalom!" Those gathered shouted expressing their good wishes.

"You are now bound to each other as though married," the scribe told them. "Miryam, you will continue to live with your family until the marriage takes place a year from now. During that time, no physical contact is allowed. Yosef, if for some reason you wish to end the betrothal, all you need do is to write out a bill of divorce dismissing Miryam from the contract. Should you die between the betrothal and the marriage, she will be your widow."

Miryam pondered the dreary future forecasted for her.

Yosef set to work building the bridal chamber in his brother's house. Hannah instructed Miryam on the ways of marriage.

"A woman must leave her father's house and cling to her husband," she told her. "Then the two become one flesh. The wife is to cook, wash, mill the grain, work the wool, nurse the infants, and in all ways look after her husband. In turn, her husband will provide food, clothing, and lodging."

Hannah smiled. "Love between a man and a woman is one of the Lord's most wondrous gifts."

Miryam blushed and Hannah took her hand. "My daughter, it is divine will that a woman should submit to her husband. The same act that brings forth children makes a man happy and keeps a happy home—but all in due time."

Miryam wondered if there would be no warmth or affection in her marriage. She knew her parents had a deep love for one another. Although they did not say it in words, she could see it on their faces when they spoke to each other. Perhaps it would be that way for her and Yosef.

The next morning was balmy as Miryam went to draw water from the well. The last days of winter had been gray and cloudy, but the days were growing longer and warmer. The crocuses were beginning to bloom, and a gentle breeze moved through the yellow-green leaves of the trees. When Miryam arrived at the well, she was delighted to see her new sister-in-law.

"Come and see the progress Yosef has made," Miri said, happily.

They put down their water jars and walked hand in hand to the house at the end of the unpaved street.

Yosef and Klofah's house was as poor as others in Natzeret—two rooms for living, dining, and sleeping. The furnishings were simple: a few small stools, a low table, a storage chest, a loom. A curtain draped the sleeping area by night, the bed used as a couch during the day. A loft supplied extra sleeping space, and a small cave-like room kept provisions fresh. An oil lamp set on a stand provided light, and a simple brazier supplied all the heat needed. The cooking was done in an outdoor oven shared with neighbors.

When Miryam and Miri arrived, the two brothers were laying flat beams from wall to wall across the rooftop. Both men had removed their outer garments. Although Miryam tried to avert her eyes, she could not help seeing Yosef's muscular arms as he swung the hammer, driving the nails into the wood.

Miri waved to Klofah who nodded, mopping his brow with the back of his arm. Yosef stopped and bowed his head to his betrothed.

"Shalom, Miryam."

"Shalom," she answered, adjusting her scarf that had fallen over her shoulders. "It looks like your house is almost finished."

"Our house," Yosef said. He rested his eyes on her so long that she felt the color rising to her cheeks.

Klofah poked Yosef's ribs, and he looked embarrassed. "Miri, where is the water you went to fetch?" Klofah called. "I would like a cool drink."

"I wanted Miryam to see the house, and I forgot my errand," she laughed. "I will come back soon."

Once they were on their way, Miri smiled at Miryam. "Did you see the way Yosef looked at you?"

"Whatever are you talking about?" Miryam asked, flustered.

"Yosef is my brother-in-law, so I do know a thing or two. Klofah tells me that Yosef has great admiration for you."

"Admiration? What does that mean? That says nothing about his feelings." Miryam threw her shawl over her shoulders and strode ahead. Miri caught up with her and twined her arm in hers. They walked in silence until Miryam asked, "How did you know Klofah was the right man for you?"

Miri sighed. "I had two husbands, and I had different feelings for both of them. But I always felt loved. Do you know your feelings for Yosef?"

"Everyone tells me that Yosef has a good reputation—that he is a hard worker— and that you can always rely on him. Everyone says that he will make a good husband."

"But Miryam, do you think you could ever love him?"

"Oh, yes—I mean—no—oh—I do not know. I scarcely know him." She was quiet for a moment, and when she spoke there was sadness in her voice. "My family has arranged the marriage, and there is nothing more to say. No one asked what I want, or what I feel. No one thinks I have an opinion of my own—not even Yosef."

"It is not our way," Miri said. She stopped and asked again. "My dear sister, do you love Yosef? Yes or no?"

3

"Good morning, daughter." Hannah covered a large batch of leavened dough with a moist cloth and set it aside to rise. Then she sat to spin yarn on a hand-held spindle.

Miryam thought it unfair that her mother worked so hard. Men sheared the sheep, but the rest was women's work—carding the wool, spinning the thread, weaving the cloth, and finally sewing garments for the family.

"I will fetch the water, Ima," Miryam said, yawning and picking up the clay jar by the door.

"Remember, daughter," Hannah called after her, "wait for the blessing that comes each day."

Miryam smiled. One of the many things she loved about her mother was the way she always looked for a blessing.

Twice a day, in the cool morning and evening, women and girls paraded down the worn path to the well. Balancing the blue-black jar on her head and steadying it with her hands, Miryam hummed as she walked along. With every step there was incredible beauty. The sky was a wonderful blue with feathery clouds that looked like the fringes on her father's garment. The olive trees were budding with foliage, and the fields were covered with poppies and daisies. The Sea of the Galil sent its warm breezes her way—or could they be from the Great Sea, the Mediterranean far to the west?

Miryam loved Natzeret. She wanted nothing more for herself than this tiny village tucked away on the slope of a hollow basin. Fifty or so one-story, flat-roofed houses, built of limestone from the nearby hills, clustered together along a rough pathway, dusty in summer and muddy in winter.

As she passed the town square where children played, she waved to her father sitting in the shade, discussing the Torah with other men. Farther along, she nodded to the older women whom she knew were gossiping about others—whether true or not.

When she arrived at the well, she realized that she was alone. That was odd. Usually there would be a number of women and girls there. Wrapping the rope around the water jar, she lowered it into the cool depths, tilting the jar to allow the water to fill it. A deep feeling of contentment overcame her, a sense that life was good and that she was blessed. A soft breeze stirred the branches of the trees. She breathed in the heady scent of roses wafting through the air. Paradise itself could not be more fragrant.

She became aware of a presence, a sense that the Shechinah, the divine glory, had enfolded her. The hairs on her neck bristled. Looking around, everything had a dream-like quality about it. The earth seemed to shimmer with the brilliance of a rainbow; scrubby plants glowed like emeralds, their leaves like turquoise, and the thorn-bushes wore bright halos of burnished gold.

"Shalom, Miryam, O grace-filled one!"

She let go of the rope. The water jar dropped into the well with a loud splash. She turned to see someone standing nearby, covered head to toe in a hooded linen garment, a golden sash across the breast. Shading her eyes from the bright light that emanated from the stranger, she tried to determine if it was a man or a woman. Whoever it was, it was like no one she had ever seen.

"Shalom, O grace-filled one," she was greeted again. "The Lord is with you."

Before she could speak, the stranger vanished and she was alone once more. Shaken, she returned home at a quick pace. She was flushed with confusion as she entered the house. Should she tell her mother what happened? Perhaps she only imagined it.

"Miryam, where is the water?" Hannah asked, surprised.

"Oh, Ima, I lost hold of the rope and the jar fell into the well."

"My dear daughter, I suppose you have too much on your mind with your coming wedding." She stood and stretched. "Not to worry; I will fetch the water. My old bones have grown stiff from sitting and spinning."

Before she could protest, her mother went out the door. Miryam sat down and taking up the spindle with trembling hands, continued to spin the yarn. Her mind raced as fast as her hands moved.

How did the stranger know my name? What does it mean that I am full of grace—that the Lord is with me? When the great leaders of the past were summoned to a task, they were promised that the Most High would be with them. Is something important being asked of me?

The room seemed to take on a luminous glow, as though someone had brought the sun into the room. Miryam dropped the spindle. The blinding radiance made her shade her eyes once more. Her visitor had returned—the face like lightning, the garments white as snow.

"Shalom! Peace and blessing."

"What is your name?" she asked, trembling.

The answer sounded like a thunderous roar. "I am Gavriel, one of seven angels who stand before the Heavenly Court."

Gavriel? Miryam knew that name. It was the angel who appeared to the prophet Daniyel with visions of the Mashiach, the anointed one. Could it be? She shook her head, trying to dismiss the foolish thought.

"Fear not, Miryam." The angel's voice was clear and strong. "You have found favor with the Lord."

Favored by the Lord? How could I be compared to my ancestors—Noach, Avraham, or even Moshe?

"Who am I to find favor with the Lord?" she asked, amazed at her boldness.

"You will conceive in your womb and bear a son, and you will name him Yeshua, and his name will be great."

Conceive a son? When? After Yosef and I are married? What does it mean that his name will be great? Will he be a rabbi? A priest? A prophet? Surely not a king!

The angel seemed to read her mind, "The Most High will give him the throne of his ancestor David. He will rule over the house of Yaakov, and his kingdom will have no end."

The throne of David? Yosef is of the tribe of David, but there is no throne, no king or kingdom.

"How can this be?" She drew in a breath. "I am a virgin."

"The power of *Ruach Ha Kodesh*, the Holy Spirit, will come upon you, and the child you conceive will be the 'Son of Elohim.'"

Son of the Most High? Not Yosef's child? Impossible! A sign! I must ask for a sign that these words are true.

"I will give you a sign," the angel declared. "Elisheva, your kinswoman, has conceived and is now in her sixth month. For nothing is impossible with the Lord."

Miryam's hands flew to her mouth. Elisheva? Pregnant? She was old and barren. If Elisheva was with child, that would be a remarkable sign. She would have to see this for herself.

The angel stood in silence, as though waiting for an answer to an unasked question.

She shut her eyes, trying to block out the apparition. It was too much to believe…yet…what if it was true? What if she was chosen to be the mother of the Mashiach? Could she stand in the way of the divine plan?

Miryam stretched out her hands as if grasping for an answer. Say yes; say no. Struggling to believe the astounding message, she repeated the angel's words: "Nothing is impossible with the Lord."

Like dewfall from the sky, extraordinary grace filled her soul, and she spoke with fervor. "I am the servant of the Lord. Let it be done to me as you have said."

She held her breath, waiting for the messenger's next words. None came. When she had the courage to open her eyes, she discovered that the angel had left her.

It was the secret night of the divine visitation. Miryam was glad to leave the heat of the house and breathe the cool night air. Climbing the staircase to the rooftop, she was surprised to see that a dove had built her nest in the eaves. The bird was so close she could reach out and touch it, but she did not want to frighten it.

"Mother bird, where is your husband?" she asked, knowing that doves mated for life. "You need not fear me. Your little ones are safe in their warm nest. I will not harm them."

The dove cocked its head to one side, seemingly unafraid. Miryam sank to the ground, drew up her knees, and hugged them. The moon made a shimmering hole through the clouds, casting its pale light. The night air was turning cold and she hunched her shoulders to keep warm. There was a rustle of the wind in the trees, almost as if the leaves were clapping their hands in delight.

Miryam pondered the mystery. *Kings and prophets longed to hear what I heard. My people have waited for the Mashiach for hundreds of years. Am I any different from other women who dreamed of being the mother of the anointed one? Surely the Lord does not love me more than them!*

She placed her hands on her womb, overwhelmed with a sense of the Spirit hovering over her like it did at the first moment of creation.

The angel said that I am blessed among all women? If the promise is true, I am blest indeed.

She gazed heavenward. The clouds had scattered, and there were more stars than she could possibly count.

Do I have the faith of Avraham who went where the Lord led him? Will the Lord lead me, too?

Fear stabbed her heart. How could she tell her mother and father? What would she say to Yosef? Unmarried, pregnant women often suffered horrible deaths.

"I must keep this to myself." She buried her head in her arms and prayed, "Adonai, Lord, if I am to be the mother of the Mashiach, if this be your will, then let it be. You have promised the one thing I need most. You will be with me. Help me to trust your promise. Help me to rest this night as a babe in your arms."

There was no bright light or hint of comfort. There was nothing but the woeful song of the dove.

4

Miryam awoke to the sound of voices in the courtyard below. Sitting up, she pressed her fingers against her eyelids, trying to shut out her worrisome thoughts. Perhaps it was only a dream. Leaning forward, she looked over the parapet, surprised to see a tall, well-dressed man talking to her mother and father. He wore a wide-sleeved, crimson-colored cloak edged with an ornate hem of blue fringe. A girdle, embroidered with gold, wound around his slim waist; a multicolored turban circled his head. His sandals were of fine leather.

"Could it be my angel?" she wondered, creeping down the stairs.

"Look Miryam, your uncle has brought us these beautiful pomegranates." Hannah held up the bright red fruit. "And he has also brought us some wonderful news."

"Ah, my daughter, do you remember your uncle?" The distinguished man took Miryam's small hands in his.

She looked at him shyly and shook her head.

"Of course you do not. You were a little girl when I saw you last. And here you are a grown woman."

"Miryam, this is my brother, Yosef from Ramatayim," Hannah

said with unconcealed pride. "Your uncle is the Minister of Tin Mines, and he has traveled all over the world—to the farthest corners of the Roman Empire."

"The Island of the Britons," he explained. "When you were a child I took you and your mother on one of my travels to see your aunt in Ain Karem. Do you remember?"

She shook her head again.

"No matter. I bring pomegranates as a blessing from Adonai, the Lord." He broke the fruit and offered Yoachim a bite. "Taste and see, brother; it is a sign of fertility."

He handed a piece to Miryam, smiling. "It will make you fruitful!"

Miryam blushed and ran her hands over her belly. Surely he could not know her secret.

"Daughter," Hannah cried, clasping her hands with joy. "A miracle has happened! After all these years, my eldest sister Elisheva is pregnant and is now in her sixth month!"

The sign! Could it be true?

"My aunt will need assistance, Ima. I must go to her immediately," Miryam said, making a great effort to remain calm.

"You are a good daughter, but the village of Ain Karem is a long way off," her mother said.

"Almost eighty miles," Yoachim added."

"I can walk. I am strong. I am not afraid."

"No, child. It is impossible for a woman to travel alone." Her father shook his head. "It would be dangerous. There are bandits on the highway. They could attack you, rob you, or worse...."

"But, Abba—" She put her hands on her hips, her chin jutting out in protest. Hannah put her finger to Miryam's lips. "Daughter, there are other women who can help your aunt."

"If you permit me to help, your problem will be settled," Yosef stepped forward. "If Yoachim agrees, Miryam can go with me. I am traveling to Yerushalayim on business, and it is only a short distance from there to our sister's house."

Yoachim frowned. "My daughter cannot travel alone with a man—even an uncle."

"And I would not think of such a thing," he said. "I have a caravan of workers and their wives. She will be perfectly safe with the women to look after her."

"Then I will give my permission for Miryam to travel with you," Yoachim answered, with some reluctance.

"Nothing is impossible with the Lord," Miryam said, smiling.

The wagon was so loaded with baggage and tin goods that there was barely enough room for Miryam. She bid her father and her betrothed a hasty farewell as her uncle helped her into the wagon.

"Come home soon," Yosef said, unhappily.

"I will," was all she could say as she turned and looked ahead.

The wheels creaked and the wagon started down the road to meet up with the caravan. They were on their way. If they paced their trip, they would see Ain Karem at sundown of the fifth day. It was longer than Miryam expected, but being that far from home would give her refuge from a difficult situation. Perhaps she could confide in her aunt. After all, she had experienced a miracle, too.

As they descended from the hills of Galil, Miryam's uncle pointed out Mount Tabor to the east rising over the lush Valley of Yizreel. Carpets of wildflowers dotted the landscape, rich with green forests and fresh water to drink. In the rainy winter months there were occasional flash floods, but the rains ended in late spring. Now there were only trickling streams, which they crossed without difficulty.

The Galil was a land of extraordinary fertility. The grape vine, fig, olive, almond, pomegranate, and citron put down their roots, making it the garden of Yisrael. Miryam remembered her father saying, "It is easier to grow an orchard of olive trees in the Galil than to bring up one child in Yehudah."

The lush countryside soon gave way to a sandy expanse of hills, deep ravines, and dusty riverbeds where a few scrub oaks and acacia trees grew. The land turned gold under the setting sun, and they stopped near the Yarden River where the men unloaded the baggage, watered and tethered the mules.

"There," Miryam's uncle pointed to a grassy place. "That is where we will spend the night."

"Uncle, are there no inns?" Miryam asked, seeing the women setting up the tents.

"The Roman inns have a bad reputation. The wine flows like water, and there are other evils that I will not mention. I will not expose you to such places."

Bundled in a coarse blanket, she lay shivering on the cold tent floor. Curled on her side, she listened to a chorus of crickets joining the sounds of nocturnal animals foraging for food. Through the tent flap, she could see a crescent moon rising in the evening sky. She gazed at its reflection trembling in the river. Was the moon cold and frightened like her? She pulled the blanket over her head, wondering what the days ahead would bring.

At the first hint of dawn, the caravan moved on. The constant bouncing of the wagon jolted Miryam's back and made her stomach feel sick. The road grew treacherous with tangles of branches and stumps of fallen trees. At one point, debris from a recent landslide made it nearly impossible to pass. She held her breath as they crossed a flimsy bridge above a swollen brook at the ford of the Yabok River.

"This is where the patriarch Yaakov wrestled the angel," Miryam's uncle told her. "His name was changed to Yisrael, the father of a people whose struggle will be without end."

Miryam understood: her struggle was just beginning.

The midday sun became pleasantly warm, and they stopped to eat a light meal and let the animals graze nearby. Then they set out again, journeying southwest of the Holy City to Ain Karem. The terrain rose, gentle at first and then steep.

Ain Karem, the 'House of the Vineyard,' was nestled on the slopes of a terraced hillside dotted with slender cypresses and clumps of purple anemones. Elisheva's husband Zecharya sold the sweet wine of his grapes in Yerushalayim.

Miryam's uncle left the rest of the caravan by the side of the road. Then he put Miryam and her bags on the back of his mule and led it up the narrow dirt road leading to the village. Nearing the top of the hill, they stopped for a view of the surrounding hills, which were turning green with the spring rains. The cool breezes brought welcome relief from the desert heat. Ahead were rows of golden-colored houses with graceful archways covered by trails of bougainvillea.

"Where does my aunt live?" she asked, leaning forward on the mule.

"There, the house closest to the spring," he answered.

Miryam shielded her eyes and looked toward a group of women, wondering if the angel's message was just a pious dream. Then she caught sight of her aunt. The full curve of her body assured her that it was true.

"Shalom, Elisheva!" Miryam called out, waving her arms.

"Go on ahead," Yosef told her, helping her down. "I will come as soon as I tether this beast."

With her skirts flying and her mantle billowing, Miryam flew up the grassy hillock, only slowing to dodge the scattered stones and ruts. Her cheeks were flushed when she reached the hilltop. Catching her breath, she called again, "Shalom, Elisheva!"

At the sound of Miryam's voice, a sudden gust surrounded Elisheva, like the breath of the Spirit. "Miryam," she cried. "Blessed are you among women. And blessed is the fruit of your womb!"

Miryam's knees grew weak. How could she know her secret?

Elisheva placed her niece's hands on her rounded belly. "And how has it happened that the mother of my Lord comes to me? For as soon as I heard your voice, the child leaped in my womb for joy."

"He is dancing!" Miryam laughed as the baby gave a sharp thrust.

"Just like King David when he brought the Ark into Yerushalayim," Elisheva said, laughing, too.

Miryam could not contain her delight. Her voice rose in a lilting song of praise. It was the song of once barren mother of the great prophet Shmuel. It was the song of David singing to his flock, praising the Most High. It was the sweet song of the dove in Natzeret.

"My soul gives thanks to the Lord, and my spirit rejoices in my Savior who has looked with favor on his lowly servant. Surely all generations will call me blessed, for the Mighty One has done great things for me, and holy is his name!"

"Dear niece, I think that you came out of the womb singing, and you continue to sing even now," Elisheva laughed with delight.

"I love to sing," Miryam smiled, shyly.

"As long as the song lasts, sing," Elisheva said.

"Shalom, sister." Miryam's uncle was coming up the walk carrying her bags.

"Dearest brother." Elisheva kissed him on the cheek. "Thank you for bringing our niece in my time of need. Come, you must be thirsty after such a long journey."

Elisheva's husband Zecharya shuffled to the door as the two women walked arm and arm up the pathway. His face was rutted by wrinkles, giving him a sad look. But upon seeing Miryam, his face brightened. He reached out both hands to greet her, but did not speak. She looked to her aunt, but she said nothing as she led the way into the house.

Elisheva poured cool water from a jug and handed a cup to Miryam and to her brother. Then she placed dishes on a mat on the floor, laying out bread, cheese, dried figs, spiced olives, cucumbers, and grapes. Zecharya helped his heavily-laden wife sit on a cushion.

"It is hard for an old tree to bend," she joked as Miryam sat beside her.

The two men sat cross-legged and they all ate from the common dish. Whenever Zecharya wanted to join the conversation he wrote on a tablet. Then he poured two cups of wine and motioned for Yosef to follow him to the courtyard where he could hear the news of his brother-in-law's journeys.

Elisheva looked at Miryam and laughed. "Whoever would have thought that a woman could conceive a child this late in life—like Sarah!"

"Like my mother," Miryam added.

"Ah yes, I am a good ten years older than Hannah, but nothing is impossible with the Lord."

Miryam started at hearing the angel's very words again.

"When you were a little girl, your mother and father came to visit when they went on pilgrimage to Yerushalayim. Do you remember?"

"Only what my father has told me. It seemed a blessed time."

Elisheva's smile widened. "Dear niece, you were blessed from the moment of your birth." She pulled her closer. "Now I will tell you how my husband lost his voice. It is an amazing tale."

Miryam could not imagine anything more remarkable than her own story.

Elisheva face grew wistful in remembrance. "Everyone thought we were the happiest of couples, but as the years passed we had no child."

Miryam nodded. Her parents had told her how sad they were when they were childless.

"There was a greater problem," Elisheva continued. "We had no son. I cannot tell you how we wept and prayed that our reproach would be taken away. My husband's name means 'Adonai has remembered,' but as we grew gray we thought the Lord had forgotten. Then one day Zecharya was chosen by lot to serve at the altar of incense in the temple."

"What does that mean? To be chosen by lot?" Miryam asked, helping her aunt to stand.

"Many of the duties in the temple are settled that way." She pressed her hands into the small of her back, grimacing. "There are numerous kohanim in Yisrael, and all the priests serve at the Great Feasts. But only one is chosen to burn incense for the morning and evening sacrifice. Their names are written on stones, then put in a jar and shaken until one falls out. The stone that bears the kohen's name is elected."

Elisheva leaned against the wall, working out the crick in her back. She went on. "While offering the evening incense, Zecharya begged the Most High to give us a child. And then a wondrous thing happened.... An angel appeared and told Zecharya that I would bear a son."

"What was the angel's name?" Miryam asked in anticipation.

"The angel's name was Gavriel."

"Gavriel!" Miryam clasped her hands to her breast. "That is the angel who appeared to me!"

Elisheva stared in astonishment. "Tell me what happened, dear child."

"The angel first appeared when I was fetching water at the well, and soon after, in our home. I was terrified, but the angel told me not to be afraid. Elohim, the Most High, had chosen me to bear a son who would save our people from their sins."

"And how could that be?"

"Dear Aunt, the power of the Holy Spirit overshadowed me. My child is to be called the 'Son of the Most High!'"

"Blessed be *HaShem*, the Holy Name." Elisheva lifted her hands in praise. After a moment of thanksgiving, she went on with her story. "The men were waiting for my husband to come out of the sanctuary and bless them. But when he did not come, they wondered who would go into the Holy Place to bring him out. When at last Zecharya appeared, he tried to signal that he had seen a vision, but no one understood him. The angel told him that he would be unable to speak until the day of fulfillment."

"Was Zecharya being punished?"

"No child, it was not punishment. It was a sign."

"A sign?"

"Yes, a sign that the promise would come true." She patted her belly. "And I know that when our son is born my husband will speak again."

Yosef and Zecharya came back inside the house. "I must be on my way, sister." I will come for Miryam on my return trip."

"No, uncle," Miryam said, firmly. "I will be staying for some time. I will find another way home."

"You are my sister's child, and I could not rest if I did not see you safely home," he said. "After I sell my goods in Yerushalayim, I will travel north to replenish my stock. I will return in three months. Does that suit you?"

She stood on tiptoes and kissed him on the cheek. "Thank you, dear uncle. The Lord will repay you for your kindness."

As the time for Elisheva's confinement grew near, she taught Miryam how to prepare for her own son's birth—what to eat, how to recline in bed, and how to pick up something from the floor.

On a cool afternoon, the two women sat on their knees at the millstone, grinding grain. "Tell me, dear aunt, will you name your son for his father?" Miryam asked, throwing a handful of grain into the mill.

Elisheva grew quiet as she rotated the upper stone about a wooden pivot fixed in the center of the lower stone. The pure white flour was caught on a sheepskin placed under the mill. "The angel told Zecharya to name our son Yochanan, 'Adonai's gracious gift.' He will be filled with the Spirit and he will prepare the people for the coming of the Mashiach."

"For the coming of my son," Miryam said as she rested her head on her aunt's shoulder. Elisheva put her arm about her. "It feels like my mother is holding me," Miryam sighed. "I miss her so."

When all the flour was ground, Elisheva poured it into a bin and carried it into the house. Miryam dusted the white powder from her hands and gown, and then went to sit beside the spring. The soft murmuring of the stream joined with the bird's song. She watched a dragonfly emerge from its gray tomb-like sheath. It opened and closed its delicate wings to dry them, and then flew skyward. At that moment, she felt the first flutter of life inside her.

Miryam leaned over the edge of the wagon, bouncing on the rough roads, flinging her from side to side making her nauseous. She breathed deeply, trying to settle her stomach. But it was the growing concern about her child that troubled her most. What would happen when she told her mother she was pregnant? What would her father say—or Yosef? How would he ever understand? She closed her eyes and tried to sleep.

"Miryam, you are home!" A familiar voice startled her awake. Yosef was grinning at her. "My little bird has flown home," he said, taking her hand and helping her down from the wagon. His smile faded when he saw her blanched appearance. "Miryam, are you ill? Was the trip too difficult for you?"

"No—I am well," she stammered, unable to look at him

Miryam's uncle came around and unloaded the baggage. "She was sick on the journey home. It seemed too much for her."

She drew her mantle about her swollen belly, wondering if he suspected anything.

"I will give my regards to your parents before I leave," her uncle said, kissing her on the forehead. "I have a long journey ahead of me to Tiberius. The hot springs there will help ease my aching bones."

"Thank you for your kindness," she said as Yosef took the parcels and bid him farewell.

"You should not have gone," he told her when her uncle had left.

"I am just weary, Yosef. I have much to tell you."

"What is troubling you?" he asked, taking hold of her arm.

"Please, Yosef." She pulled away, hating that she was unable to say more. "Come back tonight after I have rested. We will talk then."

"Yes, of course," he said, looking glum. "I will return this evening."

With a heavy heart, she watched him walk away. This was to be a happy reunion, and now she had spurned her betrothed.

Hannah was eager to hear the news when Miryam entered the house. "Did it go well with my sister and her child?"

"She had a fine son. They named him Yochanan."

"Yochanan? No one in the family has ever bore that name. Why was he not named for the father?"

"That is what Zecharya wished to call him," was all Miryam said.

Hannah started to ask more but her daughter shook her head. "Ima, may I rest a while? The journey was long and difficult. I will tell you everything when Yosef comes this evening."

When Yosef returned that night, there was an uneasy silence, as they waited for Miryam to speak. Miryam stood in their midst, wringing her hands.

"What is it, child?" her mother finally asked. "Is there something wrong with Elisheva, or with her child?"

Miryam's heart pounded as though it would leap out of her chest. There was nothing to do but to say it. "I am with child."

Yosef looked at her, dazed, unable to speak.

Her father exploded. "You are with child? Who has done this to you? What is the name of the father?"

Miryam was silent.

"If a man attacked you, you are not at fault," Yoachim said, clenching his fists. "But he must be stoned to death for disgracing a virgin of Yisrael."

Yosef slumped to the floor, holding his head in his hands.

Miryam said nothing.

Her father's face was grim, his voice menacing. "Was it your uncle? I knew that I should not have allowed you to go with him!"

"Husband!" Hannah gasped. "How can you accuse my brother of such a thing? He is an honorable man."

"No one is at fault, Abba," Miryam interrupted, her voice dropping to a whisper. "I have conceived the child by the Holy Spirit."

"What did you say?" Her father's eyes flashed.

"I conceived by the Holy Spirit," she said, a bit louder.

"Do not add blasphemy to your sin," her father shouted, and raised his hand as if to strike her.

Hannah took hold of his arm. "My daughter, how can you say this?"

Miryam looked at her with dark, mournful eyes. "An angel told me."

"An angel?" Hannah asked in a hushed voice.

"An angel!" Yoachim said in disgust. "What angel ever appeared to people like us?"

"Always to people like us," Hannah reminded him.

Yoachim scoffed. "Yes, in Yerushalayim, but whoever heard of angels in Natzeret? Why do you make up such a story? To cover your shame?"

Yoachim paced the floor. "Do you know the penalty for adultery?"

"Yes, Abba, I know the penalty." She could scarcely say the words. "Death by stoning."

Yoachim waved his hand as though finished with the matter. Miryam wondered if Yosef was also through with her. In the long, black silence that followed, she could see the pain growing inside of him.

"You are with child?" He looked up at her in bewilderment.

She heard the tremor in his voice and saw the anguish in his eyes.

"I believed that you were a faithful woman." He rose to his feet with a stony stare. "You have brought shame to this house.... You have shamed me."

"Yosef, please hear what I am saying. I have been with no man. The child is the Son of the Most High," she pleaded, taking a step toward him.

But Yosef held up his hand to stop her and left the house.

Yoachim and Hannah were standing outside the house the next morning when Yosef came up the road. He looked like a man with an urgent message to deliver. Before he reached the house, Yoachim stopped him. "Please, Yosef, do not expose our daughter to a shameful death."

His voice was gentle as he greeted them. "Please, may I come in and speak with your Miryam?"

They did not meet his eyes, but merely nodded, and let him enter ahead of them. "Miryam," Yoachim called to her, and she emerged from behind the curtain in the corner of the room. Her eyes were red and swollen. She looked a frightened bird caught in a net.

Yosef stood for a while looking at her. Outside, they could hear women talking as they passed by, and children playing in the street. But inside, there was only silence.

"Miryam, this angel of yours," he said at last. "This angel of ours.... I had a dream last night. An angel appeared to me and told me not to be afraid to take you into my home."

She looked at him wide-eyed, scarcely believing his words.

"The angel said that the Most High is the father of your child.... He shall be called Emmanuel."

"Emmanuel!" Miryam's hands flew to her mouth. "That is what the angel said: "God is with us."

Yosef took her hands in his. "Miryam, I do not understand how, or what the Lord is asking of me…asking of us. I am a simple man, Miryam, but if you will still have me, I will be a father to your son."

"His name shall be Yeshua," she said, smiling through her tears.

6

It was her wedding day. Although there would be no respite from work, Miryam was glad to have her mind occupied. The festivities would last a full week. Food had to be prepared—platters of stuffed grape leaves, seasoned olives, dates, almonds, raisins, and pomegranates. Bread must be baked, a lamb roasted, wine purchased.

In the late afternoon, she bathed so as to enter marriage in a state of purity. Her mother combed her hair and plaited it in braids on top of her head. When she was married she would never again appear in public with hair unbound. She put on the wedding dress her mother had made, a gown of blue—the color of the heavens.

"I think the Creator dressed Chavah in such a dress when she was joined with Adam," Hannah said, smiling.

Miryam wore ten silver coins on her forehead, and silver bracelets about her wrists and ankles. Her parents had saved these for her wedding, and they could not be taken from her, even as payment for a debt.

Miryam went to the doorway to watch for the bridal party. It was growing late, and there was still no sign of them. Preparing her dowry had kept her busy, but now her heart longed for that moment when he would arrive.

"Will Yosef come? Has he changed his mind?" she asked.

Hannah put her arms around Miryam's thickening waist. "Take courage my daughter. Yosef will come. He is an honorable man, true to his word." She held her mother's hands against her belly, grateful for her trust and love.

Soon, the sound of laughter and singing was heard. The light from torches bobbed up and down in the dark night, casting long shadows on the street. The groom was coming to meet his bride and her maids. Miri laughed when she caught sight of her sister-in-law's ashen face. "Today is your wedding day! It is not so terrible." She placed a garland of fresh herbs on Miryam's head. "This will ward off evil spirits." Then, taking her oil lamp, Miri grasped her by the hand and pulled her along. "Come, let us rejoice and be glad!"

Clad in their finery, the bridesmaids danced along the road and went out to meet the groom. Miryam managed a wan smile and joined the procession with her parents.

Yosef's brother Klofah went before his brother, and when he caught sight of the bride, he gave a glad cry, "Behold! The bridegroom is coming!"

Miryam's face flushed pink. She had not seen Yosef for seven days, and even in the dim torchlight she could see how handsome he looked. He was splendidly attired in a fine woolen robe with a linen headdress, his olive skin glowing with oil.

Neighbors joined the wedding party along the way, their children skipping ahead of them, shouting happily. When they reached Yosef's house, the bride and groom were seated on cushions under a canopy, a symbol of the new home they were creating together.

"Just like a king and queen," Hannah said as she gazed at the young couple.

Yosef placed a veil over his bride's face to show his intention to clothe and protect her. Then she stood and walked around him seven times, the sacred number of the days of creation.

"A good wife is far more precious than jewels," Yoachim said, looking with pride at his daughter. Then he turned to Yosef. "She is an unfailing prize. She does him good, and not evil, all the days of her life."

Miryam could see tears forming in her father's eyes. He blinked to wash them away. Then he blessed the wine. The couple drank from a common cup, the first of seven that bound them together.

"How beautiful is your love, my sister, my bride, how much more delightful is your love than wine," Yosef said, quoting the Song of Songs.

Yoachim took their hands in his. "When husband and wife are worthy, the glory of the Lord is with them."

Yosef placed a gold ring on Miryam's finger, declaring, "You are sanctified unto me with this ring according to the Law of Moshe and Yisrael."

The rabbi read the marriage contract, reciting seven blessings, beginning with praise of the Master of Creation and ending with the hope that they would rejoice like Adam and Chavah in the Garden of Eden.

Yoachim could no longer control the tears. "Yosef, this is my daughter Miryam. Take her with my blessing." Hannah handed him a pomegranate and he broke it, squeezing the ripe fruit so that the seeds poured forth in hope of a fruitful union. "May you be blessed like Avraham and Sarah with as many children as there are stars in the heavens."

Yosef took Miryam's hand. "Come into my home, my beloved among women. Blessed be HaShem forever."

"I am your servant," she answered in a soft voice. Her eyes were bright; her heart was calm. "Take me under your wing, for you are my kinsman."

Klofah signaled for the festivities to begin. The women rushed back and forth to their houses, bringing food and drink to be enjoyed by all. Joyous shouts went up and the men locked arms, stepping from side to side to the beat of drums and tambourines. They formed a circle around Yosef, and as they danced, the women clapped and sang.

While the guests continued the celebration, Yosef took his wife to their bridal chamber. Yoachim looked the other way as Yosef closed the door. Klofah stood guard, waiting for the signal that the marriage had been consummated.

In the dark entryway Yosef lifted his bride's veil and looked at her with a steady gaze. Holding her close, he kissed her forehead and cheek. Miryam pulled away.

"Have no fear, my sister, my bride," Yosef said, his voice soft. "I vow that I will not sleep with you now. Not ever. You are consecrated to the Lord. I will honor that."

He kissed her forehead once more and released her.

7

"Shalom!" Klofah greeted Yosef as he entered the workshop, clapping him on the back, making his awl go awry.

"Be careful, brother!" Yosef sucked the small wound on his hand and scowled. "Wood is scarce. We cannot afford to ruin a good piece of lumber."

Klofah seemed surprised. "Is this any way to greet your brother after a long absence?"

"I am sorry." Yosef wiped the sweat from his brow with the back of his hand. "How was it in Yerushalayim?"

"King Herod continues to enlarge the temple, and more carpenters and stonemasons are needed. You might consider going there, too."

"I hear that even the birds are in his pay." Yosef remarked with scorn.

Klofah smiled. "I have more news from Yerushalayim. An imperial decree has been issued by Quirinius, the governor of Syria."

"And what has that to do with you and me? Governors are always making pronouncements that have nothing to do with people in the Galil."

Yosef went back to work, pushing the plane against the rough plank as curls of wood fell to the ground.

"This has a great deal to do with us," Klofah said. "The governor demands all citizens to return to their place of birth for registration. Since we are of the House of David, I have already registered in Beit Lechem."

Yosef spat on the ground. "Taxation! That is what this decree is about…and finding men who are eligible for military service."

Klofah looked concerned. "What is troubling you? I have eyes to see you have been brooding."

Yosef shrugged. "As soon as I can make arrangements, Miryam and I will leave for Beit Lechem"

"Why so soon? No need to go until after the autumn harvest. Besides, Miryam does not have to go. Only men are required to register."

"Miryam is with child," Yosef blurted out.

Klofah laughed out loud. "That is no reason to be glum, brother! You should be rejoicing! When is the child due?"

33

"Miryam is now in her sixth month." He watched his brother for a reaction. "And I am not the father."

"What did you say?"

"I said that I am not the father."

Klofah's face contorted with anger. "Who has done this evil thing, defiling a virgin?"

"She has not been defiled." He grabbed his brother's arm, but he shook it off.

Miryam and Miri could hear the argument and came running.

"Yosef! Klofah! What has happened?" Miryam asked, looking from one to the other.

"Why have you done this?" Klofah demanded, pointing at her. "Why have you shamed our family?"

Miryam looked to Yosef for help.

"My brother," Yosef said, putting his arm around her. "I know that it is hard to understand. I found it so myself, but the child is not my own. Miryam has conceived by the power of the Holy Spirit."

"The Holy Spirit?" Klofah mocked. "You can accept this fantasy as true if you wish, but you cannot make me believe such lies. Take the woman and go to Beit Lechem. And I hope you never show your faces in Natzeret again," Klofah shouted, storming away.

"Leave Natzeret?" Miryam looked crestfallen. "Why, Yosi?"

"The governor has ordered a census, and I must register at the place of my birth, Beit Lechem. We can return later…after the child is born. Then no one will suspect he was conceived before our marriage."

Miryam seemed on the verge of tears. "Where will we live?"

"You can go to your aunt in Ain Karem," Miri suggested. "Elisheva can look after you while you await the child, just as you did for her. And Yosef can work in Yerushalayim, as Klofah has done."

Miryam looked frightened. "How can I have my child without my mother to assist me?"

"I will be with you," Yosef said. "I will see that you have good care."

"Listen to your husband, sister," Miri said.

"If our neighbors should find out, we will be safer somewhere else," he said.

"But we have good neighbors," Miryam protested. "No one would do us harm."

His voice was low. "Neighbors can speak friendly words, but their thoughts can be like deadly arrows, ready to strike if the opportunity arises."

"Yosef!" Miryam was astonished. "I have never heard you speak this way."

"I only speak from experience," he said. "It would be better if we leave Natzeret."

When all was ready, Yosef and Yoachim plotted the possible routes they could take. The coastal road was difficult as it did not run in a straight line from Natzeret to Beit Lechem. The trek through the mountains involved a great deal of climbing, which would be difficult for his pregnant wife. Yosef decided that they would travel east and then south along the Yarden River. Even though it would make for a longer journey, they would avoid Shomron where there were ill feelings toward the Yehudim.

"There will be many people traveling to Yerushalayim for work, so we can join a caravan. Travelling alone is dangerous, and a group will provide protection." Yosef held Miryam close to his own pounding heart. "We have to place our trust in our Lord."

8

The winter solstice was the longest night of the year. The sun seemed to have died; the days grew cold and bleak. Still, everyone knew the sun would rise again. The Romans celebrated it with *Sol Invictus*, the "Feast of the Unconquered Sun," in honor of the dazzling disc. Throngs of people paraded the streets, singing a litany to the Persian god Mithra: "Homage to Mithra, the ever wakeful one who sleeps not. We sacrifice to Mithra, the lord of all nations."

For the Yehudim, it was the month of Chislev, and the beginning of Chanukah. The festival commemorated the religious freedom won by the Maccabees, and the rededication of the temple after the Syrians desecrated it. This eight-day feast rekindled the hope of freedom for the Yehudim who lived under foreign rule.

But Yosef was not thinking of celebration. They were living in dark days, and he hoped that when the child was born the light would return. They had spent two months in Ain Karem with Miryam's aunt Elisheva. Miryam had insisted on going with him to Beit Lechem, not just for the census, but for the festival in Yerushalayim. It seemed impossible for Yosef to deny her this pleasure, but now he regretted his poor judgment. It was on this same road that Yaakov buried his beloved wife Rachel who died after giving birth to their youngest son Benyamin.

Beit Lechem had not known a winter as cold as this one. The wind seemed to scream, stripping the last leaves from the trees. Heavy clouds rolled across the dark sky, and distant thunder threatened more rain. It would be difficult enough to make their way on an ordinary day, but with the weather becoming foul, the unpaved road was turning into a quagmire.

"I should not have brought you with me. It is too close to your time," Yosef said, looking back at his wife huddled in the cart.

"Do not fret, Yosi," Miryam said. "We do not have to go to Yerushalayim. As soon as you register for the census, we can return to Ain Karem. There is still time."

There was a note of disappointment in her voice. Yosef knew how she looked forward to the Festival of Lights, but he hoped she was right that they had time.

The wheels of Yosef's cart soon clogged with mud as he joined the hordes of people pushing and pulling their baggage-filled carts through the tortuous mire, all trying to register for the census and find food and lodging before nightfall.

"Everyone must belong to David's house," one man quipped. The people laughed, remembering the illustrious king's many wives and offspring.

Beit Lechem was David's city, anointed king there by the prophet Shmuel. The town was called the "House of Bread." With two ridges at each end and a hollow between, it looked like a breadbasket set in the hills. Passing the soggy fields of harvested hay rolled into bales, Miryam saw women stooped over, gleaning leftover refuse.

"Just the way King David's great-grandmother Rut once did," she remarked.

Upon entering the town, Yosef saw a squad of Roman soldiers from the Tenth Legion. They were under a standing order to arrest anyone claiming to be the Son of David.

One of them eyed Yosef and scoffed. "That one would make a poor Mashiach."

Yosef lowered his eyes and hastened to find a place to tether the donkey. Then he and Miryam followed the crowd to the registration tables where scribes sat in sheltered booths. Yosef was dismayed when he saw the long column of people snaking down the street. He led Miryam to the end of the line where they waited for what seemed like hours, while the wind spat rain in their faces. By late afternoon they were wet and miserable. Huddling together, they blew warm breath into their cold hands. Miryam hugged her cloak close to her heavy body, her breath clouding in the air, her teeth chattering from the chill.

The sun was dipping low in the sky when Yosef signed the Roman registry: *Yosef ben Yaakov of Natzeret.* He hesitated. Should he also add, *Son of Heli*, his step-father? But in the eyes of the law, Yosef was the son of Yaakov. In either case, he was a son of David, though he dared not arouse suspicion.

The scribe looked at Yosef's signature and snorted, "Move along." The next man in line spat on the ground. It was not only the soldiers that incurred his wrath; it was the scribe who worked for the enemy for a few extra shekels in his pocket.

Yosef hustled Miryam away, not wanting to be involved in an argument. They found their rain-soaked donkey, and Yosef helped Miryam into the cart.

"Yosef," she suddenly gasped. "I fear the time is near."

He was frantic. There was no time to return to Ain Karem. How could they find a place in Beit Lechem at this hour? Most people had found lodging in their relatives' guest rooms. Others camped in the fields or sought shelter in one of the numerous caves in the limestone hillsides. Yosef knew of a kinsman who owned property in Beit Lechem, but he could not recall where it was. The houses, clustered along the narrow, unpaved streets, all looked the same. Still, he reassured Miryam that he would find it, secretly wondering if they would make it in time.

At the outskirts of town, Yosef saw a light coming from an inn, no more than a square enclosure surrounded by an open courtyard for animals and wagons. He did not want his wife to bear the child in a place known to be frequented by thieves and prostitutes, but perhaps there was someone inside who could help them.

Pushing his way through the swarms of people trying to find

shelter from the cold, he tethered the donkey to a stump by the tavern's doorway. He hated to leave Miryam alone, and he promised he would return as soon as he was able. When he entered the inn, he tried to adjust his eyes to the flickering light of oil lamps, which cast eerie shadows everywhere. The place smelled of hot grease mixed with the odor of raw sewage. He elbowed his way toward a young barmaid, and tried to make his voice heard above the din. But he was rebuffed.

"There is no room in the inn," she said, wiping her hands on her skirt.

"I am not looking for lodging," Yosef pleaded. "I wonder if someone might know the house of my kinsman Shaul and his wife Rut."

The woman seemed to know everyone in town, even the travelers, and she took Yosef to the door. "There." She pointed down the dark street. "It is not far, just at the bend in the road." Then, seeing the young man's very pregnant wife, she offered them a barley cake, drawing on the inn's dwindling supplies.

"May I ask one more question?" he asked as she wrapped the cake in a napkin. She nodded. "Do you know where I can find a midwife? Her time draws near."

"I am a midwife," she said, smiling. "I helped my aunts and cousins give birth, once even a mare. My name is Shlomit. Send for me when it is time."

He sighed in relief; he had not failed his wife in her hour of need. "Thank you for your kindness," he said as he pulled the cart down the bumpy street, hoping to find his kinsman's house.

"Hurry! The time grows short. The child presses to come forth," Miryam moaned. Even the donkey seemed to wince at her pain.

"I think we are here, dear one.... Yes...I am sure this is the house," Yosef said.

He pounded on the door, calling out, "Shaul! It is your kinsman Yosef. Please open the door."

After some time he heard muffled footsteps, and then a man appeared at the door holding a lamp high. He was short and stocky, with a ruddy face. A drab-looking woman stood in the shadows behind him, her features sharp in the lamp light.

"Forgive me if I have awakened you. I know that the hour is late. I am your kinsman Yosef."

Shaul squinted at him. "Yes, yes, I remember you—the son of Yaakov."

"Yes. My wife and I have traveled all the way from Natzeret for the census. We are desperate for lodging. Her time has come and I have money to pay."

"Pay?" Shaul grunted. "Who pays for such things? Come in, come in."

Yosef helped Miryam out of the cart. She was doubled over in pain. Rut led her into the house. As Yosef began to tie up the donkey, Shaul motioned to him.

"Bring the animal inside. It is a cold night. He deserves to be warm like the other creatures. And they keep us warm too." He lowered his voice to a whisper. "Besides, if you leave your animal outside, someone might steal it."

Yosef unharnessed the donkey, shouldered their baggage, and led the animal down the stone steps to the stalls and mangers. There was a strong odor of wet straw and animal dung from the livestock housed beneath the family's living quarters.

"I am sorry, Yosef," Shaul spread his fat hands in a helpless gesture. "I have no guest room to offer you. My house is full of men who have come for the census. All I can give you is this stable, but it is warm and you will have privacy."

"Thank you," Yosef answered. "It will do."

Rut did not seem embarrassed by their humble circumstances. "I will do what I can to help you, but I must admit I have no birthing skills. She shuffled around the stable to find some clean straw. "I had no children of my own, and Shaul always birthed the animals."

Miryam arched her back and groaned. Rut eased her onto a bed of straw, covering her with a worn blanket.

"I will fetch the midwife," Yosef said. He rushed out the door with Shaul trailing behind.

※

"Try to sleep," Rut said, rubbing the young woman's back, not knowing what else to do. Miryam was exhausted. As sleep overtook her, strange dreams filled her head. A great light appeared in the heavens. A woman, arrayed as a queen, clothed in a many-colored robe, shone like the sun. The moon was under her feet and on her head was a crown of twelve stars. The woman cried out in agony. She was about to give birth.

Then a terrifying dragon appeared. Miryam struggled to open her eyes. The red beast had ten horns and seven crowns on its seven heads. With its enormous tail it swept a third of the stars from the heavens, throwing them down to the earth. The dragon crouched before the woman, ready to devour the child when it came forth from her womb. But when he was born, he was snatched from his mother's arms and taken to a throne in heaven.

The dragon was enraged, pursuing the woman as she fled into the wilderness. Water poured forth from the creature's mouth, trying to sweep her away in a flood. But the woman was given the wings of a great eagle and she flew to safety. A loud voice proclaimed, "Now comes salvation! For the Evil One has been conquered by the blood of the Lamb!"

Furious that it had been overthrown, the dragon took its stand on the shore waiting for another opportunity to destroy the woman's son.

Miryam awoke to a terrible cry—the scream was her own. Pushing her knuckles against her eyes, she tried to shut out the dreadful dream. "The blood of the lamb, the blood of the lamb," she repeated.

Rut looked at Miryam, mystified. She was relieved when she heard the sound of approaching footsteps. "Help is coming," she reassured her.

Yosef and Shaul entered the house, along with the barmaid. Some disreputable looking women followed behind, chattering that they were there to lend support.

"I am called Shlomit," she said, lifting a lantern to get a look at her patient. "I was named for King Shlomo—but I never saw the inside of a palace."

Miryam raised herself on her elbows and peered at her; she was only a girl.

Shlomit pulled her long wavy hair into a bun, and went to work, giving Rut orders for water, oil, and salt. "Do you have any clean linen for swaddling?" she asked.

Rut climbed the stairs, sighing. "I will see what I can find."

"This is the world of women," Shaul muttered, taking Yosef outside. "We men must remain at a distance.

With the men gone, the women shared their birthing stories. "I remember the terrible pain when I bore my son," one of them said, tensing with each of Miryam's cries as if she too was giving birth. "I thought it would never stop. I was sure it would kill me!"

Another nodded. "When a woman gives birth, death crouches at the door."

A thin, bent woman shook her head. "There are evil demons waiting to devour a child as soon as it is born."

"I have heard that there is a roof-demon who slides down the eaves of the house ready to afflict the child with disease," another warned.

Shlomit shooed the women out. "Go tell your silly stories to the ignorant shepherds in the fields. They will believe you!"

Outside, the women found Yosef pacing, wringing his hands whenever he heard one of Miryam's cries.

"Your poor little wife!" a woman sighed. "It is a shame that we have to suffer just to bring another hungry mouth into the world."

Another leaned over to him, reciting her superstition. "If you do not wish any more children, you can tie a dead scorpion in a crocus-green cloth and fasten it to your wife's skirt."

Yosef looked disgusted and sent them away with a wave of his hand.

"I will escort the ladies to the inn," Shaul said, leaving Yosef alone. Looking up at the starlit sky, he was certain that there were myriads unseen. Was this how the great patriarch Avraham felt when he was given the promise of a child? *Count the stars if you can. Thus shall your descendants be.*

Gathering a few sticks from the woodpile, he struck fire from flint, blowing on the embers until they glowed bright orange. The sparks flew upwards and disappeared in the black sky.

"Just like my prayers," he said. "I hope they find their destination."

Many hours passed. Still Miryam had not given birth. She was seated on a milking stool, with Shlomit squatting in front of her, and Rut behind, giving support. With each pain Miryam grasped Shlomit's strong arms.

"Hold tight, My Lady," Shlomit said. "Now pull...Now push...Do not strain. The child will come in due time...Breathe deeply...Good... Now bear down."

Finally, with one forceful push, the child came forth in a gush of water and blood.

Rut peered at the child as Shlomit laid him on a bench. "He looks just like a loaf of bread set on a baker's rack to cool."

Miryam forced a weak smile, and lay back in her arms. Shlomit skillfully cut the baby's blue and white umbilical cord, and tied the stump with strong twine. Then she bathed him, rubbing his body with oil and salt. Wrapping him in swaddling clothes, she wound the long strips of woolen fabric around his body so that his limbs would grow straight.

"This child is very special," Shlomit beamed, as if he was the first child she brought into the world. Her eyes misted as she placed him in Miryam's arms. "I know that he is destined for something great."

Miryam covered her newborn son with kisses and touched his soft face. She felt her milk letting down, and she put her breast to her son's tiny mouth. He sucked the first yellow milk.

This child is flesh of my flesh and bone of my bones. He is the perfect reflection of his Father's glory.

Then she fell into a dreamless sleep.

9

Yosef sat on the ground, holding his head in his hands, listening for another moan from the house. But all was quiet. Soon he heard a different sound, like the bleat of a lamb, drifting out of the darkness. He jumped to his feet just as Shlomit came to the door and gestured for him to come inside.

Yosef hurried to the doorway and saw the tiny child cradled in his sleeping wife's arms. Lifting the babe so as not to wake him, he carried him to the manger, a feeding trough for animals.

"You will be warm here," he said, laying his son on the fresh straw.

But the infant's cheek brushed the splinters of the wood and he cried out in pain. Yosef picked him up again, stroking him and making soothing sounds.

Miryam awoke with a start, and Yosef placed the child in her outstretched arms.

"Forgive me," he said. "I am so clumsy."

She kissed the small scrape on her whimpering child. "Poor lamb, wounded so soon after your first breath."

Yosef knelt beside her. "I wish I could have provided a better place for you."

"You are a good man, Yosi," she said, drowsily.

He waited for the child to fall asleep before speaking. "I have been thinking. Was it not foretold by the prophet Mikhah that the anointed one would be born in Beit Lechem?"

Miryam did not answer. She was asleep, too. Yosef took the sleeping babe and put him back in the manger, taking more care this time. Then he and Shlomit went outside.

"What will you name your son?" Shlomit asked.

"His name will be Yeshua," he answered, taking a few coins from a pouch to pay her.

"Yeshua," she repeated. "That is a good name, strong and courageous."

"Yeshua was the warrior who led our people into the Promised Land. Did you know that?"

Shlomit shook her head and looked down the road.

"You are going back to the inn?" Yosef said, more of a charge than a question.

"Where else would I go?" she asked. "I have no home, no family."

"No family?"

"My mother and father died when I was very young. My brother looked after me until he was killed by King Herod."

"Killed? What happened?"

"When Herod placed a Roman eagle at the entrance of the temple, some Torah students ripped it down. The king had them dragged to his palace in chains…my brother was among them." Tears formed in her dark eyes. "He was burned alive."

Yosef shook his head. "Could someone take you in, so you do not have to go back to that dreadful inn?"

Shlomit shrugged and wiped her face with her grimy, blood-stained sleeve.

"Perhaps you can make money as a midwife," he suggested. "You seem to have a talent for it."

"Perhaps," she said.

"You could start a new life."

"Perhaps," she said again, with a wistful sigh.

She turned to leave, but Yosef took her arm. "It is late. Stay with us tonight. In the morning you can decide what to do."

"Thank you," she said, smiling slightly. "I will look in on the little mother."

"Remember, nothing is impossible with the Lord," he called after her.

Yosef stirred the embers on the fire. While he was considering the terrible life that Shlomit had led, he was startled by the sound of approaching footsteps. Looking up the dark road he could see the bobbling lights of lanterns. Some men came into view. They were shepherds—and they were led by Shaul.

Yosef could smell their stench even before they approached, their sheep's odor clinging to their filthy clothing.

"What do you want?" Yosef asked, fearing for his wife and child's safety.

One of the shepherds, a craggy-faced man, spoke for the group that stood behind him in a shivering cluster. "We were in the valley keeping watch over the flock." His foul breath turned to smoke in the frigid air. "There is always the danger of wild beasts and robbers when the lambs are born."

"Just tell him why you are here." Shaul's breath smelled of liquor.

"I will tell you soon enough," the old man said. He cleared his throat. "We were watching this star—it was so bright, brighter than any star that we ever saw. It was as though the heavens were set ablaze...."

"Yes, yes," Yosef said, trying to be patient.

"As I was saying," the old man continued. "The sky was filled with light, so much light, as bright as noonday."

A young shepherd stepped to the front. "And we heard singing," he said in awe. "The whole sky seemed to sing! It looked like the moon and stars were dancing."

"Pay no attention to this dreamer." The old man nudged him out of the way. "What we heard was the voice of an angel."

"An angel?" Yosef asked, with sudden interest.

The young man pushed his way to the front again. "At first we were terrified. But then the angel told us: "Do not to be afraid. I am bringing you good news of great joy for all the people.""

"Oh, there was not just one angel," the old man exclaimed, revealing toothless gaps in his grin. "There was a multitude of angels! They were singing, 'Glory to the highest heaven, and on earth peace among those favored by *El Shaddai*, the Almighty!'"

"But how did you know to come here?" Yosef asked.

"The angel told us that the Mashiach had been born in Beit Lechem, the city of David." The old man frowned and scratched his matted hair. "But why here? Should the Mashiach not be born in Yerushalayim?"

The young man spoke again. "We asked the townspeople if any of them had seen the angels. Some of them were rude, accusing us of letting our sheep strip their grasslands. Others said we had too much grape."

The other shepherds laughed, and the old man glared at them. "We asked many people where could we find the newborn babe, but no one seemed to know what we were talking about." His milky eyes narrowed. "You know it is strange."

"What is strange?" Yosef asked.

"I thought that there would be a great crowd when we arrived. Has no one come but us poor shepherds?"

"No one," Yosef shook his head.

"That is strange." The old man tugged at his scruffy beard. "Well, even so, we finally stopped at the inn—to see if anyone there could tell us." He pointed to Shaul. "This man told us that the barmaid went to his house to help a woman who was about to give birth. He showed us the way. And so here we are." His voice grew soft. "Is it possible to see the child?"

Yosef hesitated for a moment. Still, who was he to dishonor these poor shepherds if they were favored by the Most High? He led the way, and the shepherds entered the house. Miryam was startled awake.

"These men say that they saw an angel who told them they would find the newborn here," Shaul said, a bit unsteady on his feet. "Are you men fools as some say you are?"

"Perhaps you are the fool, husband!" Rut said, smelling her husband's liquored breath.

The shepherds seemed undeterred by Shaul's insults. When their eyes grew accustomed to the dim light, they saw the babe lying in a manger just as the angel told them.

"Come," Miryam said, as though she expected her visitors.

The shepherds knelt at once. The old man's raspy voice was gentle as he prayed, "O tiny child, we who are the wretched of the earth have been touched by your heavenly light."

The youngest shepherd carried a lamb, its warm breath making puffs of mist in the cold air. "This is my gift to him."

Miryam nodded, and he laid the lamb next to the infant in the manger. The shepherds rose and bowed, thanking Yosef for allowing them to see the child.

"We must return to our flocks," the old man said. "We left our sons in charge, mere children. We hope our sheep are still there."

"The angel told us we would find things just as they are, so we have nothing to fear," the young shepherd grinned.

As they were about to leave the house, the old man stopped and turned to Yosef. "I was wondering why we were chosen—I mean, of all the great people in the world, why would the Almighty favor lowly shepherds?"

Yosef stood in silence. Then he put his hand on the old man's tattered sleeve. "Avraham, Yaakov, Yitzchak, Moshe, and David—they were all shepherds. Yet the Most High chose them. And he chose me, too, a simple carpenter, so why not you?"

The old man nodded, and followed the others up the road. Yosef watched them disappear into the dark night. Then he stamped out the few remaining embers. As the red sparks turned into black ribbons of smoke, his thoughts turned to the many sinners in his line—even King David. Only Yosef, his namesake, was worthy of being counted a true son of Yisrael. Yet despite his ancestors' sins, whether they were important or insignificant, the Lord had chosen them.

"Like me," Yosef said in a hoarse whisper.

10

It was the eighth day after Miryam gave birth, and according to the Law of Moshe, the *Brit Milah*, the covenant of circumcision, was required of all male children. It was a sign that set them apart from all other peoples.

"Where can I find a rabbi to perform the rite?" Yosef asked Shaul.

"Rabbi Shmuel! I will go find him," Shaul said, eager to leave the house. He returned some time later, looking happy and a little red in the face. "The rabbi will come in the morning. I stopped at the inn for a bit of wine to ease my stomach."

"Just as I promised," Shaul announced the next day as he led Rabbi Shmuel upstairs to the family quarters. Shlomit was following behind and she went to Miryam's side. "I thought you might like me to be with you."

"O Shlomit, I would indeed," Miryam said.

When all was ready, the rabbi put his shawl over his head, its long fringes dangling almost to the floor.

"Blessed are You, Adonai Eloheinu, Ruler of the Universe," he chanted. "You have sanctified us with your commandments and commanded us in the ritual of circumcision."

Then he took the child from Miryam's arms and handed him to Yosef, who looked uneasy holding the squirming infant. As the foreskin was removed, Yeshua let out a piercing scream, his face bright red. Miryam turned pale, and Shlomit supported her in her strong arms.

"Is the boy harmed?" Yosef asked.

"No, no," Rabbi Shmuel reassured him as he bandaged the wound.

"Of course he would bellow," Rut muttered as she left the room. "What would you expect if a knife cut your flesh?"

The rabbi raised his voice to be heard over Yeshua's cries. "Blessed are You, Adonai Eloheinu, Ruler of the Universe, who has sanctified us with your commandments and commanded us to bring this child into the covenant of Avraham, our father."

"Blessed be your glorious Kingdom forever and ever," Yosef answered, trying to sooth the child.

"What name have you chosen for this son of Yisrael?" the rabbi asked.

"Yeshua bar Yosef, bar Yaakov, bar Mattan, bar Eleazar, bar Elichud of the tribe of David," Yosef announced.

Rabbi Shmuel frowned. "Not Yosef?" He shrugged. "But Yeshua is a good name: 'The Lord is Savior.' Yes, a good name."

"Rut, bring the wine!" Shaul shouted with glee. When she returned, the rabbi blessed the wine and put a few drops in Yeshua's mouth, tickling him under the chin to make him swallow it. Yeshua stopped crying, pursing his lips with the new taste.

A prayer of thanksgiving was recited. "Ruler of the Universe, may it be your gracious will to accept this child as if we had brought him before your glorious throne. May his heart be open to understand your holy Torah, so that he may learn it, teach it, and keep it with good deeds."

"Blessed be your glorious Kingdom forever and ever," Yosef answered.

Wine was poured for everyone, and with a rousing cry they toasted the child: "L'Chaim, to life!"

"Yeshua will be in pain for several days," Rabbi Shmuel cautioned Miryam as he departed.

"My poor boy," Miryam cooed. "I am sorry that you must suffer this way to belong to our people, Yisrael."

"The people of Yisrael have always suffered," Yosef said. "And I believe they always will. In all of life, there is loss, and in all loss, there is pain."

"And in all pain there is joy," Miryam added.

For thirty-three days after childbirth, Miryam was in a state of impurity. If she had given birth to a daughter, her time of impurity would have been sixty-six days.

"Why is there such a difference?" Miryam complained to Yosef. "All children, male or female, are gifts from the Lord."

"I believe the longer wait is because a girl has a greater capacity for holiness due to her creative powers," he said, grateful that his answer pleased Miryam.

At dawn, Yosef and Miryam began the five-mile journey north to the Holy City. Yosef pulled the donkey while Miryam and the child rode in the cart. As they climbed the hillside, they stopped to drink from one of the springs flowing from a crack in a rock formation.

"Look, Miryam," Yosef said, excited. "The almond tree is in bloom."

Miryam looked where he pointed. The tree was full of white blossoms with red eyes in the center of the petals.

"Do you know why they call it the 'Watching Tree'?" Miryam smiled, knowing how Yosef loved to explain things to her. "It is the first tree to bloom in the dead of winter. It seems to be looking around while everything else is asleep!"

"I hope it is watching over us," she said, shivering in the chill.

They continued through a winding pass to the Mount of Olives east of Yerushalayim. From there they could see the Kidron Valley and the Holy City. Yosef opened his mouth to speak, but what he saw silenced him. The city looked like a white jewel shining in the bright sunlight.

"Yerushalayim," he whispered.

When they approached the temple, Yosef averted his eyes at the sight of a Golden Eagle hung above the main entrance—the hated emblem of Roman power. Mounted soldiers watched from the sidelines, alert for any sign of trouble. Others were stationed atop the temple walls, their crested helmets flashing against the blue sky. Pilgrims passing through the gate glared at their oppressors with undisguised contempt.

Miryam shielded the infant's eyes from the bright sun as Yosef found a place where he could tether the donkey.

"We must bathe before entering the Holy House," he told her. "I am going to the men's mikveh, the bathing pools outside the Western wall," He looked around, unsure of which way Miryam should go.

"Are you looking for the women's mikveh?" a young woman asked in passing. "There is one near the Huldah gate. I will take you there if you wish."

Miryam nodded and Yosef urged her to follow her. "When you have finished bathing, go to the Court of Women and wait by the treasury boxes."

"How will I find them?" she asked.

"They are in the Court of Women; they look just like trumpets," he explained. "Do not worry. I will come for you."

Holding the infant close to her breast, she followed the woman to a dark, plastered room, a respite from the bright sunlight in the courtyard. She watched with apprehension as the women disrobed, and, one-by-one, descended the steps on the right side of the pool. After bathing, they ascended a different flight of steps on the left.

"This is a special moment for you," the Mikveh Lady told Miryam as she waited for her turn. "When you bathe you will feel reborn. Remember the words of the prophet Yechezkel: 'I will sprinkle pure water upon you, and you shall be cleansed from all your impurities.'"

After what seemed a long time, the attendant motioned to Miryam. "You may come," she said, taking Yeshua from her arms.

Miryam unloosed her hair, shyly removed her garments, and went down the steps into the cold bath.

"The water must cover your entire body," the woman warned, rocking the baby to keep him quiet. "Not a single hair can remain above the water."

Miryam crouched down below the surface of the pool. When she stood up the Mikveh Lady recited the blessing for purification: "Blessed are You, Adonai Eloheinu, Ruler of the Universe, who has sanctified us with your commandments."

Immersing twice more, Miryam emerged from the pool, dried her body, and tied up her long, wet hair. After dressing, she took Yeshua from the attendant and followed the other women to the temple precincts to rejoin their families. The crowd slowed to a crawl as they shoved and pushed, shoulder to shoulder, through the Huldah gate, then down a long decorated passageway until they emerged in the outer court. This was the Court of Gentiles where anyone could enter,

Yehudi or Gentile, male or female. Everyone murmured their admiration, but there was no time to stop because more people were pressing from behind.

Following the women, she walked up the thirteen steps leading into the Court of the Women where she found the treasury boxes, standing like golden lilies, just as Yosef said. She stood on tiptoes, trying to see over the heads of the pilgrims rushing back and forth, searching the faces in the crowd, anxious to see her husband.

The blast of the shofar startled her, announcing that incense was to be kindled on the Golden Altar in the Court of Kohanim, the priests. The fragrant aroma floated like a gray feather into the azure sky as songs of praise filled the temple.

"Let my prayer be counted as incense before you," Miryam prayed. "And please, help me find Yosef!"

When Yosef finished his purification, he went to the moneychangers who sat behind their coin-covered tables. It was compulsory to exchange foreign currency for shekels, the only coins allowed for the purchase of animals for sacrifice. After exchanging his money, Yosef stood in another line. Some of the men ahead of him were buying unblemished lambs for the burnt offering. Yosef felt the color rising in his cheeks; he could not afford the expense of a lamb. When it was his turn, he handed over the coins for two doves, the offering of the poor.

"Did you bring a cage?" the vendor asked, not hiding his contempt.

Yosef shook his head, and the vendor thrust the birds toward him. "Here! Hold them like this," he said, grasping their wings."

As he took them, Yosef felt a hand touching his shoulder. He turned to see a rabbi standing close by.

"There is no shame in offering doves," the rabbi said, with a kind smile. "A poor man's sacrifice is worth more than a thousand sacrifices of King Herod."

Miryam was beginning to panic as she watched the steady stream of people criss-crossing the courtyard. "Oh!" she breathed with relief when she finally caught sight of him.

"Come, Miryam, we must find a kohen," Yosef said, holding out the pair of birds for her to see.

Before long they came across an elderly priest assigned to the task of the purification of mothers.

"This is my first-born son…the first born of his mother," Yosef nodded to the bundle in Miryam's arms. "The Law of Moshe has commanded me to redeem him."

The kohen took one of the birds from Yosef's hands and raised it high. "This is a sin-offering in atonement for any transgressions the mother may have incurred. Its blood will be sprinkled against the sides of the altar."

Miryam wished she could send the doves skyward. "Your fate is sealed," she said softly, as if answering the doves' plaintive coo. "I cannot offer you a reprieve."

At that moment, the kohen wrung the bird's neck without severing its head from the body. Miryam felt sick at the sight.

Taking hold of the second dove, the kohen said, "This will be a burnt offering on the bronzed altar, dedicating the child's life to the Lord."

Then he took the birds to the Court of Kohanim.

A voice startled them. "You carry the fire, O most pure one, the light that never fades." They turned to see an old man, his eyes red with age and a cloud of white hair encircling his craggy face. "My name is Shimon," he said. Then, before she could stop him, he took Yeshua from her arms and raised his voice in a blessing. "Now Master, you can dismiss your servant in peace. You have fulfilled your word and my eyes have seen your salvation, a light for all nations and for glory for your people Yisrael."

The old man paused and fixed his eyes on Miryam. "This child is destined to be a sign that will be opposed by many."

She looked confused. Yeshua cause division? The angels sang of peace on earth. How could both be true?

Shimon spoke again, "And you, fair woman, a sword will pierce your soul."

She felt the color drain from her face. Her lips parted, but she could say nothing. As she retrieved Yeshua from Shimon's arms, an old woman hobbled toward them.

"My children, this is Hannah, a daughter of the tribe of Asher," Shimon said, with a respectful nod. "Her husband died seven years after their marriage, and from that time she has never left the temple, praying and fasting day and night. Everyone says that she is a prophet."

Hannah was nearly bent in two, and could barely lift her head. Miryam noticed her eyes. They were not clouded, like many elderly people. They were clear, giving the impression that she could see beyond the present day—far into the future.

With crooked fingers, she pulled the shawl away from Yeshua's face and looked with delight at the child. "This is the child who everyone awaits, the one who will release us from our bonds." Then, with hands held aloft, praising the mercy of the Almighty, she went back into the shadows from where she came.

Yosef and Miryam stared at one another in astonishment. Without a word, they left the temple and made their way home to Beit Lechem.

It was late when they arrived home. Looking toward the east, they were surprised to see an extraordinarily bright star in the sky. They stood for a while marveling at the sight. Then they went inside, and Yosef prayed the evening prayer: "Lay us down to sleep in peace, Ruler of the Universe, and spread the shelter of your wings over us."

Miryam added a quiet "Amen," and then put the child beside him. Curling next to them, she watched the slow rise and fall of Yosef's chest as he slept, his hands folded as in prayer. "Thank you, Lord, for giving me a good husband," she prayed. Then she sang a lullaby to her child, a song her mother had sung to her.

> *There are numerous stars in the sky,*
>   *let me add mine to them.*
> *There are numerous sands on the shore,*
>   *let me add mine to them.*
> *There are numerous strains to the lute,*
>   *let me add mine to them.*
> *There are numerous songs of the dove,*
>   *let me add mine to them.*

Yeshua slept contented. When he awoke, his nut-brown eyes seemed to focus on a distant horizon.

11

Far to the east, three sages observed Jupiter, the king planet, and Venus, the mother star, coming so close together that they gave the appearance of one very bright star. The men were magi, members of the priestly class of Persia's Zoroastrian religion, who believed that there was one god for all. The magi's task was to interpret the stars and the destinies they saw written there. "As above, so below," was their saying.

"The Yehudim believe that the Mashiach will appear when there is a conjunction of these planets," said Melchior, a white-bearded man from Tarsus, the oldest of the three.

"The trajectory points to Yisrael," added Gaspar, a ruddy, bearded man from Arabia.

Balthazar was swarthy and beardless, the youngest. He came from Ethiopia. "We must see this with our own eyes."

The astronomers agreed to make the journey, taking with them three offerings—gold, frankincense, and myrrh. Gold would purchase necessities, and frankincense would be burned at shrines and temples for their protection. And if one of them died on the way, myrrh would perfume the body until it could be buried.

"The gifts will help us discover whether the child we seek is to be a king, a priest, or a prophet," Melchior said. "If he takes gold, he will be a king; if frankincense, a priest; and if he chooses myrrh, he will be a prophet."

The magi traveled with an entourage in a camel caravan, taking with them tents, bedding and food for the long journey there and back again. Pitching their tents by day, and moving on at nightfall, the wondrous star could be seen shining over the desert like a luminous jewel. They watched in awe as it zigzagged across the sky and then resumed its normal course.

Traveling westward, they went through the pass of Moab into Yericho, where the River Yarden met the Dead Sea. They crossed the river and went on to Yerushalayim. A dark cloud had descended upon the city so that they could no longer see the star.

"Surely it is a sign that a new king will be born in the great city," Melchior said as the caravan came to a halt. "If the child has arrived, someone here will know of it."

In the early morning they went to the temple and found a kohen on duty in the outer Court of Gentiles.

Melchior bowed low. "We have come to offer tribute to the newborn king of the Yehudim."

"More lunatics in search of the Mashiach," the kohen muttered as he went to summon the *Kohen HaGadol*. Moments later, the High Priest strode into the court.

"Who is it you are looking for?" he demanded, at this interruption.

"We have seen the rising star of the newborn king and have followed it here," Melchior said.

"I know nothing of such a sign," the High Priest scoffed. "I do not trust foreigners who think they can interpret the divine will by reading the stars. But I will inform the king, and if he wishes, he will have an audience with you."

Herod was in no mood to deal with stargazers. He was not well, and he was weakening by the day. Still, he wondered if there was some truth to what these three were after. Reclining on an ornate, upholstered couch, he eyed his visitors with suspicion.

"It is a comfort to know that a new ruler is being divinely sent to take the place of an old man," the king said, feigning interest in their quest. "If you find him, I hope you will do me the courtesy of sending word so that I can do him homage."

The magi agreed.

As they went on their way, they were guided once again by the star. Following its course, they went across the swift-flowing Kidron, south toward the Valley of Hinnom, and up the winding road near the potters' field, a burial ground for strangers. After a journey of 1,000 miles, the magi arrived at the place where the star had led them—Beit Lechem.

"Where do we go from here?" Gaspar asked.

"There is an inn," Melchior said. "Perhaps some travelers can tell us where we might find the child."

The arrival of the caravan created a great commotion. "My barmaid never ceases talking of the special child she helped deliver," the innkeeper said, pulling at his thin gray beard. "But I do not know how he can be different than other children in this poor town."

Leaving their traveling companions at an inn, the magi went to the house of Shaul, where the innkeeper had directed them. Hearing the noise, Shaul rushed outside to see what was happening. Rut appeared white-faced behind him, astonished to see three men dressed in fine raiment dismounting their ornamented camels.

"Who are you?" Shaul spluttered.

"My name is Melchior," the oldest man said. "And this is Gaspar and Balthazar. We are astrologers from the east. For more than a year, we have followed a star to find the child of divine destiny."

"Who might that be?" Shaul grunted.

"We have come to honor the newborn king of the Yehudim," Balthazar said.

Shaul laughed. "First there were shepherds who claimed that the Mashiach could be found in my home, and now you say he is a king? Perhaps you mean to go somewhere else, to one of the fine palaces in Yerushalayim."

"No, no. The star has led us here—to this house," Gaspar said.

Shaul looked doubtful, but held the door open and led them upstairs. Yosef and Miryam were speechless when the men entered, overwhelmed by their noble bearing.

When the magi saw the child sitting on his mother's lap, they fell to their knees in reverence. "So, heaven's fire has fallen this far to earth," Melchior said.

"Are you kings?" Yosef stammered.

"No," Balthasar smiled. "We are sages from the east. We have followed a star to this place."

"We have brought gifts to honor him," Gaspar added.

"Gifts for a poor man's child?" Shaul scoffed.

"A gift for a king," Melchior corrected him, his piercing eyes set beneath a thatch of white eyebrows. He held out a beautiful casket, plated in gold and covered with enameled birds and flowers. Opening it with care, he presented Miryam with a small packet of gold dust.

Gaspar brought forth a jar of frankincense. "A gift for a priest. When it is burned, it will release a fragrance like perfume."

"A gift for a prophet," Balthazar said, opening a vial of myrrh from Ethiopia.

Miryam turned pale when its death-like scent permeated the room.

But Yeshua clapped his chubby hands in delight and reached out, as if eager to take all three gifts.

"He is truly the one we are looking for—king, priest and prophet," Melchior said, delighted.

"And who would believe it?" Gaspar asked. "We did not find him in a royal palace or in a holy temple, but in this lowly cottage in an obscure village."

With respectful homage, the magi left. Yosef looked at Miryam, his face full of dread. "I wonder how long it will be before the news of these men will reach the royal throne."

"Wake up!" Melchior cried out, trying to rouse Gaspar and Balthazar.

Balthazar opened his eyes and tried to focus. "What is it?"

"I was warned in a dream about Herod's evil intentions. He does not want to worship the child—he wants to kill him."

The three men took dreams seriously, and made preparations to leave in haste. Avoiding the royal palace, they went by another way. The star appeared once more as they set out on their journey, its tail reaching from the highest point of the heavens to the earth below. The magi followed its light all the way home.

12

"Why do you not stay longer?" Shaul asked Yosef, pleased with all the attention his home had received. "There is no need to return to Natzeret. There is plenty of work for a carpenter in Yerushalayim."

"We have been here over a year," Yosef answered, remembering his brother's harsh words when they left. How could they return to Natzeret?

"But this is the Shabbat," Shaul said. "We should not be talking of work. The Shabbat is a foretaste of the world to come."

"And what might that world look like?"

"There would be no need to work," he replied, smiling at the thought. "We would not worry about money—what shall we eat, what shall we wear? We would have time to rest, to pray, to study, to enjoy our family and friends—to enjoy life! That is what we will be doing in heaven!"

For the Yehudim, the Shabbat was the most important ritual observance, the only one commanded in the Torah: "Remember the Shabbat, and keep it holy." To keep the seventh day holy, work was prohibited. No meals were cooked; seeds were not sown, and the harvest was not reaped.

On the eve of the Shabbat, Shaul and Yosef attended a brief synagogue service. Walking home in the cool night air, Shaul mulled over the lesson. "The rabbi said that when a man comes home from synagogue he is accompanied by two angels—a good angel and a bad angel. If everything is in readiness, and the home is peaceful, then the good angel says, 'So may it be next week,' and the bad angel replies, 'Amen, so may it be!' But if the meal is not prepared, and the home is in disarray, the bad angel says, 'So may it be next week,' and the good angel answers, 'Amen, so may it be!'"

"The good angel will triumph in your home." Yosef clapped him on the back. "Everything will be as it should be."

The Shabbat, like all holy days, began at sunset when three stars appeared in the sky. When the sun slipped behind the hills, casting a purplish shade on the earth, two Shabbat lamps were lit: *zachor*, to remember, and *shamor*, to observe the law. As mistress of the house,

Rut lit the lamps. Covering her eyes, she prayed in an expressionless voice, "May the radiance of Adonai shine forth from one end of the universe to the other."

Then she fetched a small bowl and filled it with water. When hands were washed, a cup was filled with wine. As head of the house, Shaul recited the *Kiddush*, the prayer sanctifying the wine: "Blessed are you, Adonai Eloheinu, Ruler of the Universe, who created the fruit of the vine."

All responded: "Amen!"

Shaul drank from the cup, passing it around the table while singing: "Come, my beloved, let us go out to meet Queen Shabbat." Then he prayed over the loaves of bread. "Blessed are you Adonai Eloheinu, Ruler of the Universe, who brings forth bread from the earth."

All answered: "Amen!"

After their simple meal of boiled fish and vegetable stew, Shaul remarked, with some bitterness, "It is said that King Herod eats three and sometimes four meals a day, followed by a drinking bout."

"And people mock his red face and large belly," Rut said, eyeing her husband.

Yosef tried to lighten the mood. "There is a proverb. 'Better is a dinner of vegetables where there is love than a fatted ox where there is hatred.'"

After the meal, the family talked late into the evening, singing and clapping their hands, much to the enjoyment of Yeshua, who was wide awake.

Shaul and Rut bid them "Shabbat Shalom" when at last they retired.

※

Yosef woke with a start. For a moment he did not know whether he was awake or asleep. "Miryam, get up!"

She opened her eyes and stared at him, afraid to ask what was wrong.

"I had a terrifying dream," he whispered.

"What sort of a dream?" She lifted herself on one elbow, wiping sleep from her eyes.

"An angel told me to take you and the child to Egypt."

"Egypt? Why Egypt?"

"I do not know. The angel only said that King Herod intends to find the child and kill him."

"Kill him?" Miryam gasped, struggling to her feet.

Yosef was already packing his carpenter's tools and their few possessions. Miryam dressed in the darkness. She went to a small trunk, opened it, and unrolled a blanket. Wordlessly, she held out the gifts from the magi for Yosef to see.

He nodded, adding them to their bundles. "They might be useful on our journey."

Shaul entered the room, still in his nightclothes. "What is happening, brother?" he asked, bleary-eyed.

"We must leave," Yosef said. "King Herod intends to do away with our child."

"Why would Herod want to kill your child? How do you know this?"

"I had a dream," was all Yosef could say.

"A dream?" Shaul laughed. "You had a dream and you are ready to leave? Perhaps there was too much spice in the stew."

Soon Rut joined them, holding an oil lamp in her hand. The flame cast an eerie glow on her dour face.

"My brother and sister," Yosef said. "I cannot expect you to understand. I only know that the dream was real and we must go."

"It is still the Shabbat," Shaul protested. "You cannot travel on the Shabbat."

"If the Lord sent an angel to tell us to flee on the Shabbat, then we must go," Yosef said, embracing Shaul. "Thank you for your kindness. We will never forget you."

As Miryam picked up her sleeping child, he woke and began to whimper.

"You will have to keep him quiet," Yosef warned.

"Shush, shush, shush," she whispered, rocking him.

Rut fumbled around for some cheese and bread. Wrapping the food in a towel she handed it to Yosef along with a jug of wine.

"May the Lord reward you," Miryam said. Rut awkwardly kissed her on the cheek. Shaul placed his hands on Yosef's shoulders and prayed. "May the Most High be your dwelling place. May he command his angels to guard you in all your ways."

Gathering their baggage, Yosef opened the door and peered out into the silent street. The stars were beginning to fade, and he knew they would have to hurry before daylight. When it appeared that all was clear, he fetched his drowsy donkey, leading it up the stairs from the manger and outside. After hitching the beast to his cart, he helped Miryam climb in with the child.

Shaul and Rut stood in the doorway, shivering in the black night. The wind moaned and Rut drew her night dress close about her. "I am cold. Can we go inside?"

Shaul looked disgruntled. Then, waving goodbye, they went inside and closed the door.

Yosef covered Miryam and the child with straw, placing the bundles to hide them. The child stirred. Miryam opened her dress and put her breast to Yeshua's mouth.

"Please, holy angels, keep my little one quiet," she prayed. She held him so close she was afraid she would smother him.

Yosef held fast to the donkey's reins as he led it down the empty street. The beast, often slow and stubborn, hurried along, seeming to understand the urgency of his task. In the shadows, Yosef could see a lone soldier guarding the gates of the village. Yosef's lips moved in silent prayer.

"Halt!" The young officer's hand was on the hilt of his sword. "Who are you? Where are you going? What do you have in the cart?"

"I am a carpenter," Yosef said. His heart was beating so hard he was sure the guard could hear it. "My business is finished here and I am looking for work in another town."

He fished among the baggage for his tools. The soldier looked apprehensive. Yosef held up his hand. "Look," he said, holding out a plane, an awl and a hammer for him to see.

"Why are you out at this hour?" he snarled.

"I must get an early start," Yosef said, trying to hide his shaking hands. "I want to reach the next town before other laborers take whatever work there is."

The soldier grunted. "Move along then."

Yosef bowed his head in gratitude, pulled on the reins of the donkey, hurrying away from Beit Lechem. When they were well beyond the city walls, he spoke in a low voice, "Miryam, I think we are safe now."

She lifted a bit of the straw. "Yosef, we must stop to pray!"

"Pray? There is no time," he whispered back, trying to cover her with straw again.

Miryam pushed the straw aside. "Look, there is the tomb of Rachel," she said, her eyes pleading.

Yosef sighed. "There is no hope of changing your mind once it is made up."

For hundreds of years women had come to Rachel's tomb, pouring out their hearts to the Mother of Sorrows—barren women; women who miscarried or aborted their child; mothers of sick and dying children; mothers of wayward sons and daughters. Weeping, they would catch their tears in tiny cups and place them on the tomb. When the exiles were driven from their homes, they passed by Rachel's tomb, pleading that one day they would come back from the land of the enemy.

Yosef wanted to believe that the Lord would bring them home, too. Looking around to be sure that they were alone, he helped Miryam to get out of the cart. As soon as she knelt beside the tomb, she began to weep.

"My name is Miryam," she sobbed as though Rachel could somehow hear her. "I have come to ask you to pray to the Holy One of Yisrael to protect our child. Holy is his Name. Holy is my child."

The couple knelt in silence for some time, until Yosef insisted that it was time to go. Helping Miryam to her feet, and then into the cart, he covered her and the sleeping child with straw.

As they continued their journey, the bright yellow sun rose, warming their cold bodies. Yosef nodded to a farmer, already at work plowing his field. The farmer raised a hand in greeting. It almost seemed like a benediction.

Mile after weary mile, they plodded along the never-ending desert road. Yosef prayed, trying to understand. *Why are you sending us to Egypt—the land that made slaves of our ancestors? What will await us in that foreign land? How will we survive? We have never traveled this road before. How will we find our way?*

The howling wind was the only answer.

13

How long has that accursed star been there? Why did those foreigners see it and my councilors did not?

King Herod raged over the thought that there might be a rival to his throne. Called the 'Great" by his admirers, Herod was despised by the populace who called him the Idumean 'slave' of Rome. A man of mixed ethnic origins, his father, Antipater, was an Idumean, and his mother, Cyprus, a Nabataean, daughter of an Arabian sheik. But Herod held allegiance to no one, not to the Romans, or to Zeus of Olympia—not even to the Holy One of Yisrael.

From his terrace, Herod studied the night sky, as black as his mood—except for one bright star. He sent for his advisors, demanding that they give him answers. The scribes poured over the ancient scrolls. One of them declared: "Seventy-six generations have passed since creation. It is said that the Mashiach will deliver Yisrael in the seventy-seventh generation." He peered at Herod. "I believe that it is this generation."

"Pfaw!" Herod shouted, raising his hand as if to strike him. "A fool would know that!"

Another scribe gave Herod an anxious look. "The oracle of Balaam said that a star will rise out of Yaakov and his scepter will spring from Yisrael—and he will rule over all people."

An elderly scribe sucked a tooth. "The scriptures say that the Mashiach will come of the seed of David, from Beit Lechem, where King David was born."

"Why do you tell me this now?" Herod cried. "Why did you not warn me before those foreigners arrived? What good are you? I should have you all killed."

The scribes fled down the passageway. Herod screamed after them. "When the Mashiach arrives he will come as a grown man, not as a helpless infant." His voice rose to a fevered pitch. "And the Mashiach will not make his appearance in an unimportant town like Beit Lechem! He will come on a cloud, announced by the trumpeters of the temple—which I built!"

He staggered out to his terrace, scanning the heavens again. He was seventy years old and ill; he knew there were many waiting to sit on his throne, above all his son Antipater. He had already rid himself of his sons, Alexander and Aristobulus—executed for treason. For a moment Herod dwelt on the thought of killing Antipater, too. First, he must tend to this so-called "King of the Yehudim." How old was this upstart? Was he old enough to be a threat? The census might provide the answer.

Coughing up yellow phlegm, he spat. The mucus landed on a startled sentry below.

"You," he shouted. "Come up here at once."

Herod stormed inside his quarters, waiting for the guard to arrive. The man stood trembling as Herod scribbled an order. "Take this to the Roman tribune in the Fortress Antonia. I want the names of all families with infants two years or less." The guard scurried away to do his bidding.

Herod paced the floor like a mad man until the guard finally returned. He squinted at the scroll. His eyes were failing and he was unable to make out the names. Growing angrier, he called for the chief guard.

"I order you to send soldiers to Beit Lechem—and every town and village in the area. Spittle flew from his mouth. "Kill any male child you find under the age of two. Tear the obnoxious bastards from their mothers' arms and run them through with the sword. Or cast them from the cliffs. I do not care, just so they are all killed!"

Herod's soldiers had been standing around all day in the freezing cold, huddling over a charcoal fire in the brazier. With Caesar's army in control, they felt impotent. What good were they but to stand at attention like eunuchs, with only ceremonial duties to perform? What use was a sword if not put to some purpose? And so, when the order came, they went.

An icy wind blew in the gray streets and thunderclouds swept from the north as the soldiers set out at a fast pace. Some rode horses, their hooves flinging clods of earth into the air, their hides rippling as though in anticipation of their heinous mission. A rider approached the first house where a mother stood in the doorway nursing her child.

"Your son?" the soldier asked, leaning forward on his mount. The mother nodded in frightened confusion. Without a word he snatched the infant from her arms and dashed him to the ground. The child lay unconscious, the milk running from its little mouth. His mother shrieked as the soldier ran him through with his sword.

Hearing the screams, a neighbor ran from her house carrying her infant; another toddler clung to her dress. The soldier grabbed the terrified boy by the hair and cut his throat. The mother stifled her cry in fear for the rest of her family.

"Your son?" the soldier pointed his sword to the babe in her arms.

"My daughter," she lied, her voice quavering.

The solder ripped the shawl that covered the baby, exposing the genitals. With swift thrusts he pierced both the boy and the woman's heart before moving on to find his next victim.

The dead woman's husband came running from the house. Seeing the bloody scene, he clutched his head and fell to his knees sobbing. All around people fled. The horsemen pursued them, swinging their swords at anyone in their path. Women screamed as they struggled to hold on to their children. Some of them fell to the ground and were trampled to death.

House after house, street after street, the horrible deed was repeated until twenty infants of Beit Lechem were massacred. By late afternoon, a sad procession moved to the graveyard on the hillside. Some men held their shrouded wives' bodies in their arms, while others carried their dead sons, their hopes and dreams for the future forever lost. Mothers followed behind, walking in an unsteady gait, like sleepwalkers hoping to awake from a nightmare. A sound like none other arose—a high-pitched wailing, beginning in their hearts and moving to their throats, mourning the cruel and sudden death of their children.

Indifferent to their lamentation, Herod's soldiers marched out of Beit Lechem, carrying their weapons as if they were advancing on an enemy army. When they came across a farmer working in his field, the leader barked, "Have you seen a man or a woman with a child pass this way?"

"Oh, yes." The farmer waved a hand toward his field, freshly sown with winter wheat. "They came by a long time ago as I was harvesting my grain."

The soldier snorted and struck the farmer a heavy blow with the back of his hand.

Yosef and Miryam set out toward the great desert, doing what their ancestors had done throughout their troubled past. When persecution or famine made life intolerable in Yisrael, the Yehudim sought refuge in Egypt, more than 200 miles away, a route well-traveled by camel caravans. On an ordinary day, they could walk twenty miles, but with a slow moving donkey pulling a cart over rough terrain, they could not travel that fast.

When evening drew near, Yosef looked for a safe place where they could spend the night out of the relentless wind that blew sand in their faces. There on a hilly ridge was a small cave that would suit their needs, the opening large enough to accommodate the donkey and cart. Yosef helped Miryam down, and then unhitched the donkey. While Miryam held her child, he coaxed the stubborn animal up the hill. Pushing it from behind, Yosef got the beast inside, and pulled the cart as far back into the cave as it would go. Then he went outside to cover their tracks.

Miryam stooped and looked into the dark cave, trying to protect Yeshua's head from the low ceiling. The cold, dank air had a tomb-like smell, yet she felt as if she was stepping into the womb of the Holy One. They would be safe here.

The couple felt their way along the wall as their eyes adjusted to the dim light. Yosef spread a blanket on the ground and poured a little wine from the skin. Together they ate a simple meal of bread and cheese. Exhausted from the day's ordeal, they settled near the donkey whose body would keep them warm against the winter chill. Yosef enfolded his wife and child in his arms, drawing them close. He could feel Miryam's heart beating against his chest, the boy's soft breath keeping rhythm with his own.

"Miryam," Yosef said, after some time. "I have been thinking about the story of my ancestor Yosef. He was betrayed by his brothers and sold as a slave in Egypt. But the Pharaoh made him his advisor. Instead of the chains of slavery, he wore a gold chain around his neck." Yosef paused for a moment. "He was someone important; I am just a poor carpenter."

"You are more precious than gold to me," Miryam whispered.

He patted her hand. "When Yosef's brothers repented, he told them, 'You meant it for evil, but the Lord meant it for good.'"

"I do not understand how good can come from this evil," she said in a forlorn voice.

"Do you remember the promise the Lord spoke to Yosef's father, Yaakov?" Without waiting for an answer he continued. "The Lord said, 'Do not be afraid to go down to Egypt, for I will go with you and I will bring you back.'"

She gripped his arm. "Do you really believe that? Do you believe that all of this is the will of the Lord?"

"One day we will know. For now, the Lord will send his angels to guard us on our way. You will see."

"There are no angels to protect us here," she wept. "The angel left me before the child was born."

"The Lord will not fail us, dear one," he said, trying to reassure her.

"You are my angel now." She rested her head on Yosef's shoulder. He stroked her hair, and in a few moments she fell asleep, worn out from the journey. Yosef prayed that the angels would be with them.

The rising sun cast a finger of light into the cave, and played on Yosef's face. He opened his eyes, shivering in the cold. Standing up, he stretched his stiff limbs, then feeling his way along the wall, he reached the farthest recesses of the cave where he relieved himself. Returning to his sleeping family, he drew the blanket close around them.

The sound of voices outside startled him. Miryam awoke and Yeshua stirred. Yosef put his finger to his lips and Miryam held her son close to quiet him. Getting down on his hands and knees, Yosef crawled toward the cave's entrance. He drew a sharp breath when he saw a detachment of Herod's soldiers making their way toward them.

"Search that cave," the leader ordered. "If the ones we are looking for are not hiding in the cave, there may be bandits in there."

Yosef prayed silently. *Lord, protect us. Do not deliver us to the wild beasts.*

A soldier was about to enter the cave when he noticed a gossamer web, sparkling with frost, spun across the opening. "Look! The spider's web is unbroken," he said. "Anyone going into the cave would have torn it." He stamped his feet on the frozen ground as he waited for his orders.

The captain pulled the horse's bridle, turning it away. "We have done enough. Let us return to Yerushalayim."

When Yosef was certain the soldiers were gone, he murmured a prayer of thanksgiving. "Truly the Lord is our shield, the Holy One of Israel, our refuge, our Lord in whom we trust."

Yosef looked in wonder at the giant web covering the cave's entrance, the sun sparkling on hundreds of dewdrops. Cradling her child, Miryam crept alongside him.

"Like precious pearls," he said to her. "If I could, I would make you a necklace with them."

"And what would I do with such an ornament?"

He took her hand and looked at her as though he had never seen her before, her fine straight nose, the sweet curve of her mouth, her eyes the color of black obsidian. "I have the finest pearl in the world, a pearl of great price."

She blushed and turned her attention to the child. "Look, my little lamb." She touched the web and the spider scurried off to some dark corner.

"I hate to destroy such a beautiful thing," Yosef said, sliding his hand down the web to make a way out. Yeshua opened and closed his little fist trying to grasp the strands as they floated in the breeze.

Yosef peered out of the cave. Squinting in the bright sunlight, he cried, "Miryam! Snow! That is why our tracks were not seen. It is a miracle."

Miryam looked with awe at the white blanket covering the stony ground. The only tracks were those of the soldiers leading away from them. She closed her eyes and prayed. "The angel of the Lord encamps around those who fear him, and delivers them."

14

Day after day, Yosef and Miryam endured the scorching heat, and, by night, the bitter cold of the rugged wastelands. Worse were the fierce *Khamsin* windstorms that filled their nostrils and throats with suffocating dust. If they could not find a grotto for shelter, then there was nothing to do but wrap their heads in their mantles, turn their backs to the wind and wait for the storm to pass.

When the sandstorm died down, Yosef shaded his burning eyes from the sun, which glowed like a silver disc through the dusty haze. He could barely make out some rough-looking men approaching.

"Robbers," he said, panic in his voice.

In a moment, the men surrounded them. One of the men, who seemed to be the leader, barked, "Give us whatever you have in that cart." Miryam hugged Yeshua, knowing that their hidden treasures would put their lives in danger.

"Abu," a young boy said to his father. "Look, they are only a poor family. What could they have that we would want? We have more to give them than they could give us."

His father thought for a moment, and then exhaled deeply. "Let them go."

Seeing kindness in the young brigand's eyes, Miryam summoned the courage to speak to him. "What is your name?"

"Dismas," he answered, touching Yeshua's head with his grimy hand. "If we ever meet again, please do not forget this hour."

The robbers moved on, and Yosef and Miryam continued their arduous journey, grateful once more for divine protection. They lost count of the days. Had another Shabbat passed without their knowing it? Travelling south along the east branch of the Nile, they spied a town in the distance.

"We can stop there and rest," Yosef said. "Perhaps we will find food and lodging."

When they approached the city gates, they stopped to stare at the shrine of Bast, the lion-headed war goddess. While looking at its grotesque shape, a man and his son began setting up a stall to sell their produce. As Yosef eyed the colorful bounty of fresh figs, cucumbers and melons, the older man looked at him with distrust.

"Ghareeb?" the boy asked in Arabic.

Yosef gestured, hoping he would be understood. "We…are traveling…to Egypt…we have no food."

"You welcome to take what you need," he answered in broken Aramaic.

"May the Almighty repay you for your kindness," Yosef said in gratitude, but before he could take anything, the earth began to tremble.

"Earthquake!" the boy shouted as everyone ran for cover.

When the shaking stopped, the townsfolk were astonished. The temple of Bast had crumbled amid a great cloud of dust.

"I saw this man looking at our shrine with 'al ayn,' the evil eye," the old man said, coughing and spitting out debris from his mouth. "These foreigners have inflicted us with this misfortune. The goddess can no longer live here."

Yosef was not afraid of the idol; it was only stone, made by human hands like his. But he feared for his family's safety. They left in haste, the shouting and cursing ringing in their ears.

By the middle of the day, the merciless sun scorched the surface of the desert and beat down on their heads, making them feel as though their life's breath was being drained away. The journey was taking its toll, and there were many more miles to travel. Yosef prayed as he walked, putting one sand-filled sandal in front of the other. He tried to draw courage from the Lord's promise to Moshe when the people crossed into the Promised Land: "Be strong; have no fear, because Adonai Eloheinu goes with you; he will not fail you or forsake you."

At last they found shelter under a lone tree. While Miryam changed the baby's swaddling clothes, Yosef opened the wineskin. He tasted the last dregs, his lips dried and cracked. The wine had gone sour and he spat it out.

"Why did the Lord bring us out to the desert to die?" he wailed, sinking to his knees, and lifting his hands in despair.

Miryam knelt beside him, surprised at his sudden despair. "Yosi, Yosi, the Lord will bring us through this. We were not brought out to the desert to die but to live."

He held his head in his hands and rocked back and forth. "I am not Moshe. I cannot call down bread from heaven or make water spring from a rock. There are no quail for us to catch." He swept his hand across the barren landscape. "Look. There is not a green blade anywhere!"

She looked on helplessly as tears rolled down his face into his beard.

"Miryam," he sobbed. "We have gone too far to turn back. Where are we going? Where is the pillar of fire or the cloud to show us the way?"

"All will be well, dear Yosi," she said. "We have the child of the Most High with us."

Yosef wiped his tears with the heel of his hand, and wrapped his arms around her. As he raised his eyes, there, above them, were fresh dates in the fronds. He jumped up, shook the tree and the fruit fell to the ground.

"The sages say that adversity wears a precious jewel on its head," he said as they ate.

She smiled and added her own adage. "As an apple tree among the trees of the wood so is my beloved among men."

His eyes widened at this unexpected affection, but Yeshua's insistent cry interrupted them. He was hungry, too. Miryam sat in the shade of the tree to tend to him. *How long before my milk dries up and I have nothing to give him?*

When Yeshua finished nursing, Yosef played with him, swinging him round and round. Yeshua held fast to his father's neck, squealing with delight. "Abba, Abba."

"Miryam! Did you hear?" Yosef hugged and kissed the boy. "Yeshua called me 'Abba!'"

She frowned and put her hands on her hips. "I gave birth to him, nursed him, hovered over him like a mother bird, helped him take his first steps, worried for his life, and now the first word he speaks is not 'Ima,' but 'Abba!'"

"Do not fret, mother bird," Yosef said, laughing. "Your son knew you from the first moment he opened his eyes."

With the cooling twilight, they continued their journey—Yosef leading the weary donkey, Miryam and the child bouncing in the cart. Yosef made no complaint as he plodded along, not even when his blistered feet burned with every step. Darkness fell, and the desert grew cold again. Finding a sprawling shrub that could give them protection, he spread a blanket on the ground and wrapped another around Miryam and the child. Huddling together, they looked up at the stars, which looked like lamps in the black dome above them.

"Look at that," Miryam said, pointing to a great sweep of stars flooding the sky. "It looks like the angels spilled milk in the heavens."

"They call it the 'River of Heaven,'" Yosef said.

For a long time they looked skyward without saying a word. The moon glowed like a fine gem amidst the canopy of stars above them.

"Yosi," Miryam murmured.

"Yes, my dear," he answered, gazing at a shooting star blazing across the sky.

"How was it possible for those men from the East to follow just one star? There are so many."

He stroked his beard. "Because they were wise men."

Miryam smiled and curled close to him, making a pillow of her arms. While she and Yeshua slept, Yosef kept his eyes on the heavens. "Lord, you who dwell in the tent above us, I pray that you will watch over us."

When they awoke, the sky was bright and the stars had faded away. Yosef suddenly recognized the large shrub that sheltered them.

"Miryam!" he cried. "This is a broom tree."

She looked at him sleepy-eyed. "What makes it so special?"

"The broom tree is the thorn-bush, the most humble of plants. That is why the Most High chose it to reveal his glory to Moshe. Miryam, the Lord is in this place and we knew it not."

At that moment, he felt something fall on his brow. Taking the white substance, he turned it over in his hand. "Manna."

"What is it?" Miryam asked.

"That is what the nomads call this stuff," he said, laughing. "Manna means, 'What is it?'"

"Can you eat it?"

He put it to his tongue. "It tastes sweet, like honey."

"But where did it come from?"

"Insects have left some sort of substance in the bark—look." He stood and bent a thorny branch for her to see. "When the wind blows, the dried pieces fall to the ground."

Miryam leapt to her feet. "The Lord has sent us manna from heaven!"

Yosef grabbed both of her hands and swung her around until they were dizzy. When they fell to the ground, their child's eyes flew open, startled. Another piece of manna fell on her gown and she put it to his mouth. He smacked his lips eager for more.

"Come little one, let us collect the manna." She lifted him high in the air. "We who have little will gather much."

15

Yosef blinked, trying to clear the sweat from his eyes. Was that a glimmer of water in the distance? Or was it just a mirage? No, there was an oasis, like a blue jewel shimmering in the tawny desert. The clear air carried the sounds of shepherds herding their flocks of sheep and goats. Their shouts and whistles mingled with the low moaning of camels as their drivers urged them along.

The Bedouin considered the camel a gift from Alláh. They depended upon them for their existence. They ate its meat, drank its milk and used its urine as a tonic to protect their hair from parasites. Its fur was woven into flaps for tents, and its hide was used to make sandals, water bags, and even troughs for the camels to drink.

Bedouin called them the "Ships of the Desert" because of the heavy loads they carried for trade from southern Arabia to Egypt. Camels were well-made for desert travel. Their broad feet kept them from sinking into the sand, and they could close their nostrils to keep the sand out of their noses. The animals tolerated thirst for long periods, grazing on thorny desert shrubs that even sheep and goats passed over.

But when the camels smelled water, in their frenzy, they knocked over their drivers and anything else that stood in their way. After the animals slaked their thirst, the herdsmen tapped them with long poles, urging them to lie down so they could unload their goods. The camels crouched on their forelegs and folded their hind legs under their heavy bodies.

"They look like they are praying," Miryam whispered with amusement as she and Yosef approached.

"Be careful," one of the herders warned. "Camels can expel the contents of their stomachs toward anyone they think is threatening them."

"*Salām*, peace be with you," a young man said, with a slight bow, touching his forehead and heart. "My name is Ali," he said, smiling, his teeth as white as his headdress.

The couple looked surprised to hear him speak their native Aramaic.

"I speak many languages," he explained. He filled a water bag and handed it to Yosef, who gave Miryam a drink, first. "A drink of water and a safe place to stay means the difference between life and death in this desert land. We give food and shelter to others, because one day we might need it ourselves."

When their thirst was quenched, Yosef led their donkey to the watering hole. The camels kept a wary eye on him as Yosef spread a blanket beneath the shade of a date-palm. Then he and Miryam sat down to rest.

"Everything is either thirsty or hungry," Yosef mused, watching birds squabbling for the ripe fruit above them.

In the late afternoon, the women set up their long, black tents, woven from goat hair.

"When it rains, the weave does not let the water in, and the inside remains cool in the heat of the summer," Ali explained.

While the women worked, the men set about digging a fire pit to cook the meal, using dry camel excrement for fuel. Iron plates were placed over the smoky fire for the women to bake *abud*, a simple mixture of flour and water shaped into flat cakes. Ashes settled on the dough as it cooked, and when it was baked, the ashes were shaken off and the warm bread passed around.

"The Bedouin believe that any guest is the guest of Alláh," Ali told them. "We have a saying: 'Eat bread together and be friends forever.' Offering bread is a sacred law, and it is a violation to decline it. The bread might be a coarse barley loaf, but it is still bread, the best a poor man can give."

Miryam and Yosef poured a little water over their hands and wrists as was their custom. Then, taking a piece of bread, they closed their eyes in a silent prayer of gratitude. The Bedouin frowned at this extravagant waste of precious water, but they recited their own prayer finishing with, "Alláh be praised." Folding the bread over at the end, they spooned the vegetables from a common dish. Dried dates were then passed around and washed down with sweet wine.

Twilight gave way to the deep blue of the sky, and a silvery moon rose over the horizon, flooding the darkness with its lamp. Ali joined Yosef and Miryam by the fire, watching the flames sending red and gold sparks into the star studded sky.

"From the time we were very young, every Bedouin has learned how to navigate over the trackless desert, using the stars to guide them. That is what made us a nation of great merchants," Ali said.

As everyone began to settle in for the night, an aged man gathered the children to tell them a story. The adults were also eager to listen. The storyteller was thin and bent, with fleece-white hair and a dark, wrinkled face. Yet when he smiled, the corners of his eyes crinkled, making him appear very kind.

"I will interpret the story if you like," Ali said.

The storyteller cleared his raspy throat. "Once there was a sultan named Shahryār. He had a beautiful wife, but, when he discovered that she was unfaithful, he had her executed. Then he came to the conclusion that all women were unfaithful."

Yosef glanced at Miryam, knowing how close he came to sentencing her to death.

"Now, the sultan scorned women. So he began to marry one maiden after another, only to execute each one, until none were left but the beautiful Scheherazade. Against her father's will, she offered herself as the sultan's bride. Scheherazade had read a thousand books, and so on their wedding night, she told the sultan a story—the Voyage of Sinbad the Sailor, Aladdin and his Wonderful Lamp, the Merchant and the Genie, Ali Baba and the Forty Thieves, and many, many others." The storyteller took a swig of water.

"Scheherazade was very wise. When she told the story, she did not end it. Thus the sultan was forced to keep the young woman alive so that he might hear the end of the story the next night. And what do you think happened?"

The children looked amused. They had heard the story many

times before.

"The next night, as soon as Scheherazade finished the tale, she began another. And so it went for a thousand and one nights!"

The storyteller smiled with satisfaction, and the children clapped in approval.

Miryam looked downcast. "She wanted what we all want—to live."

Ali smiled and held out his hand, wanting to be paid for his service. Yosef took a coin from his purse and gave it to him. Ali bowed low, and, as he started to leave, turned back. "The Bedouin have a proverb: 'All sunshine makes a desert.' The land on which the sun always shines becomes an arid place where no fruit grows. Only the rain produces the crop—and only sorrow brings forth good fruit." Then he touched his forehead and heart, and, with a slight bow, retired to his tent.

Yosef was taken to the men's tent, and Miryam was shown to the women's tent. One of the women spoke Aramaic, and she invited her to sit on the carpet beside her. "I was wondering," Miryam asked, nestling Yeshua in her arms. "Why are there so few infants traveling with you?"

It was some moments before the woman could speak. "Life is hard in the desert. Is there anything as terrible as watching your child die? To hold your dead son in your arms? To bury him in a grave and leave him there?"

"I cannot imagine what that would be like," Miryam said, shaking her head.

"I hope you never will find out," the woman said, reaching out to caress Yeshua's cheek. Then she covered her face with her hands and wept.

Miryam lay awake for a long time pondering the proverb Ali had told them. It seemed that he had read their troubled hearts. She gazed at the pin-prick holes in the top of the tent, which looked like stars shining in the heavens above. "Heavenly Father, watch over my child," she prayed.

As sleep began to settle over her, she listened to the sound of tent flaps whipping in the wind while the herdsmen serenaded their camels.

You have traveled far and wide.
You have walked over hot desert sand.
You have carried precious cargo.
May you sleep well; may you sleep well.

16

For thousands of years, the civilization of Egypt had been woven from the strands of migrating people with various philosophies and religious beliefs. Among these were the Yehudim. They were the *tefutzah*, people who had been scattered throughout the world after Cyrus, King of Persia, liberated them from exile in Babylonia. Many settled in Alexandreus at the mouth of the river Nile. The city was named for the Macedonian King Alexandros, called 'the Great,' who spread the Greek culture to Egypt.

After Roma, Alexandreus was one of the largest cities in size and wealth. It was a cosmopolitan city with wide avenues, and an enormous temple dedicated to Augustus Caesar. At one time its renowned library, containing hundreds of thousands of volumes, included the Greek translation of the Bible. But during a great battle, Julius Caesar set fire to his own ships; the fire spread, burning the docks and destroying the library.

To Yosef and Miryam, Egypt was a mysterious land of false gods who were honored with festivals and processions. Yosef averted his eyes from a statue of the god Sarapis, who he heard had been consulted on behalf of King Alexandros when he was dying.

"Idols," Yosef scoffed. "I wonder what it was like for our ancestors who lived in this pagan land."

Tugging on the reins of the donkey, he tried to hurry it along, but noticed that the beast was limping.

"Yehudim," a tall, silver-haired man snarled in Greek as they passed. "Any time there is a problem in the world you come pouring into Egypt. You should stay home and stop filling our country with your refuse."

Yosef did not understand him, but knew his meaning.

"Are you visitors?" a woman asked in Aramaic. She carried a toddler, and was big with another child.

"We are refugees," he answered, glad to hear his own tongue spoken.

"Are you hungry?" she asked, kindness in her voice.

He nodded. Judging from her tattered clothes she was not much better off than they were.

"Please. Come to our home and share our meal."

She led them toward her modest mud-brick house. He thought it looked like one of the tombs they passed in the desert, but he was grateful for her hospitality. Unbridling the donkey, he led it to a watering trough, where it drank thirstily. Miryam leaned forward, whispering into the donkey's long ears, "Thank you, dear friend, for keeping us safe on our journey." The animal lifted its head and looked at her as if it understood. "Take your rest," she said, patting his graying muzzle.

They followed the woman into the one room home the family shared. Yosef paused at the doorway, touching the *mezuzah* affixed to it, kissing his fingers in respect for the Law of Moshe. Then he touched it again and, putting his fingers to Yeshua's lips, he said, "May Adonai guard you in your coming and in your going."

"My name is Devorah," the woman said, as two more ragged children came to greet them. "And this is my husband Benyamin."

As Yosef embraced him, he looked up at the shafts of dust-filled sunlight streaming through the lightly thatched roof. Pigeons perched on the beams, and there was a strong smell of dung.

"Ah, my doves," Benyamin smiled. "They are happy to sit up there and raise their families. And we are happy to eat them."

Miryam offered to help Devorah prepare the food, and she set Yeshua down on the earthen floor where he crawled underfoot.

"Let me tell you a story about the dove." Yosef sat on the floor and pulled Yeshua onto his lap. The children quickly gathered around him.

"Once, in the days of Noach, the people were so sinful that the Almighty wanted to destroy them. But Noach was a good man, like your father."

He nodded to Benyamin and the children beamed.

"Well, one day, the Almighty told Noach that there would be a great flood, and that he should build a boat, large enough for every sort of animal. And Noach did as he was told, and, two by two, all the animals marched into the boat."

"Even lions?" one boy asked.

"Even lions," Yosef said, patting the boy's head. "So, one day the flood came, and it destroyed everything on earth, except Noah and his family—and the animals in the boat. Now, when the storm was over, Noach wanted to see if the land was dry. So he sent out a raven. But this raven was not smart. It just flew to and fro over the water and soon returned to the ark. Then Noach looked around for a better bird.

The ostrich was so big it could not fly, and the peacock was so proud he thought only of himself. So Noach thought of the most loving bird he knew—the dove."

He smiled at Miryam, and she smiled back.

"Noach knew that if he sent out the dove, it would return to its nest on the ark with food for its young. And that is what happened. The dove returned with a green olive branch in its beak, and Noach knew that the land was dry."

"Ow! Something bit me." Benyamin yelped and rubbed his thigh. The children giggled behind their hands. "Tell me Yosef, why did Noach bring fleas and spiders into the ark?"

"I think there should be room for all creatures," Miryam said, trying to hide her smile. As she looked down, she caught sight of a little spider climbing up the hem of her skirt. "Oh!" she exclaimed, with a little jump.

"Is there no room for spiders, my dove?" Yosef asked, smiling.

Miryam frowned. "Do you think that spider followed us all the way to Egypt?"

Benyamin looked puzzled, but turned to Yosef. "Did you know that there was once a sacred bird here in Egypt, said to have lived for five hundred years?"

"Five hundred years?" Yosef shook his head in amazement.

"Yes, it is true—or so the legend goes."

"What bird was that?"

"The bird was called the phoenix, a beautiful bird with bright plumage and a tail of scarlet and gold. It is said that when the bird felt death approaching, it built a nest of frankincense, myrrh, and other spices. When the phoenix entered the nest, it caught fire, and the bird died in the flames."

The children looked at him, dismayed.

"Ah," said Benyamin, smiling, "from the ashes a new phoenix arose, with the power to bring the dead to life. What do you think, children? Can the dead be brought back to live again?"

"It is not possible for the dead to rise," the oldest child said.

"Is it possible, Abba?" the youngest asked.

"Come, no more stories," Devorah said, laying out earthenware bowls on the floor. After blessing their simple fare, a large cup of beer was passed around and everyone drank from it.

Yosef and Miryam thought it tasted bitter but they did not let their host know. Yosef leaned back on an elbow and looked up at the openings in the roof. The birds had left their whitewash on the beams. He hoped none would drop on them.

"You are wondering if our house will blow over in a storm," Benyamin said. "Have no worry. It seldom rains in Egypt. The weather is always the same—sunlight and warm breezes one day, and the same the next day."

Yosef nodded and made a sign to Miryam that they had overstayed their visit.

Benyamin waved his hand. "Please, our home is humble but you are welcome to spend the night. In the morning, I will help you find lodging. I know a widow, a good woman, whose children are grown and live far from home. For a small fee, I am sure she will find room for you in her house."

It rained all through the night, and the families huddled together trying to keep dry as best they could.

"Perhaps I took divine providence for granted," Benyamin apologized in the morning.

"No apology is necessary," Yosef protested. "One never knows what the weather will bring."

After a modest meal, they went outside. There in a sad heap was their donkey, tethered to the post where he died. Miryam rushed to his side and knelt on the ground, heedless of the mud. "My dear friend," she wept, stroking the animals matted head. "How could we forget you and let you die this way?"

Devorah knelt beside her, holding her close.

Benyamin helped Yosef put the beast on his cart, and together, they hauled it to a nearby ravine where they dumped the body. When they returned, Benyamin led Yosef and Miryam to the home of the widow Avigal, a slight woman, bent over with age. Though unused to having a child in her home, she was grateful for the extra income.

Benyamin kissed Yosef on both cheeks. Then he wished them Shalom, promising that they would meet again.

"They are a poor but happy family," Yosef said, watching them walk away.

"Like us," Miryam said.

"There is something I can do for them. The Lord gave me the skill of carpentry, so I can fix their roof. Even if it seldom rains, it will keep the pigeon droppings from falling upon them."

"A good *mitzvah*," she agreed.

"You will find many so-called philosophers and orators there," Avigal warned Yosef as he and Miryam set out for the market. "And each one will try to convince you that he alone knows the truth."

Yosef thanked her, and beckoned to Yeshua who reached for his hand. The boy was two years old now, and when Yosef was not carrying him he toddled beside him wherever he went. Miryam slung a cloth bag over one shoulder, and followed behind them.

Even before they reached the marketplace, the smell of pungent spices wafted toward them. Blocking their way was a small boy prodding his goats with a long stick. Some men were pushing carts, peddling their goods. Women carried baskets on their heads, loaded with vegetables and fruit. Others lugged earthen vessels filled with milk.

Miryam marveled at the number of small shops lining the street—carpet weavers, leather crafters, and butchers, and stalls offering pottery, clothing, jewelry, and all sorts of trinkets. Other vendors displayed their goods on blankets. Voices rang out as the buyers tried to outshout the sellers, bantering and bartering in strange accents: How much is that? Too much money! I will give you half!

She stopped to inspect some dried okra hanging on strings, and bins stuffed with fresh vegetables. "At home in Natzeret I grew my own vegetables in my own garden," she complained.

Yeshua held up his hands, and she picked him up, balancing him on one hip. While Yosef went to examine some tools, she went a little farther where canopies shaded an array of colorful bolts of fabric, dyed red, gold, blue and purple. As she stopped to admire the cloth, she overheard women speaking Aramaic.

"They say that the infants were torn from their mothers' arms. There was scarcely a family whose blood did not flow because of the massacre."

"Forgive me," Miryam ventured. "Where did this terrible thing happen?"

The woman seemed annoyed by the stranger listening to her

conversation. "It was in a town called Beit Lechem. A caravan just brought reports of the slaughter."

"Who did this?" Miryam asked with a look of horror on her face.

"Herod." She spat on the ground. "They call him the builder king, but he is the butcher king. His soldiers killed all the boys in the town under the age of two."

"Why would Herod do that?"

"They were looking for a child whom Herod thought would seize his throne."

Miryam hoisted her son to her shoulder, drew her head-scarf close around him, and walked away. If they knew she was from Beit Lechem, they would wonder how she escaped the slaughter. Now she understood. The angel told them to flee to Egypt to escape Herod's sword.

"Miryam!" She was startled to hear a familiar voice calling her name. Who would know her in this foreign land?

"Miryam!" A girl was running toward her, cheeks flushed. "I said to myself that I would find you today. And I did!"

"Shlomit?" Miryam cried. "Can it be you?"

"Yes, it is me." Shlomit beamed at Yeshua. "Look at your son! How he has grown."

Miryam gave Shlomit a warm embrace. "Oh, it is so good to see you again. But what are you doing in Egypt?"

"Your husband told me that I should start a new life. I thought about it for some time. And then something terrible happened."

"The slaughter of the children in Beit Lechem?"

"You have heard?"

"Only now."

"I was so afraid that...." Shlomit stopped and bent to kiss Yeshua. "I went to the house of Shaul, and he told me that you fled to Egypt. So I decided to follow you."

"You traveled all that way alone?"

"I am not as brave as that," Shlomit laughed. "I came with a caravan of refugees. Some of them lost a child and could no longer stay where that murderer ruled."

"And where are you living now?"

"I have no home. I have a little money and sleep wherever I am invited."

"That is not wise," Miryam said. "I will talk to Yosef. You must come and stay with us."

17

"How I miss Natzeret," Miryam told Shlomit, gazing at the scraggly shrubs outside the door. "The field flowers are beginning to grow in the Galil. It seems a lifetime since I bade goodbye to my mother and father. I fear that their faces are beginning to fade from my memory."

With a great sigh, she set about preparing curds and honey for Yeshua. Shlomit held the child on her lap, and he looked up at her with bright eyes. Yosef was out in his workshop, and Avigal had gone to fetch water, unhappy that there was yet another mouth to feed.

Shlomit wiped Yeshua's sticky face and hands and sat him down on the earthen floor to play. "I will go down the road and help Avigal carry the water."

Miryam took the bowl to wash it. Humming a little tune, she took no notice when Yeshua toddled out the door, escaping her watchful eye.

A loud wail startled her. She looked around; Yeshua was not in the house. Had he followed Shlomit? She rushed outside and found him a short distance away, sitting on the ground nursing a skinned knee. Miryam sat next to him and wiped the tears from his cheeks.

"Poor boy, Ima is here to help you," she cooed, laying his head on her shoulder. Spitting in the palm of her hand, she rubbed it on the wound. "This will take the sting out until I can put some oil on it."

He looked up at her with teary eyes as she brushed back the dark curls around his face. "You have lost one of your sandals," she said. "Come, help Ima find it."

She stood and set him on his feet. Taking him by the hand, they walked only a few steps when he squealed with delight.

"My shoe," he said, tugging his mother's hand, pointing to his sandal lying near a thorn bush.

"There it is you clever little man," she said, fetching it. "Now, let us go into the house and fix you up."

Miryam sat him on the table and poured a little oil on his scraped knee. Scolding him gently, she tied the sandal onto his foot. "See, you must not leave Ima's side or you will get hurt or lost."

"My, my, what happened to you my son?" Yosef asked, coming into the house.

Yeshua looked at him with tearful eyes and pointed to his injured knee.

Yosef bent down to examine it. "If that is the worst that ever happens to you, you will have an easy life. But it is too nice a day to spend inside. Let us go for a walk."

Forgetting his injury, Yeshua put his arms out to Yosef, who scooped him up and set him on his shoulders.

"Like a shepherd and his lamb," Miryam mused as they left the house.

Shlomit and Avigal were returning from the well, and Miryam called to them. "Come with us for a walk, it is a beautiful day."

"Yes, it is beautiful today, but what about tomorrow?" Avigal grunted, taking the water jar from Shlomit. "Go along. Someone has to work today." Shlomit did not hesitate to join them.

A cool autumn breeze sent dead leaves flying in the wind as the seasonal change enveloped the land. When they drew near the center of town they heard music. A rowdy band of screeching boys rushed past, and Shlomit chased after them. Miryam moved close to Yosef, glad that he was holding Yeshua in his arms. Soon they came to the public square where they saw a traveling troupe putting on an amazing exhibition. With tremendous energy, the dancers slapped their ankles and stomped the earth in time to the pounding drums and clanging cymbals.

A tall, mahogany-skinned man with large gold earrings stepped into the center of the square. He leaped and twirled, kicking one foot as high as his head and then kicking the other, his hands clapping together under each thigh to the beat of the drum.

A juggler followed, and then a magician, pretending to perform spells, swaying back and forth and chanting incantations. Miryam drew back when he held up a chart covered with diabolical looking images.

A young boy produced a wicked looking asp from his bag. "This is snake that poisoned Cleopatra when Mark Antony was defeated in Alexandreus." He held it up for all to see. "She put snake to her breast, like this."

He held the creature to his own chest, to the astonishment of the crowd. Petting and kissing the snake, he walked among them, his hand outstretched to be paid for his bravery.

"The snake has been defanged," Yosef said when the boy came

toward him, and he shooed him away.

The performance was finished. The dancers and musicians walked among the crowd taking up a collection. A tall, graceful African woman approached Miryam.

Bowing low, she seized her hand and kissed it, but Miryam drew it away.

"Why would I not kiss de hand of a holy woman?" she asked in her clipped tongue. Then she smiled at Yeshua. "I travel all over da' world an' I never see such a beautiful child." You are special child, you know dat? You will make de—how you call—de idols of Egypt—you will make dem fall down. You destin' for great tings."

Miryam was taken aback. A special child destined for great things? The very words that Shlomit spoke when Yeshua was born.

The woman reached into a little pouch in which her donations were kept. Miryam shook her head. "No, you must not give him money."

The woman smiled, her white teeth flashing against her dark skin. "I not give him money. I give him sumting bettah." Fishing around in her pouch, she pulled out a small white amulet and placed it in Yeshua's hand, closing his fingers around it. "On dis stone is written a name known only to you."

Miryam watched as Yeshua turned it over and over in his hands as though trying to read an unseen inscription.

"There is nothing on the stone," Yosef said, snatching it away.

"Mine!" Yeshua wailed.

"Ahh! Only da child can read da name," she laughed. "But not now. No, not now. When he be older, den he will know da name."

The drummer changed his beat, signaling it was time to move on. The woman circled among the people, collecting more coins before disappearing in the crowd.

Yosef started to throw the stone away, but Miryam took it and put it in the bag she carried. "I will keep it for him. Perhaps one day it will mean something to him."

"You have to be careful, Miryam. It may be some sort of sorcery. Perhaps there is a spell attached to it."

"I do not think so. The woman meant to be kind."

"Amulets are worn to ward off evil," he said, sternly. "We do not need its protection. The Most High watches over us."

She said nothing more as they made their way down the coast

road. Yeshua soon forgot about the stone and ran ahead. Yosef and Shlomit gave chase.

Before long they came to the seashore where brown-skinned, half-naked children ran and called to one another. Their mothers sat by the shore washing clothes in the foamy surf. Yeshua stopped every so often to pick up as many shells as his little hands could hold, examining their shape and color. When they reached the docks, they watched men loading grain on boats to be sold in faraway lands.

"Look." Yosef pointed to the colossal lighthouse on the eastern point of Pharos Island. "It must be one of the wonders of the world."

"Do you see that statue on the top?" a nearby sailor asked.

They craned their necks and shielded their eyes.

"That is Poseidon, the god of the sea, and there beneath his feet is the great furnace. The column of smoke directs us to port, even when we are many miles out to sea. And the light from the fire guides us by night."

Miryam gazed at it with yearning. "I pray that there will be a light to guide us home."

Then she unlaced Yeshua's sandals. He seemed delighted to feel the warm, gritty sand beneath his bare feet. Yosef picked him up and ran across the beach into the surf. Holding Yeshua by his arms, he let his feet dangle in the lacey white waves as he squealed with delight.

"Which one of you is the child?" Miryam called out, happy to see her husband laughing and playing.

"Look Miryam," Shlomit cried a few moments later. "Your son is making little birds from the wet sand. They look as if they could fly away at the clap of his hands." Then she danced along the shore, only stopping to pick up shells to add to Yeshua's collection. Miryam watched, fascinated by her wild, free spirit.

She never walks if she can run. I think that she will dance her way through life.

Miryam walked on, breathing the fresh air. The sea sparkled in the golden Mediterranean sunlight, and tangles of shiny seaweed washed up on the white sand. The sky was filled with hundreds of birds starting their annual migration—storks, cranes, and white-breasted kingfishers, all flying in formation. Some of them seemed to stand still in the air, their graceful wings supporting them against the wind. Others skimmed the water's surface looking for prey. A flight of pink flamingos trailed through the air, and swallows wheeled in graceful patterns from sky to earth spinning against the cloudless sky.

A spindly-legged ibex stepped along the shore, probing the sand for food with its long, slender bill. One marched along with his head tilted back, its high-pitched voice sounding like laughter.

"Oh, my," Miryam cried as a huge bird with an enormous pouch waddled into view. "Whatever can it be?"

A woman passing by explained. "That is a pelican, a bird that lives in the wilderness of the River Nile. It is a bit far from home. May I tell you something interesting?" Before Miryam could answer, she went on. "The mother bird is so devoted to her young that she opens her side and feeds her brood with her own blood. Can you imagine that?"

"Any mother would give her blood for her child," Miryam answered.

A sudden breeze came up from the harbor, spraying a rainbow-colored mist, leaving its salty taste in Miryam's mouth. Threatening clouds passed over the sun, casting dark shadows as a gray fog rolled along the watery horizon. The ominous dream she had the night Yeshua was born returned—the horrifying dragon, taking its stand on the shore, waiting to devour her child.

A clap of loud thunder startled her, and she recoiled as if stepping on a snake. "Yosef," she called, giving him a start. Putting Yeshua on his shoulders, he walked back to her.

"What is it, Miryam?" he asked, looking at her anxious face.

"It looks like rain. We should go home," she said, clutching her scarf to keep it from blowing away. Yosef and Shlomit looked disappointed and Yeshua began to wail. But at Miryam's insistence, they gathered their belongings and set out just as the first raindrops began to spatter.

When Miryam put Yeshua to bed that night, she took the stone from the bag and held it in her hand, rubbing its smooth surface. *What if Yosef is right? What if the stone is dangerous?* Yet she could not bring herself to throw it away. Putting it back in the pouch, she placed it in the chest along with the gifts from the magi. She sat by her sleeping child, elbows on her knees, her chin in her hands, pondering what the future might hold for her son.

18

Yosef shook Miryam awake. "Herod is dead."

"Dead?" Miryam rubbed the sleep from her eyes.

"The angel told me in a dream that the one who sought the child's life is dead. We can return to Natzeret."

"We are going home?"

"Yes, my dove, we are going home." He held her close. "I will go and make the arrangements." Putting on his cloak, he left the house, leaving Miryam to ponder another miracle in her heart.

As soon as Yosef reached the marketplace, he heard of Herod's death; people were talking about it everywhere.

"Herod went mad before he died," he overheard one man say. "After killing the infants, he consipired to kill his own son and heir, Antipater."

"The king wanted to be sure that no one would plot to take his throne," another said.

"When Herod died there was a lunar eclipse, a blood moon boding evil. It must have been a horrible death—gangrene and fever."

"And when he collapsed in his palace, did any of his councilors and officers come to his aid? No, not one. They just stood and watched him die."

"He got what he deserved," another snarled. "He choked to death, in the same way he murdered his sons."

"I heard it said that the emperor would rather be Herod's pig than Herod's son," the first man smirked. The others laughed.

But Yosef did not laugh. "Then who is king of Yehudah now?"

"Herod willed that his son Archelaus would be ruler. But he is no king—just another puppet dancing on the string of the emperor."

"Archelaus is worse than his father. He hates the Yehudim, calling us a filthy race," a man added bitterly.

Yosef shook his head. "And the Galil? Who will rule there?"

"It is reported that it will be Herod's son, Antipas."

Life would be less threatening in the Galil. Yosef would take his family to Natzeret as the angel told him.

"There will be no need for us to trek across the desert to Yisrael," Yosef announced when he returned with their provisions. "I have saved enough money for a boat trip."

Miryam looked both pleased and relieved. "A boat trip! I have never been on a boat in my life."

"Nor I," said Shlomit. "I will go with you to Natzeret."

"It is a small village, not at all like Alexandreus," Yosef cautioned. "If you come with us, I hope you will be content there."

"I will be content anywhere," she sighed.

When they were packed and ready to leave, Miryam bid Avigal goodbye, kissing her and thanking her for her hospitality. Another farewell. They seemed endless.

At the port, gulls swooped about the waterfront as ships of every kind loaded and unloaded their cargo—metals from Spain, fine leather from Gaul, pottery from Greece, spices and perfumes from the Orient. The streets were crowded with merchants, their servants pulling wagons of goods, and their slaves, almost bent to the ground, laboring under the heavy loads on their backs.

Yosef looked around to find the ship's captain who booked their voyage. He was dismayed when he saw him standing in the bow of a frail old vessel bumping against the pilings of the wharf.

"Do you think it is safe?" Miryam clutched his arm. Yosef did not answer as he shouldered his way through the swarms of people scrambling to board the boat.

Shlomit carried Yeshua, struggling to keep her footing as she followed Miryam up the swaying gang plank. Yosef came after them, pulling their heavy cart, which threatened to overturn and dump them into the choppy, gray water that lapped beneath their feet.

While the baggage and trunks were loaded, the pilot tried to keep order, shouting to the scores of passengers of every color and nation crammed into the boat along with various livestock. Finally, they set out to sea. The wind filled the billowing sails, and the captain set a straight course northward along the coast. Shlomit hitched Yeshua onto one hip and stood arm in arm with Miryam who gazed out to sea, longing for a glimpse of home.

The boat lagged behind schedule due to a strong headwind that whipped the sea into frothy whitecaps. At times the vessel heaved so forcefully that they feared they would be dashed into the waves. Yeshua laughed, thinking it great fun, but Shlomit was seasick.

"Take him." She shoved the boy toward Miryam, and pushing her way through the crowd at the railing, hung her head over the side of the boat and retched.

"Will the boat sink?" Miryam asked, feeling queasy herself.

"You know the story of Yonah the prophet, yes?" Yosef asked.

"Yes I do," Miryam grimaced. "The sailors threw him overboard and he wound up in the belly of a whale."

"Oh, no," Yosef laughed. "I only meant that Yonah's name means 'dove,' and a dove always returns to its home."

"Yes, and a dove is always ready to take flight again . . . like us." Miryam rubbed an elbow bruised by the boat's tossing. "But I do not want to fly anymore. I just want to go home and stay there."

The rickety vessel sailed with great difficulty. Finally, after passing Mount Karmel, they arrived at the port of Haifa. When they disembarked, Yosef emptied the dust from his shoes, following the custom when returning from a pagan land. Then falling on his knees, he kissed the ground and gave thanks to the Lord for the safe voyage.

"I am just happy that we are on dry land again," Miryam sighed.

It was a long walk from the port to Natzeret. Yosef's arms ached as the cart bumped along the road, rutted by the harsh winter.

"Miryam," he said, stopping to catch his breath. "When Yeshua is older, I will teach him the stories my father told me and his father told him. Above all, I will tell him the stories of his ancestor, King David."

Miryam nodded. "And I will tell him of Sarah and Rivka and Rachel, and of Devorah and Yehudit and Rut. And, of course, Miryam, and how she sang and danced when the children of Yisrael were led out of Egypt." Suddenly she realized, "Oh, Yosef, we too have left Egypt and are returning to the land as the Lord promised."

At last she saw the low blue hills of Natzeret in the distance.

"Soon I will see the faces of my beloved parents," she said.

Yosef frowned. "I am thinking of Klofah, saying that he hoped he would never see our faces in Natzeret again. What will he do now that we have returned?"

"Klofah is your brother, Yosi. All will be well," Miryam said, with a reassuring smile. But Yosef still looked troubled.

The village seemed drabber than she remembered. Still, it was like a dear friend that she had not seen for a long time. They were home.

As soon as they arrived at the well in the center of town, one of the women recognized them. Throwing her arms about Miryam, she kissed her. "When you left Natzeret, you were a mere girl. And now you return as a grown woman!"

"Is this your son?" another woman asked, smiling at Yeshua who stood at his mother's side. "He looks exactly like you."

"Yes, he is the image of his mother," Yosef said, looking uneasy.

"I will send word to your brother of your return," she told him, running off before he could stop her.

"Surely your brother's love for you has not changed," Miryam told him.

Before long, they saw Klofah coming and, with reluctance, Yosef went to meet him. The brothers stood looking at one another, and then without a word they embraced and wept, their tears mingling on their faces.

"Seeing your face is like seeing the face of HaShem," Klofah said between sobs. "Forgive me. I should not have spoken such harsh words."

"We will not speak of it again," Yosef said through his tears. "We have enough enemies without having more under our own roof."

Klofah's wife, Miri, and the children soon joined them, and she and Miryam fell into each other's arms kissing one another, weeping with happiness.

"Your son is beautiful," Miri said, touching Yeshua's soft cheek.

"Are these your sons Yaakov, Yosef, Shimon, and Yehudah?" Miryam asked Miri. "How you have grown since last I saw you."

The boys looked at one another, embarrassed.

"And these are my daughters, Lysia and Lydia—twins! We are doubly blessed." Miri beamed as two little girls toddled over to Miryam. "We have been busy while you were gone!"

Miryam laughed, and then felt apprehensive. "Is it well with my mother and father?"

By the grave expression on Miri's face, she knew the news was not good.

"We did not know where to find you," Miri said, her lips quivering. "We sent word to Elisheva but there was no answer. This is not how I hoped to welcome you, but bad news does not wait."

Miryam turned pale as Miri tearfully told her everything that had taken place. "Your father became very ill and died soon after you went away, and your mother did not live long without him. Hannah smiled on death as she drew near to her eternal reward."

Miryam could not restrain her grief and she let out a wail. "We should have come home sooner."

Yosef gripped her hands, trying to comfort her. Breaking free of his hold, she fell to the ground, pounding the earth with her fists.

No one spoke as they walked to the burial ground near the olive orchard. There was no family tomb, so Yoachim's and Hannah's graves were marked by a simple pile of stones. Neighbors joined the family as each person placed a stone on the graves, a sign that the deceased were not forgotten. Yeshua watched with curiosity, and then picked up a stone and placed it on top of the pile.

Miryam smiled, but her heart was heavy with memories. "My mother taught me how to bake and spin and sew. She sang to me, played with me and cared for me when I was ill. My father was my hero. He never complained of his suffering." She buried her head on Yosef's chest, weeping.

"May the Almighty comfort you," Klofah said, and then he and Miri left the family to mourn alone.

It was some time before Miryam was willing to go to her parents' house at the other side of the village. She wept again when she saw it standing empty, overrun by weeds.

"We should live here," Miryam urged Yosef. "Your brother's house is full and there will be peace if you live apart."

"And do not forget me!" Shlomit insisted.

"How could we ever forget you? I pray that this will be the last of our wanderings," Miryam said.

Soon, they threw themselves into setting up their household, toiling every day to repair the ravages to the little house. After patching the roof, Yosef worked on the stone outbuilding that would serve as a workshop, wondering how the town could support two carpenters.

Pausing from his work, he looked at the spindly tree near the house that refused to leaf out. "One day we will sit under our own fig tree. Until then, we have several laying hens, sheep for wool, and a goat for milk and to keep down the underbrush."

"You can tell that goat to stay out of my garden," Miryam said crossly, pulling weeds from the arid soil. "I want to plant some flowers."

"Flowers? We cannot eat flowers."

"I love roses in particular," Miryam answered, ignoring his objection. "Roses make everything beautiful, as if they were dropped from heaven."

Yosef surveyed the land, hands on hips. "I think I will build a little wall around our home."

"A wall, Yosi?" She stood and brushed the soil from her hands and skirt. "We have nothing to fear from our neighbors. Why should there be a wall between us?"

He looked solemn as he often did when giving one of his little sermons. "A wall is like the law, Miryam. It puts a hedge around us to keep us from breaking the smallest decree. Then we will not transgress the important *mitzvot*. Our families will dwell in peace if we each one knows the other's borders."

"You cannot shut people out, Yosef," she said, with a slight frown.

He was about to say more when they heard Shlomit calling. She was lugging a heavy basket from the market. Yosef took it from her and carried it into the house. Miryam went back to weeding.

Shlomit's eyes were bright with excitement as she squatted beside Miryam. "I have something to tell you. I met a wonderful man in the marketplace."

"Shlomit," Miryam cried. "What were you thinking, speaking with a strange man in a public place?"

"Oh, this is not the first time we have met," she smiled, pulling a weed or two. "He often comes to Natzeret to sell his fish in the market. His name is Zavdai, a widower with two young sons—Yaakov and Yochanan. Let me tell you, they are rowdy fellows. Zavdai is a fisherman from Kfar Nahum."

"A fisherman?"

"Oh, he is not just a fisherman. Zavdai owns his own boats and hires laborers to fish for him. He has a factory for making anchors, weights, hooks, and needles for mending the nets—all sorts of things. Caravans often stop at Kfar Nahum to purchase Zavdai's dried fish."

She leaned forward, a twinkle in her eyes. "Zavdai told me that whenever he goes to Yerushalayim to sell fish for the pilgrim feasts, there is no one to care for his sons. So that is why he asked me to marry him!"

Miryam jumped up, and Shlomit followed. "Marry a man that you scarcely know? That cannot be. You must be betrothed for at least a year."

"Oh, he has no time for that."

"Do you have love for him?" Miryam asked, remembering her sister-in-law's question when she and Yosef were betrothed.

Shlomit shrugged. "You know very well that it is not a question of love. We marry someone who will provide a good life. It is the way things are."

"What are you ladies talking about?" Yosef asked as he came out of the house.

"Shlomit has met a fisherman in the market and intends to marry him," Miryam said before Shlomit could say anything.

"I was hoping for your approval," Shlomit said eagerly, but her face fell when she saw Yosef's stern look.

"Shlomit, as your guardian I feel responsible for you." His voice was firm. "I must meet this man and then we will see what will be."

Shlomit took both their hands in hers, her eyes darting from one to another. "My dear friends, do you not see? Perhaps this is why the Lord brought me here. I will no longer be a burden to you. I will have a husband who will take care of me all the days of my life. Zavdai has agreed to come to meet you as soon as he finishes his work in the market. Then you will see what a good man he is."

"You do have a wandering heart," Miryam said, knowing she could not dissuade her.

"My wandering heart has found a home," Shlomit said.

19

The rabbis had a saying that they first received the Torah at their mothers' breasts. Yeshua's education began with his mother, who imparted the old truths handed down to her. She taught him prayers on awakening: "From the rising of the sun to its setting the name of the Lord is to be praised," and before going to sleep: "Into your hands I commend my spirit."

Miryam taught him their sacred traditions, the meaning of daily activities and dietary laws. He learned the value of money by watching his mother, lamp in hand, searching the house for a lost coin, and how relieved she was when she found it. He knew a good deal about his heritage before he left his mother's side.

Yosef was obliged to teach his son a thorough knowledge of the Torah. "The first thing in the morning, you must bind your head, your heart and your hand with the words of the Torah," Yosef told his admiring son who watched him fix the *tefillin*, leather boxes, on his forehead and arm. "We do this to bind ourselves to Adonai Eloheinu." Wrapping Yeshua in his *tallit*, his prayer shawl, he murmured, "My son, when the Ruler of the Universe created the world he embraced it, just as I am embracing you."

But the law was also taught by example. One evening, after the Shabbat service, Yosef walked home with Yeshua at his side. Passing a man whose ox had fallen into a muddy ditch, they went to help him, even though work was prohibited on the Shabbat. It took a long time to get the animal out, and it was very late when they arrived home, their clothes soiled and their hands grimy.

"You missed a wonderful meal and great songs with your family," Miryam said.

Yosef winked at Yeshua, "We have been singing in our hearts all the way home."

Natzeret was a small town, but it was fortunate to have a *Beit HaSefer*, a primary school for boys under thirteen years of age. No history was taught other than the history of the Yehudim and their deliverance from Egypt and Babylon. Students did not learn mathematics; they watched their fathers as they measured and calculated. Understanding the times and seasons were important for planting and harvesting the crops, but discerning the movements of the sun, the moon, and the stars was the concern of pagans. There was no physical exercise—running, riding, boxing, wrestling, swimming, and hunting were left to the Greeks and Romans.

"It is time for Yeshua to learn his letters," Rabbi Reuven told Yosef. "You are a good craftsman, and can afford the small fee for your son's education."

Yosef agreed, and soon after he took his son to the synagogue. "My sons, keep your eyes upon your teacher," the rabbi said when the students turned to see who had come in. Waving his hand for Yosef to leave, he motioned to Yeshua to join the other the boys sitting cross-legged in a semi-circle on the floor.

The rabbi handed Yeshua a reed pen and pot shard. The ink had been collected from the soot of olive-oil lamps and diluted for writing. The students could not afford papyri or wax tablets.

"My sons, it is a privilege to read and write," Rabbi Reuven said, walking up and down in front of the cabinet where the Torah scrolls were kept. "Do you know what is said of Esav and Yaakov, the sons of Yitzchak? They went to school when they were your age. And when they finished their thirteenth year, they parted. Esav entered the houses of idols, and Yaakov joined the older students at the *Beit HaMidrash*."

Yeshua was impressed. He did not want to end up like Esav; he wanted to be like Yaakov and learn to interpret the law.

"My sons." The rabbi stroked his long beard. "Pour over the Torah again and again, for it is the gift from our father, Moshe Rabbenu, our great rabbi. There is no better pursuit than this, for all wisdom is contained in the law. Do not depart from it, even when you grow old and gray—like me."

The first text that Yeshua committed to memory was the *Shema*, an oath of loyalty to the Lord, to hear and obey the covenant: *Shema Yisrael. Adonai Eloheinu, Adonai, echad.*

"Whoever receives the law with a sincere heart, will receive the kingdom of heaven," the rabbi told his students. "Where there is a *minyan*, ten righteous men, and the law is remembered, the Lord will come and bless them."

Yeshua's brow furrowed. "Ten? Cannot the Lord be present to five—or three—or two? Cannot the Lord be present to just one?"

The rabbi looked annoyed. "Yeshua, students do not question their teacher."

The other boys snickered, and the color rose in Yeshua's face, knowing he had been scolded.

When the boys settled down, the rabbi wrote out the alphabet for the class, explaining why some of the letters had straight figures, others had double figures, and why some letters were written in a different way when they appeared at the end of a word than at the beginning.

"The letters we use in writing are called the '*Aleph Bet*,' because of the first two characters. The twenty-second, and last letter, is '*Tav*,'" the rabbi said.

"Rabbi," Yeshua interrupted. "Can you tell us the meaning of the letter Tav?"

The master drew in his breath. "My son, it is said that the prophet Yechezkel saw a vision of six executioners and a man dressed in fine linen carrying a writing case. They were summoned to destroy all the idolaters in Yerushalayim. The ones who were spared were those marked with the Tav on their foreheads, like this," he said, marking an x on Yeshua's forehead with his thumb.

Rabbi Reuven was anxious that his young students should commit the whole Torah to memory. "A good student has a memory like a deep well that loses not one drop." With great patience, he taught them to pronounce each word with care. "Every word is a jewel with seventy faces that we should turn, and turn, and turn again, so that it will speak to our lives." The rabbi regarded the Torah as a delicacy. One day he placed a dollop of honey on the boys' lips as he recited from the *Tehillim*, the Book of Psalms. "How sweet are your words to my taste, sweeter than honey from the comb." The boys smacked their lips. "But I wonder. Do you savor the honey more than the word?"

Another time, he lifted a small lamp. "Your word is a lamp to my feet and a light to my path." He also showed them a beautiful pearl, saying, "A merchant can search the whole world over and never find anything as precious." Taking a gold coin from his purse, he said, "Truly, I love your law more than fine gold." His aged eyes sparkled when they were able to repeat the commandments, counting them one by one on their fingers.

He stressed the blessings of obeying the law and the consequences of disobedience. "What is the thing that you should avoid most in life?"

"*Ayin HaRa*, an evil eye," one boy answered.

"A disloyal friend," said another.

But Yeshua answered, "*Yetzer HaRa*, to do evil."

The rabbi nodded. "And what is the most desirable thing to strive for in life?"

"*Ayin Tovah*, a good eye," said the first student, looking smug.

"A good neighbor," said the second.

Yeshua jumped to his feet. "*Yetzer HaTov*, to do good!"

"This answer is best," the rabbi said. "We must strive to do good, not evil. But this is almost impossible here on earth. It is a struggle that will go on until the Mashiach comes."

Yeshua enjoyed the rabbi's riddles most of all. "How can a person tell when the darkness ends and when daylight begins?"

The students thought for a moment, and one put forward an answer. "It is when there is enough light to see an animal in the distance and be able to tell if it is a sheep or a goat."

Another ventured, "It is when there is enough light to see a tree, and know whether it is a fig or an oak."

The old rabbi shook his head and said, "No. It is when you can look into the face of a man and recognize him as your brother. For if you cannot recognize the face of your brother, the darkness has not yet lifted, and the light has not yet come."

One afternoon, when the class finished, the rabbi came out of the synagogue with Yeshua at his side. Yosef and Miryam were there to meet him.

"Is it going well, rabbi?" Yosef asked. "Is Yeshua a good student?"

The rabbi threw up his hands. "Your son seems to think that he knows more than his master!"

Miryam pulled Yeshua's chin. "My son, you do not yet have a beard, and already you think you are a rabbi?"

Yosef placed his hand on his son's shoulder. "Yeshua, your place in school is to learn, not to teach."

The rabbi smiled. "Nevertheless, the mark of a good student is the ability to debate well. How can we learn if no one disagrees with us?"

Every day after school, Yeshua turned the rabbi's lessons over and over in his mind. But there were times when he was not content with knowledge; he wanted to know the moral lesson.

"Why does the Torah say that we are the chosen people and other people are not?" he asked one day after class.

"Because Yisrael has accepted the yoke of the law that other people are unwilling to bear. Out of all other people, Yisrael is dearest to the heart of the Lord."

"Does the Lord not love all people?"

The rabbi sighed. "Yeshua, do you think you are different than other boys?"

He bit the corner of his lip, looked down, and then blurted out, "Yes, rabbi. Sometimes I feel that I am like no one who has ever lived. I feel that I have come from somewhere else, high above the firmament. I do not understand why, but I do think I am different."

The rabbi lifted an eyebrow. "Yes, my son. I do believe you are. Now go join your schoolmates."

Klofah's son Yaakov sneered as Yeshua came toward them. "You think you know more than the rest of us. But you do not know how to play our games."

Yeshua drew himself up. "I have no time for your silly games. You sit in the marketplace calling to the girls, 'We played the flute for you, and you did not dance.' And they answer back, 'We wailed for you, and you did not mourn.' You are never satisfied."

The boys scoffed, kicking the dust with their sandals.

"Let me tell you a story," Yeshua said.

The boys gathered around; Yeshua told good stories.

"There once was a town where the boys loved to tease their schoolmates. One day, a great bear came out of the woods," he said, crouching low. Then he sprang forward, curling his hands like claws. "Grrrrrr! The bear ripped those boys to pieces and ate them all!"

The youngsters fled, and Yeshua swaggered home. When he neared his house, he saw his mother standing at the door with her hands on her hips.

"What were you saying to those boys that scared them so?"

He was surprised that she had been watching. "I was just telling them a story."

"Well, whatever it was, you gave them quite a fright." She gave him a gentle swat. "Go help your father in the workshop if you need something to keep you out of trouble. And I do not want to see you strutting around that way again."

Raising her eyes heavenward she sighed. "He is your son, Lord!"

20

There was a long break after morning classes at the synagogue until study resumed in the afternoon. The boys ran to the town center, pushing and shoving each other, showing off their strength to the girls who passed by with their arms about each other's slim waists. The men wagged their heads, predicting the youngsters would come to no good end.

Yeshua was nearing ten years of age, tall and lean, with dark curls encircling his fine features. While any number of girls would welcome his attention, he was content to join his father and the other men in the town square.

"I hear that Archelaus is no longer *ethnarch* of Yehudah," one man said of the Roman occupation of their land. "He was deposed and exiled by Augustus."

Another shook his head in dismay. "He was a butcher king, like his father, massacring our people in the temple during Pesach."

"So, to whom do we owe our allegiance?" Yosef asked.

"The Emperor no longer trusts us to rule ourselves," the first man answered. "He has appointed a *procurator* to govern Yehudah."

Yeshua sat back on his heels, listening to the men discuss their changing world. Picking up a sharp stick, he scratched out the alphabet in the dirt, erasing each letter with the palm of his hand before beginning another.

Rabbi Reuven came from the synagogue and, with difficulty, squatted beside him. "Remember, my son, the Shabbat law says that you cannot write more than one letter of the alphabet."

Yeshua stopped writing and erased his work. The rabbi chuckled. "But of course, this is not the Shabbat and writing is permissible. So go back to your work. I am pleased to see your interest in learning." Then he gave Yosef a wry look. "I believe your boy was born before Noach."

A gruff voice interrupted. "Rabbi, Caesar behaves as if the Almighty gave the law to the Romans!"

"The Almighty gave the law to Yisrael," the rabbi assured him.

"Our only hope is that that the Mashiach will come soon," the man muttered.

"And if the Mashiach should come to Natzeret?" another glowered. "Where do you think he would end up—nailed to a tree!"

An old man spat on the ground. "Nothing good ever comes from Natzeret."

Yeshua looked up in surprise. "Rabbi, who is the Mashiach? When will he come? Will we recognize him?"

"Questions! Questions! Always questions," the rabbi said. "So tell me, my scholar, did the Almighty answer all of Iyov's questions? No! Of course, no! Some things remain a mystery. It is said that the Torah is so shallow that a flea can walk through it, but it is so deep that a camel cannot wade through it. But when the Mashiach comes, he will be our teacher and answer all our questions. Until then, who can know the mind of the Almighty, eh, Yeshua?"

Yeshua began to speak again, but Yosef motioned him to be quiet.

The rabbi waved his hand. "Your son has the right to know such things now that he is in school."

Yosef took a deep breath. "My son, there are many ideas of the Mashiach. Some say he will be a great king like David who will bring forth an age of peace and plenty."

"I hear that the Mashiach will be the High Priest," one of the men disagreed. "He will lead the people to true worship of the Almighty."

"And the Zealots say that the Mashiach will lead the people in a rebellion," another added, a gleam in his eyes. "He will set his foot upon the eagle's neck and drive the Romans from the land."

Yosef scowled. "Why do you speak of such things? Do you want to bring the Roman Empire down on our heads? We have enough trouble without talking of revolution."

"But why would they hang the Mashiach on a tree?" Yeshua persisted.

"Because of the things those rebels have done," Yosef answered. "The Romans want to make an example of anyone who causes trouble—just like they did with the followers of Spartacus."

"Who is Spartacus?"

"Spartacus was a slave who led thousands of other slaves in a revolt against the Romans," the rabbi said. "He died in battle, and his followers were nailed to crosses along the Appian Way as a warning to others who might be tempted to rebel."

"The most wretched of deaths," one of the men grimaced.

"This is no discussion for a young boy," Yosef said. "It is better not to speak of such things."

But Yeshua knew what crucifixion meant. His father and uncle often worked in nearby Tzippori, bringing back tales of the Yehudim who had raided the royal armory there. Roman revenge had been swift—burning the town to the ground, selling the people into slavery, and crucifying the rebels along the roadside.

"But where will we find the Mashiach when he comes?" Yeshua asked.

"Let me tell you a story," the rabbi smiled. "A man once asked the same question: 'Where will I find the Mashiach?' And Eliyahu, the prophet, told him, 'Go down to the city gates and you will find him there.' But the man said, 'There are many people at the city gates, how will I recognize him?' Eliyahu told him, 'You will find him among the lepers.' 'What is the Mashiach doing among the lepers?" the man asked, and Eliyahu answered, 'He is bandaging their wounds.'"

"Yes, I am sure that is what the Mashiach would be doing," Yeshua said.

Leaving the men to their discussion, he had the urge to climb the hill, lie down in the warm sun and think about everything he heard that day. Lost in thought, he ambled along the narrow, dusty footpath that strung the homes of the village together. Passing beneath the trees, he stopped to watch the autumn leaves—yellow, brown, orange—falling one-by-one to his feet. He jumped and grabbed a low branch and swung. Then he shuffled down the road, kicking pebbles. A mother hen gathered her chicks under her wings, unconcerned for her own safety. *Like my mother*, he thought.

Soon he began the slow climb up the hill. When he reached the top, he savored the view below—sheep and goats grazing among clumps of thistles; the fields plowed for the winter crops of barley and wheat; the orchards picked bare of their fruit; and grape vines sending their barren tendrils along the hillside.

Yeshua looked to the north, where he saw Mount Hermon lifting its snow-crowned head over the rolling hills with their changing patterns of ochre and brown. To the south, he could see the Valley of Yizreel, which divided the hilly areas of the Galil and Shomron. From his studies, he knew that the fertile plain had been a scene of conflict from ancient days. There, Devorah and Barak fought side-by-side, Gideon won his victories, and Eliyahu challenged the prophets of Baal. King Shaul had been defeated there, and King Yoshiyah was killed in battle against the Pharaoh of Egypt. There too, the struggles for freedom took place in the glorious days of the Maccabee warriors.

Yeshua looked to the east and saw the sun flashing off the helmets of a Roman legion marching toward a distant post. To the west he could see the coast of Tyre and the "Way of the Sea," the road that connected the seaports of the Mediterranean, the "sea in the middle of the earth." Yeshua wondered how the Romans could call it 'Our Sea' when the Almighty had created everything.

Leaning up against a tree, he breathed in the sweet smell of scarlet poppies and anemones that swayed in the gentle mist drifting from the Sea of the Galil. *Why do we worry about gold and silver? The lilies of the field do not toil or spin; yet the meadows are clothed with their beauty, better than the fine robes of kings.*

A covey of quail startled him as they burst from the underbrush. As they fluttered away, he bent down to study the great variety of insects scrambling from leaf to leaf. He wondered where they were going in such a hurry. A spider was spinning a web and a fly flew into it, trapped in its filmy strands. He watched as the spider climbed down the web and wrapped its prey in a gauzy shroud. *Like my people, caught in a web of suffering.*

Yeshua stood up, stretched out his arms, and began to spin in a circle, until he was dizzy. The whole world seemed to whirl beneath his feet. He fell down on the coarse grass, still damp from the morning dew. Rolling onto his back, he crossed his long legs and locked his fingers under his head. He gazed up at the white clouds scuttling across the blue dome above. Butterflies danced in the sunlight's beams, and its warmth fell like a blessing on his face. His eyes grew heavy as he listened to the bees buzzing from flower to flower. *Why do flowers need bees? Does everything need something else?*

Then he heard the song birds. Opening his eyes and squinting against the sun, he saw a little bird perched on a branch above him. *There seems to be no worry in the lives of birds. Why do people not put their trust in the Lord the way birds do?*

A soft slithering sound frightened him, and he jumped to his feet. There close by was a poisonous viper. He could see its yellow eyes, the dark V-shape on its head, and the brown diamond markings along its body. The viper curled up, lifted its head and hissed, ready to strike should he come near.

Yeshua had no such intention. He ran down the hill as fast as he could until he came to his house. Removing his sandals, he brushed the dirt from his feet.

"What is it my son?" Miryam asked, seeing his flushed face.

"I saw a snake in the field, on the hilltop," he said, catching his breath.

"What were you doing up there?"

"The snake was so close I could touch it," he said, without answering her question.

His mother handed him a cup of water. He sat down at the table and sipped the water, his face pensive. "That is the way it is with evil, is it not, Ima?"

"What do you mean?" she asked, brushing back the moist curls clinging to his forehead.

"Evil is like a snake, always ready to attack, ready to poison our hearts with wicked thoughts and deeds, striking us when we are not watching."

Miryam was unable to speak, so amazed at her son's growing wisdom. She went to the door and looked out. Shafts of sunlight were streaming to the ground, like swords.

Yeshua went and stood at her side. "The snake brought darkness into the world, and darkness creeps into us as well," he said. "But darkness cannot overcome the light, can it, Ima?"

21

"Good Pesach!" Yosef greeted Klofah and his family as they came to the door.

"Good Pesach," Klofah said in return, happy that he could share the feast with his brother.

The Feast of Pesach was celebrated on the fifteenth day of the month of *Nissan*, in the spring, commemorating the exodus of the slaves in Egypt. Earlier in the day, Yeshua watched his father dip a branch of hyssop into a basin and mark the doorposts and lintels of the house with the blood of a year-old lamb.

"The blood recalls the night when the Angel of Death passed over the houses of the Yehudim, while slaying the first-born sons in Egypt," Yosef told Yeshua as blood trickled down the sides of the doorway and drained into the ground.

"Does the blood protect our house, too?" Yeshua asked.

"Yes, my son, the blood protects our house, too."

Miryam hurried to finish the cleaning and cooking before sunset when the feast would begin. Matzah had been baked, and every scrap of chametz, leaven, had been removed from the house.

"The leaven reminds us to get rid of the puffed-up pride in our souls," she cautioned, as Yeshua arranged pillows around a mat on the floor for the Seder meal.

When all was ready, Yosef announced to his guests: "At Pesach, every one of us goes out of Egypt, as the proverb goes: 'Our forefathers waded in the water and our feet are wet.'"

"But first we must wash our hands," Miryam said, presenting a bowl of water and a towel. "We do this to consider what we are about to eat."

"What do you mean, Ima?" Yeshua asked.

"It means that tonight we are going to eat our history, my son," Yosef told him. "Now it is time to usher in the Holy Pesach. The lamps must be lit before the sun is set."

Everyone reclined on pillows. Then Miryam cupped her hands in front of her eyes, and prayed, "Blessed are you who sanctified us through your commandments and commanded us to kindle the lights of the festival."

Yosef looked at his family, the lamps casting a warm glow on their faces. "Our ancestors suffered in the darkness of slavery. The light of Pesach is the light of freedom."

Miryam passed around a plate of *maror*, bitter herbs, which they dipped in salt water. Klofah frowned when the boys tasted the sharp flavor and made a face. The girls giggled, and they were scolded, too.

Yosef poured a cup of wine, the first of four served at the meal. Though the wine could be diluted, he liked to serve it just as it came from the vat—rich and strong.

"We drink the wine not to become drunk," he warned the children. "Wine is meant to gladden the heart and should be drunk with reverence. Each cup represents the Lord's promises: sanctification, deliverance, redemption, and restoration."

"This is the Cup of Sanctification, the *Kiddush*, by which we proclaim the holiness of the Lord." He offered everyone a sip from the cup and prayed, "Blessed are You, Adonai Eloheinu, Ruler of the Universe, Creator of the fruit of the vine."

He uncovered the matzah, which had been broken into three pieces. Taking the middle piece, he broke it in two.

"When we dishonor our bodies, our souls die within us, and we too become broken." He tucked the larger piece into a napkin and winked at the children. "This is the *Afikoman*. It will be hidden, and after the meal, you must search for it. The one who finds it will receive a copper coin—a great fortune!"

The children clapped their hands with glee, but Yosef signaled for quiet. "Now we will tell the story of our deliverance. Even if we know all things in the Torah, it would still be our duty to tell the story."

"Abba," Yeshua spoke up.

"Yes, son?"

"Abba, the rabbi said that the world stands on a three-legged stool—the first leg is the Torah, the second is worship, and the third is our mitzvot, our good deeds. The rabbi said that those who do not uphold those things behave as if the Lord does not exist. Do you think that is true?"

Yosef put his fingertips together and thought for a moment. "It is true, my son, that a stool would tip over if one leg was missing. Now, please allow me to continue."

He chanted the *Haggadah*, retelling the story of the exodus.

My father was a wandering Aramean.
He went down to Egypt with a small household
*　　and lived there as an alien.*
When we became strong and numerous, the Pharaoh imposed
*　　hard labor on us.*
We cried to Adonai Eloheinu, and he heard our cries,
*　　saw our affliction*
and brought us out of Egypt with an outstretched arm.

Yosef finished with a somber recital of the ten plagues. At the announcement of a plague, he dipped a finger into the wine and watched the ruby-colored drops fall from his fingertips. "We do this as a reminder that our happiness cannot be complete when anyone suffers."

The solemn mood changed as he lifted his voice, chanting praise for the gifts the Lord had bestowed on them. Everyone responded: *Dayenu*—"It would have been enough!"

"If the Lord had brought us out of Egypt…"

"Dayenu!"

"If the Lord had split the sea for us…"

"Dayenu!"

"If the Lord had given us the commandments…"

"Dayenu!"

"If the Lord had given us the Shabbat…"

"Dayenu!"

"If the Lord had built the temple for us…"

"Dayenu!"

Then Yosef declared: "It is because of what the Lord did for me when I came out of Egypt."

"Were you in Egypt, Abba?" Yeshua interrupted.

Yosef looked uneasy, remembering their terrible flight from Herod. "It was a long time ago, when you were very young. But everyone lives in a place of bondage, and needs the help of the Lord to be released."

Then he looked at the other children. "Now, since Yeshua is the youngest son at our Seder, he will ask the Four Questions. Each question represents a different child, and I want you to think: Which child are you?" Yosef's frown made them squirm. "The first is the wise one, who wants to know all the details of the Pesach. Next is the wicked one, who does not celebrate the Pesach, and will learn the penalty for that. Then there is the foolish one, who only wants to know what is necessary, and no more. And last is the one who is unable to ask a question, because he does not know enough to know what he needs to know."

Yosef turned to Yeshua, hoping that he would remember all he had been taught.

Instead, Yeshua asked, "Abba, does the Lord love just the good and wise children, and not the wicked and foolish ones?"

"Yeshua," he warned. "Do you not have other questions to ask?"

Yeshua sat up straight. "Abba, I want to ask the Four Questions."

"Yes, my son?"

"Abba, why is this night different from all other nights? On all other nights we eat leavened bread. Why do we eat unleavened bread on this night?"

"We eat unleavened bread because on the night we departed from Egypt, there was no time to make the dough rise with leaven. And so it was baked into hard crackers, the matzot."

"Abba, on all other nights we eat all sorts of vegetables, but on this night we only eat bitter herbs. On all other nights, we do not dip our vegetables in salt water, but on this night we dip the herbs twice. On all other nights, we eat sitting upright, but on this night we recline."

Yosef pointed to the horseradish. "We eat *maror* to show the bitterness of slavery in Egypt. We dip our vegetables into salt water for the tears we shed. We recline as a sign that one day we will take our rest as free men and women."

Klofah scowled. "And from generation to generation we are still oppressed. How can we live in peace with the Romans when their hands are in our purses, and their swords are to our backs?"

Yosef heaved a sigh, and poured a second cup of wine. "This is the cup that commemorates our deliverance from Egypt." Before passing it, he prayed, "Blessed are You, Adonai Eloheinu, Ruler of the Universe, Creator of the fruit of the vine."

Hands were washed again, and each person broke a piece of matzah, dipping it in the sweet *charoset*, the gray apple mixture resembling the clay used to make bricks for the Pharaoh's storehouses. Yosef raised the matzah for all to see. "This is the bread of affliction that our fathers ate in the land of Egypt."

Dunking a hard-boiled egg in salt water, he mused, "I once asked the rabbi why we eat eggs on Pesach, and he answered, 'Because eggs symbolize the Yehudim. The more an egg is boiled, the harder it gets.'"

"Like me!" Klofah laughed.

Miryam and Miri brought forth the roasted lamb. The pungent aroma caused everyone to "oooh" and "ahhh." A third cup of wine was poured.

Yosef declared, "This is the cup of redemption, our reminder that we are saved from our sins." Again everyone took a sip as Yosef prayed, "Blessed are You, Adonai Eloheinu, Ruler of the Universe, Creator of the fruit of the vine."

A portion of the fourth cup of wine was then poured into a cup decorated with grapes. Placing it before an empty space, he said, "This is the cup of restoration. We drink it in anticipation of the prophet Eliyahu's return, announcing the coming of the Mashiach." Then he rose from the table, opened the door and prayed, "O Compassionate One! Make us worthy of the day of the Mashiach and the life of the world to come."

Everyone raised their voices and sang the *Hallel*, praise for the Lord's loving-kindness.

> *Give thanks to Adonai Eloheinu, for he is good;*
> *his steadfast love endures forever!*
> *Let Yisrael say, 'His steadfast love endures forever.'*

Yeshua did not sing; his attention was focused on the open door. "Ima, perhaps the Mashiach has come and no one knows it."

Miryam looked stunned, even as everyone else shouted, "Next year in Yerushalayim!"

22

Yosef was a *tekton*, a craftsman, skilled in both wood and stone work. In Egypt, he had learned to make furniture—chairs, tables, beds, chests, and even a desk. Each one was a delight to his wife and the envy of her neighbors. Soon women begged their husbands to buy pieces from Yosef, and his carpenter shop flourished.

"Whoever does not teach his son a trade is teaching him to steal," Yosef quoted the proverb to Yeshua as they worked together. Through Yosef's skillful guidance, his son learned to make bins, troughs, plows and yokes. A sign above the door read: "My yokes fit well," and men came from the surrounding area to buy them.

Yosef usually had enough work to occupy his time, but when there was no work in Natzeret, he would go with Klofah to the surrounding towns and villages.

"I heard that Herod Antipas is rebuilding the town of Tzippori," Klofah told him, coming into the shop. "He plans to make it the 'Ornament of the Galil.' He is in need of craftsmen for masonry and carpenters for banquet tables and couches."

"All for the pleasure of the rich," Yosef sighed.

"There will be a long queue of men looking for work," Klofah said. "I want to get there before the others, so I plan to take my sons and leave today. Will you go with me?"

"I will go tomorrow, when I finish this job." He pointed to a storage chest. "Now that Yeshua is no longer in school, I can take him with me."

Rising before dawn, Yosef woke his son. While Yeshua washed and dressed, Yosef watched Miryam sleep. Her dark hair fell over her face. His heart swelled with love for her. Before he left, he whispered, "Sleep, my beloved."

Tzippori was four miles from Natzeret, just an hour's walk. As the sun began to rise in the east, Yosef cast a wary eye at the reddish glow in the sky. "It is going to be a stormy day."

"How can you tell, Abba?" Yeshua asked. "It is very pleasant now."

"Breathe deep. What do you smell?"

Yeshua took a breath and smiled. "It smells like rain."

"Look at that cloud rising over the Great Sea," Yosef said, pointing west. "That means it will be wet and cold. If the wind blows from the desert in the south it will bring the scorching heat. It is important to pay attention to such things. Did you see the red sky this morning?"

Yeshua nodded.

"You can always tell the weather by reading the signs of the sky. Do you know the weather proverb?"

"You have told me many times. 'A red sky at night is the shepherd's delight. A red sky in the morning is the shepherd's warning.'"

The land rose swiftly. Yosef became winded and slowed their pace. They walked in silence until they reached the crest of the hill. Yosef stopped. "Who would build a house where the drainage is so poor?" he asked, looking at a cottage under construction in a sandy hollow. "The winter rains will turn the gully into a swamp, and the house will be swept away by the floods. A house needs firm bed rock to withstand a storm."

Yeshua furrowed his brow. "Abba, if it is easy to read the signs of the weather, is it also easy to read the signs that the kingdom of heaven is at hand?"

Yosef did not reply. He was not sure how to answer.

Yeshua burst through the doorway that evening, his face flushed with excitement.

"Your clothes are soaking wet," Miryam scolded.

"Abba said it would be a stormy day and he was right. But it has stopped raining."

His mother dried his hair with a towel. "And where is your father?"

"He is coming. He told me I could go ahead. His steps seemed slower today." He pushed the towel away. "I am almost dry. And so is my mouth."

She poured a cup of goat's milk and handed it to him. "I put honey in the milk to sweeten the taste." She went to the door and peered down the road. "Your father has seemed weary of late. I hope that he is not ill."

"No, Ima, I am sure that he is well. He is just tired from working so hard." He went to a corner of the room. Stripping off his wet clothes, he pulled a dry tunic over his head.

When he returned, he slid into a chair and took a long gulp. "Ima, you should see all the wonderful things in Tzippori. King Herod's palace has walkways with marble pavers and there are mansions for the rich. There was another large building…I think it is called a basilica. It covered an entire city block!"

She sat beside him and cupped her chin in her hands. "I have never been to Tzippori."

"Ima, there were shops in the building," he chattered between swallows. "But they did not face out to the street, they were inside…. You could look through the open doors and see all the fine things for sale…. And you could walk from stall to stall and never get wet from the rain."

"What did they sell?"

"You can buy anything you want, if you have the money."

"What did they sell?" she asked again.

He counted on his fingers. "Wheat, olives, grapes, wine, figs, pomegranates, dried fish, herbs, onions, and spices…. Now I am hungry!"

She rose and looked out the doorway again but there was no sign of Yosef. Then she mashed olives and bread in a bowl and waited while Yeshua ate.

"What else did they sell?" she asked him.

"There were all sorts of things, Ima. There were pots and pans, and baskets, and colored bottles and jewelry, and even carved ivory furniture."

Miryam sat down, anxious to hear more.

"The floor down the center of the building was paved with little pieces of tiles, and there were pools of water at each end—with live fish. I stopped to watch as they swam by. I tried to catch one, but I took pity on it and let it go." He paused, seeming to gather his thoughts. "Oh! And there were tapestries woven with pictures of hunters and fights between animals and people. I counted over forty scenes. There was one tapestry with a picture of the Greek god Dionysius…and people drinking wine and making love!"

"Yeshua!" Miryam sat upright, the color rising in her cheeks.

"That is what someone told me they were doing."

"I do not know what your father thinks of all this."

Yeshua picked up the empty clay bowl and ran a finger around its rough edge. "Ours looks drab by comparison with the splendid things we saw in the house of a very rich man. There was a garden, right inside, and his guests were lying on couches, eating from silver bowls!"

"What is this talk?" Yosef asked, touching the mezuzah on the door post.

"Yosef." Miryam said. "I was so worried."

Wordlessly, he went to his shop and put his tools away. When he returned, his face was gray, and he was perspiring. Miryam poured him a cup of water. He drank and then sat down heavily. Putting his elbows on his knees, he looked up at her.

"Yeshua was just telling me of all the wonderful sights you saw at Tzippori," she said. "Perfume, jewelry, silver and ivory...."

"I do not think I will take Yeshua to Tzippori again," he interrupted.

"Why, Abba?" Yeshua asked. "Was I not of help to you today?"

He shook his head. "It is not because of your work, my boy. You are learning the trade well."

"Then why?"

"There are too many temptations." He cleared his throat. "There was a Roman theater for thousands of spectators. Only the Almighty knows what goes on in such places. When we stopped to eat our meal, Yeshua was nowhere to be seen. I found him climbing up the rows of seats in the amphitheater."

Yeshua protested. "I wanted to see the view. From up there you can see the Valley of Yizreel, and even the Great Sea...."

"And there was this house, a mansion," Yosef continued. "We went inside to repair the windows. And there were pleasure-seeking men with...painted women...who were...public women."

Yeshua started to ask what his father meant, but Miryam shushed him.

"One of the women reached out and touched Yeshua's cheek. 'Beautiful' was all she said, but her smile was shameless."

Miryam put a protective arm around her son's shoulder. "He *is* beautiful."

Yosef stood suddenly. "Yeshua, come with me."

Yeshua's face reddened as he felt his father's strong hand on his shoulder.

"He meant no harm!" Miryam called after him.

Yosef turned and looked sternly at her. "It is my duty to teach our son the laws of Yisrael. Remember Izevel, who painted her eyes and adorned her head? She drove her husband to do what was evil in the sight of the Lord."

"Yeshua will not sin!" Miryam stood her ground. "He is the Lord's son, Yosef. He will not sin! Do you hear me, Yosef?"

He shoved Yeshua ahead of him by the scruff of his neck. "I can hear you. All of Natzeret can hear you."

As they headed toward a clump of sycamore trees, Yeshua wondered what his mother meant. Why was he not capable of sinning?

Yosef motioned for him to sit on the ground, and squatted beside him.

"You are angry with me, Abba, yes?" he asked.

"You know the proverb," Yosef answered. "The Lord loves those he reproaches and chastises the son he favors." He was silent for a moment, and, when he spoke again, his voice was gentle. "The Torah says that we must take heed lest our hearts be deceived and we turn aside to serve other gods and worship them."

"Yes, Abba, those are the words of Moshe."

"You are growing into a man, my son, and you must understand that people are not always what they seem to be. There are women who will try to lead you away from Moshe's commands."

"Like Izevel?"

Yosef nodded. "She urged her husband, the king, to sin by going after idols. And she tried to kill the prophets of the Lord. Remember the story of Eliyahu?"

"Yes, but all women are not like that, are they? Ima is not like that."

"No, your mother is not like that."

"Ima is more beautiful than any of the painted women I saw in Tzippori." Yeshua said. He paused and looked anxious. "Will I go with you go to Tzippori again?"

"Yes, son. You will go to Tzippori again."

They sat in silence, until Yeshua asked, "Abba, do you hear that sad song?"

Yosef tilted his head to hear the plaintive call of a dove.

CooOOoo-woo-woo-woooo.

"Is that why they are called mourning doves?"

"To our ears their cries are sad," his father said. "But that does not mean that the doves are mourning. They are very happy when it is the mating season."

When his father stood, Yeshua grabbed his sleeve. "I want to ask you another question."

"Of course."

"Does a woman need a man to have a child?"

"Who told you such things?"

"Yaakov," Yeshua answered, embarrassed. But he persisted. "Is it true, Abba?"

"Yes, it is true. Just like the birds in the nest, and the animals in their stalls, human beings mate also."

Yeshua wanted to know more but Yosef stopped him. "Come! That is enough talk for now. Let us see what your mother has prepared for us to eat."

The two rose, and Yosef put his arm around Yeshua's shoulders as they walked back to the house. Miryam was waiting in the doorway, her hand to her chin.

"Yes," Yosef said, with a light in his eyes. "Your mother is blessed among women."

23

A steady winter rain fell throughout the night. The branches of the fig tree banged against the house, and the flickering oil lamp made strange shadows on the walls. Unable to sleep, Miryam prayed.

Yeshua was sick. He had returned from Tzippori soaked to the skin. By nightfall he was pale and shaking with a chill, barely touching the hot broth she encouraged him to drink. Miryam sent him to bed, lit a lamp, and placed it by his bedside. "This will keep the demons away," she told him. "No harm shall come to you."

Twice during the night, Miryam rose to cover Yeshua. Now, hearing a soft moan, she went to him and laid her hand against his cheek. He was hot to the touch; his damp hair clung to his forehead. Fear gripped her heart. She had seen other mother's children die from such fevers.

"Please be well, my sweet child. Be well." Kneeling beside his bed, she held his hot hand and prayed. "I will stay at your side until I know you are well."

At last it was dawn. Miryam felt his clammy forehead. "He is cool."

Yosef sighed with relief. "Let him sleep. It will do him good. I will go to work alone. If he is well tomorrow, he can join me."

She wrapped some cheese, raisins, and olives in a napkin, along with thin slices of day-old bread. Yosef gathered his tools and supplies.

She followed him out to the rain-drenched courtyard. A pale sun ventured from behind the clouds, the slate-gray sky washed clean by the showers. It was still early and very cold; no one else was on the street. Drawing her mantle close to her body, Miryam looked with dismay at the fig tree lying in a puddle where it had fallen in the storm.

"No fruit ever will ever come from you again," she said.

"I will dig it up when I return," Yosef promised, surveying the ragged trunk.

She waved goodbye as he trudged down the muddy street to meet Klofah and his sons. Then she gathered up some dry dung and grass, put it in the open-air oven, and lit a fire. Although exhausted from her sleepless night, she returned to the house to prepare the daily bread.

Bread-making was so much a part of Miryam's routine that she could not imagine a day without it. Taking a lump of fermenting dough from yesterday's baking, she mixed it with three measures of flour and a little salt, honey, and oil in a wooden bowl, kneading the dough until all was leavened. After the dough rose, she punched it down to let it rise again, and then shaped it into a loaf for baking. Sometimes she coated it with olive oil so it turned glossy brown when baked. Today, she sprinkled it with aromatic seeds, which gave the bread a spicy flavor.

While the dough was rising, she thought of her mother, who taught her the importance of bread, a gift from the Almighty. Her mother taught her that life could not be hurried. The dough needed to be worked for a period of time, and needed time to rest or it would not rise. So too, she must have time to work, time to rest, and time to pray.

By the mid-morning, the fragrant smell of baking bread wafted from the courtyard. Miryam heard Yeshua stir.

"Are you awake?" His long eyelashes fluttered and he yawned. "There is fresh bread if you are able to eat."

He rose, shuffled to a chair, sat down, and rested his head on the worn, scarred table.

"Did you wash your hands?" she asked without raising her eyes from her work.

He looked at her drowsily, and then got up and went to the basin. Breaking the thin sheet of ice that formed during the night, he washed his hands in the frigid water. Returning to the table, he slid again into the chair.

"Did Abba go to work?" He ran his fingers through his hair, trying to wake himself up.

"Your father left early." She broke bread into a clay bowl. Pouring a little goat's milk over it, she set it on the table in front of him. "He thought it best for you to rest. He said that if you are well tomorrow, you can go with him."

He nodded and tried to say his morning prayers. Soon he gave up. Giving simple thanks, he picked up a chunk of bread and shoved it into this mouth.

"Ima, I had a strange dream." Warm milk dribbled down his chin.

"What did you dream?" she asked, sitting down beside him.

Wiping his mouth with his sleeve, he leaned back in his chair, tipping it on two legs.

"Yeshua, sit up straight," she ordered. "You will hurt yourself if you fall."

He did as he was told. He took another mouthful, and rubbed his head.

"Does your head ache?" Miryam asked, putting her cool hand on his forehead.

"No, Ima, I am trying to remember my dream." When he spoke again, his words were slow. "In my dream, I saw the heavens open. There was a white horse…the rider's name was 'Faithful and True.' He wore many crowns on his head, and his eyes were like flames of fire." He paused for a moment. "The rabbi told me that the Mashiach would tread the wine press of the Almighty's wrath…and that his garments would be dipped in blood. That is what I saw in my dream."

Miryam shuddered, remembering her own dream the night Yeshua was born.

He looked at her, his eyes questioning. "Ima, the rider had a two-edged sword, sharper than any Roman sword. But he did not wield it. The sword came from his mouth."

The sword of Shimon! She thought. *It is always there!*

"Ima, I have heard men talk that when the Mashiach comes, he will wage war against our enemies. But I think that the power of the

Mashiach will be truth and justice—the sword that came from his mouth."

"Please stop, Yeshua. I do not want to hear such things."

"There is something more," he said, leaning forward. "In my dream, the Mashiach had a name written on his robe and on his thigh. The name was: 'King of Kings.'" He sat pondering this, resting his chin on the palm of his hand, and then spoke again. "Ima, when I awoke this morning, I thought that I was the rider on the white horse…but how can that be? I am not a warrior."

"Talk no more of this dream." Miryam pushed her chair away from the table and stood. "Are you well enough to come with me to draw water?"

Yeshua sighed. "I will come with you, but I hope no one sees me doing women's work."

She threw her scarf around the back of her head and shoulders, and they went out the door. She realized how tall her son had grown. He was nearing his twelfth year. How did the time pass so quickly?

As they made their way down the muddy road, Miryam held the hem of her skirt to keep it out of the mire. Yeshua hopped over the puddles. She was glad to see that he was still a child.

"Shalom, Miryam," Naftali called out as he passed by, holding the hand of his blind son.

"Shalom," Miryam replied. "Look how fresh and clean everything is from the rain's bath."

"Listen to the rustling of the leaves," Yonatan said. "It as if the trees are clapping their hands."

When they went on their way, Yeshua closed his eyes, put his hands out before him, and tried to walk.

"What are you doing?" Miryam scolded.

"I was just wondering what it would be like to be blind." He opened his eyes and looked at her. "It is like being in a dark room. But when you come into the light, you are no longer in darkness."

"It is a terrible thing to be blind," Miryam whispered. "You must not mock Yonatan."

He hung his head. "I know it is terrible to be blind. When I open my eyes I can see, but for him it is still black. I am sure that the Mashiach could give light to his eyes. What a wonderful thing it would be to heal the blind."

They walked a while longer. Yeshua seemed lost in thought. Finally, he said, "If I were blind like that boy, I would have to stay at your side all of my life, like Yonatan."

"That will not happen. Before long you will go out into the world, and make your way on your own." She linked her arm with his, longing to keep him close by her forever.

"Ima," he said, after they had drawn the water. "Do you know that a camel has a third eyelid?"

"Wherever do you get such ideas?"

"When there is a desert storm, the third eyelid closes to keep out the sand."

"The only thing I know about camels is that they spit when they are annoyed. So if you ever see one, you had better stay out of its way."

"Did you ever see a camel?"

"We saw many camels when your father and I were in Egypt."

"I do not remember going to Egypt."

"You were just a babe." She looked at the dusty road beneath her feet, remembering their harrowing journey.

"Why did we go there?"

"We felt safer in Egypt," she tried to explain. "There were some bad people in Yerushalayim."

"King Herod."

"Yes."

Yeshua thought about this for a moment. "Ima."

"Yes?"

"Do you know why a camel holds its head up high?" She shook her head. "A camel holds its head high for it alone knows the sacred name of the Holy One."

"Is that so?"

"Ima, I know the sacred name of the Holy One." He stopped, and took her hand. "In my dream the Holy One's name was 'King of Kings.' But I think that it is 'Abba,' the name I call my father. Yes, I am certain. The Holy One's name *is* 'Abba.'"

Before they reached home, a misty rain began to fall. "Look Ima, a rainbow," Yeshua said, pointing. "Some say that when you see a rainbow it means that the Lord has put down his bow. Do you think the Lord has a bow?"

"The rainbow is a promise that the Lord will never again flood the earth," Miryam said. "There is a blessing said upon seeing a rainbow. But she did not recite it; instead she sang out.

> *"Blessed are you, Most High, Ruler of the Universe,*
> *who remembers the covenant,*
> *and is faithful to your promise."*

"You have a blessing for everything," he laughed, catching a few raindrops in his mouth.

Miryam put her hand on Yeshua's shoulder to hurry him along. But he stopped and looked at her with a wise expression.

"We cannot stop the rain, Ima. It is there to remind us that there are some things in life that we cannot change."

24

Miryam went outside to milk the goat, which she did twice daily, morning and evening. After pouring grain into a bucket, she let the goat out of the pen, and it went straight to the feed. Placing another bucket under its udder, she sat down on a stool. With smooth, rhythmic motions, she squeezed one teat and then the other. From time to time, she looked down the road to see if Yosef and Yeshua were coming from Tzippori. The sun was dipping low over the blue hills and they were late.

When the bucket was full, she gave the goat a scratch under the chin and led it back to its pen. She took the bucket to the house, and wrapped a shawl around her head and shoulders. Then she walked to Klofah's house at the end of the street.

"Any sign of the men?" Miryam called to Miri, who was preparing the evening meal with her daughters.

Miri came to the door, wiping her hands on her apron. "Supper will grow cold if they do not come soon. I wonder what can be keeping them."

"Perhaps their work was unfinished and they needed to stay another day."

"Surely Klofah or Yosef would send word if they were delayed," Miri fretted as she returned to the house.

Miryam walked back and forth, watching the road until she caught sight of the men. They were walking fast, all talking at once. Yosef was pulling the cart and Klofah's sons were running alongside, but Yeshua was not with them. By the look on their faces, she was certain that something dreadful had happened. She gasped when she saw a man sprawled in the cart. When they drew closer she could see that it was Klofah.

"Sister, come quickly!" Miryam called out.

Miri rushed outside to the cart. Blood gushed from her husband's gaping wound. She cried out in anguish and fell to her knees.

"What happened?" Miryam asked.

"We were working on a water tower," Yosef said, trying to catch his breath. "We were hoisting bricks with pulleys and ropes…the scaffold…it collapsed without warning…. Most of us escaped serious injury…except Klofah…. The bricks fell upon him and we had to dig him out." His face was drained of color. "I think my brother is dead."

Klofah's sons gently lifted their father's lifeless body, brought him into the house and laid him on his bed. Yosef bent down and felt his brother's neck for a pulse. Nothing. He put his ear close to his mouth and listened for a breath. Again, nothing.

"I am so sorry, dear sister," he said, closing his brother's eyes.

Miri's shriek pierced the stillness. "My husband! Why have you left me? What will I do without you?"

"We never know when we are made to pay the debt of Adam's sin," Yosef mourned.

With a loud wail, Miri put her head on her husband's chest. Lysia and Lydia sobbed as Miryam held them in her arms. Their brothers tried to be brave but looked frightened.

Neighbors heard the commotion, and soon filled the house. Miryam left them to console the family and went outside to look for Yeshua. He was not there. What if something happened to him, too? She paced back and forth, wringing her hands. At last she saw him plodding along. He was in no hurry. Although thankful that he was safe, she scolded him when he drew near.

"Where were you? You should have been here! Your uncle is dead. Perhaps you could have saved him!"

But he only looked confused. "I was tending to the injured men in Tzippori."

She pulled him close and kissed him, asking his forgiveness. It was not yet his time.

The funeral procession moved slowly through the cold, harsh dawn. Miri and her daughters walked ahead, followed by Miryam, Shlomit, and the other women. It was believed that woman had brought death into the world by sin, and so women must lead the mourners to the graves. The men walked behind, their heads bowed, carrying the body to its burial place. No coffin, just an open litter. Yosef began to chant *Kaddish*, the mourner's prayer.

"May HaShem be blessed forever and to all eternity. May there be consolation on those who dwell in the dust."

"Amen," the others intoned.

"May there be abundant peace from heaven, and life upon us and upon all Yisrael."

"Amen."

Short speeches were made in honor of Klofah. The women sang a lament, their plaintive wailing adding to the grief. "Depart in peace," they said.

"Have no fear, my sister," Yosef told Miri. "I will provide for you and your children."

"You are my kinsman, and I know you will not leave us bereft," she wept.

"What happens when a person dies?" Yeshua asked, summoning the courage to interrupt the rabbi's reading. He had finished school, but he still had a thirst to learn the Torah beyond discussions at the dinner table or the marketplace.

Rabbi Reuven rolled up the scroll and put it in the Torah cabinet. "My son, some understand death as a place where the righteous live in the world to come—*Olam HaBa*. Others say that the afterlife is a shadowy place called *Sheol*, where the dead wait until the coming of the Mashiach when they will be resurrected. And some do not know what happens after death."

"What do you believe?"

He pursed his lips. "I believe that life does not end with death. We live on in the memories of our loved ones."

"Rabbi, does the prophet Daniyel not say, 'Many who sleep in the dust of the earth shall live forever'?"

"This is true, my son, but as Rabbi Yaakov once said, 'It is better to spend one hour doing good deeds in the present world, than to be in everlasting shame in the next.' We must prepare ourselves for the world to come."

"How can I prepare myself?"

The rabbi looked at him with a steady gaze. "My son, this world is like an entrance hall to the world to come. Prepare yourself through study of the Torah and by your mitzvot, and then one day you will be worthy to enter the banquet hall."

Yeshua sat at the door stoop pondering the things the rabbi told him.

"Come inside and eat something," his mother said when she returned from helping Miri deal with her grief.

Yeshua wanted to think more on what the rabbi told him, but he was hungry, so he followed her into the house. She dipped a piece of flat bread in honey, and handed it to her son. He licked the sticky substance from his fingers.

She smiled and poured a cup of fresh goat's milk. He sloshed it down, the drops like tiny pearls on the hairs of his upper lip.

"Your beard is growing," she said, taking his chin in her hand. "You are becoming a man."

He drew himself up. "Will we be going to the temple to celebrate the Pesach?"

"It may be possible," she said. "Your father and I will discuss it."

"I must go. I am a man now." He stuck out his chin. "I have an obligation."

"So grown up, my son?" she asked. A strand of dark hair fell across his forehead and she pushed it back.

"Ima, I am not a child," he said, brushing his hair forward.

"Yes, you are a man now," she sighed. "And since you are a man, you are the one who should speak to your father about Pesach."

25

Three times a year, the faithful were commanded to go up to Yerushalayim to celebrate the festivals of Pesach, Shavuot, and Sukkot. Distance prevented many from attending all three, but most tried to make Pesach. The journey from Natzeret to Yerushalayim would take four or five days, depending on the pace. Families and friends traveled together, camping overnight. Men pulled decorated carts that carried the older women who tended the very young. Some women rode donkeys and some went by foot, the boys running ahead, the girls laughing and skipping behind.

Miryam and Miri walked hand in hand as they did when they were younger, enjoying the sight of tender green of corn and barley in the fields, the wild anemones flowering along their path. At times, they had to move aside for the ox teams hauling huge slabs of limestone for the ongoing building projects in Yerushalayim.

The pilgrims came in a never-ending procession, like a surging river. When they were about ten miles from the Holy City, they went up a steep ascent to a ridge where they caught their first glimpse of the city. The entire caravan halted. In size and ornament, the temple that Herod restored surpassed the one King Shlomo built. Sitting atop two hills, rimmed by great protective walls, it was the most beautiful place Yeshua had ever seen. It gleamed like a jewel set high above the old city of David.

"There is a proverb," Yosef said. "Anyone who has not seen Herod's temple has never seen anything beautiful." He turned and looked at Miryam. "But of course they never saw my wife."

From the ridge they could see the white marble villas of the kohanim and the palaces of the rich, their homes like patches of snow against the houses in the lower city, yellowed from years of sun and wind.

The pilgrims began their descent along the narrow road, which sloped toward the Tyropean Valley. Someone called for a song. As though directed by an invisible choirmaster, their voices rose in the air above the clapping of hands, the clanging of cymbals, and the ringing of tambourines.

> *I was glad when they said to me, "Let us go to the house*
> *of the Lord!"*
> *And now our feet are standing within your gates,*
> *O Yerushalayim.*

As the sun began to set, the pilgrims began to look for a place to settle. Those who had family or friends found lodging, while others rented space. Yosef set up camp among the groves on the Mount of Olives, along with countless families clustered in tents and temporary shelters. As they worked, they could hear the sounds of stones being finished at the quarry, mixing with the voices of men chanting prayers in the temple. Other voices were heard—the ominous cries of the Roman guard keeping watch from the Antonia tower, named for General Marcus Antonius.

By nightfall, the hillsides around the city flickered with the red glow of numerous campfires. Pungent aromas filled the smoky air as the women prepared the evening meal. Everyone stopped their work when a trumpet blast called them to prayer; their voices rising in songs of gratitude for their safe journey.

> *I will offer to you a thanksgiving sacrifice*
> *and call on your name.*
> *I will pay my vows to the Most High*
> *in the presence of all his people,*
> *in the courts of the house of the Holy One,*
> *in your midst, O Yerushalayim!*

When they awoke at dawn, the sky was pearl-white above the city rooftops. After a simple meal of bread and figs, Yosef and his family went to bathe in the mikvot outside the temple walls. Afterwards, they made their way down the street, hoping not to be separated by the swarms of strangers speaking in many languages.

Yeshua stared at the massive walls Herod had built to support the sanctuary. Various grasses filled the crevices between the stones where doves made their nests. At intervals along the walls were ten gates leading into the temple courts—the Golden Gate on the east side, another gate on the west, four on the north and four on the south. Roman soldiers stood guard atop the temple walls, watching for any disturbance. Yeshua was dismayed to see the lame and blind begging for alms along the walls. They were barred from entering the temple because their afflictions were thought to be a curse.

Climbing the monumental staircase, the pilgrims passed over the street and shops below. Yeshua gaped at the soaring, fifteen-story sanctuary sheathed in white marble, the sunlight gleaming off the gold façade, making the temple blaze like the sun. A series of buildings, set upon massive supporting walls, rose terrace above terrace, each enclosed court holier than the preceding one.

Pushing his way through the mob, Yosef urged his family to move along to the four southern gates named for the prophetess Huldah, who once preached there. On the steps, would-be prophets tried to outshout each other. One man babbled senselessly. Another cried: "Repent! The day of the Most High is coming, the great and terrible day!"

Yeshua tugged on Yosef's sleeve. "Abba, the rabbi says that we should repent one day before our death. Does he mean that we will know on what day we will die?"

"No, no," Yosef answered. "The rabbi only meant that we should repent today, lest we die tomorrow."

A croaking voice startled them both. "Alas for you!" He pointed to Yeshua. "The day of the Almighty is coming, a day of darkness and gloom!"

"Abba," Yeshua said, panic rising in his voice. "What is he saying? Is it the end of the world?"

"My son, there have always been people who predicted the end of the world. And there always will be." He smiled and clapped him on the back. "But look! We are still here!"

Another man with wild, matted hair raged, "The Most High hates your festivals, and takes no delight in your burnt offerings!"

Yeshua frowned. "Why is he condemning us for bringing offerings to the Most High?"

"Do not be troubled," Yosef answered. "There are always those who rebuke others for their good works. It is not a new battle. Only the names change. Now, enough questions, yes?"

Yeshua protested but Yosef put a finger to his lips. "No more. We must look to ourselves and go to the Holy One with clean hands and a right spirit."

Passing through the gate, Yosef and his family made their way down a long decorated tunnel, dark as a cave despite flaming torches along the way. The driving crowd pressed in on them until they emerged into the largest of the temple courts, the Court of Gentiles. Coming out into the bright sunlight, Yeshua stared open-mouthed at the spectacle—hundreds of kohanim in their white linen robes and tubular hats were hustling to and fro over the blue marble floor, which had the appearance of the Great Sea. Crowds of people were buying and selling, their voices buzzing like bees around a hive as they haggled over the price of salt, flour, wine, oil, or incense for temple offerings. Guides were directing pilgrims, advising them where they could purchase sacrificial lambs for the Pesach. The pungent smell of blood and burnt fat from animal sacrifices filled Yeshua's nostrils. He thought the place looked and smelled more like a giant bazaar than the holiest place on earth.

Yeshua stopped to read one of the inscriptions posted:

"No foreigner may pass within the wall around the sanctuary. Whoever is caught, the guilt for the death that follows will be their own."

He was about to ask his father why there was such a harsh judgment on the Gentiles, but Yosef motioned to his family to follow him to the money-changers. "We must exchange our Roman coins for shekels."

"Why, Abba?" he asked, craning his neck to see the coin his father pulled from his pouch.

Yosef showed him the imperial seal and stamped image of Caesar. "Remember the commandment against graven images."

After changing his money, Yosef told Miryam and the girls to wait while he and the boys went to stand in a long line to purchase a lamb for the Pesach meal.

"Please hurry back," Miryam urged as the men rushed away.

Yosef glowered when he heard the price "That is higher than what they charge outside the temple."

"Look at this lamb," the vendor said. "You will never find such a spotless, unblemished one like this."

Yosef sighed and paid the fee. Taking the small creature into his arms, he went to look for Miryam and the girls. Yeshua followed behind, searching the lamb's sad eyes, wondering if it knew what its fate would be.

When the family was reunited, they followed Yosef into the Court of Women, the beginning of the sanctuary. There were several chambers. In one, lepers washed before being presented to a kohen who would decide if they were fit to return to society. In another, Nazirites had their long hair trimmed after completing their vows. A third chamber stored oil, wine, and flour, and a fourth held wood for sacrificial purposes.

The court was not exclusive for women; it was open to all Yehudim, natives or visitors from abroad. Even a ritually unclean kohen was allowed in the women's court to perform his various duties. But women were permitted no further.

Above the din, Yeshua heard voices singing. He tried to see where it was coming from, and saw a number of kohanim gathered on the semi-circular steps leading to the Court of Men. Their arms were outstretched in prayer, and their voices rose in a glorious chorus.

> *It is good to give thanks to the Lord,*
> *to sing praises to your name, O Most High;*
> *to declare your steadfast love in the morning,*
>   *and your faithfulness by night.*

Yosef smiled at his wife. "It is said that Adam and Chavah sang that song on the first Shabbat in the Garden of Eden."

"Look." She pointed to one of the large, lily-shaped collection boxes. "That is where I waited for you when we brought Yeshua to be consecrated. I was so worried. I thought you were lost."

"And you must wait here again while we take the lamb to be slaughtered," Yosef told her, juggling the wriggling animal in his arms. "We will return as soon as we can."

Miryam reached out to touch the lamb. "Do not get lost."

The Women's Court, the *Ezrat Nashim*, was divided from the *Ezrat Yisrael*, the Court of Men, by a wall along the west side. Yeshua was proud that he was now a son of the law and did not have to stay with the women. Running ahead, he skipped up the flight of fifteen steps leading to the courtyard for male worshippers.

"Yeshua, what do you think you are doing?" Yosef called, aghast at his behavior. "You do not run in the temple. This is holy ground!"

Miryam turned to Miri and said under her breath, "My father once told me that I skipped up the temple steps as a child. I cannot help thinking how much alike we are."

Yosef handed the lamb to his son when he returned to his side. "See that you mind me."

Miri's boys followed behind, jabbing at Yeshua as he obediently walked up the stairway to the Nicanor Gate. He stopped to stare at the bronze doors, glimmering with a golden hue.

"Abba! Is this the gate called 'Beautiful'? Can the gates of heaven be more beautiful than these?"

"I am sure that they are," Yosef replied. "Though it is has been said that miracles have been performed at these doors."

A low, stone rail set off the Court of Priests, the *Ezrat Kohanim*, from the Court of Men. Two great columns flanked the doors leading into the sanctuary, a small rectangular structure divided into two chambers. The first chamber was the *Hechal*, the Holy Place, where the kohanim burned incense, trimmed the lamps of the large, seven-branched *menorah*, and offered the Bread of Presence on the Shabbat.

In front of the Holy Place hung a heavy veil embroidered in rich colors of blue, white, scarlet, and purple thread, depicting the whole vista of the heavens. On the other side of the curtain was the innermost sanctuary, *Kodesh HaKodashim*, the Holy of Holies. Only the Kohen HaGadol could enter this sacred place, on Yom Kippur, the Feast of the Atonement. Although it once contained the Ark of the Covenant, it was now empty. There, in the impenetrable darkness, the High Priest asked forgiveness for himself and for the sins of Yisrael.

Three blasts from silver trumpets announced the beginning of the sacrifice. Yeshua stood with his father at the balustrade, appalled at the gruesome sight of animals being sacrificed on the great altar of holocausts. Accessed by a ramp, the altar stood fifteen-feet high, the top almost hidden by a great cloud of smoke. A bronze laver stood alongside the altar for the kohanim to wash their bloodied hands and soiled feet before entering the sacred presence.

As the sacrifices were about to take place, each man in turn brought his lamb, tied its fore legs to its hind legs, and suspended its head and breast over the low railing. The kohen laid his hand upon the lamb's head and said a prayer over it. Then, with a quick motion of a blade, he slashed the animal's throat, collecting its blood in a basin.

When it was their turn, Yosef motioned to Yeshua. He took one last look at the lamb's pitiful eyes, and then laid it over the rail. He thought it remarkable that it made no sound when the knife was put to its throat. Other animals would bellow.

"Like a lamb led to the slaughter, he did not open his mouth," Yeshua murmured, watching the creature's life ebb away.

The kohen took the blood and splashed it around the base of the altar in atonement for sins. Two nostril-like holes at the corner of the altar captured the blood, washing it down a water channel that flowed out into the Kidron brook. Another kohen fetched the carcass and took it to a place where it would be butchered. A short time later, he returned with several pieces of meat. He gave a portion to Yosef who offered thanksgiving, then gave the rest of the meat to the kohen.

As they left the men's court, Yosef and the boys were pushed and shoved by a great surge of men struggling to get through the Nicanor Gate to meet their families. Yeshua was almost knocked down by a boy who rushed past him, ragged and barefooted with a great chain about his neck.

"Is he a slave?" Yeshua asked.

His father nodded. They watched the boy dart through the throng, leap over the balustrade, and run up the ramp to the altar of sacrifice. Clinging to the horns of the altar, the lad cried, "Sanctuary! Sanctuary!"

"What is it you are asking?" an elderly kohen demanded.

Yeshua strained to hear the boy, who was sobbing like a little child.

"Give me sanctuary. Do not return me to my master. Sell me to someone else if you want, but please release me from this fiend."

The kohen leaned forward and put his ear close to the lad's mouth so he could hear what sort of abuse he suffered.

"What happened to him?" Yeshua asked.

But Yosef shook his head. "I will tell you about it later. Such things are an abomination and should not be talked about in the Holy House of the Most High."

As the kohen took the young man to his chambers, Yeshua wondered.

How can a building be more honored than people? It is an abomination for one man to own another. I must talk to the teachers of the law.

Yosef and his family left the temple, returning to the campsite. There they ate their roasted lamb prepared with bitter herbs. When the last of the Pesach songs faded, they began to make preparations for the night, the women setting up tents in a separate area from the men. Yeshua decided that he would wait until dawn and then go back to the temple. He planned to stay only a short time, until he had a chance to speak to the scholars. Afterward, he would return to camp, hoping that no one would notice his absence.

Early in the morning, he found the doctors of the law sitting on colorful mats in Shlomo's Portico, a roofed, colonnaded gallery, running along the eastern wall in the Court of the Gentiles. Drawing near, he could hear the scholars holding their students spell-bound with their wise argumentation. Young and old were seated side by side. All were allowed to speak and ask questions in turn. When Yeshua spoke, everyone was surprised to hear such wisdom from a boy of twelve years.

26

"Soon we will be home," Miryam said as she loaded the cart for the journey back to Natzeret. She looked around for Yeshua, thinking he might help her, but then smiled. He was a man now; he would be with the other men.

It was mid-morning when the women's caravan began to move north. The men followed. In late afternoon, both groups stopped to rest near a caravansary where the animals could be watered. As Miryam and the other women began to prepare the meal, she saw Yosef coming toward her. He was alone.

"Where is Yeshua?" she asked.

He shrugged. "I have not seen him all day. I thought he was with you."

"No, he is not. Wherever can he be?" she asked in alarm.

They set about searching the camp, asking relatives and friends if they had seen him. They looked everywhere, but there was no sign of the boy.

"Could we have left him behind?" Yosef wondered.

"Surely he would have tried to find us," Miryam said, panic rising in her voice.

"I must return to Yerushalayim," Yosef said.

"I will go with you," she said, and he agreed.

Leaving Miri and her children in the camp, they set out for the Holy City in haste, asking pilgrims along the way if they had seen a lost boy.

"So many youth pass this way," a man said. "It is impossible to tell one from the other."

The sun began to sink behind a ragged line of trees and the sky turned red, purple, and pink. They trekked along what seemed like an endless road. Soon it would be dark.

Her mind raced. *Where are we to go? What are we to do? This road can be dangerous at night. So many caravans pass this way. Perhaps he was taken, like the slave boy in the temple. What if a robber attacked him? What if he is lying in a ditch, injured…or….*

Night fell. They came upon another caravan camped by the roadside. Had anyone seen a lost boy? No one had.

"Please stay with us," a man implored. "There is nothing you can do until dawn."

Reluctantly, Miryam and Yosef agreed. Unable to sleep, they spent the night in prayer.

"Turn to me and be gracious; give strength to your servant," Yosef prayed.

"Save the child of your serving girl," Miryam wept.

In the morning, they set out at a fast pace. It was late afternoon when they arrived in Yerushalayim. A crowd streamed out of the city gates. They searched the face of every boy passing by, but their son was not among them. Frantic, they went up and down the city streets, peering into every shop along the way. Soon they were lost in the narrow, winding alleys.

"Have we passed this way before?" Miryam wondered.

"It is getting dark, and all the shops are closing," Yosef said, discouraged. "Let us go to the camp on the hillside and look again when it is light."

When they arrived at the campsite, the sun was setting behind the distant purple mountains of Moab. Wrapping themselves in their outer cloaks, they lay on the hard ground. They prayed throughout the night, their prayers sometimes punctuated by the cries of shepherds tending their flocks.

"Please, please, merciful Father," Miryam prayed. "We have lost our little lamb; please help us find him."

As the sun rose, they started out once more in the cold, pale dawn. All morning they looked for their son but did not find him. Fear gripped Miryam's heart; they held one another in despair.

"Let us go back to the temple," Yosef suggested.

"Why would he be there?" Miryam asked.

"I do not know where else to look."

When they arrived at the temple, most of the pilgrims had returned to their homes. The Court of Gentiles was nearly empty. Kohanim were climbing the steps to the inner courtyard, where they would feast on a sacrificial meal in their private quarters.

Yosef and Miryam scanned the courtyard, but Yeshua was not there.

"Let us go into the Women's Court," Yosef proposed. "And if he is not there, I will see if he is in the Court of Men."

As they crossed the court, Miryam glanced toward the Portico of Shlomo. A number of men were sitting in a circle under the roofed arcade. Perhaps one of them had seen their son. As they approached the portico, they could hear everyone talking at once, gesturing wildly, their voices rising in a feverish pitch. They seemed to be arguing, but when Miryam and Yosef drew closer, they realized they were merely discussing the Torah. And there in their midst was Yeshua, listening to them and prodding them with questions.

Miryam gasped with relief, and just as quick, became upset. "Son, why have you treated us like this? Look, your father and I have been searching for you in great anxiety."

The men turned at the sound of a woman's voice.

"Three days!" Yosef almost shouted. "We have been looking for you for three days!" We thought you were lost…for all we knew you might have…."

Yeshua seemed surprised. "Why were you searching for me? Did you not know that I must be in my Father's house?"

Yosef looked at Miryam in distress, but she understood. She had made her decision to accept her calling long ago. Now Yeshua must make his. But he was young. Did he truly know who he was?

On the long road back to the caravan, Miryam pondered the events of the day. "What if we lost him?" she whispered to Yosef, her voice filled with dread.

"Did we really lose him?" Yosef asked through clenched teeth. "Did he not go on his own without our permission?"

Miryam put her arm through his. "Are you angry because Yeshua strayed, or because of what he said—that he must be in his 'Father's house'? Yosef, no man could be a better father to his son than you."

"The boy was my responsibility and we came close to losing him," he answered. "Why did I fail?"

Yeshua had been walking a short distance behind, and he caught up with Yosef, seeming to have forgotten his misdeed. "Abba, I was asking the rabbis why everyone says, 'the temple, the temple,' as if it was the greatest thing on earth."

Yosef's eyes narrowed. "You have shamed me in front of those scholars. What will they say, 'Yosef's son instructs the scribes'? You should think before you say such things!"

"But Abba, it is the truth," Yeshua exclaimed. "We think that the temple is the only place where the Most High can be worshipped, but it is just a building made by human hands. Did the prophet not say that heaven is the throne of the Most High and the earth is his footstool?"

"I told you before. I do not want you to talk that way. The temple is the House of the Holy One." Yosef shook his head and walked on, his hands clasped behind his back.

There was a long tense silence; then Yeshua turned to his mother, "Ima, I did not mean to upset Abba. I am only saying...."

Miryam grabbed him by the arm. "What did your father just tell you?"

Yeshua lowered his voice. "Ima, what I wanted to say is that the Lord is everywhere. When the clouds come down and touch the earth, I can see his hand at work...."

Miryam gave him a warning look but he persisted. "When I see the rising star in the morning, and the beautiful colors of the sunset at night, I know that the Lord is here." He motioned to the reddening sky. "But so many people are blind to His presence."

He grew quiet for a moment. Miryam was glad that she did not have to shush him again. All at once he tugged at her sleeve. "Ima...."

Miryam sighed. "Yes, my son?"

"Ima, the temple is not the only place where we can hear the voice of the Lord. We can listen to him every day—in the wind blowing through the trees, in the song of the birds in the morning, and their last song at night. If you turn over a stone it will shout praises to the Lord's goodness."

Bending down, he picked up a pebble and tossed it as far as he could. It landed near his father, startling him.

"Son, go make amends with your father," she ordered.

Yeshua went to his side, looking repentant. "Abba, I did not mean to be rude. I made you angry, yes?"

"You made me very angry, yes," Yosef snapped.

"Forgive me please, Abba. It is just that I want to learn so much," Yeshua pleaded.

Yosef looked into Yeshua's dark eyes and nodded. "Yes, I forgive you, my son. But you should not say such things about the temple of the Holy One."

Yeshua furrowed his brow. "Abba, *we* are the temple of the Holy One, whether we are tall or small," he said, holding up his hand to measure his height with his father's. He stopped and searched his face. Had he offended him again?

Yosef smiled, and Yeshua added, "Abba, I will make it my custom to go to worship at the temple. I know that the elders have a great deal to teach me . . . but they have something to learn also."

Yosef threw up his arms and marched ahead.

When they reached the camp, Yaakov ran to meet them, his spindly legs and arms flying. Taller by a head, Yaakov leaned close to Yeshua's ear, whispering loud enough for Miryam to hear, "Did you get in trouble?" Yeshua screwed up his mouth and said nothing. "Will you be punished?" Yaakov snickered. "I am sure that you will be."

"Come, let us have a footrace," Yeshua challenged him. Yaakov forgot his taunt, and together they sprinted away.

"Yeshua! Yaakov!" Yosef shouted as they ran some distance ahead.

"Do not go too far," Miryam called, afraid of losing her son again.

27

Yeshua followed the grain of the wood, shaving it with the plane to make it smooth. The sweet smell filled his nostrils. Now in his twenties, he had learned his trade from boyhood, standing at his father's side, copying his every move. He learned to drive a nail; to use a level; to drill a clean hole; to choose what wood worked best for a yoke or plow; and how to wait for the green wood to dry.

Yeshua hummed as he worked. His father seemed to enjoy the pleasant tune as he sharpened a tool at the stone wheel.

"You should sing too, Abba," Yeshua urged. "It will give you joy, and it will give the Lord joy to hear you sing."

"I do not have a good voice. It is your mother who has the song."

"The Torah tells us to make a joyful noise. The important thing is to sing!"

Yosef gave a little laugh and tried to hum along. But all of a sudden, he stopped to catch his breath. He cleared his throat and tried to say something, but a deep cough rattled his thin frame.

"You work too hard." Yeshua took the tool from him. "Let me finish. You must rest."

Yosef had little strength, and offered no resistance. Wiping his brow with the back of his hand, he left the workshop in a coughing fit.

Yeshua worked late into the afternoon. At length, he laid aside his tools, took off his apron, and hung it on a peg. He could smell a savory stew cooking as he strode across the courtyard.

"Dinner is almost ready," Miryam said as he entered the house.

His hands felt cramped, and he stretched out his muscular arms. The setting sun streamed through the doorway, throwing his shadow across the floor. Miryam stood still and stared. It was the shape of a cross.

"What is it, Ima?" he asked.

She only shook her head. Then she lit the evening lamp and set the stew on the table. Yeshua looked at his father who was sitting at the table, gaunt and pale. He seemed to have grown worse month by month.

"It is too much…too much," Yosef said, leaning forward, putting his elbows on his knees.

"What is too much?" Miryam asked, kneeling beside him.

"I am just tired. It will pass," he said, pressing her hand with his.

Yeshua cut a wedge of fresh bread, placed it before his father, and sat down beside him. With a weak voice, Yosef blessed the food. Several times he leaned forward to speak, but the only sound was a husky rasp. With trembling hands he dipped the bread into the stew, but after a few mouthfuls he pushed back his chair.

"I am not hungry," he said, trying to rise from the table. "I have a job I need to finish."

"You have done enough," Yeshua said, placing a firm hand on his shoulder. "The work can wait another day."

"You must rest," Miryam pleaded, stroking his hair, now threaded with gray.

He touched her cheek, tracing the curve of her face. "My dove."

Then, standing with great effort, he shuffled out to the workshop.

Yeshua and Miryam finished their meal, exchanging worried looks. At first there came familiar sounds from the workshop, the sawing and sanding. Then suddenly there was nothing. Only silence—and then a groan.

"What was that?" Miryam asked.

They sat motionless, listening.

"There it is again." Miryam's face blanched with fear.

They rushed to the workshop and found Yosef slumped over the workbench, his white-knuckled fists clutching his chest.

"Yeshua! Your father," Miryam cried. "Oh, no! . . . Yosef!"

Yeshua took hold of his father, and led him back to the house. As he laid him on the cot, Yosef's eyes rolled back in his head. Yeshua knelt beside him, unsure of what to do—except to pray.

Miryam knelt beside her son. "My beloved, what is the matter?" When there was no answer, she placed her ear close to his mouth.

"Are you ready for me to die?" he asked in a hoarse whisper, struggling to breathe.

"Oh, Yosi," she wept. "Please do not leave me. How can I live without you?"

But he only murmured the prayer he had said all his life: *"Shema Yisrael…Adonai Eloheinu…Adonai echad."*

"You are a good man," she sobbed. "I love you."

Yosef answered her, forming the words without making a sound. "And I love you."

There was a rattle in his throat and then a slow hissing sound. His eyes became dark and glassy. She took his calloused hands in hers, kissing the small scar left by an awl that had slipped.

She clung to him and wept until she had no more tears. Then Yeshua closed his father's eyes, stood, and with hands upraised, prayed the song of David.

You are a shield around me, my glory,
and the one who lifts up my head.
I cry aloud to you, and you answer me from your holy hill.
I lie down and sleep; I wake again, for you sustain me.

Miryam put her head upon her husband's chest and whispered in his ear as though he could hear. "You are the song that sings in my soul."

Yeshua bent down to give his father a final kiss. "One day you will be raised on high, and people will call you blessed among men."

Miryam knelt in silence. When she stood, Yeshua embraced her. "I will go and make the preparations," he said.

"Your father was good to me and my family when Klofah died," Miri told Yeshua, helping Miryam wash and anoint Yosef's body. "I could never thank him enough for his kindness."

Yeshua cleaned under Yosef's nails, the rough hands soiled with years of toil.

"That is women's work, my son," Miryam protested, wiping her eyes with her sleeve. "Touching the dead will make you unclean."

"He is my father. How could his death defile me?"

When he finished, he cut one of the fringes on the corner of his father's tallit. "The dead are no longer bound by earth's laws," he said. Then he wrapped Yosef's body in fine linen and covered his face with a napkin.

Miri sprinkled Yosef's body with aromatic spices, and her sons placed him in a long wicker basket and lifted it to their shoulders.

On the way to the graveyard, flute players played their dirge while women beat their breasts, wailing, "Alas! Alas!" Miryam walked in silence, her head bowed. Yeshua followed.

When the procession arrived at the tomb, he placed the decayed remains of his brother and parents in ossuaries to make room for Yosef's body. Then he lifted his father from the bier and laid him on a shelf inside.

Miri's sons rolled a stone in place, and it closed with a thud. The tomb was then whitewashed as a warning that it was contaminated.

Each of the mourners took their leave, expressing their sympathy.

"May Adonai Eloheinu comfort you for the sake of Yerushalayim."

"May you have no more pain."

"May you only have happiness."

Miri looked sadly at her sister-in-law. "The Angel of Death has dipped his sword into our hearts."

28

Spring came; the days grew longer; the winter winds quieted; the trees put forth their yellow-green foliage. It was a sunny morning as Miryam stepped out of the house. She breathed in the cool scent of growing things. She stopped and stared at the stump of the old fig tree.

"Look, Yeshua! It is sprouting shoots."

He fingered the fresh leaves drenched in dew. "The prophet said it well. 'If a tree is cut down, there is hope that it will sprout again.'"

From the time of Yosef's death, Miryam had noticed a growing restlessness in Yeshua. He continued his carpentry work, but no longer with joy. He was tired of complaints and unpaid debts. At times, he wandered up into the hills to be alone. Often, he closed shop early and went to the synagogue, returning long after his mother had gone to sleep. Now and then she observed him reading the sacred scrolls the rabbi lent him, the golden glow of the oil lamp illuminating the yellowed pages.

Sometimes she sat by his side as he read out loud, watching him follow the text with his long, tapered fingers. Little by little, she began to understand the strange markings on the page. Her heart swelled with love as he read the Song of Songs, his voice filled with such tenderness it seemed that he was singing to his bride.

"Ah, you are beautiful, my beloved, ah, you are beautiful; your eyes are like doves!"

It made Miryam sad to think that her son might not marry. He told her that a wife would be a distraction to the path he was on. But he never explained what path he meant.

Her neighbors often clucked their tongues, wagging their heads and whispering to each other behind their hands.

"Most men are married long before this."

"Surely there are young women in the village who catch his eye."

"Does Yeshua not know that marriage is a sacred duty?"

"The rabbis say that an unmarried man is always thinking of sin."

"Is Yeshua studying to be a rabbi?"

"What is it my son?" Miryam asked one day, seeing Yeshua hunched over at his workbench, his back to her.

"The days go by, one Shabbat follows another, and then one day everything changes," he said, turning to her.

"What has changed?"

"These hands of mine." He turned and held them out to her. "They are intended for some other purpose than wood and stone. But what? I wish I knew what I was meant to do."

Miryam took a deep breath. She should have told him. She had tried many times, but had failed. "Come into the house, Yeshua. There is something I must tell you."

He followed her and he sat down at the table, his head bowed, his hands folded on his lap. Miryam was silent, trying to find the right words.

"I wanted to tell you this for some time." She sat down beside him. "Are you listening, Yeshua?" she asked, her voice gentle but firm.

He looked up, a bewildered look on his face. "Tell me what?"

"Before you were born, an angel came to me." She twisted a strand of her long, dark hair. "The angel gave me a message concerning your birth."

"An angel? In Natzeret?"

"The angel told me that your birth would be a miracle. You were conceived…." She stopped. How could she put something unexplainable into plain words?

"Your father, Yosef…his seed did not bring you into being."

"Ima, you are not saying…?"

"No, no, my son." She felt embarrassed that the thought he might be illegitimate would cross his mind. "It was the Holy Spirit. The Spirit overshadowed me. Do you understand?"

He looked at her blankly.

She rose and went to the small chest in the corner. She touched it lightly, remembering that Yosef had made it for a wedding gift. Lifting the lid, she searched for a pouch she had placed there long ago. He watched as she rummaged until she found it. Going to him, she opened the pouch and dropped a small white stone into the palm of his hand.

"Do you remember this?"

He shook his head, running his fingers around the stone's smooth surface.

"A woman gave it to you when we were in Egypt," she said.

"I remember music and dancing, a dark-skinned woman." He stared into the distance. At last he spoke, "Ima, why did we go to Egypt?"

"It was when King Herod ruled over Yehudah. When he heard that a special child was to be born, he was afraid."

"Afraid of what?" Yeshua asked, leaning forward, clutching the stone.

"Afraid that the child . . . that you . . . would take his throne."

"Me? I am no king. Tell me, Ima: Why did we go to Egypt?"

She looked into his questioning eyes. "After you were born in Beit Lechem, there was a massacre. All the boys under the age of two were killed. Herod did this because of you."

"Because of me?" He stared at her in disbelief.

Miryam covered his hand with hers. "The woman who gave you the stone said there was a name written on it, and one day you would know what it meant. I can see nothing. Does it have any meaning for you?"

In the long silence that followed, Miryam watched him clench and unclench the stone in his fist. Then he spoke in a low voice. "Son of Yahweh."

It was the name that no one dared pronounce. To Miryam, it sounded as natural as "Father."

Throughout the night, Yeshua tossed fitfully, brooding over the meaning of the Holy Name. Rising before dawn, he went to wake his mother.

"Ima, I have come to a decision," he said. "I am going to Yerushalayim to study with the doctors of the law."

She sat up. "Dear son, you have put aside everything to look after me when your father died. You must go and find your destiny."

"I might be gone for some time," he said, searching her face.

She got up and helped him pack a few things. "Perhaps you should also go to your cousin. The last time you met Yochanan, you were both in the womb. His father announced at his birth at he would be will be called prophet of the Most High, and would go before the Lord to prepare his ways."

"Why was I never told these things?" Yeshua asked, bewildered.

"I wanted to tell you…but it never seemed the right time…until now." She wrapped some cheese, bread and dates in a napkin and put it in his bag.

"And my cousin, Yochanan, where can I find him?"

"I have heard that from the time his mother died he has lived in the settlement at Qumran…near the Dead Sea, I believe. You may find some answers…and perhaps some comfort."

Yeshua made no reply. He kissed her lightly on the forehead, and then left the house. He did not look back.

When Yeshua arrived in Yerushalayim, he went straight to the temple where he studied diligently with the Torah Master each day. One afternoon he found him walking with a scribe in a shaded colonnade. "Rabboni, I want to grasp the wisdom of the Torah so that I can understand what is required of me."

The Torah Master stroked his long white beard. "The sages liken the Torah to a goad that directs the ox along the furrow. So, too, the words of the Torah direct those who study them, leading them from the path of death to the path of life."

"But the scholars seem to take more delight in arguing about the law than its practice."

"My son, there are several groups of Yehudim, each one with different understandings of the *Halakhah*—the path that one walks." The old man pointed to the corridor ahead.

The scribe spoke up. "The *Tzaddikim* accept only the written Torah, rejecting the belief in angels and demons. Neither do they believe in the resurrection of the dead as we do."

The Torah Master pursed his lips. "We are the Perushim, the 'people of the book,' the *Am HaSefer*. When our people returned from exile, our devotion to the law is what saved us."

"Moshe Rabbenu, our teacher, gave us the written Torah," the scribe explained. "But there are also six hundred and thirteen oral laws that have been passed down the generations to cover every possibility of infidelity to the written law."

"Do the rabbis not have a saying that the Lord's mercy is two hundred and fifty times stronger than the Lord's justice?" Yeshua asked.

"Of course. Mercy restores right relationships with the Lord and one another. Yet, we must put a 'hedge' around the Torah," he said. "By putting ourselves behind the hedge, we are able to avoid falling into the pit of sin."

"I understand." Yeshua nodded. "But it seems to me that the scholars have lost their sense of proportion, raising the hedge higher, forever complicating the precepts. It is like straining the wine to avoid swallowing a tiny gnat, thereby swallowing a camel."

The Torah Master laughed. "My son, do not look at the vessel but at what it contains."

Yeshua looked at him somberly. "No one puts new wine into old wineskins. The fermenting wine will burst the skins and be lost. New wine must be put into fresh wineskins."

The old man frowned. "Have you abandoned our traditions?"

"It is not a question of putting aside my faith," he argued. "On the contrary, to say that I am no longer a Son of the Law is like denying my father. But it matters not if a bird is held by a heavy chain or a silken cord. It is still not free."

The Master squinted. "You have heard of the renowned scholar Hillel?"

"Yes, Hillel opposed the severe interpretations of the law of his colleague Shammai."

"That is true!" The old man's ancient eyes brightened. "Hillel knew that brotherly love is the fundamental principle of the Torah. I will tell you a story, eh?"

Before Yeshua could answer, the Master went on. "There once was a certain Gentile who asked Shammai if he could summarize the law while standing on one foot. Shammai thought he was a fool and sent him away. And so the Gentile went to Hillel and asked him the same thing. And do you know what Hillel told him?"

Yeshua shook his head.

"Hillel told him, 'What is hateful to you, do not do to your fellows. This is the whole law; the rest is mere commentary. Go and learn.'" The Torah Master beamed. "And that is what I say to you. Go and learn, and may the love of Yisrael remain in your heart forever."

29

Yeshua stood on the banks of the Yarden River, wondering if this was the place where his people crossed into the Promised Land. He continued along the river valley to the northwestern shore of the Dead Sea, fifteen miles east of Yerushalayim. The fierce summer heat was scorching, and a yellow haze hung over the salt-crusted lake. He thought of his beloved Sea of Galil, teeming with life. But here was this useless sea in which nothing lived—no splashing fish, no song birds. No creature could drink of its acrid water.

Putting his hand up to protect his eyes against the sun's fierce glare, he looked toward the northernmost limits of Yisrael where the waters originated on the snowy slopes of Mount Hermon. From there it poured into the Sea of Galil, emptying into the Yarden River, and ending in the Dead Sea. He stooped, cupped some of the water in his hand, and let it fall through his fingertips.

What is the difference between these two seas? The same good water is in both. Yet for every drop of water that flows into the Sea of the Galil another drop flows out. The Galil gives and so it lives, but the Dead Sea hoards every drop and has no life. How like the soul—without living water it dies.

Walking a mile inland, he could see the dry plateau of the Qumran settlement. He looked up at the caves in the sheer cliffs. He was curious to understand why his cousin Yochanan would live in this isolated place.

When Yeshua arrived at the commune, he found it alive with activity—craftsmen making baskets and leather goods, weaving cloth at looms, or firing pottery in kilns. Others were baking bread, tending bee hives, or gardening.

One of the elders showed him around. "We are known as the Essenes, the Holy Ones. We are dedicated to a life of self-denial, and abstinence from worldly pleasures. Most of us aspire to live a celibate life. We regard ourselves as the 'Sons of Light' in opposition to worldly people, the 'Breakers of the Covenant.'"

As they walked along, the elder pointed out the abundant crops tended by members of the community. "We view life as a garden from which we harvest the knowledge we need to reach the Eternal Garden," he told him. "As we cultivate our gardens, we are creating a veritable kingdom of heaven on earth. Here there is no maker of weapons of war, nor do we trade in merchandise. No work is considered superior to any other."

At midday, Yeshua was invited to join the community in the dining room, which also served as an assembly room. Before the meal, the members immersed in a daily ritual bath, after which they donned a clean garment. Thus purified, they assembled in the common room, sitting at three rows of tables where they ate their frugal meal in silence. After prayers, they returned to their work until evening.

It was some time before Yeshua was introduced to his cousin Yochanan, a member of the higher group of ascetics. Tall and raw-boned from the austerities he practiced, his dark hair was pulled back, revealing long side-curls at his ears.

Yeshua extended his hand. "I am your cousin, Yeshua ben Yosef. Your mother, Elisheva, was the aunt of my mother, Miryam."

Yochanan did not take his hand. "How did you find me?"

"My mother told me that your mother brought you here."

Yeshua waited for an answer. When Yochanan finally spoke, his voice was filled with bitterness. "I only know what they told me. I was very young when Herod ordered the massacre. My mother fled from the soldiers, hiding me in a cave in the hillside. She told me that we survived by drinking from a stream until the danger passed. She feared for my safety, and was afraid to return home. Knowing that the Essenes adopted orphans, she brought me here to Qumran. They promised her that I would be trained to live a virtuous life according to 'The Way.'"

"The Way?"

"The Essenes' way is to reject pleasures as evil. They esteem conquest over passions to be a virtue. Their piety is extraordinary."

There was silence between them. At length, Yeshua asked, "And your father?"

Yochanan's eyes clouded over. "My father, Zecharya, was one of the kohanim who served in the temple. When Herod learned that my father had an infant son, he had him arrested and interrogated as to my whereabouts. My father refused to answer, and Herod had him slain in the very place he once offered incense and prayed for a son."

There was a cold glint in his eyes when he spoke again. "The wise sage Ben Sira said, 'Forgive your neighbor the wrong he has done, and then your sins will be pardoned when you pray.'" He shook his head. "I am trying to do that, Yeshua, but it is hard."

Abruptly, he turned away. "We will speak no more of this. If you like, I will have one of the elders of the community enlighten you as to the rules of the group, their way of life, and their beliefs." Yochanan spoke to a slim man with a graying beard, and then introduced him as the "Overseer."

As his cousin slipped away, Yeshua wondered. *Why did Yochanan speak of the Essenes as though he was not a member of the community? He has lived here most of his life.*

"Our founder was the 'Teacher of Righteousness.'" The Overseer looked Yeshua over. "Our teacher understood the secret knowledge of the Holy One."

The two walked in silence until the Overseer spoke again. "There are two groups within our community. The higher group rejects all human relationships apart from spiritual fellowship. The lower group is composed of householders who regard marriage as a mystical union and seek to live a pure life. Nevertheless, everyone has been assigned an angel, even the lowliest ones. One must not despise the weak."

Continuing down the corridor, the Overseer took Yeshua to their vast water system, which was divided into several waterways carrying water throughout the complex.

"Like the rivers in Eden," Yeshua remarked.

The Overseer did not answer him. He continued, "Water is precious in the desert, as you know. During the occasional winter storm, a dam diverts the rainwater into an aqueduct leading to the cisterns. The water is stored there for drinking and ritual baths."

Abruptly, the Overseer stopped. "Our path is not an easy one. When a novice desires to enter our community, he is on a three-year period of probation, learning our doctrine and correct conduct. Not until he has successfully undergone this apprenticeship is the candidate officially accepted. After his novitiate, he vows to possess no personal property, giving all his belongings to the community. Only then can covenant immersion take place. Our Manual of Discipline warns that no one can be cleansed by a mere ceremony, unless he has already turned from the deceit of sin. If he remains unrepentant, he must be cast out into the darkness—with the other sinners."

Before Yeshua could comment, the Overseer gave him a piercing look. "Until the day when the Mashiach comes to slay the wicked of the earth, our community here at Qumran is the temple, the Holy House of Truth in Yisrael."

Yeshua looked bewildered. "Why is another temple needed when the temple is still standing?"

The old man's eyes narrowed, his jaw tightened. "The kohanim and their rituals have become corrupt and must be replaced. If you choose to live as a member of Qumran, you must accept our rule. There are punishments imposed on violators." Then he smiled, thinly. "But take heart, our rule ends with praise to the Almighty."

As the years passed, Yeshua found a sense of peace under the discipline of the Essenes. Although he was not ready to commit, he continued to participate in the communal life.

"Let the angels prepare your bread," one of the elders told him in the kitchen. "Crush your grain and make thin wafers, as our forefathers did when they departed Egypt. Put the wafers beneath the sun, for the fire of the sun that gave life to the wheat will give life to the bread and to the body."

Because Yeshua was a carpenter, he worked mostly with wood or stone. He often made deep bowls, incising concentric circles on a lathe. He also made vessels from limestone, which was found in abundance in the area.

The Overseer examined a new pot. "The reason we use stone is that pottery becomes ritually unclean and must be broken and never used again. However, stone vessels retain their purity and need not be discarded."

When it was discovered that Yeshua was able to read and write Hebrew, he was given the task of copying the community's manuscripts. His superiors explained that if some disaster should befall them, the scrolls would be sealed in pottery jars and hidden in the nearby caves.

Every afternoon, Yeshua climbed the stairs to the scriptorium on the second floor. A musty odor filled his nostrils as he walked along. The walls were lined with niches filled with parchment scrolls made from the skin of sheep or goats. The scroll that he had been working on was still lying on the plastered writing table, piled high with manuscripts.

While the narrow windows, set high in the walls, let in some light, he lit an oil lamp. The flickering glow bathed the table and floor around him. Clearing a work space, he sat on a bench and slowly read a troubling passage out loud.

> *They killed the Prince of the Congregation,*
> *the Branch of David....*

Who was this Prince and why did they kill him?

Rolling up the scroll, he stood and returned it to its niche. Searching through numerous parchments, he found the community's Manual of Discipline and carried it to the table. He unrolled it and sat down. Trimming his reed pen, he dipped it in the ink well and began to copy a passage. He stopped short.

> *He went out from the dwelling place of the men of perversion*
> *in order to go to the wilderness to prepare the way of him, as*
> *it is written, "In the wilderness prepare the way, make straight*
> *in the desert a road for the Holy One."*

The prophet Yeshayahu had said something similar. He went to the alcove where the longest scroll was kept. Carefully unwinding it, he searched for the passage. His eyes moved from right to left, until he found the text he wanted.

> *A voice cries out: "In the wilderness prepare the way of the*
> *Holy One, make straight in the desert a highway for him.*
> *Every valley shall be lifted up, and every mountain and hill*
> *be made low; the uneven ground shall become level, and the*
> *rough places a plain. Then the glory of the Holy One shall be*
> *revealed, and all people shall see it together, for the mouth of*
> *Adonai Eloheinu has spoken."*

Rolling back the scroll to the beginning, he searched for other passages that might enlighten him.

> *For a child has been born for us, a son given to us; authority*
> *rests upon his shoulders; and he is named Wonderful*
> *Counselor, the Almighty, Everlasting Father, Prince of Peace.*
> *The spirit of the Lord shall rest on him, the spirit of wisdom*

and understanding, the spirit of counsel and might, the spirit of knowledge and the fear of the Lord.

As Yeshua read, Yochanan entered the room unseen and sat against the wall. When Yeshua finally noticed him, he became concerned. Something had been causing his cousin anguish, although he never spoke of it. In fact, they rarely spoke, only seeing one another at meals and even then they ate in silence.

Yochanan brought the tips of his fingers to his lips and drew a deep breath. "I did not know this all at once, but I began to understand. Eliyahu was told that he could not remain in a cave and still be a prophet.... And I cannot stay shut up in a monastery if I am to proclaim the word of the Holy One."

He stood and walked over to Yeshua placing a hand on his shoulder. "My brother, I have decided to leave Qumran. I feel called to go out into the wilderness. The old world is crumbling, and there is a message of a new world that I must announce."

He reached down and covered Yeshua's hand with his. "It would be a shame for someone like you to be shut away from the world."

"What must I do?" Yeshua asked.

"A man must make his own decisions."

"And then?"

"And then you will do whatever the Lord asks of you." Yochanan turned and started to walk away. Then he stopped. "But you must know that whatever path you choose will involve suffering."

30

Yochanan went out to the wilderness near the Yarden River to proclaim the coming of the Anointed One, the Mashiach. It had been 400 years since a prophet had spoken. People wondered if there would ever be another. Or would the voice of the Holy One be silent forever?

"Repent. The kingdom of heaven is at hand!" Yochanan cried out, his voice loud and strident. His words were filled with frightening depictions of divine judgment, images drawn from the desert, covered with stubble as dry as tinder waiting for a spark to set it ablaze. "Every tree that does not bear good fruit will be cut down and thrown into the fire. Wheat will be gathered into his barn, but he will burn the chaff with unquenchable fire."

Yochanan's message stirred the people. They came by the hundreds to be immersed in the river by him. Before long he became known as "the Baptist." His followers claimed that he was not just a prophet, but the Mashiach. When the High Priest in Yerushalayim heard of this, they sent some Perushim to investigate.

"We want to know who you are," one of the emissaries demanded. "Tell us so we can give an answer to the one who sent us."

"If you are wondering if I am the Mashiach, I am not," the Baptist answered, his voice stern. "And you would not recognize him if he was present among you."

"Well, then, what are we to think? Are you Eliyahu the prophet?"

"I am not!"

"Do you claim to be the prophet that Moshe Rabbenu foretold?" another asked.

He denied this, too.

"Who are you?" The man lashed out. "What have you to say for yourself?"

Yochanan glared at his opponents. "I am a voice crying out in the wilderness. Let anyone with ears listen!"

"Tell us, if you are not the Mashiach or any of the prophets, why do you baptize? Are you suggesting that the chosen people need to be cleansed by you?"

To their horror, the Baptist compared them to the snakes and scorpions that scurried out of the thorny underbrush. As they disdainfully walked away, he called after them. "You brood of vipers! Who warned you to flee from the wrath to come? Repent! The kingdom of heaven is at hand!"

Someone in the crowd shouted, "What then should we do?"

The Baptist's words were harsh. "Whoever has two coats must share with one who has none. If you have more food than you need, share with those who have none. Be faithful and honest in your duties. Do not extort money from anyone by threats or false accusation."

His answers distressed some, and they walked away.

Yeshua heard Yochanan's thunderous voice long before he came into view.

"I am baptizing with water," he bellowed. "But there is one among you who you do not recognize, and I am not worthy to untie the straps of his sandals."

Yeshua was surprised to see that his cousin was no longer the aloof individual he met at Qumran. He had abandoned the long white tunic of the Essene community. Dressed in a short garment of camel's hair, his waist girded by a leather belt, he looked the image of the prophet Eliyahu. Yeshua wondered if he also ate locusts and wild honey as the prophet did.

Yochanan's eyes widened when he saw Yeshua coming toward him.

"Baptize me," Yeshua said, wading into the reedy marsh along the riverbank.

"You have no need of repentance," Yochanan said. "It is I who should be baptized by you."

Yeshua took his hand. "Baptize me. It will fulfill all righteousness."

For a long moment they stood looking at one another. Then Yeshua slipped off his outer garment and stepped into the shallow river, kneeling on the glimmering stones beneath the surface.

Yochanan laid his hand upon Yeshua's head and pushed him down under the water. When he emerged, he came up gasping for air as though coming from his mother's womb. The sunlight sparkled in a halo of droplets about his head, his hair shining black as a raven. At that moment, it seemed as if the heavens were torn open; a pale dove swooped down, finding its dwelling within him.

A voice from above roared, "You are my beloved Son, with whom I am well pleased." Some thought it was a thunder clap or the cry of birds. Only Yeshua knew it was the voice of his Father. Yet there was no applause and no coronation procession.

Yochanan saw it happen, something that only the eye of the soul could see. "It is good! It is very good," he shouted with joy.

"I want to be your follower." Yeshua clasped his cousin's hands.

"You do not need anyone to teach you." Yochanan shook his head. "The anointing you have received from the Spirit will teach you all things."

Yeshua left his cousin by the river, his message of repentance still ringing in his ears. Led by the Spirit, he went into the wilderness beyond the Dead Sea, its chalk-white stones glowing like a vast furnace. The air hung heavy with the smell of sulfur and bitumen—the odor of Sodom and Gomorrah. Many called it 'The Devastation,' a desperate place where life and death met—the scarcity of food and water, the unrelenting sun, the danger of wild beasts. Vultures wheeled above the jagged slopes, waiting for the opportunity to take their prey.

Yeshua watched the sun rise high above Mount Nebo, the place where Moshe had glimpsed the Promised Land. Yisrael had spent forty years in the desert before taking possession of the land. Now Yeshua would spend forty days, praying and fasting, to prepare for a mission he did not yet understand.

Bathed in sweat, his stomach gnawing with hunger, doubts flooded over him. An insidious voice whispered in the howling desert wind, "If you are the Son of the Most High, command these stones to become loaves of bread."

Weak from hunger, Yeshua answered with the one weapon he had—the scriptures. "It is written, 'One does not live by bread alone.'"

In an instant Yeshua saw all the kingdoms of the world, shimmering like a mirage in the heat. A snake-like sound hissed, "All these nations have been given to me, and I give them to anyone I please. Just bow down and worship me and they will be yours."

"All creation belongs to my Father," Yeshua shouted. "For it is written: 'Worship the Lord and serve him alone.'"

Shutting his eyes against the glaring sun, he saw himself standing on the pinnacle of the temple above the Royal Portico—a sharp drop to the Kidron Valley below.

"If you are the Beloved Son, throw yourself down from here." The sinister voice continued its taunt, using Yeshua's own weapon against him. "For it is written, 'He will command his angels to guard you in all your ways. They will bear you up, so that you will not dash your foot against a stone.'"

Yeshua cried out, "The scriptures also say, 'Do not put the Most High to the test.'"

He would work no miracles for his advantage, only for his Father's reign. In a loud voice that seemed to shake the desert floor, he commanded: "Be gone, Satan!"

The tempter left him, but Yeshua knew that he would spend his life doing battle with this enemy.

Yeshua returned to the Yarden River where he had been baptized. Now the area was deserted. Yet he could still hear the Baptist's command: "Repent! The Kingdom of Heaven is at hand!"

With sudden realization, he knew his mission: to heal and transform the world by bringing forth his Father's reign. It would not be an earthly realm, as many supposed. It would begin in people's hearts and embrace all who were willing to be faithful subjects.

Yeshua went in search of his cousin. He found him at Beit Ani, near the mouth of the Yarden. Trailing behind the Baptist were two fishermen. They had come to Yerushalayim to sell fish to the kohanim. One was Andreas, the brother of Shimon, and the other was Yochanan, the son of Zavdai, the husband of Shlomit. Both had been attracted by the Baptist's fiery preaching.

Upon seeing Yeshua, the Baptist called out to them, "Look! There is the Lamb of the Most High! He is the one who will take away the sins of the world!"

Yeshua knew what he meant. From the time of Moshe, Yisrael had been redeemed by sacrificial blood. Was that what his Father wanted of him?

At once, Andreas and Yochanan changed their loyalties, and followed Yeshua.

"What are you looking for?" he asked them.

"Rabbi," Andreas said, "we want to know where you live."

"Come and see," he answered.

31

"Who does Yeshua think he is, preaching to others?" Yaakov asked Miryam when her son returned to Natzeret. "His father was a carpenter, and his son should be a carpenter. A man can be no more than his father."

"He should be home caring for you," Yaakov's brother Yosef complained.

"Do you think Yeshua has been possessed by an evil spirit?" Shimon asked.

"Perhaps he has gone mad," Yehudah wondered.

Yaakov was indignant. "He has brought shame to our family."

"Do you agree with your sons?" Miryam cast a sharp look at Miri, but she did not answer.

"I hear that Yeshua is preaching at Naftali's house," Yaakov grumbled. "I am going to judge for myself."

"I will go with you," Miryam insisted as he left the house.

"Come and hear the preacher," a neighbor called as others joined him. Yaakov and Miryam followed along. When they arrived at the house, they were surprised to see a great number of people pushing and shoving, trying to get close to the teacher.

"Wait here," Yaakov told Miryam, elbowing his way through the crowd. But she took hold of his cloak and trailed close behind, edging in near the doorway. Standing on tiptoes, she could barely see her son seated in the center of the room. But she could hear his solemn voice.

"If a kingdom is divided against itself, that kingdom cannot stand. And if a house is divided against itself, that house will not stand."

Yaakov's face reddened with anger and he called out, "Your mother and brother are here looking for you!"

Yeshua stood and spread his hands toward those around him. "Who is my mother? Who are my brothers? Whoever does the will of my Father in heaven are my brothers and sisters and mother."

Yaakov took Miryam by the arm. "Yeshua has shamed you in public. I told you that he would bring dishonor to our family."

Yeshua came to the door as Yaakov led Miryam away in tears. A woman in the crowd cried out to Yeshua, "Blessed is the womb that bore you and the breasts that nursed you!"

"Blessed rather are those who hear and obey the word of my Father," he called after his mother. But she was already gone.

It was late in the evening, and Miryam left the oil lamp burning in hope that her son would return. She felt hurt and betrayed. She had always obeyed the will of his Father. What would have happened if she had said "no" to the angel?

She was still awake, combing her long, gray-streaked hair, when she heard Yeshua enter the house. She glanced at him. He said nothing about the earlier incident. Although she wanted to admonish him, her hurt turned to pity when she saw how tired he looked. There were dark circles under his eyes as though he slept very little.

She tied her hair into a bun at the back of her head. "Why do you and your followers sleep in the fields like wild animals?"

"Foxes have dens, and birds have nests, but I have nowhere to lay my head." He slumped into a chair.

"You always have a home with me."

He loosened the leather laces of his sandals and looked at his grimy feet. He placed one dirty foot across his knee and examined a blister.

Miryam looked at him with concern. How many miles had he walked that day? Without a word, she fetched a basin and filled it with the remaining water in the house. Then she knelt at his feet and bathed them.

"Thank you, dear mother," he said, enjoying her comforting touch. "But you are not my servant that you should wash my feet."

"I am your handmaid." She smiled up at him.

"I am sorry, Ima," he said.

"Sorry?"

He leaned forward, his elbows on his knees. "I did not mean to hurt you, but my family is now those who believe in me, whether or not they are of my blood."

His words pierced her, but she did not answer. Drying his feet with a towel, she threw the dirty water out the door.

"Come sit beside me." She motioned to the cot. He rose with a sigh and sank down next to her, his dark hair falling in waves against her shoulder. Soon he drifted off to sleep in the shelter of her arms. As she pondered this mystery, her heart pleaded: *Do not let him go out into the world. Hold on to him.*

In the morning he was gone.

32

It was many months later when Yeshua returned to Natzeret. News of his powerful preaching and miraculous healings had spread. On one Shabbat, he was invited to teach in the synagogue. Miryam went with him, along with Miri and her sons and daughters. The women went to the back of the unadorned room where the elderly and infirm sat. Yeshua joined the other men who were seated on a beautiful woven carpet at the front.

Two white-haired elders rose from their benches and spoke with Yeshua. "We have been discussing a difficult passage."

"What is it, my friends?" Yeshua smiled.

"In the scriptures, King David said, 'The Lord says to my Lord: sit at my right hand.' What do you think? Will the Mashiach be the son of David?"

"The Mashiach is not David's son," Yeshua said, firmly. "He is David's Lord. The Mashiach will not repeat David's conquests. He will be a servant of all."

The two men nodded as though they caught his meaning. As they took their seats, all eyes turned toward the ruler of the synagogue who entered the room.

Aharon was a gray-bearded man with stooped shoulders and a deeply lined face. Walking with difficulty, he went to the front of the synagogue. Facing south, so that his prayers would be directed toward the Holy City, he began the service with the Shema, calling the people to be attentive to the Torah: "*Shema Yisrael. Adonai Eloheinu, Adonai, echad.*"

A litany followed, blessing the Lord for His steadfast love toward the sinful people. Then Aharon went to the veiled cupboard, before which burned a small menorah. Removing the Torah scroll, he raised it high, and, in a raspy voice, prayed: "May the Torah give us length of days; may the Torah be a fountain of water for all who thirst; may the Torah bring us the Mashiach in our own time!"

Then Aharon rewound the scroll to the first book of scripture, *Beresheet*, and read:

Elohim tested Avraham, saying to him, "Avraham!" And he said, "Here I am." Elohim said, "Take your son, your only son Yitzhak, whom you love, and go to the land of Moriah, and offer him there as a burnt offering on one of the mountains that I shall show you."

Aharon looked up from the scroll and peered at one of the elderly men seated along the wall. He was snoring so loud that his head bobbed up and down.

"Abner." The old man woke with a start. "Even though you cannot stay awake, I am glad that your head is able to nod in agreement."

There was muffled laughter, and Aharon motioned for silence. Finishing the reading, he asked the attendant to remove a lengthy scroll from the cabinet. Beckoning Yeshua to come forward, he asked him to read the Haftarah, a selection from the prophet Yeshayahu.

"Who is that?" a nearly blind man whispered as Yeshua stood and walked to the raised platform.

"Yeshua ben Yosef," was the hushed answer. "He left us as a student and has come back as a teacher."

Yeshua went up to the lectern, covered his head with his white tallit, and taking the heavy scroll from the attendant's hands, unrolled it with care. Scanning column after column, he found the passage. He looked at the prophet's words for a long time, and then read:

> *The Spirit of the Lord is upon me, because he has anointed me to preach good news to the poor. He has sent me to proclaim release to the captives and recovering of sight to the blind, to set the downtrodden free, and to proclaim the year of the Lord's favor.*

Everyone knew the meaning of the prophet's words. The coming of the Mashiach would be a Jubilee Year, a time for the cancellation of debts, the release of prisoners and slaves, and most amazing of all, a time when the lame would walk and the blind would see.

Yeshua rolled up the scroll, gave it back to the attendant, and sat down on the Chair of Moshe. He could feel everyone's eyes fixed upon him, anticipating his interpretation of the prophet's message. Looking around the room, he studied the faces of his neighbors. He knew what he wanted to say, but would they accept it? After a few moments, he spoke in a loud, clear voice, "Today this scripture has been fulfilled in your hearing."

The silence that followed was intense; no one seemed to breathe. Was Yeshua declaring himself to be a prophet like Yeshayahu or a liberator, like Moshe? Did he think he was a healer or miracle worker like Eliyahu or Eliysha?

Then the sound of hissing filled the room. "Pshaw!" Aharon jumped to his feet. "How dare you compare yourself to the great prophet!"

Another cried out. "Is this not the son of Yosef the carpenter?"

"Are not his brothers and sisters with us? Is that not your mother?" A man pointed at Miryam, who flinched.

Aharon crossed his arms and glared. "How could someone like you make such a claim?"

But Yeshua only shook his head. "You will probably quote me the proverb: 'Physician, cure yourself,' and say, 'Do here in your own town the things that we heard were done in Kfar Nahum.' But the truth is, there were many widows in Yisrael in the time of Eliyahu when a famine fell on the land. Yet the prophet was sent to none of them, but to a Gentile woman in Tzidon. And there were many lepers in Yisrael in the time of the prophet Eliysha, but none of them were cleansed except Naaman the Syrian—a Gentile."

"Gentiles? What is this?" Aharon shouted. "How can this upstart say that the Holy One of Yisrael would do more for outsiders than his own people?"

"The Gentiles are nothing but dogs," an old man bellowed, clapping his hands over his ears.

Everyone began shouting at once, filling the air with vile words. Little children looked on in fear; some clung to their mothers' skirts. Miryam clutched Miri's arm. She looked at her in confusion, not knowing what to do.

In a blind rage, the men grabbed Yeshua by the scruff of the neck and hurried him out of the synagogue. Miryam, Miri, and her daughters followed, watching as they dragged Yeshua to the brow of the hill above their town.

"My sisters!" Miryam shrieked. "I think they mean to hurl Yeshua off the cliff."

But suddenly, the maddened crowd stopped as though held back by a powerful force. Yeshua passed calmly through their midst.

33

Yeshua was no longer able to preach in the synagogue. So the open air became his pulpit. From time to time, he returned to his home in Natzeret, but Miryam saw him less and less. Month after month went by with no word from him. Often she wandered through the empty house, speaking his name. In his presence her world was filled with song. Now the music was stilled.

She was grateful whenever her sister-in-law came to visit. The two would talk for hours. Today they sat in comfortable silence while mending their worn clothing.

"It is so strange," Miryam finally spoke.

Miri looked up from her sewing. "What is strange?"

"You raise a son, you teach him, you pray for him. Then he is gone, with no word from him. Is he well? Is he sick? Is it too much for a mother to know what her son is doing?"

Miri pushed a long needle through the piece of goods with her calloused fingers. "I have learned to put my memories in a safe place. Then when I need them, I take them out to comfort me."

Before Miryam could answer, a familiar voice called out. It was Shlomit. "How good it is to see you," Miryam cried, falling into her friend's warm embrace.

"I cannot stay long," Shlomit said, hanging her scarf on a peg near the door. "I have come to Natzeret with Zavdai on business. The fishing trade is thriving and we are very busy."

"What is the news from Kfar Nahum?" Miryam asked, pouring a cup of cold water for her.

"Someone you know is there." Shlomit's eyes danced with excitement.

"Who?"

"Yeshua!"

"What is he doing in Kfar Nahum?"

"He is preaching. And my sons, Yaakov and Yochanan, are his *talmidim*, his disciples."

Miryam's mouth fell open. "My son is a rabbi?"

"Yes, there are twelve men who learn from him," Shlomit beamed. "But I must tell you, my husband is not happy that his sons have gone off, leaving the work for him." She paused to take a sip of water, and sat down. "My sisters, I hope you will believe what I am about to tell you." She searched their faces. "Yeshua heals the sick."

The two women could only stare at her.

"It is true! Some men brought their crippled friend to him while he was teaching in our home. There was such a large crowd that they could not get through the door. So they carried the man to the top of the house and dug a hole in the roof. You can imagine our surprise when we looked up and saw a man coming down on a stretcher. Can you see it? All that thatching falling upon us? I laugh when I think of Zavdai's face when he saw the lame man lying right at Yeshua's feet."

Miryam and Miri were speechless.

"And there is more that will amaze you." Shlomit leaned forward. "When Yeshua saw the faith of the lame man's friends, he told the cripple that his sins were forgiven."

"He forgave sins?" Miryam asked, surprised.

"The scribes called it blasphemy, saying only the Almighty can forgive sins. But Yeshua knew what was in their hearts, and he asked,

'Is it easier to say your sins are forgiven or to say stand up and walk?' Then he said something that no one expected.... He said that the Son of Man had authority to forgive sins. He told the cripple to stand up, pick up his mat and go home. And the man stood up."

"He stood up?" Miryam gasped.

"He stood up! Everyone was shouting and praising the Lord. None of them had ever seen anything like that. And I never did either."

Shlomit finished her water and put the cup on the table. She furrowed her brow. "What do you suppose Yeshua meant by calling himself the Son of Man?"

"I do not know," Miryam said, shaking her head. "I have heard nothing from my son for a long time, and now you come with this news. It is too much."

An uncomfortable silence washed over them. Then Shlomit spoke again. "When my husband finishes his work here in Natzeret we will return to Kfar Nahum. Is there a message I can take to Yeshua?"

Miryam stood and went to the writing table that Yosef had made upon their return from Egypt. She ran her hand over the smooth, dark surface of the desk, remembering how often he sat there writing bills for his customers. There were still writing materials in the little cubby holes—a pen with its worn nub, a powdery ink cake, and a few pieces of yellowed parchment. She pulled up a stool and sat down, tapping her fingers on the table. "I wish I could write a letter to him," she sighed.

"You can tell me what you want to say," Shlomit promised. "I will put your words into my heart and give them to him."

Miryam stood up and folded her arms. "When you see my son, tell him that if it is not too much to ask, to please send word that he is well. You will tell him this, yes?"

Shlomit winced and Miryam shook her head. "No...just tell him that I miss him and that I wait for the day of his return. Tell him that I send my love and my prayers."

Then Miri added, "Oh, and please remind him that my daughter Lydia's daughter is getting married in Kanah next month. Tell him that his aunt will be disappointed if she does not see him there."

A wedding feast was a festive occasion with rich foods and wine that were not always available in places of poverty. The wedding was held on the third day of the week and could last until the following Shabbat. It seemed that everyone in the village had gathered for the celebration, and many more came from afar. Lydia's sister Lysia and her husband, Cleopas, journeyed all the way from Ammaus in the south.

Miryam looked around to see if Yeshua had come. She was delighted when he finally arrived, but was dismayed that four of his followers had joined him.

"We do not have proper wedding garments," one of them, a large burly man, gestured.

"You are clothed from the inside, Shimon," Yeshua told him, putting his arm around the fisherman's broad shoulders. "Come, let us eat."

Miryam watched in astonishment as Yeshua's talmidim began to grab food and drink. It was as though none of them had eaten in a long time.

When Shimon had his fill, he wiped his hands on his sleeves and took a long drink of wine. Turning to the rabbi, he asked, "If the Creator made the universe in six days, what has he been doing since then?"

"He has been busy arranging marriages," the rabbi said, his voice edged with sarcasm.

"Ach," Shimon scoffed in his big voice. "Arranging marriages is a simple task."

The rabbi stiffened. "I assure you that arranging marriages is as difficult as parting the Red Sea."

Shimon poured himself another cup of wine. Yaakov glared at Yeshua, angry with him for bringing his rag-tag followers along.

When the music began, Yeshua called out to him, "Come, brother! This is no day to be glum. Come, enjoy the dance."

Reluctantly, Yaakov joined the other men who encircled the groom, dancing to the beat of drums and tambourines. Women formed their own circle, clapping their hands and stamping their feet. Miryam stood near the doorway, tapping her foot to the rhythm of the music. She felt a stirring within her, the same feeling as when the angel appeared to her in Natzeret. It seemed that something new was about to happen.

She was surprised when Miri and the groom's father came toward her, seemingly agitated.

"I thought that I had provided everything necessary for my guests," the father said. "But it seems that almost all of the wine has been drunk."

"And the feast still has several days to go," Miri said. "It would be a shame if our guests do not have enough to drink. Without wine there is no joy."

Miryam was mortified. Did Yeshua's friends cause the wine to run short? Making her way through the crowd, she waited until Yeshua danced close by and then motioned for him.

"What is it, Ima?" He stopped and mopped his forehead with his sleeve.

"They have no wine," she said.

He folded his arms across his chest, studying her face. "Woman, what concern is that to you and to me? My hour has not yet come."

She flinched. *Woman? Was she no longer "Ima?"* But it did not matter. The people needed wine, and she was sure that he was the one who could supply it.

She had helped him take his first steps as an infant. Now she must help him take a far more important step, prodding him like a mother bird, encouraging her fledgling to take flight. She looked into his eyes, as deep as the vessels standing near the doorway. Turning to the household servants, she said, "Do whatever he tells you."

Yeshua looked at her for a moment. Then he beckoned the servants. "Fill the jars with water."

"There is already enough water in the jars for the guests to wash," one of the servants protested. "But if you need more, we will do as you say."

Yaakov stood nearby watching, but said nothing.

When the servants returned from the well, Yeshua told them to fill the jars to the brim. Then he leaned over the jars and breathed… *Ruu-ahhh*…a sound such as the wind might have made when it swept over the waters at creation.

He turned to the servants. "Now draw some out and take it to the chief steward."

They looked puzzled but did as they were told.

The steward took a big gulp and broke into a huge grin. He called to the groom. "Most people serve the good wine first. Then, when the guests have become drunk, and no longer care what they are drinking, they serve the inferior wine. But you have kept the best wine until now!"

Yaakov looked at Yeshua in bewilderment. "Why did you choose to perform this miracle…here…in this village…at a wedding? You could have fed the multitudes or made sick people well. You could have raised someone from the dead. Why did you choose this time and this place?"

"My brother, I have come that you might have an abundant life." Yeshua put his arms around him—Yaakov was close to tears. "Do not weep. Guests cannot mourn as long as the bridegroom is with them, can they?"

34

"Natzeret no longer seems like home," Yeshua told Miryam when they returned from the wedding. "Our friends and neighbors lack faith in me. The time has come for me to move on."

She turned away so he would not see her tears.

"Ima." He touched her shoulder. "I cannot leave you in this place. We will go to Kfar Nahum. I will set up a home for you there."

Would it always come to this—leaving one home and going to another? Natzeret, Beit Lechem, Egypt…and now where?

But she would do what he said—no matter what it cost. She had said "yes" to the angel many years ago, and she would say "yes" again.

Rising in the icy dawn, Miryam walked through the house. The rooms overflowed with memories—he place where she grew up, the home that she and Yosef shared. For most of her life she lived in peace with her neighbors, but now they swarmed her son like locusts. Few of them came to say goodbye.

"It is time to go, Ima." Linking his arm through hers, Yeshua led her to the doorway. She did not look back.

Together they traveled through the Valley of the Doves, also called the "Valley of the Robbers," as bandits often plundered caravans there. As they rounded a bend, tiny white doves cooed in their cotes among the rocks. Miryam shielded her eyes and looked at the cliffs. *The doves might have their nests, but there is no place I can call home.*

"Ima," Yeshua said, hoping for a smile. "Kfar Nahum was the home of the prophet Nahum. It is called the 'Village of Comfort.'"

Miryam found it difficult, but managed a slight smile.

"Ah, listen, Ima," he said, pointing to the birds flying from place to place. "During the great flood, the dove had the honor of bringing glad tidings. When it found land, it returned to Noach with an olive leaf in its beak."

Miryam nodded.

"You see, Ima, it is a good sign. We will find comfort and peace in our new home."

She was not sure this was true. But to quiet her troubled spirit, she began to hum, her sweet voice rising softly.

"What is that song?" Yeshua asked. "It sounds like the harp strings of heaven."

"It is the song of the Lord," she said. "The tune is implanted in my heart."

"And what is the song of the Lord?"

"The song is your song."

"Then I will sing it, too, like the birds, without words."

He tried to hum along but soon laughed. "Ima, I think it is *your* song."

"Perhaps it belongs to both of us," she said, her eyes brightening.

They walked in silence until Yeshua spoke again. "Ima, your song has taught me a lesson today."

"And what is that?"

"I learned that the disappointments and sorrows of life can become a song."

Kfar Nahum was not a large town, but it was important enough to quarter Herod's peacekeeping force. From the garrison, the centurion could move his troops to key cities along the Via Maris, the seaward road running along the Mediterranean coast to Egypt.

The town had a somber appearance, the houses of dark basalt blocks where poor families crowded together. Scanning the hovels, Miryam thought that they looked like rabbit warrens. *Will one of these be my home?*

It was not long before people heard that Yeshua had returned to Kfar Nahum, and that his mother was with him. Shlomit was the first to greet them.

"My dear friends," she said, with a warm embrace. "You must come and stay with me. I want to repay you for your kindness in sharing your home with me. There is plenty of room now that...." Her mood darkened; she seemed upset. "You have not yet heard, but my dear Zavdai has died."

"How did he die?" Miryam took her hand.

"A great fever came upon him. Many in the town have been afflicted by it." She looked at Yeshua. "I know that my husband would not have died if you had been here."

Before Yeshua could speak, a man approached, his face filled with fear. "Rabbi, my name is Yair. I am the leader of the synagogue. I have one child, a daughter. She is only twelve, and she is dying. Can you help her?"

"Show me the way to your home," he said.

Miryam followed with Shlomit and her sons, Yochanan and Yaakov, trailing behind. Soon a curious crowd began to press in on Yeshua. Among them was Shimon, the fisherman. Everyone was trying to get close to the man known to be a healer.

At the edge of the crowd was a woman who had been suffering from hemorrhages for twelve years. Her name was Veronika.

A man in the crowd recognized her. "Woman, you are unclean, Get out of here!" He pushed her, and she fell to the ground.

She was not deterred. Crawling like an animal, she crept up behind Yeshua. Her hand shook as she reached out to grasp one of the tassels on the corner of his garment.

"Who touched me?" he asked, looking around.

The crowd murmured denials.

Shimon was astonished. "Master, there are many people jostling you on every side. Why do you ask who touched you?"

"Someone touched me, for power has gone out from me."

"I touched you," Veronika admitted, trembling. "And when I did, I felt something course through my body. I knew at once that the flow of blood had stopped."

The men looked embarrassed by her confession, but Yeshua's voice was kind. He helped her to stand. "Daughter, your faith has made you well. Go in peace."

Veronika looked at him in amazement. "I have a little money, and I will give it all to you. Perhaps I can be one of your followers."

The crowd laughed at this incredible notion, but their attention was soon diverted by a man running toward them. When he reached the synagogue leader, he bent over, trying to catch his breath.

"I have a message for you," he said, panting. Yair looked fearful. "Your daughter has died; there is no need to trouble the teacher any longer."

Yair broke into convulsing sobs. "Do not be afraid. Have faith that your child will be saved," Yeshua said. "Show me the way to your home."

When they neared the house, they heard the sad tones of flutes and the wailing of mourners. Ignoring the din, Yeshua entered Yair's house, along with Shimon, Yochanan and Yaakov. Miryam and Shlomit kept near the doorway, waiting to see what Yeshua would do.

Yair led him to his daughter's lifeless body. The mother was draped over the child, pleading for one more word from her silent lips.

"Do not weep," Yeshua told her. "Your daughter is not dead, but sleeping."

"Sleeping?" The woman's face was contorted in grief. "Look at her. She is dead!"

He did not reply. He took the child's cold hand and spoke to her gently. "*Talitha Cum*, little girl, get up."

Everyone gasped as the girl awoke. As if awakening from a dream, she struggled to rise. Her astonished parents kissed her and held her.

"She is hungry," Yeshua smiled. "Give her something to eat."

For days, no one could talk of anything but the miracles they had witnessed. On the following Shabbat, Yair invited Yeshua to teach in the synagogue. Miryam took her place with the other women, remembering the terror in Natzeret. But the women nodded and smiled at her as they listened to her son's powerful preaching. Perhaps she would find a peaceful home in Kfar Nahum after all. But her reverie was interrupted by a loud shriek.

"We know who you are, Yeshua of Natzeret. Have you come to destroy us?"

The man was alone, yet he kept speaking as though there were many with him. His face was a gray-green color; his body contorted and writhed; his claw-like hands scratched the floor in a desperate attempt to rid himself of the fiend that possessed him.

The people were horrified. It seemed that such demons lurked everywhere, ready to do them harm. The wretched creatures lived in tombs and deserts where their terrifying howling could be heard at night. They hovered around the bride and bridegroom, around women in child-birth, and around the lone traveler. There were demons of blindness and deafness, of leprosy and paralysis. Wars and disasters were attributed to them. Their evil-eyes could turn good fortune into bad.

There were exorcists who used elaborate incantations and magic spells to expel demons. Yeshua used none of these.

"What is your name?" he asked.

"Legion," the man croaked. He stood and took hold of Yeshua's cloak, clutching it at his throat.

"He mocks the Roman legions," one man whispered loud enough for all to hear. Others nodded knowingly.

Yeshua kept his eyes focused on the screeching man. "Be silent! Come out of him!"

At once, the man collapsed to the floor. The color returned to his face and he lay still. People gathered around, amazed.

"No one has ever seen anything like this before."

"What sort of man is this?"

"Where did he get his authority and power?"

"He commands the unclean spirits, and they come out!"

An elder interrupted their praises. "It is the Shabbat! Healing is not permitted."

"The Shabbat was made for man, not man for the Shabbat," Yeshua answered. "That is why the Son of Man is Lord—even of the Shabbat."

The elder was angered all the more, and while he argued with the synagogue leader about his meaning, Yeshua slipped out the door. Visibly shaken, Miryam caught up with him. Shimon tagged alongside as they walked down the pathway in silence. Just then, one of Herod's officers approached them.

Frightened, Miryam turned to Shimon, grasping his arm. "Do you think he will arrest Yeshua for causing a disturbance?"

Shimon patted her hand. "No need to worry. The centurion is a friend of the Yehudim. He helped to build our synagogue, and even paid to have the walls adorned with beautiful mosaics of stars and palm trees."

"Peace be with you, rabbi," the officer said, bowing to Yeshua. "My name is Caius. I have heard of your authority over sickness. I have authority myself. When I speak a word of command, my troops do what I say." The officer paused, looking distressed. "I have a servant who is very dear to me. He is paralyzed, in terrible pain."

"I am sure that you have a number of servants. If one dies you can get another," Shimon said brusquely.

The officer looked uncomfortable. "Perhaps I should not have troubled the Master."

"Show me the way to your home," Yeshua said.

"Sir," the centurion hesitated. "I am a Gentile. I know that, as a Yehudi, you cannot come under my roof. Say but the word, and my servant will be healed."

Yeshua looked at him in admiration. "I tell you that I have not found such faith in all of Yisrael. Go home. It will be done for you according to your faith."

Shimon watched as the awestruck centurion set out for his home. Then he said to Yeshua, "Master, I know that it is still the Shabbat, but may I ask a favor?"

"Ask what you will," he said.

"My mother-in-law Yehudit is not well. Can you restore her health?"

"Let us go to your house."

As they walked the short distance from the synagogue, Shimon explained. "After my beloved wife Rivka died, her mother remained with me. But Yehudit seemed to lose all interest in living. She recently became ill with a great fever—the same illness that killed Zavdai. Now she is so weak that she cannot get out of bed."

When they reached the house, Shimon stepped aside, allowing Yeshua to enter. Miryam watched as Yeshua went to the woman's bedside and laid his hand on her feverish forehead. Yehudit opened her eyes.

"Are you the one my son follows?" she croaked.

Yeshua nodded as the woman tried to raise herself on one elbow. "Ever since Shimon left his fishing business, no money has come into this house. How do you expect us to live when you take away our livelihood?"

Shimon looked embarrassed, but Yeshua seemed glad to see her feisty spirit. Taking her by the hand, he lifted her from her sick bed. In an instant the fever left her. Yehudit stood for a moment, struggling to regain her balance, trying to understand what happened.

"Teacher, you have brought me up from the pit of Sheol," she said, grasping his hand. "What can I do to repay you?"

"You owe me nothing, dear lady. I only ask that you serve my brothers and sisters."

"Then I must prepare something for them to eat," Yehudit said, taking his instructions literally.

"It is the Shabbat," Miryam said, coming to her side. "Do you have anything at hand that we can serve?"

Yehudit rummaged in her cupboards, and soon the women set out a simple meal of bread, olives, and cheese.

"Master, there is nothing I can do to repay you," Shimon said as they ate. "But I can invite you and your mother to stay with us."

"I thank you, my friend," Yeshua said. "But I do not need a house. The green pastures will do for my bed, and the sky is my canopy."

"Look." Shimon spread out his large hands. "There is plenty of room for you."

Miryam caught her son's eye. Yeshua sighed, "I cannot ask you to share my frugal life, Ima." He turned to Shimon. "Thank you for your hospitality."

Miryam was happy to have a home, and Yehudit was thankful that there was another woman to assist her. They talked happily after the meal, until two stars in the sky signaled that the Shabbat was over. As they began to clear the table, they heard the noise of a crowd gathering outside the house. No longer bound by the Shabbat law, many were bringing their sick to Yeshua in hopes of being healed.

He rose to his feet, looking weary. He had spent the day healing, and each time he had been drained of some of his power.

"My Father gave the day for work, and work is to be laid aside in the evening. But it is not to be." He heaved a sigh. "I cannot rest while others suffer."

When he went outside, he found what he expected: the unrelenting demands of people bringing the lame, blind, and deaf. He set about laying his hands on each of them. And they were cured.

At daybreak, he left the house to find a deserted place. Perhaps he could find peace in seclusion. Yet the people came looking for him, and when they found him they pleaded, "Stay with us! Stay with us!"

"I must proclaim the good news to others," he told them, "for I was sent for this purpose." It was clear he would have to go farther afield to spread his message.

35

Miryam could smell the salted fish long before she arrived at the market. She watched the fishermen pull their heavy nets ashore, piled high with the night's catch. A woman carelessly threw a pail of fish-heads aside. Miryam tried to get out of the way, but some of the waste splashed on the hem of her skirt. The woman did not seem to notice. Others passed by with expressionless faces. Miryam smiled at them, but they did not return her greeting.

Once again, she felt as though she had been transported to a foreign land where no one knew her name. She thought she would find a friend in Shimon's mother-in-law, Yehudit, but the woman spent her days grieving for her dead daughter, repeating her endless tale of woe. Miryam wondered if that was why Shimon and his brother Andreas were so eager to take to the road with Yeshua. As she walked along the fish stalls, Miryam wondered where she could find a friend in this place.

"My name is Mariamene," a woman said, smiling. "But everyone calls me Magdala because I am from the fishing village of that name not far from here."

"My name is Miryam, from Natzeret," trying to make it sound like an important place.

Miryam liked the young woman immediately, and soon they became friends. Magdala taught her how to deal with the fishmongers, how to bargain with them, and how to choose the freshest fish. But Magdala's soft, slender hands looked unused to hard work. Miryam wondered how she knew so much about fish.

"My husband owned a prosperous business," Magdala explained. "He shipped dried fish and fish oil to wealthy people across the Great Sea, as far away as Roma." She bit the corner of her lip. "After my husband died, I was grief struck, upset by the smallest things. My family thought I had lost my mind and that I could not manage alone. I knew that I had to leave that place and start a new life. So I sold the business and moved to Kfar Nahum."

Miryam looked at her with sympathy. She knew how hard it was to start a new life.

"My reputation did not escape me," Magdala said ruefully one day. "At times, I was unkempt from long nights of wakefulness, and people wondered if I partook of strong drink or was insane."

"I believe none of that," Miryam assured her. But there were times she found it hard to understand her troubled friend. Sometimes Magdala would laugh when there was nothing amusing. Other times there were dark circles under her eyes from inconsolable weeping.

"I do not know what is happening to me," Magdala told her, twirling a lock of hair around her finger. "Perhaps it is true what people say, that I have demons inside of me." She smiled ruefully. "Or even seven demons."

"Oh, that cannot be," Miryam said.

"It must be so. Why else would I behave as I do?"

Miryam held out her arms and Magdala fell into them.

"There is something I did not tell you." Magdala began to weep. "Before my husband died, I found that I was with child. It was the happiest time of my life. But when my husband died, I wondered how I could raise a child alone, as a widow. And then...." Her body shook with sobs. "And then a new grief overtook me. My son was stillborn. He never saw the light of day. I did not dream that my heart could be broken so soon again. It was more than I could bear."

"Hush, hush," Miryam whispered.

"Before I buried my child, I held him in my arms. I touched his tiny hands and feet and looked at his wonderful face. He was so perfect. Why did he have to die? The world is cold and merciless." Magdala could speak no more.

Miryam rocked her in her arms. "It must be a great sadness for a woman to lose a child," she said, wiping the tears from Magdala's face. "My son Yeshua has gone to Yerushalayim for the Feast of Dedication and will be home soon. Many say that he is a healer. Perhaps he can help you. Would you like to meet him?"

"Yes, I would," Magdala said, looking hopeful. "I would give anything to live a happy life."

It was winter. Yeshua walked in the portico of Solomon, trying to keep out of the cold winds in the open courtyard. He remembered sitting there as a young boy, discussing the finer points of the law with the scholars. Now they circled like a pack of wolves.

"How long will you keep us in suspense? If you are the Mashiach, tell us in plain words."

"I have told you," he sighed. "The works that I do in my Father's name testify to me, but you do not believe, because you are no sheep of mine. My sheep hear my voice. I know them, and they follow me. I have other sheep who do not belong to this sheepfold, and they will listen to my voice. Then there will be one flock, one shepherd."

"There is only one flock—here in Yisrael," one of the scholars said in disdain.

"My sheep have been given to me by my Father and no one can snatch them out of my hand," Yeshua told them. "A hired hand, whose sheep are not his own, sees a wolf coming and runs away, leaving the sheep for the wolf. This is because he works for pay and has no concern for the sheep. I am the good shepherd. A good shepherd lays down his life for the sheep. Truly, I say to you, I know mine and mine know me, just as the Father knows me and I know the Father." He drew a deep breath, for he knew that his next words would provoke them further: "The Father and I are one."

Outraged, the scholars took up stones and clenched them in their fists, ready to cast him from the temple.

"I have shown you many good works from the Father," Yeshua said, putting up his hands as a shield. "For which of these are you going to stone me?"

One of the scribes was so angry his veins were popping. "It is not for good works that we are going to stone you, but for blasphemy. You are only a human being, but you are making yourself a god."

"I tell you again, so that you may know and understand: The Father is in me and I am in the Father."

They rushed at him, but he escaped. The seed he hoped to sow had fallen on the stony hearts of his enemies.

Yeshua returned to Kfar Nahum, relieved to be at home. He was surprised when Miryam brought her young friend to him. "What can I do for you?" he asked, looking with compassion at Magdala's beautiful but distressed face.

"My friend has been grief-stricken ever since her husband and child died," Miryam said. "At times her sorrow causes odd behavior. Will you pray for her to be well?"

Yeshua placed his hand upon Magdala's head. He seemed to look deep into her soul. "Come out of her foul spirits, and release her," he commanded. Her body stiffened, her eyes filled with fear. He gazed at her with love. "My daughter, your faith has healed you."

"I feel peace," Magdala said, calmly. "I have not felt this way in years. How can I repay you?"

"What is given freely is freely received," he told her.

"I have some money," she insisted. "I want to give it to you for what you have done for me."

"My disciples and I would be grateful for your help," he said, smiling.

She looked pleased, but suddenly exclaimed, "I want to go with you on your next mission."

He stared at her in disbelief. *A women on my mission? What would my talmidim think? Would they accept her as an equal?*

"I promise not to be a burden," she said. "I will contribute what I can from my resources."

Before he could answer, Miryam put herself between them. "I will also go with you, Master. I will not be left behind again. I have spent years longing for home. Now I will put the past out of my mind and look to the future. I will follow you wherever you go."

36

"Beware of the road that is easy," Yeshua called to his talmidim. They were struggling up a winding path tangled with brush. "The wide road leads to destruction, and there are many who take it. The road that is narrow leads to life. But few there are who find it."

He had new concerns: his mother, Magdala, Miri, Shlomit, and the wives of some of his followers, were now traveling with them. Moreover, Photini, a woman of questionable character, had recently joined them. It was well known that she had been married five times, not counting the man she lived with before she became a follower of Yeshua. Some called her "the woman from Shomron," as if she were the only woman from Shomron, as though she had no name at all.

Yehudah looked at Photini with disdain. "Has Yeshua not heard of the proverb that a man who teaches the law to his daughters teaches her folly?"

"Yeshua accepted me, even though you do not," she said with a stony gaze. Then she turned to the women. "I met the Master at a well. He was sitting there in the hot, noonday sun, as though waiting for me, and no one else. I was wary. A woman alone with a man? You never know what might happen."

The women eyed one another. Their look showed that they were certain Photini knew what she was talking about.

"At first, I thought the Master was a prophet. He could read my heart. He told me everything I ever did." Her face flushed. "After a while, I knew that he was more than a prophet. I had come to the well many times, but my thirst was never satisfied. When he spoke, it was as though there was a living spring deep inside me, waiting to be realeased. And it has been flowing ever since." The other women fell silent, their expressions betraying the same stirring within their hearts.

There was another woman: Yochanah, the wife of Herod's chief steward Chuza, who looked after the king's financial interests and royal properties. Tall and elegant, fine-boned with black, oiled hair, Yochanah had eyes the color of onyx.

"When Chuza was at his winter residence in Yericho, I left him," she told them. "I took Shoshanna, my maid with me."

"A woman who leaves her husband is a scandal," Miri said.

"My husband set me free with a large sum to avoid scandal." Yochanah's dark eyes flashed. "I could no longer abide his philandering with women much younger than me. He lusted after Herodias' daughter, just as Herod did. I was heartsick when Herod had the Baptist killed. I will never forget the bloody dish bearing his head."

The women looked at her in horror.

"I will help the teacher in whatever way I can—money, food, a horse." Yochanah said. "What can I do?"

She noticed the women admiring her earrings, each with an emerald and pearl set in gold. She took them off and handed them to Yehudah who ogled them.

"I want you to sell these and give the money to Yeshua for his mission. They will fetch a great price," she said.

Then she turned to the women, "Get rid of any suspicions you might have about Manaen, Herod's foster brother. He did not leave the court because of me. He too wants to be a follower of the Master."

Then, as the path straightened and ran through a clearing, she walked ahead with the bearing of royalty.

They were now only a short distance from Yericho, the last stop on the road to Yerushalayim. Beyond the city, a steep road descended to a barren desert where bandits often waited to ambush travelers. Yeshua decided that they would rest before the arduous journey ahead.

Yeshua reclined with the men, but Yehudah sat alone in a black mood, plucking the heads off weeds. He was from the southern town of Kerioth, and harbored a smoldering hostility toward the other talmidim who were Galileans. To him, they were the *Am HaAretz*, the people of the land, whose rustic ways he detested.

"Dear sister, you are as pale as the moon," Miri said as she poured a drink of water for Miryam. When she had satisfied her thirst, Miri took her by the arm, and led her to a grassy knoll where they sat in the shade with the other women.

As they prepared to eat their sparse meal, Yeshua bowed his head in a prayer of thanksgiving. Observing his solemn devotion, Andreas had the courage to make a request: "Master, teach us to pray as the Baptist taught his followers."

A smile spread over Yeshua's face. "My friends, when you pray, do not pray in fear, as though our Father is a tyrant, ready to punish your every misdeed. Our Father is loving, kind and merciful—as near to you as your breath," he said, touching his lips.

"How then shall we pray?" Shimon insisted.

"Pray in this way," Yeshua said, closing his eyes and lifting his hands.

> *Our Father in heaven, holy is your name.*
> *Your kingdom come, your will be done,*
> *on earth as it is in heaven.*
> *Give us this day our daily bread.*
> *And forgive us our debts, as we have forgiven our debtors.*
> *And do not bring us to the time of trial,*
> *but deliver us from the evil one.*

When he opened his eyes, his talmidim were looking at him in amazement.

"Is that all?" Shimon asked with surprise. "It is such a simple prayer."

Yeshua smiled at his followers. "I want you to realize that you are children of our heavenly Father. You can come to him with all your needs."

※

Shlomit looked at Miryam "I am going to ask your son if he would do me a kindness." Although Shlomit was less agile than when she was young, she jumped to her feet.

Miryam rubbed her aching legs as she watched her friend go to the place where Yeshua was resting. Shlomit knelt before him for a brief moment, and then returned, looking shamefaced.

"What happened?" Miryam asked.

Shlomit looked mortified. "I asked Yeshua if my sons Yaakov and Yochanan could sit at his right and left hand in his kingdom."

"You did not!" Miryam exclaimed.

"I did!"

"And what did he say?"

"He said that I did not know what I was asking."

Miryam shook her head in mild amusement. Shlomit slumped down alongside her.

"Mother!" Yaakov looked irate as he and Yochanan came to her. "How could you ask such a thing? Now we must make amends for your behavior."

Shlomit's face reddened as her sons approached Yeshua, but he put up his hand to stop them.

"Are you as willing to share my suffering as much you are my glory?" Yeshua asked.

"We are!" they answered.

But Yeshua's eyes were dark. "You will indeed drink the cup I am about to drink, but to sit at my right and left hand is not mine to grant. It is reserved for those chosen by my Father."

Embarrassed, the brothers slipped away.

Yeshua stood and beckoned Magdala to sit with him apart from the others. She joined him and they spoke for some time.

"He talks to her but not to me," Shimon grumbled as he passed Miryam.

"Magdala says that she understands his heart better than the rest of us," Miryam said.

When Yeshua returned to the group, Shimon's face was redder than usual. "Why do you speak with Magdala more than to us? We have left our homes and families to follow you."

Yeshua looked saddened by his outburst. "Shimon, Shimon, truly I tell you, there is no one who has left family for the sake of the kingdom who will not receive more in this age, and in the age to come."

Then he called them all together.

"Are we going to be rebuked for our mother's ambition?" Yochanan whispered to his brother as they joined the others.

"I want to teach you something important," Yeshua said, looking at his followers. "Do you know the way that masters lord it over their servants?"

They all nodded. They knew how those in authority treated their subjects.

"I want you to know that it cannot be that way among you," he told them. "If any of you wants to be great, then you must first be a servant to all. I came to serve, not to be served. I give my life as a ransom for many."

"What do you mean?" Shimon looked mystified. "Do you intend to sacrifice your life…like a lamb for a sin offering?"

"Remember what I have told you," Yeshua said as he signaled them to continue their journey. "Servants are not greater than their master. If they persecuted me, they will persecute you."

Yericho was a pleasant oasis, situated on a trade route, a stopping place for caravans. It was called the city of palm trees, since its generous streams watered the soil and date palms grew in abundance. At one time, Marcus Antonius gave its royal plantations to Cleopatra. Her marble palace was now used as a Roman garrison.

When Yeshua and his followers came to the city gates, a blind beggar heard the commotion.

"Who is passing by?" he cried out.

"It is the prophet from Natzeret." Shimon told him.

The blind man was ecstatic, and shouted to attract Yeshua's attention, flailing his arms in a wide arc.

Shimon looked at the man with pity. "Rabbi, whose sin caused this blindness?"

"Someone must be at fault," Andreas said. "Was it his sin or the sin of his parents?"

"Everyone knows that punishment is visited on the children of the sinner," Yehudah grumbled.

"Sin is not the cause of blindness," Yeshua said, looking at Yehudah. "The blind are those who say, 'I am free from guilt,' and refuse to come into the light."

The blind man called out again, "Son of David! Have pity on me!"

A city official tried to silence him, but nothing could stop him from shouting.

"Call him here," Yeshua ordered.

"Have courage. He is calling you." Yochanan helped the man to his feet. The blind man took off his cloak and threw it aside. Holding his hands in front of him, he groped his way to Yeshua, following his voice.

"What is your name?" Yeshua took the man's hands so he would not stumble and fall.

"I am called Bar Timai."

"What do you want me to do for you?"

"Is it not obvious what the man needs?" Yehudah muttered.

Bar Timai reached out to touch Yeshua's face, running his grimy hands over the fine features. "Master. I want to leave this darkness so that I might see."

Yeshua looked at him with compassion, and then touched his eyes. "Go. Your faith has healed you."

Bar Timai stood still, blinking at the bright sunlight, momentarily stunned. Then, clapping his hands and hopping up and down, he shouted, "I can see! I can see!"

"Come, follow me," Yeshua said. Without a word, Bar Timai trailed behind him as they went down the road.

"Just what we need, another beggar to feed," Yehudah complained.

As they were about to enter Yericho, Yeshua noticed a stirring in the branches of a nearby sycamore tree, although there was no wind. He looked up and saw a man perched on a limb, smiling and waving.

"I heard the preaching of the Baptizer," the man called down, unabashed by his awkward position. "But I wanted to see this new preacher who has set everyone's tongues wagging."

"Why are you up in the tree?" Yeshua asked, amused.

"I am not very tall, so I was unable to see over the crowd. I did not want to miss this opportunity, so I climbed the tree. It was easy because the trunk is short, like me," Zakkai grinned.

"Who is this man?" Yeshua chuckled.

"That is Zakkai," a passerby said, spitting to show his disdain. "He is the regional tax-collector for the Roman government."

"Zakkai, I want to dine at your house today!" Yeshua called to him.

"Are you going to eat at a sinner's house?" Yehudah asked, incredulous.

"Look you!" Zakkai cried to Yehudah as he scrambled down from the tree. "I give half of my goods to the poor. And if I have ever taken anything by fraud, I will give it back four times over."

Yeshua looked at the man in admiration. "I have not come for those who believe they have no need for repentance, but for those who recognize their need to change their lives." Clapping the man on the shoulder, he said, "Zakkai, today salvation has come to your house."

When Yeshua resumed the journey, much to Yehudah's dismay, Zakkai was among them. As they passed through the city, the streets were lined with people eager to catch a glimpse of the celebrated healer. "Shalom al Yisrael! Peace to Yisrael," they called out.

"Teacher, what must I do to inherit eternal life?" a scribe called to him.

Yeshua stopped, wondering if the man was setting a trap for him. "You are a scholar of the law. You know what is written. So tell me, what do you read there?"

"You shall love Adonai Eloheinu with all your heart, and with all your soul, and with all your strength, and with your entire mind," the scribe answered, self-satisfied.

"And what else does the law say?"

"And you shall love your neighbor as yourself," he quickly added.

"That is correct." Yeshua congratulated him. "Upon these two commands the law and the Prophets hang."

"And who is my neighbor?" the scribe probed.

"Let me tell you a story," Yeshua said. "There once was a man on the road from Yericho to Yerushalayim. As you know, it is a dangerous road, and the man was attacked by robbers and left half dead."

The crowd drew near.

"Now by chance a kohen came by on his way to the temple. He knew that touching the bloodied man would make him unclean, and he would be unable to perform his service. And so he crossed to the other side of the road. Likewise, one of the Leviim saw the man, and he too passed by." Yeshua paused, building suspense. "Just then, a man from Shomron approached."

The people looked at one another as though a villain had suddenly slipped into their midst. Yeshua fixed his gaze on them. "Now, when the man from Shomron saw the injured man, he was moved with pity. He poured oil and wine on his wounds, and putting him on his own mule, he took him to an inn. Before leaving, he told the innkeeper that he would repay him on his return for whatever he spent for his care."

Yeshua surveyed the scribe and asked, "Now tell me, which of these three was a neighbor to the man who fell into the hands of robbers?"

The scribe stammered, "I suppose…it was the one who showed him mercy."

"Then go and do likewise!"

The scribe walked away, looking displeased.

Just then, a young man dressed in costly garments approached. "Good Teacher, tell me please. What must I do to inherit eternal life?"

"You know the commandments," Yeshua told him. "You shall not commit adultery. You shall not murder. You shall not steal. You shall not bear false witness.…"

"I have kept all these commands since my youth," the man interrupted.

"Then there is only one thing missing."

The man looked perplexed. "What more can I do?"

"Sell all that you own and give the money to the poor. Then come, follow me."

When he heard this, the man walked away dejected.

Yeshua shook his head. "How hard it is for the wealthy to enter the kingdom of heaven. It is easier for a camel to go through the eye of a needle."

They were astounded and asked him, "Then who can be saved?"

"What is impossible for mortals is possible for the Lord," Yeshua told them.

Shimon spoke up. "Look, we have left everything and followed you. What will we have in return?"

"Your heavenly Father knows what you need," he answered. "But strive first for for his kingdom and his righteousness, and all these things will be given to you as well."

His countenance darkened. "So, do not worry about tomorrow, for tomorrow will bring troubles of its own."

37

"Why must you go to Yerushalayim? You know your enemies await you there," Miryam pleaded with her son, but he did not answer. "Do you hear me? Please listen when I talk to you."

"When we get to Beit Ani," he said, "I want you to remain there. You will be safe with our friends should something go wrong."

But she seemed rooted to the ground. "No. I am safe when I am with you." Yeshua knew that nothing would move her once she made up her mind.

They had not gone far when a man came running up. "Marta sends word to you that her brother Eleazar is very ill. He is at the point of death."

Yeshua did not reply. He seemed to be in communion with someone beyond himself. At length he said, "Tell my friends that this sickness is not unto death. Eleazar is sleeping." Then he turned to his talmidim. "I am going to Beit Ani to awaken him."

"Master," Shimon protested. "If he is only sleeping he will recover."

"Eleazar has died," he said, plainly. "And for your sakes, I am glad that I was not there so that that you may believe. Let us go to him."

"We know that you have the power to cure sickness," Shimon said, hurrying to keep pace with Yeshua's steady stride. "But is it possible to raise someone from the dead?"

"And if you do this, how long will it be before all of Yehudah hears of it?" Mattityahu said, alarmed.

"Let us go to Beit Ani," Toma sighed audibly. "So that we may die with him."

But to their surprise, Yeshua stopped at nearby Beit Pagey instead.

"Master," Magdala asked, "why are we wasting time when your friends need you?"

"I am hungry," Yeshua said, looking up into the twisted, barren branches of a fig tree. He turned his eyes toward Yerushalayim. "May no one ever eat fruit from you again."

"Master, it is not the season for figs," Magdala said. "How can you expect it to bear fruit?"

"Let me tell you a parable." He called his followers and they gathered around. "There was a man who had a fig tree in his vineyard that did not bear fruit. So he said to the gardener, 'For three years I have come looking for fruit on this fig tree, and I found none. Cut it down.' But the gardener begged, 'Master, let it be for one more year while I dig around it and fertilize it. If it bears fruit next year, well and good, and if not, I will cut it down.'"

He looked at his talmidim. "Do you understand?"

They were expressionless.

He ran his hand through his thick, black hair as if deeply disappointed at their inability to discern his meaning. When he spoke again, his words were ominous. "My people had a chance to bear fruit, but they failed."

Miryam's legs ached as they finally climbed the narrow path to Beit Ani. She was breathing hard, and sweat ran in rivulets down her back. Stopping to shake pebbles from her sandals, she was relieved to see that Marta's house was only a short distance away.

"My brother has died." Marta came running to meet them. "Did you not receive my message that he was ill?"

Yeshua nodded.

"Then why did you not come at once? Now it is too late." As soon as she had spoken, she seemed to regret her words and she wept. "Yet I know that the Almighty will give you whatever you ask."

"Marta, your brother will rise again," Yeshua said, taking her by the hand.

She pulled away. "I know quite well that he will rise on the last day. But today he is dead."

"I am the resurrection and the life. And everyone who believes in me shall never die."

She stared at him, and then ran back to the house, calling her sister, Miryam. The mourners followed her, assuming that she was going with her sister to weep at the tomb. Instead, she fell at Yeshua's feet, sobbing. "My Master, if you had been here, my brother would not have died."

He lifted her to her feet. Seeing her tears, he too wept.

"Look how he loved him," one of the mourners said.

But another disagreed. "If he thought so much of Eleazar, why did he tarry so long before coming?"

"I heard that he opened the eyes of the blind. Could he not have prevented his friend from dying?" another complained.

"What is the good of healing strangers if he cannot save a friend?" the first man fumed.

Yeshua looked saddened by their lack of understanding. "Where have you laid him?"

"Come and see," a young boy told him. He led the way to the far end of the garden.

"Roll away the stone," Yeshua ordered when they came to the tomb.

The lad scratched his unruly hair. "If you want to take another look at Eleazar, you will no longer recognize him."

"Master," Marta said, wringing her hands, "the stench of death is upon him. He has been in the tomb for four days and his spirit has left him."

Yeshua searched her face. "Did I not tell you that, if you believe, you would see the glory of the Most High?"

Several men took hold of the stone and rolled it away with great effort. Bending down, they peered inside, trying to make out the form of Eleazar's body resting on a low niche.

Yeshua lifted his hands, and raising his eyes, he prayed, "Father, I thank you for hearing me. I know that you always hear me, but I want my people to know that you sent me." Then he cried out in a voice that even death was powerless to oppose. "Eleazar, come out!"

The people watched in terror as the man rose to his feet and staggered out of the tomb. He was bound hand and foot, his face encircled with a linen cloth.

"Even death submits to his power," one of the men said, astonished.

"Unbind him and let him go free," Yeshua told them.

For a moment the crowd stood open-mouthed. Then, two men rushed to remove the bindings. Marta and her sister fell upon their brother, kissing and embracing him even before the wrappings were fully removed. Everyone was overjoyed, laughing and crying and clapping their hands. Soon, women began to bring their children to Yeshua so he could bless them.

"The Master has more important things to do," Yehudah rebuked them.

"Let the children come to me," Yeshua said, kneeling and stretching his arms toward them. "Only those who become like a little child are worthy of heaven's reign."

Miryam watched with delight as the children scampered to him. Taking each one in the crook of his arm, he kissed them, laid his hands on their heads, and blessed them. Yet there was sadness in her heart, knowing that she would never hold grandchildren of her own.

"We are forever in your debt," Marta exclaimed. "Let us give a dinner in your honor." Turning to Yeshua's mother, she asked, "Will you come and help us?"

Miryam was exhausted, but she took Marta's arm and together they went inside. While Marta fried fish, Miryam laid out milk, dates, and figs.

Marta's sister seemed unconcerned about cooking and serving. Leaving the work to the other women, she went outside to join her brother Eleazar. Marta was irate. She went out and found Yeshua reclining on a low couch, enjoying wine with his friends. Everyone was talking about the miracle they had seen that day. And there was her sister—sitting at Yeshua's feet.

"Master, my sister has left me to do all the work by myself. Tell her to help me," Marta demanded.

"Marta, Marta," Yeshua sighed. "You are worried about so many things. There is need of only one thing—to seek the kingdom of heaven before all else. Your sister has chosen the better part, and it will not be taken from her."

Marta's face reddened and she returned to the kitchen. Her sister rose to her feet and followed, and the men thought she had a change of heart. They scarcely noticed when she returned, carrying an alabaster jar. Without a word, she broke the vial's neck, knelt down at Yeshua's feet, which were stretched out behind him, and poured the oil over them. Then she loosened her long hair and let it fall to her waist in black waves. Tears mingled with the precious oil as she kissed his feet and dried them with her hair. The air was filled with the fragrance of oil of spikenard.

The men shifted in their places, embarrassed by the young woman's display of affection. But Yeshua seemed touched by her devotion.

"Such an extravagant gift is only lavished on a king or High Priest," he said, rising from the couch. "But this anointing means much more."

"Why has this perfume been wasted?" Yehudah asked, his long thin fingers touching his moneybag. "It might have been sold for over three hundred denarii, and the money given to the poor."

"Leave her alone," Yeshua said, unable to hide his irritation. "You will always have the poor with you, but you will not always have me."

Yehudah went to the corner of the garden to sulk.

"Do you see this woman?" Yeshua called after him.

"Of course I see her," Yehudah hissed.

"She has done what she could. She has anointed my body for its burial."

The talmidim stared dumbstruck at one another.

Yeshua looked on his friend, who shared the same name as his mother, with love. "I say to you, wherever the good news is made known, what she has done will be told in her memory."

"I only did what I knew I must," Miryam murmured. "It is unimportant to me whether I will be remembered or forgotten."

38

Leaving Beit Ani, Yeshua traveled resolutely toward Yerushalayim. His talmidim trailed behind, their clothes covered with the yellow dust raised from his sandals. His entire being seemed to be taken up with the struggle to bend his will to the will of his Father. Would dying be the only way to defeat death?

Along the way, a group of lepers approached them. Keeping their distance, they called out in desperation, "Master, have mercy on us." Their breath was wheezing and foul.

Yeshua was moved with compassion. "Go and show yourselves to the kohanim in Yerushalayim," he simply told them.

The lepers looked at one another. Were they healed? It seemed too much to hope for, but they did as they were told. Before long, one of them returned. He was a man from Shomron.

"Look at my hands! They are like new." The man held them out for everyone to see. Then he prostrated himself at Yeshua's feet, praising the Almighty for his mercy.

"Your faith has made you well," Yeshua told him. Then he looked around. "Were not ten made clean? Where are the other nine? Have none of them returned to give thanks except this foreigner?"

Deeply disappointed, he lifted the man to his feet and sent him on his way. Yeshua and his talmidim had gone just a short distance when some Perushim came to him with a warning. "You had better get away from here. Herod has expressed a desire to meet you, but we believe he wants to set a trap for you."

Yeshua's eyes narrowed, unsure of their intent. "Foxes are cunning, but they get caught all the same," he said, quoting a proverb. "I am sure that Herod's real motive is, like his father's, to eliminate any threat to his power. So, go and tell that fox that I will go on doing my Father's work today and tomorrow, and on the third day I will finish my work."

"If your work will be finished in three days," one of them sneered, "then Herod will have nothing to worry about. No one will ever hear of you again."

Yeshua turned to his followers. "I tell you, my friends, do not fear those who kill the body. The one you should fear is the one who can destroy both body and soul in the fires of Gei Hinnom. Yes, I tell you, fear that one."

The talmidim looked frightened. Gei Hinnom was once the place of child sacrifice to the pagan god Moloch. Now the cursed valley was a refuse dump. A pall of acrid smoke hung over it, the stench carried for miles.

"Do not be afraid," Yeshua reassured them. "Are not five sparrows sold for two pennies? Yet not one of them is forgotten in the sight of your father." He rubbed Shimon's balding head. "Even the hairs of your head are counted, so do not worry. You are of more value than a flock of sparrows."

The talmidim laughed, but Yeshua's face was now ashen. Taking the twelve aside, he said, "I want to tell you again, so you will not be distressed by what will happen. I will undergo great suffering at the hands of the elders and chief priests and scribes, and they will put me to death."

His friends looked at one another in horror.

"You cannot announce your own death," Yehudah growled. "It is said that the Mashiach will live forever!"

Yeshua ignored him and turned to Yaakov and Yochanan. "I want you to go to the village ahead, where you will find a donkey and her colt. Untie them and bring them to me."

"But Master, what will the owner think?" Yaakov asked.

"Just say that I have need of them, and he will give them to you."

In a few hours, Yaakov and Yochanan returned with the animals. Just as Yeshua had said, the owner had given them freely.

Yeshua took off his cloak and spread it across the donkey's back. Then he lifted his mother onto it. He handed the reins to Yochanan. Yeshua mounted the colt, hooked his feet under its soft belly, and prodded it toward Yerushalayim.

Passing by the fig tree, the talmidim were astonished to see that it had withered to its roots.

"Every tree that does not bear good fruit is cut down and thrown into the fire," Yeshua said.

They continued their way, climbing the winding road up the eastern slope of the Mount of Olives. Coming to a level place, Yeshua signaled for them to stop. Spread below them was Yerushalayim with its enormous sanctuary, courtyards, porticos, and Tower of David. Now the poet-king slept with his forefathers on the slopes of the Kidron valley, their white tombs hedged by dark cypresses. When Yeshua was a boy it was a wondrous sight, but now it seemed insignificant, a mere speck on the horizon.

A sob rose in his throat, a deep sadness for his people. "Yerushalayim, Yerushalayim, the city that kills the prophets and stones the messengers sent to it."

He shouted as if the city might hear him. "You hypocrites! You say, 'If we had lived in the days of our ancestors, we would not have taken part in shedding the blood of the prophets.' Their blood cries out from the ground. You cannot escape the coming wrath."

He wept with the passion of a spurned lover, with the broken heart of a father grieving for his lost child. "How I desired to gather your children together as a hen gathers her brood under her wings. But you were not willing to hear my voice."

His grief turned quickly to anger. "Yerushalayim, Yerushalayim! The days will come when your enemies will hem you in on every side. They will dash you to the ground, you and your children within your walls. They will not leave one stone on another, because you did not recognize the time of my coming."

The talmidim looked at one another. The city of David? The temple of the Holy One? How could it be possible that they would be destroyed as Yeshua said?

Yeshua tugged on the reins of the colt and picked his way down the rocky slope of the Mount of Olives and up the opposite bank of the Kidron Valley.

Thousands of pilgrims had come for the Feast of Pesach. Many were on the lookout for the one thought to be the Mashiach. Rumors of miracles had spread throughout the city—multiplying bread in the wilderness, giving sight to the blind, curing lepers, and, most astonishing of all, raising a man from the dead. When they saw Yeshua coming with his entourage, someone bellowed the words of the prophet Zecharya: "Rejoice, O daughter Tziyon! Shout out, daughter of Yerushalayim! Look! Your king is coming, riding on a lowly colt!"

The Roman cavalry looked with contempt at this rabble-rouser astride the foal of a she-ass. But people began throwing their cloaks on the road for him to tread upon. A shout went up: "Hoshana! Hoshana to the Son of David!"

"What are they doing, Yochanan?" Miryam asked.

"They are proclaiming him king, the promised Son of David who will restore Yisrael to its place among the nations," he said.

But Miryam looked at her son with dismay. He seemed sad and alone in the center of this jubilant multitude.

Soon everyone was caught up in the frenzy, shouting, "Hoshana! Save us!" The crowd overflowed on either side of the road, swelling like the waves of the Great Sea. A swarm of children joined the parade, running in and out of the festal procession. People began to pull branches from palms along the way, spreading them on the road, creating a green carpet. Others waved and shouted with boughs in hand: "Hoshana to the Son of David!"

The shouts grew louder. "Son of David! Hoshana!" Their cries echoed across the narrow canyon and against the massive stones of the city walls. "Hoshana! Save us!"

Someone in the crowd cried out, "The Kingdom of the Almighty is at hand!"

"Ah hah!" Yehudah cried, his fist in the air. "Now it begins! Now he will reveal himself as the Mashiach."

Shimon grabbed hold of his sleeve. "You know that Yeshua warned us not to tell anyone."

Yehudah clenched his teeth and pulled his arm from Shimon's grasp. "Pshaw!" he said, spewing spittle. Shimon wiped the contamination from his face. The other talmidim gave Yehudah sharp looks, and fell in line behind Yeshua.

When they neared the temple, a great crowd was already milling about. When they saw Yeshua and heard the adulation, they went out to meet him, merging with the coming procession, making the road impassable. The crowd shouted praises; even the children called out, "Hoshana to the Son of David!"

"Do you hear what the people are saying?" a Perush called loudly as Yeshua passed by. "Rebuke them! Put a stop to this blasphemy."

Yeshua shouted back at him. "Have you not read: 'Out of the mouths of babes you have fashioned perfect praise?' I tell you, if they are silent, these very stones will cry out."

Another Perush shouted to the crowd, "Do you believe the foolish tale of a man raised from the dead? You are following a false prophet, and look at what is happening. The whole world has gone mad."

The crowd surged past, chanting, "Hoshana! Son of David! Blessed is the one who comes in the name of the Most High! Hoshana in the highest heaven!"

The procession halted at the eastern gate of the temple, called Golden. It was believed that the Mashiach would enter Yerushalayim by this gate when he came.

The crowd cleared a pathway for Yeshua.

He leaned forward on the colt, trying to be heard above the shouting, "Yochanan, I want you to take my mother to Beit Ani and wait for me there."

Then he dismounted, made his way through the crowd, and walked up the steps to the Golden gate. One man, thin as bones, raised his hand in warning. "The Day of the Most High is near! It will not be a day of rejoicing, but a day of gloom."

Had that day come? Yeshua wondered.

39

The Court of Gentiles was always crowded, but at Pesach it was teeming with pilgrims from all over the world. Yeshua entered the temple. What he saw raised his wrath—the porticos, filled with people exchanging foreign coins for shekels; the courtyard, a market where animals were bought and sold for sacrifice; the hideous din of voices buying and selling; the bleating of sheep and bellowing of cattle in their pens; and birds squawking in their cages. It sounded and smelled more like a barnyard than a sacred place.

Enraged, he found some cords used to tether the animals. Fashioning a whip from them, he drove out the animals, smashing the dove coops and letting the birds fly free. "Get these things out of here!" he shouted, overturning the tables of the moneychangers. The coins bounced into greedy hands quick to catch them.

Yeshua was incensed. "It is written: 'My house will be called a house of prayer for all people.' But you have made it a den of thieves!"

"We should strike now," Shimon the Zealot said in a menacing voice, his hand moving to the dagger beneath his cloak.

"What are we waiting for?" Yehudah asked.

"Would you spill the blood of our own people?" Mattityahu clenched his teeth in anger. "If you do this, the Romans will destroy us."

The kohanim and the scribes came running, furious at the disruption of the feast. "By what authority are you doing these things?"

Yeshua knew that they were trying to force his hand. If he said that he was acting under his own authority, they would declare that he was a mad man. If he said that he was acting on the authority of his Father, they would charge him with blasphemy.

"I will ask you a question," he said. "If you can answer, then I will tell you by what authority I do these things. Tell me, did the baptism of Yochanan come from heaven, or was it of human origin?"

The religious leaders looked concerned, fearing that they might fall into a trap themselves.

"If we say, 'from heaven,' he will ask why we did not believe him," one of the kohanim whispered.

"But if we say it was of human origin, the crowds will protest, for they regard the Baptist as a prophet," a scribe countered.

So they answered in unison: "We do not know."

"Then neither will I tell you by what authority I am doing these things," Yeshua told them.

He started to walk away when one of them called out, "What sign can you show us for doing this?"

"Here is your sign." He pointed to his breast. "Destroy this temple, and in three days I will raise it up."

The kohanim and the scribes scoffed. "The temple has been under construction for forty-six years, and you say you can raise it in three days?"

He knew that they failed to understand his meaning. How long would they refuse to believe in him? At that, he left the temple with his talmidim.

On the outskirts of the temple, Andreas asked, "Why did you say that you would raise the temple in three days if it was destroyed? These blocks of stone seem indestructible."

"Do you see all these things?" Yeshua asked, pointing to the massive buildings. "I tell you, one stone will not be left upon another. It will all be thrown down."

"Rabbi, if the temple is destroyed, will that bring about the end of the world?" Shimon asked with dread.

"And what will be the sign that this will take place?" Andreas added.

Yeshua was weary of questions about signs and times. "Beware that you are not led astray. For false prophets will come in my name saying, 'I am he!' and, 'The time is near!' Do not believe them. When you hear of famines and earthquakes, and rumors of insurrections and wars, do not be alarmed. These things must take place first, but the end is not yet. That day and hour, no one knows, neither the angels of heaven, nor the Son, but only the Father. Therefore, you must be ready, for the Son of Man is coming when you least expect."

Seeing their troubled faces, he said, "Do not lose heart. Remember, I have told you these things before they happen. Heaven and earth will pass away, but my words will not pass away."

Yeshua and the twelve spent the night at Bet Ani, and in the morning, they returned to the temple and went to the Court of Women. He wanted to sit in peace after the turmoil of the previous day. As the pilgrims passed by, he observed well-dressed men throwing sizeable offerings into the collection boxes. When a poor woman came along, she dropped in two lepton, the smallest of all coins.

Yeshua turned to his talmidim. "Did you see that woman? Her offering is greater than all the others." His followers looked surprised. "Do you want to know why? Because the others gave what they could spare and still had money left over. But the woman gave everything she had to live on."

A crowd was beginning to grow around him, so he began to teach them. "On the Day of Judgment, everyone will stand before the great King."

"Who is the great King?" someone asked. "Is he the king of Yisrael or the Romans?"

"Will we be judged on how well we have kept the law, or how we failed?" another asked.

Yeshua answered, "The great King is the Lord Most High. All the nations will be gathered before him, and he will separate people one from another as a shepherd separates the sheep from the goats, the sheep at his right hand and the goats at the left. Then the King will say to those at his right hand, 'Come, you that are blessed by my Father, inherit the kingdom prepared for you from the foundation of the world. For I was hungry and you gave me food; I was thirsty and you gave me to drink. I was a stranger and you welcomed me, naked and you gave me clothing. I was sick and you took care of me, in prison and you visited me.'"

His disciples looked at him in confusion. "Master, when did we see you hungry and thirsty?"

"And when did we welcome you as a stranger, or see you naked and gave you clothing?"

"And when were you sick and cared for you or in prison and visited you?"

"Indeed, I say to you, if you did it for the least among you, you did it for me." Yeshua's eyes narrowed. "But, I tell you, whosoever did not do these things will go into eternal punishment, but the righteous, to eternal life."

"Teacher," a man said, with an ingratiating smile, "we know that you are sincere, and teach the Law of Moshe with truthfulness."

"Yes, what is it you want?"

"Teacher, what do you think? Is it lawful to pay taxes to the emperor, or not?"

"Why do you keep putting me to the test?" he asked, exasperated. He knew that if he told him to pay the tax to Caesar it would support the emperor's sovereign claim. If he told them not to pay the tax, it would be reported to Herod that he was in allegiance with those seeking to overthrow the empire. So he said, "Show me the coin used for the tax."

The man fumbled in his purse and handed him a denarius, the silver coin minted by the emperor. Yeshua turned the coin over in his hand and read the inscription engraved on it. "Tiberius Caesar, son of the Divine Augustus!" Holding the coin so all could see he asked, "Whose head is this?"

They all answered at once: "Caesar's."

He tossed the coin back to its owner, saying, "Give to Caesar what belongs to Caesar. And give to the Almighty what belongs to him."

"And what is that, Teacher?" someone asked.

"Your lives belong to the Almighty, not to Rome," he answered.

"The chief priests will soon hear of this!" a member of the Sanhedrin shouted as he hurried off to tell others.

"The people regard Yeshua as a prophet," the Herodian muttered. "How can we arrest him without provoking a riot?"

One of Yeshua's talmidim overheard them. "What will you give me if I betray him to you?"

It was Yehudah of Ishkerioth.

40

"Where should we go to prepare for the Pesach?" Shimon asked Yeshua.

"Take Yochanan with you and go into the city," he told him. "Find a man carrying a water jar. He will lead you to a house with a furnished room ready for the meal."

"Carrying water is the task of women and slaves," Shimon grumbled as they left. They were surprised when they found the man as Yeshua said, and even more so when they discovered that he was a servant of Nakdimon ben Gurion, a wealthy, distinguished member of the Sanhedrin.

The servant led Shimon and Yochanan to a large house in the 'upper city,' an area higher in elevation than the temple mount. Herod Antipas, Kayafa the High Priest, and his father-in-law Annas lived there in Roman splendor, their luxurious dwellings separated by wide streets and plazas.

"Shalom," Nakdimon greeted them. "You are welcome to stay in my home during the festival."

The house was two-stories high, encircled by a courtyard with splashing pools and a terraced garden with flowers and fruit trees. Inside there was a large paved vestibule that led to furnished guest rooms and living quarters for servants. The floors boasted fine Greek mosaics, and the walls were decorated with beautiful frescoes.

Nakdimon led them up a wide stone staircase to the formal dining room where the Paschal meal would be held.

"This room is often used by the Sanhedrin for discussions," he told them. "It is called a 'triclinium.'" He pointed to the three couches arranged around the table. "The fourth side, as you can see, is open for ease of serving the guests."

"How do you know our Master?" Shimon asked.

Nakdimon drew a deep breath. "I spent my life observing every detail of the scribal law. When I heard of the 'Prophet of Natzeret,' I was curious. I must admit that I was afraid of what my fellow members of the Sanhedrin would think. So I came to Yeshua at night."

He paused for a moment, and then laughed. "When Yeshua told me that I must be born again, of water and spirit, I was astonished. I wondered, how could I reenter my mother's womb? Yeshua answered as though I was a child in a school room. He said, 'If the simple things of the earth are beyond you, how will you be able to understand the deep things of heaven?' He explained that rebirth only comes from the Holy Spirit. Not long after, I was baptized and became his follower—even though in secret."

Shimon and Yochanan completed the arrangements, and then went to the temple to purchase a lamb to be sacrificed at the mid-afternoon service. They waited for some time, until it was their turn to present the lamb. When it was killed, skinned, gutted, and skewered on a long stick, they carried it back to the house to be roasted.

Soon the guests began to arrive. The women were overwhelmed by the size and the beauty of the home.

Miri whispered to Miryam, "I am sure that Nakdimon's house does not impress Yochanah since she is used to the court life of Herod's palace."

While the men went off to bathe, the maid servants led the women to a smaller bathing pool where they immersed in the soothing waters, enjoying the perfumed oils set out for their use. When they finished, the maid brought them fresh clothing. Miryam looked at the clean linen dresses. She had forgotten how shabby she looked.

After dressing, the women went to the kitchen, insisting on helping with the meal preparations. Without much discussion, each one found a task that needed to be done—boiling eggs, chopping parsley, cutting apples, and mashing raisins, nuts, plums, and cinnamon together with wine. The women worked all afternoon, their happy voices blending with the clattering of pots and pans.

Miryam enjoyed making the matzot. With sleeves pulled to her elbows, she worked the flour and water, kneaded the dough, and formed it into a ball. After she rolled the dough into flat cakes, she poked holes in them and laid them on a tray for the servants to take to the baking ovens. Pouring cool water over her hands, she recalled the miracle at Kanah when the water was changed into wine.

The water saw him and blushed. She smiled at the memory, and wondered. *Will something happen to change the bread?*

When three stars appeared in the night sky, silver trumpets were blown from the temple, announcing that the Paschal meal could begin. The large oil lamp hanging from the ceiling cast a golden glow on the table laid out with fine dishes, bowls, and cups.

Although Yeshua was accustomed to dining with both men and women, he made it known that he wanted to eat this Paschal meal with his talmidim. The others would eat in an adjoining room. As the guest of honor, Yeshua was to recline between Shimon, who acted as the host, and Yochanan, his assistant. Instead, Yeshua told Yehudah to take Shimon's place.

"He did not arrange the meal and help with the preparations," Shimon fumed, blocking Yehudah with his thick body. But Yeshua asked Yehudah to sit where he was told. Shimon stomped to the opposite side of the table and sulked. "I wonder which one of us is the greatest," he said in a voice loud enough for all to hear.

Yeshua did not speak about his friend's behavior. He gazed at his followers, his face grim and drawn. "How I have longed to eat this Paschal meal with you," he said.

Everyone expected the customary washing of hands to follow. But, to their surprise, Yeshua rose from the table, took off his outer robe, tied a towel around his waist, and poured water into a basin.

"My friend, I want to wash your feet," he said, kneeling before Shimon, who was still brooding.

Shimon looked surprised. "This is the work of a servant. You will never wash my feet."

"Unless I wash you, you will have no share in my inheritance," Yeshua insisted.

Shimon stuck out his calloused feet. "Then, Master, wash not only my feet but also my hands and my head!"

"One who has bathed does not need to wash." Yeshua said as he continued washing the feet of his talmidim. He stopped at Yehudah. "But not all of you are clean."

He stood up and put on his robe. "Do you know what I just did? You call me 'Master' and so I am. A student does not deserve more honor than a teacher, or a servant more than a master. What I did was an example. As I have done for you, so you should do for each other."

He observed a quick movement in the corner of the room. His mother had parted the curtains to watch from the doorway. He glanced at her with love, knowing that she alone understood what he had done.

He sunk down on the couch, and there was weariness when he spoke. "I tell you truly, one of you will betray me."

Miryam covered her mouth, failing to stifle a cry.

"Betray you?" Yaakov asked. "All along we have been worried about our enemies. How could one of us betray you?"

Yochanan seemed overcome by sorrow and leaned back on Yeshua's breast. Shimon motioned to him, to ask Yeshua of whom he was speaking.

So Yochanan asked, "Master, who will betray you?"

Yeshua did not answer. Instead he broke a piece of bread, dipped it in the dish of bitter herbs, and handed it to Yehudah who was reclining on his other side. Yehudah's hands trembled as he took the morsel.

"Surely it is not I, rabbi?" he asked with a twisted smile.

"You have said so," Yeshua answered in a low voice. "Do quickly what you are going to do."

Yehudah rose from the table and left the room, his footsteps echoing as he went down the stairs and out into the dark night, the door slamming behind him.

Shimon looked puzzled. "Did we forget something for the meal?"

Yeshua did not answer. He lifted the first cup of wine, the Cup of Sanctification, praying, "Blessed are You, Adonai Eloheinu, Ruler of the Universe, Creator of the fruit of the vine." Then he passed it around the table. As his friends drank, he recounted the story of Exodus.

"Pharaoh was obstinate, refusing to allow the slaves to go free. The message of Pesach is that we can escape from our 'house of bondage.' One day we will all be free in the Promised Land."

He poured a second cup of wine, the Cup of Deliverance, praying, "Blessed are You, Adonai Eloheinu, Ruler of the Universe, Creator of the fruit of the vine." He gazed around the table as they all drank from the cup. "My friends, I will be with you just a little while longer."

Toma looked troubled. "Master, where are you going?"

"Where I am going, you cannot follow. But you will follow later."

"Master, why can I not follow you now?" Shimon asked. "I am willing to go wherever you go—and even die for you!"

"Will you lay down your life for me?" Yeshua fixed his eyes on him. "My friend, you have stood by me in my trials; however, Satan desires to sift you like wheat. I have prayed that your faith may not fail. But I tell you, Shimon, before the cock crows in the morning, you will deny me three times."

Shimon stared at him in disbelief.

"Do not let your hearts be troubled," Yeshua said with compassion. "In my Father's house there are many dwelling places. I will come again and take you to myself, so that where I am, there you may be. And you know the way to the place I am going."

"Master," Toma said, "we do not know where you are going. How can we know the way?"

"I am the way, and the truth, and the life," he said. "No one comes to the Father except through me."

"Master, show us the Father, and we will be satisfied," Philippos pleaded.

"Have I been with you all this time, and you still do not know me?" Yeshua asked. "How can you say, 'Show us the Father'? If you know me, you know my Father also."

The talmidim fell silent, bewilderd by his words.

"I will not leave you orphaned," he promised. "I will ask the Father, and he will give you another Advocate to be with you forever."

"Who is this Advocate? Who will stand beside us if you are not here?" Mattityahu asked.

"I speak of the Spirit of truth, who will abide with you and in you as your comforter and guide. I have told you this beforehand, so that when it occurs, you may believe."

He wanted to say more, but his thoughts were interrupted. His mother had entered the room with the unleavened bread. Her hands were trembling as she placed the platter in front of him. She stood transfixed. In place of the blessing usually said, he took the bread and raised it for all to see. "This is my body, which is given for you. Do this in remembrance of me."

Then he broke the bread. The cracking sound startled Miryam so that she retreated behind the curtain.

After passing the bread from hand to hand, Yeshua poured a third cup of wine, the Cup of Redemption. Once again, instead of the traditional blessing, he said, "This cup that is poured out for you is the new covenant in my blood." When they all drank from it, their faces glowed.

"I give you a new commandment," he said. "Love one another as I have loved you. By this everyone will know that you are my followers, if you have love for one another."

He poured the fourth cup of wine, the Cup of Restoration, but he did not drink. "I will never again drink of the fruit of the vine until that day when I drink it anew in my Father's Kingdom."

Then, raising his voice, he sang the Great Hallel with a passion they never heard before. "Give thanks to Adonai Eloheinu, for he is good, for his steadfast love endures forever."

The others joined him, their voices full of melancholy. "His steadfast love endures forever."

When they had sung the hymn, Yeshua rose from the table and beckoned them. "My hour has come! Let us spend this night in prayer."

"Was everything prepared as you wished?" Nakdimon asked as Yeshua passed through the vestibule.

Yeshua put his hand on his host's shoulder. "My friend, you have great wealth. If you wish to enter the kingdom of heaven, sell your possessions, and give the money to the poor. Then you will have treasure in heaven."

Nakdimon said nothing as he watched the men leave.

Miryam came down the stairs just as the door closed behind Yeshua. Opening the door a bit, she watched him disappear into the darkness. Over the sleeping city the full moon of the Pesach had risen, barely seen through the ragged clouds drifting across the sky. She wrapped her arms close around her, afraid what this night might bring.

41

Yeshua led his followers through the narrow, sloping streets, then down a stepped pathway leading out of the city. They crossed the causeway above the Kidron brook where the waters rushed underfoot. Beyond the valley, the massive walls of the temple appeared blue-white against the dark sky.

At the foot of the Mount of Olives was a small garden belonging to one of the wealthy women who followed Yeshua. He often went there to pray. The garden was called Gat Shemanim, the 'oil press,' so named because of a cave that housed the press for the autumn olive harvest. By spring, the cave was used for storage or rented to pilgrims during the Pesach festival.

A chill was in the air, but the cave was warm and dry with a cistern for water. It would be a good place for Yeshua and his followers to rest during the night. Together they entered the cave and lit the oil lamps, their shadows creeping across the walls.

"Where is Yehudah?" Shimon asked, looking around.

No one seemed to know—or care. Sated with heady wine, they began to prepare for sleep. But Yeshua motioned to Shimon, Yaakov, and Yochanan to come to his side.

"My hour has come," he said, his eyes dark and brooding. "Remain here and keep watch with me while I go outside and pray." Pausing, he added, "I tell you, a grain of wheat must fall into the earth and die, or else it remains nothing more than a single grain…. But if it dies, it bears much fruit."

"Is the Master predicting his own death?" Yochanan asked, in a hushed voice.

No one dared answer.

Yeshua walked to the mouth of the cave, stopped, and looked back at his talmidim. "Stay awake with me." Then he went outside.

The silvery-green leaves of the olive trees trembled in the breeze. Sinking down on his knees, he clutched his head in despair. It felt like death was upon him. He could breathe it in the icy air and hear it in the Roman sentinel's cry from the Tower of Antonia.

"Abba, Abba," he prayed in a hoarse whisper, "Give me a sign that you are with me."

He waited but the only sound he heard was the chirping of crickets and snoring from the cave.

"Abba," he prayed with clenched fists, battling the two natures within him—divine strength and human weakness. "Why was I chosen? And for what? To be alone and abandoned? To never have what other men have—a wife and children to console me in old age, to be with me at the hour of death? What more do you want? What profit is there in my death? If I go down to Sheol, will the dust praise you there? Will it tell of your faithfulness? Abba, hear my prayer and come to my aid!"

Still there was no answer, no consolation from heaven or from earth. He returned to the cave's entrance—all of the talmidim were asleep.

"Could you not stay awake with me one hour?" he asked, but there was no answer. He shook his head dejectedly. "The spirit indeed is willing, but the flesh is weak."

Leaving them again, he fell prostrate on the ground. "I have given my body and blood for my people." His sweat fell like drops of oil pressed from olives. "Father, I taught my followers to pray 'your will be done.' Can I drink this bitter cup and say, 'Your will be done,' when I want to shout, 'Save me from this hour?'" He bowed his head in resignation. "No, it is for this hour that I have come. Father, glorify your name."

A clap of thunder startled him. A voice spoke from heaven. "I have glorified it, and I will glorify it again."

He stood up, his senses alert, listening to a distant murmur. But it was not his Father's voice, nor was it a chorus of angels. A mob of soldiers and temple guards were slowly snaking up the hillside, the red glare of their torches flickering in the darkness. The moon appeared from behind the clouds, and a shadowy figure emerged. Yehudah was coming toward him.

42

Miryam awoke to the sound of loud thumping on the door. At first she thought she was dreaming and then realized the knocking was real. Wrapping a shawl over her shoulders, she headed down the cold stairway. She was barefooted and her long hair hung unveiled, but the knocking seemed urgent, and she did not go back. Before she reached the vestibule, her sister-in-law Miri was behind her, awakened along with the servants.

Nakdimon was already at the door. "Who is there?"

"It is Yaakov," the muffled answer came.

Nakdimon unbolted the door and the young man rushed into the house, breathing hard as though someone was chasing him.

"What is it?" Miri asked her son.

"It is Yeshua," he said, his face pale.

Nakdimon bolted the door.

Yaakov answered their unspoken question. "They have arrested him."

Miryam's hands flew to her mouth. "Arrested? Why would they arrest my son?"

Yaakov took her arm. "When we went to the garden to pray, the temple police and the elders came to arrest him." He paused as though afraid to say the words he must. "Yeshua was betrayed.... He was betrayed by one of us."

Miryam looked wild-eyed at him. "Betrayed? Who would betray him?"

"Yehudah Ishkerioth," Yaakov said, hanging his head in shame. "It seems that Satan found his way into his heart."

Miryam caught her breath. "Where did they take him?"

"To the house of Kayafa, the High Priest."

Miryam could only mouth the word: *Why?*

"They wanted to question him about breaking our law." His voice was angry. "But they are the ones who broke the law. Trials should not be conducted during the Pesach—and not at night. This should not be."

Miryam draped her shawl over her head and started toward the door.

205

"Where are you going?" Yaakov cried. "You cannot go outside. It is dangerous."

"I am going to my son," she said. "Will you go with me?"

"I will, if you promise to wait until the morning," he said. "There is nothing we can do now."

A call had gone out for select members of the Sanhedrin to assemble at Kayafa's palace, a hillside villa he shared with his father-in-law Annas. Usually, they met in the Hall of Hewn Stones in the temple, but this was a secret trial. Two notable members were absent: Yosef Beit Ramatayim and Nakdimon. But Kayafa and most of the Sanhedrin were of the same mind—Yeshua must die.

Throughout the night they argued the law, looking for evidence to convict him.

"That man is endangering public peace," Annas muttered. "If we let him go on like this, everyone will come to believe that he is the Mashiach."

Annas was short and slight, but his presence was commanding. Everyone knew that he was the real power behind his son-in-law Kayafa.

"If that so-called prophet dies at our hands, his followers will rise up in rebellion, and the Romans will come and destroy our temple and our nation," he argued. "Do not forget King Herod's slave who declared himself a king and organized an uprising. It took three Roman legions to suppress them. Two thousand of our people were crucified."

Kayafa made a calculated decision. "It is better for one man to die than for the whole nation to perish."

"But what would be the crime?" a member of the Sanhedrin asked. "We have found nothing against him."

Kayafa spoke up. "Perhaps we could bribe someone."

Yeshua was brought before the council, hands bound. It was evident from his bruises that the guards had beaten him.

"Why did you come out with swords and clubs to arrest me as though I were a bandit?" he asked, as though it was the Sanhedrin on trial. "Day after day I sat in the temple teaching, and you did not take hold of me."

Kayafa stood up and strutted, his hands on his wide hips. "What crime do they testify against you? Have you no answer?"

Yeshua was silent.

Two witnesses were brought forth, the minimum required to make a criminal charge. Both looked disreputable.

"That man over there," one of them said, wagging a finger at Yeshua.

"Yes, yes," Kayafa said, irritated. "What do you have to say about that man?"

"He said: 'I will destroy the temple!'"

The other man pushed him aside. "I heard him say it with my own ears. Not only that, he said that he would rebuild the temple in three days."

There was a loud gasp from the assembly.

A soldier escorted the two men from the chamber, slipping each of them a coin for their trouble.

"What do you have to say for yourself?" Kayafa asked Yeshua when they left.

"Why question me?" he was defiant. "Ask those who heard me, not those you paid to lie."

One of the officials struck him across the face. "Is this the way you answer the High Priest?"

Reeling from the blow, Yeshua regained his footing. "I spoke the truth, so why did you strike me?"

Indignant, Kayafa demanded, "Tell us. Are you the Mashiach?"

"Your own lips have said it," he answered.

"Blasphemy! You have insulted the majesty of the Holy One." Kayafa gnashed his teeth and tore his garments. "What further need do we have of witnesses? He has condemned himself."

One of the elders spat in Yeshua's face. Others fell upon him, hitting him with their fists. Blood spurted from Yeshua's nose. "Put him in the dungeon until we can take him to Pontius Pilatus," Kayafa ordered. "He will decide this case."

The dungeon was hewn out of bedrock beneath the palace floor. A hole, large enough for a body to pass through, was the only way in or out. Yeshua was tied with ropes under his arms and lowered into the pit. There he would hang throughout the night. A grate clanged shut, emitting a dim light overhead. Footsteps echoed on the stone floor above.

Yeshua felt as though his arms would pull from their sockets. Hours passed. Delirium set in—a man in a river—a woman at a well—hands reaching out—the lame, the blind, and the deaf, pleading to be healed. In the dark horror, he prayed the most desperate psalm he knew.

> *O Holy One, incline your ear to my cry.*
> *You have put me into the depths of the pit,*
> *in regions dark and deep.*
> *Your wrath lies heavy upon me.*
> *Why do you cast me off?*
> *Why do you hide your face from me?*

43

Pontius Pilatus was not a tall man, but he gave the impression of being taller. Looking down his long, thin nose with disdain, he distanced himself from those he governed as "uncultured peasants." Aside from commanding the military forces, he was the province's chief judge. He alone had the right to impose capital punishment. His term had been fraught with briberies, injustices, and executions without trial.

Pilatus spent most of his time in the coastal town of Kaisereia, but during major festivals, such as Pesach, he traveled to Yerushalayim to be sure the peace was being kept. As a rule, he would take up residence in the Antonia Fortress, but when his wife, Claudia Procula, accompanied him, they stayed at the palatial residence of Herod Antipas.

Herod had built an incredible fortified palace to provide protection for the upper city. Two buildings each contained huge banquet halls, baths, and accommodations for hundreds of guests. The palace was surrounded by groves of trees and pools with bronze statues spouting water. The extensive, well-tended gardens had an atrium with numerous cotes for doves, which Herod was fond of raising.

Very early in the morning, Pilatus heard a commotion. Irritated that his morning bath has been disturbed, he called for his wife. Claudia came to her husband's side. Looking through the window, she observed a manacled man being dragged through the courtyard below. Claudia looked distraught. There were dark circles under her eyes.

"Did you take a sweet Alban to help you sleep?" he asked, stroking her flaxen hair.

"Yes, but it did not help. It only brought about a nightmare."

"What was it, my dear?" He kissed her neck, catching the scent of rose oil on her skin.

She gripped Pilatus' robe. "I suffered much in the dream I had about that man. He is innocent and I want you to have nothing to do with him."

"Have no fear," Pilatus soothed her. Yet he could not help thinking of Caesar's wife, Calpurnia, who had such a dream. Ignoring her warning not to go out on the *Idus Martii*, he met the assassins' daggers.

"The laws of these people are no concern of mine," he said abruptly. "We will settle the case in quick order."

He leaned out the window and called to one of the guards. "Tell the Sanhedrin that I will meet with them at the palace gates." He turned to Claudia, his voice cold and hard. "The Yehudim think that they will be defiled by coming into the palace, but they are the ones who pollute the ground they stand on."

"What accusation do you bring against this man?" Pilatus demanded when the Sanhedrin gathered.

Kayafa bowed his head in feigned respect. "That man is Yeshua of Natzeret, my lord. He is guilty of blasphemy, claiming to be the Mashiach, the anointed one of the Yehudim."

"There is no basis in Roman law for such a charge," Pilatus said with a scornful look. "Judge him according to your own law."

"It is not lawful for us to put anyone to death." Kayafa bowed again, hoping to flatter. "You must be aware that this man has stirred up the people all over Yehudah by his teaching. Now he has followers everywhere."

Pilatus had heard enough. "The last thing I need is a rebellion during the high feast. Is this man a Galilean?"

"He is, my lord."

"Then he is under Herod's jurisdiction. Take your prisoner to him."

Herod looked pleased. "The Roman Governor sent this man to be judged by me?"

"Yes, my lord," Kayafa answered.

"I have wanted to meet Yeshua for some time." Herod was stretched out on his couch, wearing a sleeveless tunic, eating roasted quail presented on a golden charger. Tossing the bones to the floor, he wiped his greasy mouth and hands on a piece of bread. With some effort, he stood and surveyed the bound prisoner before him.

"You do not look like a prophet to me," he said, circling his prey like a fox. "If you are a prophet, tell me my fortune."

Yeshua did not answer, nor did he lower his eyes, keeping them fixed on the king.

"I have heard that you are a wonder-worker," Herod said, sneering. "So perform some magic for me."

Yeshua looked at him with contempt.

Kayafa was infuriated. "This man stirs up the people saying that he is a king. He incites them to rebel."

Herod pulled at his beard. "A king?" He called one of his servants. "Fetch one of my old robes."

The servant disappeared and returned a moment later with a worn garment. Herod ordered him to drape it around Yeshua's shoulders and bow to him.

Yeshua remained silent.

Herod spewed spittle into the prisoner's face. "Beat him. Then send him back to Pilatus!"

"Why have you brought him back to me?" the Roman governor demanded.

"The prisoner refused to answer the king's questions, so he ordered us to return him to you," the guard answered.

"Imbeciles," Pilatus muttered as he went out to meet with the Sanhedrin again. The judgment seat, an enormous chair, had been carried to the courtyard. With great pomp, he sat down. Word of the trial had spread throughout the city, and a large crowd had gathered at the palace gates. Among them were Miryam, Magdala, Shlomit and her son Yaakov.

Miryam stood on tiptoes straining to see Yeshua, but was surprised to see Shimon and Yochanan. "What are they doing in the courtyard?"

"The servants must have let them in," Yaakov answered. "They often sell fish to the household for high feasts."

Before long, they saw Yeshua being dragged and made to stand before Pilatus. Miryam gasped. Her son's face and lips were bruised, his left eye swollen shut. Blood ran from his nose, down his chest and legs, pooling around his naked feet.

A woman cried out. "This man is innocent! He healed me of an issue of blood that I had for twelve years."

"Our law does not permit a woman to give testimony," one of the Sanhedrin scolded.

"He is innocent, I tell you," she protested as the guards led her away.

Pilatus grew impatient. "You are wasting my time with your accusations."

But Kayafa was not easily dismissed. "This man has been subverting our nation by his claim to be a king."

Pilatus looked at Yeshua with disdain. "Are you the king of the Yehudim?"

Yeshua raised his bloodied head and looked at the governor. "Do you ask this on your own, or did others tell you about me?"

Pilatus was irritated by his impudence. "Your own nation and the chief priests have handed you over to me. They charge you with claiming to be their king."

"My kingdom is not from this world. If it was, my followers would be fighting to keep me from being handed over to you. But my kingdom is not from here."

"So you are a king?"

"It is you who say that I am a king. I came into the world to testify to the truth."

"What is truth?" Pilatus scoffed.

"Everyone who desires the truth will listen to my voice."

"I am the judge, not you," Pilatus raged. "Do you know that I have the power of life and death over you?"

"You would have no power were it not given from my Father in heaven."

"Blasphemy!" Kayafa ran to the gates and called to the crowd. "You have heard for yourselves! This man condemned himself with his own mouth. What do you say?"

"Crucify him!" The crowd roared.

Miryam put her hands over her ears and closed her eyes.

Pilatus held up his hands. When order was restored he addressed the crowd. "It is our custom to release one prisoner during the festival—a gracious act by your governor. A man called Barabba is being held in the Fortress Antonia, charged with rebellion. Shall I release *him* or *this man* standing before you?"

The people shouted, "Release Barabba!"

Pilatus appealed to them again, but they shouted over him: "Release Barabba! Release Barabba!"

"His supporters must have been bribed," Yaakov whispered to Miryam. Her face had grown white with terror.

Pilatus tried to make his voice heard above the tumult. "What crime has this man committed? I have found no grounds for his death."

"Crucify him!" The shouting was louder now. "Crucify him!"

"Shall I crucify your King?" Pilatus asked.

"We have no king but Caesar!" someone shouted. Soon the rest of the crowd took up the cry.

"Release Barabba," Pilatus ordered his soldiers.

He ordered a basin and towel to be brought to him. There, in front of the multitude, he washed his hands. "Let this dirty matter be on your hands, not mine!" He turned to the guards. "Flog him! Perhaps that will satisfy their blood lust."

Stripped to his loin cloth, Yeshua's hands were tied to a wooden stake. One of the guards brought forth a short, braided leather whip sewn with sharp sheep bones. Two men alternated striking Yeshua's back, legs, and buttocks, peeling off ribbons of bloody flesh.

Yaakov held Miryam's head against his shoulder, trying to muffle his agonized cries. But each lash sent sword after sword into her heart.

When they were finished, the soldiers were drenched in sweat. Thirty-nine stripes had left their victim short of collapse. They untied him, and he crumpled to the ground. The soldiers laughed. "So this weak man claims to be a king!"

Pulling Yeshua to his feet, they put his robe on his bloody shoulders, and a reed in his hand as a scepter. One of them twined some thorny brambles into the shape of a crown, ramming it onto his head. Fresh blood spurted from his wounds, ran down his face, mixing with the saliva the soldiers spat upon him.

"Hail, King of the Yehudim," they said, kneeling in mock homage.

Pilatus returned to the courtyard and pointed to his blood-spattered prisoner. "Here is your King!"

"Anyone who claims to be a king sets himself against the emperor," someone in the crowd shouted.

Pilatus was shaken. He had hoped to evoke the sympathy of the crowd, but their thirst for blood would not be quenched. He grabbed Yeshua by the hair and pushed him toward the soldiers.

"Take him to be crucified," he yelled. Venom almost dripped from his mouth.

44

"Prepare a sign and hang it around the neck of the prisoner," Pilatus ordered his guards. "Write in Hebrew: *Yeshua of Natzeret, King of the Yehudim*. So that no one will misunderstand the penalty for pretending to be a king, write it in again in Latin and Greek."

Kayafa protested. "This man is not the King of the Yehudim. You must write: This man *said* I am the King of the Yehudim."

"What I have written, I have written," Pilatus answered arrogantly. He thought a moment and then added, "There are two bandits in prison. Take them to be crucified with your king. They can be his subjects."

The sky was dull and gray as the procession left the palace courtyard. It was led by the *exactor mortis*, the centurion in charge of carrying out the sentence. Yeshua's arms had been stretched out on the crossbeam, tied and balanced on the nape of his neck. His body shuddered with pain as the rough-hewn beam tore at the gaping wounds on his shoulders. Blood seeped through his garments.

Four battle-hardened soldiers goaded him with whips. Staggering out of the courtyard, Yeshua glanced at Shimon. His look was intense, but there was no anger, only pity. Shimon did not return his gaze. Turning away, he wept.

"Yeshua," Miryam called out, clasping her hands to her heart as if to keep it from bursting.

But he passed by and did not look her way.

"He does not hear you." Yaakov held her close.

"Let me go to my son," Miryam cried.

"There is nothing you can do," he said. "Come, I will take you home."

"No! No!" She struggled against him. "I must go to my son. I will not desert him."

"I cannot let you watch him die," Yaakov said.

Just then Yochanan came through the gate.

"Please, take me to my son," she begged. "Yaakov will not go with me."

Yochanan pushed his way through the crowd and released Yaakov's hold on Miryam's arm. "I will take her. You can go with Shimon and the other cowards."

Without a word, Yaakov slipped away into the crowd.

Yochanan put his arm around Miryam to protect her from the mob that followed the death march.

"Who are those men?" she asked, pointing to the other two carrying crossbeams.

"They are criminals to be executed along with Yeshua."

"He will be with sinners in death as he was in life," Miryam said mournfully.

The procession had barely begun when the palm branches littering the road pitched Yeshua forward, slamming him face-down. Before Yochanan could stop her, Miryam pushed through the crowd.

"Yeshua!" She knelt beside him and took his face in her shaking hands. There was a deep gash on his brow where it hit the pavement. His nose appeared to be broken.

"Ima," he groaned through parched lips.

"Woman! Go on your way!" A soldier pulled her to her feet and shoved her aside. Yochanan caught her and they were swallowed up in the throng.

"I would carry the cross on my back if I could," Miryam wept.

The centurion studied his prisoner. He looked too weak to carry the crossbeam; he would need help if he was to make it up the hill. Searching the crowd, he spied a stout, dark-skinned man. A tap from one of the soldiers, and he was forced to carry the instrument of death.

"I only came to Yerushalayim to do business with my son," the man complained, helping Yeshua to his feet. "I do not know who you or what you did to deserve this. It looks like you are carrying the weight of the world on your back." With a grunt, he picked up the beam and placed it on his massive shoulders. "Strange, it does not seem as heavy as I imagined."

"Move on!" the soldier barked.

Winding their way across the upper forum, they turned onto a street leading to the Gennath Gate in the north wall of the city. The narrow street was lined with stalls on either side of the path. Few of the vendors paid attention. They had seen such sights before. The great Shabbat was approaching and they had to sell their produce and lambs whose blood was soon to flow.

Making their way through the crowd, Yeshua fell on the rough pavement again. Before the soldiers could stop her, a young woman rushed forward, crouched beside him, and pressed her veil to his bloodied face.

"This is no place for whores," a soldier spat, yanking her hair and pushing her aside.

Clutching her veil, she joined the other women gathered at the gate. All of them were beating their breasts and wailing at the pitiful sight.

"Daughters of Yerushalayim," Yeshua's voice was hoarse. "Do not weep for me. Weep instead for yourselves and for your children. The days are coming when they will say, 'Blessed are the wombs that never bore, and the breasts that never nursed.'"

A sharp boot to his back thrust him forward again. Raising his head, blood ran into his eyes, nearly blinding him. "If they do this when the wood is green, what will happen when the tree is dry and rotting inside?"

"Get up!" A soldier jabbed him with the blunt end of a spear.

Exerting his remaining strength, Yeshua rose from the ground. The procession made its way up the steep, rutted path to an abandoned quarry called *Gulgota*, "the Skull." Miryam stopped short. The place indeed gave the impression of a human skull, its cavernous mouth grinning at her as if to say, "You will find no life here, only death."

A small crowd had gathered on the hill, the curious and the sadistic who enjoyed other people's suffering. Scornful of the helpless men, they gave thanks that they were not among those nailed to the cross. A few came to mourn, huddling in small silent groups cordoned off by the military. So many had been killed on this hill—husbands and sons, fathers and brothers—and now three more.

Some women followers of Yeshua also stood afar—Magdala, Shlomit, Miri, Yochanah and her maid Shoshana. All were struck dumb with grief.

Miryam passed through the crowd, edging her way closer to her son. Magdala and Shlomit followed.

"We better stay back," Yochanan warned.

"Dear friend, you do not want to see this," Magdala pleaded with her.

Miryam did not answer. She moved forward, steadily, stopping only when she heard the prisoner's terrible wails. Then she edged close to the executioners. It was worse than she imagined. Two men were already nailed to the stakes, writhing in agony. Miryam had never heard such sounds.

"I am here, dear friend." Shlomit took Miryam's arm. "I saw your son draw his first breath, and I will be with him to the last."

One of the soldiers pushed her away, almost knocking Miryam to the ground.

The centurion in charge stepped forward. "Let this woman alone. She is his mother!"

Miryam wondered how he knew, but he looked at her with kindness as he held forth his sword and allowed her to pass.

"My name is Caius," he told her in a low voice, so only she could hear. "I was stationed at Kfar Nahum. My servant was ill. Your son cured him."

Her eyes misted. She remembered.

"I am truly sorry about this day," he said. Then, as though he had never spoken to her, he returned to his work.

Yeshua's body was stretched out on the ground. She watched in horror as the soldiers drove long spikes into his wrists, tearing through nerves and muscles. He groaned—the pain too deep for him to scream. Hoisting the crossbeam by a pulley, the soldiers attached it to the upright beam fixed in the ground.

"Here is your throne, O King," a soldier mocked, positioning Yeshua's thighs on a wedge attached to the post. Then, bending his legs up and backward, they drove a spike through his heels. This time, there was a terrible gasp and his eyes rolled back in his head. Blood flowed from his feet, trailing down the wood of the cross.

Miryam clasped her hands to her heart; a vice seemed to crush her chest, making it difficult to breathe. For a brief moment, it appeared that it was not the wood holding him but the arms of his Abba in heaven.

The soldiers squatted in the dust bickering over Yeshua's clothing. Miryam felt sick—it was the seamless tunic she wove for her son.

Would they tear it in pieces and divide it among them? No, they were throwing dice for it.

Angry voices hurled insults and abuses at him.

"You would destroy the temple and build it in three days, save yourself!"

"If you are what you say, come down from that cross! Then we will believe and become your followers!"

"Ha! He saved others; he cannot save himself."

Yeshua took no part in the hatred surrounding him. There was no cry of vengeance from his lips. Instead he uttered a simple prayer. "Father, forgive them, for they don't know what they're doing."

One of the crucified began to berate him. "If you are the Mashiach, save yourself—and us!"

"Do you not fear the Holy One?" the other rebuked him. "We are getting what we deserve, but this man has done nothing wrong." Then, with great difficulty, he turned his head toward Yeshua. "My name is Dismas."

Dismas? Miryam faintly remembered. *If we ever meet again, please do not forget this hour.*

"Will I find forgiveness for my crimes in your kingdom?" Dismas implored.

Those around the cross laughed and cursed. "There will be no pardon for the likes of you!"

"Remember me when I come into your kingdom," Dismas begged Yeshua.

Yeshua's voice was barely audible. "Amen, I say to you. Today you will be with me in Paradise."

"Mercy, Lord! Have mercy!" Miryam was choked with sobs. "My son has shown mercy to this condemned man. Can you not have mercy on him?"

She looked up at the roiling sky. Where was the angel who once appeared to her? "You said I was favored," she cried out. "What favor is it to watch my son go to his death? You told me not to be afraid. But I am afraid. I am numb with fear. You left me, never to return. Where are you now?"

Yochanan came forward to hold Miryam, lest she collapse in grief. Yeshua gazed glassy-eyed at them.

"Woman, behold your son," he said.

Woman? That is what he called her when he changed water into wine. But now there was no celebration, only mourning.

"My son," he told Yochanan. "Behold your mother."

Miryam understood. She would not be left alone; Yeshua's family was hers. Her tears ceased. She waited. She had waited for his birth, and now she would wait for his death. There was nothing else to be done. She listened to her son's strained breath, the weight of his body slowly crushing his lungs until only a faint whisper of air could be heard. In vain she tried to breathe for him, her lips parting with his every gasp.

All else was silent except the howling wind, moaning with all the earth.

44

Miryam stood, watching and waiting, hour after hour. Vultures wheeled overhead, waiting for the victims to take their last breath. Her son had been crucified at the third hour, nine o'clock in the morning. From noon on, the sun seemed to hide its face. Dark clouds slid across the sky as though the angel of death passed over.

"An evil sign," someone shouted, fearful of the eclipse. "A blood moon!"

"It is the day of darkness foretold by the prophet Amos," another cried.

At the ninth hour, Yeshua cried out in a loud voice. *"Eli, Eli, lema sabachthani?"*

"Is he calling for Eliyahu, the prophet?" one of the bystanders asked.

"Let us see whether he comes to save him," another sneered.

Yeshua's lips moved. Miryam scarcely made out the words. "Father, into your hands I commit my spirit."

Magdala clutched her head. "Is there something you can give him to deaden the pain?"

One of the soldiers filled a sponge with *posca*, water mixed with vinegar. He put it on a branch of hyssop and lifted it to Yeshua's mouth. He refused it.

"He will drink the dregs of suffering to the last bitter drop," Miryam wailed.

Suddenly Yeshua cried out, his voice strong. "It is finished!"

"Finished?" Magdala wept. "It is too soon. Your work is not done. Your message has not been heard by all."

With a terrible sound like rushing wind, Yeshua breathed out his spirit. His bloodied head fell to his chest.

A strong gust swept Miryam's veil, wrapping it around her body like a shroud. Her legs buckled and she fell to her knees. "If this is a dream, let me wake!" She lifted her hands to the pitiless sky.

All creation joined in her rage. Darkness overshadowed the land. A driving rain began to fall, mixing with the tears of the mourners. The earth trembled and then shook with violence.

"Earthquake!" People rushed for cover. "Earthquake!"

"We must go," Yochanan said, lifting Miryam to her feet.

"No! I want to die on this hill with my son," she sobbed.

The earth shook again, and the centurion cried out, "This man was innocent! Truly, he was God's Son." The guards gaped in disbelief. How could a Roman soldier proclaim such words?

Miryam remembered Yeshua's words. *When I am lifted up from the earth, I will draw all people to myself.* If a pagan centurion could believe, perhaps her son's death was not in vain.

When the shaking ceased, soldiers came forward with clubs and broke the legs of the two men crucified with Yeshua. Unable to support their bodies, their lungs collapsed under the weight—a great hissing breath announced their deaths.

The centurion motioned to one of the soldiers, a lancer. "Pierce this one's side as proof that he is dead."

Water and blood gushed from Yeshua's heart, splattering upon Miryam and the lancer. She tried to cry out, but no sound came forth. Until now she had never dreamed of the full extent of the words of the old man in the temple so many years ago. The sword sought her out, running its blade through her heart.

"We want these bodies removed before the Shabbat," one of the kohanim demanded.

Anxious to end the affair and go home, the soldiers yanked the nails from the hands and feet of the two brigands, just as they had pounded them into their flesh a short while before. The bodies fell face-forward with a sickening thud.

They were about to release Yeshua from the gibbet when Yochanan stepped forward. "Let me help you," he said, unafraid of the soldiers' hostile stares. Yet they allowed him to support Yeshua's limp body as they laid him on the ground.

Miryam fell to her knees and cradled her son in her arms. His face was so marred, almost unrecognizable. Kissing his bloody brow and stroking his matted hair, she spoke into his ear, hoping he could still hear her voice. "You are my beloved son."

But Miryam's son, the Son of the Most High, was silent. David's harp would sing no more. Only the mournful wind played its dirge.

"Mother," Yochanan said, softly. It sounded right to call her that now. She did not respond. "Mother," he spoke again, bending over her.

Finally, she looked at him. He tried to loosen her grip from Yeshua's body.

Magdala leaned down. "Miryam, there is nothing more we can do here. Your gown is soaked in blood. Let us go home and I will help you bathe."

Miryam looked at the blood. The pungent smell filled her nostrils, yet somehow it was sweet. "Long ago I held a blood-soaked lamb in my arms. It died, too."

Magdala looked at Yochanan in bewilderment. "Miryam," she said again, trying to persuade her. "Your bloody clothes make you unclean. You must wash."

"No!" Miryam said—her voice firm. "My son's blood does not defile. His blood saves us!"

"Mother," Yochanan said firmly. "The Shabbat is almost upon us. We must lay him to rest. Nakdimon has brought us a man who has offered his tomb."

An elderly man dressed in finery stepped forward, bowing. "It would be an honor to place your son's body in my tomb. It has never been used by our family."

"Do I know you?" Miryam asked, bleary-eyed.

"I am your uncle, Yosef Beit Ramatayim. Do you not remember

me? I took you to visit your aunt, Elisheva, when she was with child. I became wealthy from the broken backs of the tin miners, but I left that cursed trade. Since I am a prosperous citizen, the council was glad to have me as a member."

Miryam caught her breath. "You are a member of the Sanhedrin? Did you sentence my son to die?"

He cleared his throat, looking downcast. "Dear daughter, I did not agree with the verdict and sentence of the court. When I heard your son speak, I came to believe that he was a great teacher, a prophet, the...."

"The Mashiach." Miryam finished what he lacked the courage to say.

Nakdimon intervened. "Miryam, your uncle and I did not take part in the wicked plot. The council met during the night. We were taken by surprise and had no time to act. When I came to Yeshua's defense, they scoffed at my appeal as if I was an ignorant peasant." He hung his head. "Seeing your son on the cross has stirred me as nothing else has ever done."

Miryam turned to her uncle. "And now you want to bury my son in your tomb?"

"Forgive me for my boldness, but I have already sent word to the governor and asked for his body. As a family member I have the right to claim my relative, your son. Pilatus had no objection. So if you will allow me, my servants are here to prepare your son's body for burial. Otherwise the Romans will...."

Yochanan held up his hand to prevent him from speaking further. Miryam's uncle was silent for a moment and then motioned to his servants. "Look here. I have a mixture of myrrh and aloes, which I offer for your son's anointing. It is a small thing, but all I can do right now."

Magdala and Yochanan managed to separate Miryam from Yeshua's body, and together they helped her stand. Touching her uncle's hand, she looked at him with gratitude.

The light was fading and the servants went to work. Miryam watched as they followed their master's directions. They washed the corpse, removing every trace of blood from its many mutilations—the thorny head wounds, the torn flesh on back and shoulders, the bloodied holes in hands and feet, the gaping gash in his side. Then they anointed the body. A sweet fragrance filled the air.

When they finished, they brought forth a great linen winding sheet. Laying it full length on the ground, they lifted Yeshua's body, placed it on the shroud, crossed his lifeless arms in front of him, and covered him head to foot. A face cloth was secured with more windings.

Miryam looked at Magdala, grief struck. "Once I wrapped my child in swaddling clothes, so that his little arms and legs could not thrash about. He was warm and safe in my arms, and now he lies alone on the cold earth."

45

The tremors continued to shake the earth, yet the world went on as it had before. The day seemed to drag, trailing its gray mantle. Finally, the sun dipped below the hills. The Shabbat was over.

Many of Yeshua's talmidim had returned to their farms and to their fishing. There were family responsibilities that needed attention. Nothing was left for them now; their hopes of a restored kingdom were as shattered as their hearts. Their feelings of cowardice only added to their grief.

Magdala and Yochanan stayed with Miryam in Nakdimon's house. The dwelling was dimly lit, as if it too shared the heartache of the terrible day. At first Magdala was furious, blaming the one who had betrayed Yeshua and those who put him to death. Anger turned to sorrow, silent tears falling on her face, etched with pain.

Miryam pressed her fists against her brow. When she closed her eyes she saw three dark crosses against the angry sky. She could still hear the sound of hammers and mocking voices.

"Tell me what happened after they arrested Yeshua," she finally asked.

Yochanan looked downcast.

"Tell me," she repeated.

He struggled to tell her what he had witnessed. "After they arrested your son, they brought him to the palace of Kayafa," he said. "Since I am known to the High Priest, I was able to enter the house."

Nakdimon interrupted. "As the saying goes, 'Woe to the house of Annas! Woe to their serpent's hiss.'"

Miryam looked at him in a daze.

"Forgive me. I only meant to say that when your son cleared the temple of the buyers and sellers, he also attacked Annas."

"Annas?"

"Yes. Annas made a fortune from the profits on the temple sacrifices. So he was eager to take revenge. But what he did was a mockery of justice."

"Yeshua was not afraid of them," Yochanan said. "Even when one of the officers struck him, drawing blood."

Nakdimon put his finger to his lips.

"I am sorry," Yochanan said. "I should say no more."

"Tell me everything," Miryam insisted.

"But Miryam!" Nakdimon protested.

Miryam glared at him, and Yochanan continued his account. "They held Yeshua in the chamber beneath Kayafa's house. He hung in that pit all night long."

The pain on Miryam's face was so heartbreaking, Magdala left the room sobbing.

"Is there more?" Miryam asked.

Nakdimon shook his head. "I did not stay after that."

Yochanan spoke up, "In the morning, they brought Yeshua up from the pit. I barely recognized him he was so...." He fell silent for a moment, then continued. "When they summoned Pilatus, the Sanhedrin hurled accusations against him. Every charge was a lie—that he was a rebel; that he incited the people not to pay their taxes; that he would destroy the temple; that he claimed to be a king. But Pilatus did not take their claims seriously. He knew a revolutionary when he saw one, and Yeshua was not one of them."

"So everything depended on Pilatus?"

"No. The people cried for Yeshua's crucifixion, shouting, 'Crucify him.'"

Miryam put up her hand. "No more, Yochanan. I was there."

Magdala returned to the room, her eyes like black holes. She kissed Miryam's forehead and the mother's tears began to flow again.

"Hush." Magdala folded Miryam's slight body in her arms. For a long time, the two rocked back and forth. Tears washed both of their faces.

A knock on the door startled them. Nakdimon peered through the shuttered window.

"It is a Roman soldier," he said under his breath.

A gruff voice came through the locked door. "Is this the house of the mother of the crucified one?"

"Who comes to our house at this late hour?" Nakdimon shouted back.

"My name is Longinus from Cappadocia," the man answered. "I am not here to harm you."

Miryam regained her courage and gestured to Nakdimon to open the door.

"What more can they do to me now?" she said, wiping her tears with the palm of her hand.

"It is too dangerous," Yochanan said. "It may be a trick."

"Let him in," Miryam ordered.

Nakdimon slid back the bolt, opening the door a crack. The soldier made no move to enter.

Magdala gasped. "I know who you are. You are the man who pierced the side of my Master."

The soldier looked at Miryam. "My name is Longinus. I know there is no excuse for what happened, but I want you to know that I was only following orders."

"There is a higher authority that we obey," Yochanan said, his voice cold.

"I do not know your god," Longinus said. "I can only tell you what happened today. May I come in?"

Nakdimon opened the door wider. "Bring some water for our guest," he told his servant.

The boy went to the kitchen and soon returned. The soldier took a sip from the cup, wiping his mouth with his sleeve.

"As I said, my name is Longinus. I am a lancer. Indeed, that is what my name means." His eyes darted to Magdala. "I am a friend of Caius, the centurion. Did you hear him when he cried out, 'Truly, this is the Son of God?'"

"Yes, I heard him," Miryam said.

"My Lady, I want you to know that the blood of the crucified healed me." The soldier's smile revealed several missing teeth.

"My son healed you?"

"Yes, when I pierced the side of your son." He paused, looking ashamed. "My vision had been cloudy for some time, and I was afraid the captain of the guard would discover how poor it was. If I was released from the army, I had no place to go. I know nothing but soldiering. So I did the best I could. But when I pierced your son's side, his blood fell into my eyes. I was almost blind, but now I can see."

Miryam took Longinus' rough hands in hers, the same hands that pierced her son's heart, and looked into his eyes. She was startled by their clarity.

"My words are true," he said. "You can trust me."

"I know you tell the truth," she said. "Now you must live in truth. There must be no more killing, no more warfare for you."

Longinus began to protest.

"The Most High will provide for you," Miryam promised.

He bowed low and kissed her hands. "Thank you. I will try to do as you say."

When he was gone, Miryam and Magdala sat together, pondering their visitor's account. All at once, Miryam sat upright. "Do you hear the sound of weeping?"

"It sounds more like a wail to me," Magdala said, standing.

Yochanan slowly opened the door. A woman was sitting on a bench in the courtyard, her face marred by grief. She wore no veil; instead, she clasped her head-covering to her breast.

Miryam started outside, but Yochanan stopped her. "I will go to her."

Ignoring him, she stepped across the threshold. Magdala and Yochanan fell in behind.

"I know who you are," the woman told Miryam through her tears. "You are the mother of the healer."

"Yes, I am." She shivered. "Will you come inside? It is very cold out here."

The woman stood and came with her.

"Child, what is causing you such sorrow?" Miryam asked, putting an arm about her slight shoulders.

The woman tried to compose herself, and explained. "Yesterday, I was doing my household chores when I heard loud voices. I ran into the street and, to my horror, I saw a procession of men on their way to be crucified. One of them was so weak he could hardly stand, let alone walk. He carried a sign: *Yeshua of Natzeret, King of the Yehudim.*"

"What is your name?" Magdala pressed the woman.

"I am called Veronika."

Yochanan looked at her for a moment. "Are you the woman who called out in the house of the High Priest?"

"Yes, I am. They told me that the law did not permit a woman to give testimony, and they led me away—roughly, I must say."

"How do you know my son?" Miryam asked.

"I was visiting my kinswoman in Kfar Nahum who told me of a healer who might help me. I had suffered from a bloody flow for twelve years and spent all that I had. But I only grew worse. I was desperate. When the healer passed by, I reached out to touch him. I was cured of my affliction immediately."

"Yes, I remember," Miryam said. "I was there. What are you doing in Yerushalayim?"

"This is my home," Veronika said. "I always wanted to repay your son. And when I saw him in that sad march of death, I knew that I would never have another chance. But what could I do? I had no water to ease his thirst. Then I thought of my veil. I could wipe the wounds on his face."

Miryam reached out to her, but Veronika shook her head. "Somehow I had the courage to go to him, even though the soldiers kept pushing me back. With all my strength I rushed forward, and before they could stop me I pressed my veil to his face. The soldiers knocked me to the ground. One of them struck me, but I scarcely felt the pain. I just held my veil to my breast as I am doing now."

Miryam smiled. "I know that my son will reward you for your kindness."

"He already has," she said through her tears.

She held out the veil for all to see. Imprinted upon it was Yeshua's countenance.

Miryam looked faint and Magdala helped her to a chair. She sat down hard, staring at the bloody image. Then she took it from Veronika's hands and held it to her breast.

Shimon Kefa struggled for some time before he summoned the courage to face his master's mother. How could he look her in the eyes after what he did—or what he did not do? He paced in front of the house. Finally, he tapped on the door. After several attempts, a servant let him inside.

Shimon had rehearsed his speech. But when he saw Miryam's ashen face, he dropped to his knees and buried his head in her lap. "Forgive me. I have betrayed your son. Three years I followed the Master. I thought I would stand by his side to death, but I failed him."

She lifted his tear-streaked face. "My son forgives you, Shimon. And I forgive you."

"He knew I would fail him," he wept. "I thought I was so brave, yet I could not even stay awake when he asked us to watch with him. Our eyes were so heavy from the wine."

"We all fell asleep in the garden." Yochanan admitted. "When I awoke, I hoped it was just a terrible dream."

There was an agonizing silence. Then Shimon stood and spoke. "When they came for the Master I behaved like a wild man, swinging a sword. I do not even know how to handle one."

"What were you doing with a sword?" Miryam asked.

"I brought it with me, thinking I could defend Yeshua if there was trouble." He shook his head. "What was I thinking? Yeshua told us that if we lived by the sword, we would die by the sword."

"What did you do?"

"I struck a servant of the High Priest."

"Did you kill him?"

"No…I cut off his ear. The blood was terrible, spurting like a fountain.… Then Yeshua touched the man's head and the blood stopped."

"I know the man," Yochanan said. "His name is Malchus. He is a servant of the High Priest. I often dealt with him when I sold fish to Kayafa's household."

"Malchus was healed? Yet he joined in arresting my son?" Miryam asked in disbelief.

"No…yes, he was healed," Shimon stammered. "Malchus walked away. I think he was sorry to be part of that mob. Some say his heart was changed by the miracle." He furrowed his brow. "Yeshua said a strange thing to me. He said, 'Am I not to drink the cup my father gave me?' Before I could ask what he meant, they arrested him. They bound him like a slave and led him away."

Yochanan swallowed hard. "They say that Yehudah betrayed him for thirty pieces of silver—the price of a slave."

Shimon heaved his massive shoulders. "We all betrayed him.

Falling asleep, denying him. We all betrayed him."

No one spoke for a long time.

"And Yehudah, what happened to him?" Miryam finally asked.

Yochanan hesitated. "I have heard that he killed himself, hanging from a tree. They said that the weight of his body broke the branch. When he fell, he landed on the road. A cart ran over him."

Miryam closed her eyes. Her voice was faint. "Do you know who Yehudah's mother is?"

"I do not know who is mother is," Shimon said, "but his father is surely the devil."

"So it seems," Yochanan said.

"My son forgave everyone from the cross," Miryam said, her voice now strong. "Did you not hear him?"

Yochanan took Miryam's hand. "Dear mother, I believe that if heaven's gatekeeper banned sinners from entering, you would open a window for them."

She turned to Shimon. "And you, what did you do after they arrested my son?"

"Yeshua was taken to Kayafa's house, and I followed at a safe distance. When I arrived at the gate, Yochanan was already inside. He spoke to the guard, and he allowed me to come into the courtyard. I joined the servants who were warming themselves by a brazier. I was so cold.... I do not think it was the morning chill." Shimon stole a glance at Miryam.

"Two of the servants asked me if I was Yeshua's talmid. I was afraid, so I answered that I was not. A third said my accent betrayed me as a man from the Galil. But I denied even knowing him.... And at that moment the cock crowed, just as Yeshua had said."

Miryam looked steadily at him. "My son is counting on you to strengthen your brothers."

"But I have no strength," Shimon moaned. "Look how I failed your son. He called me a rock, but I am nothing more than shifting sand. I am weak. I am a coward. How can I strengthen anyone?"

"Have faith, Shimon. My son gave me the strength to bear this terrible time. He will strengthen you."

46

A crowd filled the upper room at Nakdimon's house—120 in all, including Yeshua's mother and a number of other women.

"Greetings, daughter." Yosef Beit Ramatayim embraced Miryam when he entered the room. "Did you feel the earthquake?"

"I thought the tremors would never stop," she answered.

"The ground shook so fiercely that some say tombs were opened, the dead rose and appeared to many," her uncle said.

"He has destroyed the power of the grave," Miryam said. Still, she wondered why her son had not appeared to her.

He sat down beside her. "Now that Yeshua has given the tomb back to me, I have been thinking. One day I will lie in that tomb. What will your son think of that?"

"He will say to you, 'Because I live so shall you live.'"

"I know I can depend on that," he said, smiling.

"We never thought that Yeshua would die," Miri's daughter, Lysia, moaned. "We had hoped...."

"We hoped that he would have been the one to save Yisrael," her husband, Cleopas, finished her thought. "We were returning to our home in Ammaus, seven miles from Yerushalayim. The sun was setting and we were blinded by its light.

"Perhaps it was our grief that blinded us," Lysia mused.

"In any case, we did not recognize the stranger at our side," Cleopas said.

"A stranger?" Miryam asked.

"Yes. At first we did not know who he was. But as we walked together he explained all the things about himself in the scriptures—beginning with Moshe."

"He told us that it was necessary that the Mashiach should suffer so as to enter into his glory," Lysia said with sadness.

Miryam looked distressed. "Necessary? Why should it be necessary for anyone to suffer as my son did?"

"When we were close to home we were afraid that he would leave us," Lysia hastily added. "So we pleaded, 'Stay with us.'"

"And so he did," Cleopas said. "And when we were seated at table, he took bread, blessed it, broke it, and gave it to us."

"It was in the breaking of the bread that we recognized him," Lysia said, brightening. "It was Yeshua! How our hearts burned within us."

"Yeshua?" Miryam asked.

"Yes, but then he vanished from our sight!" Cleopas sighed.

"We did not recognize him either when he appeared to us," Shimon spoke up. "The Master was standing on the shore calling out, telling us to cast our nets on the other side of the boat. We did as he said and we caught a great haul of fish—so many that our nets were breaking."

"I knew that it was Yeshua," Yochanan said.

"But I was the one who jumped into the water and swam ashore," Shimon protested. "Three times he asked me if I loved him. I told him that I did, but all he said was, 'Feed my sheep.'"

"I recognized him when he spoke my name," Magdala said. All eyes turned in her direction. "After the Shabbat, Miri and Shlomit went with me to anoint the Master's body. We wondered who would roll away the stone."

"We were surprised to find the tomb open and empty," Shlomit said.

"There was a young man, dressed in a white robe, sitting beside the tomb," Miri added. "He said to us, 'Why do you look for the living among the dead? He is not here. He has risen as he said.'"

"You both were terrified and fled," Magdala accused them. "I stayed. I heard a voice asking, 'Woman, why are you weeping?' I thought it was the gardener, and I asked where they laid Yeshua." She paused, her eyes were glistening. "When he spoke my name I knew that it was my Rabboni, my teacher. I was overjoyed and wanted to embrace him, but he told me I was to go to my brothers and tell them that he had been raised from the dead."

Shimon's expression showed his displeasure. "And why did the Master speak to a woman and not his talmidim?"

"I do not mean to dishonor you, brother, but I am a talmid, too," Magdala answered, her voice growing cold.

"Do you think that makes you more worthy than the rest of us?"

Magdala's eyes flashed. "Why did you not believe me when I told you that Yeshua was alive and that I saw him?" She turned away in disgust. "Men never believe the testimony of a woman."

Shimon exploded. "Are we supposed to believe the words of a disturbed mind like yours?"

"What do you think?" She looked wounded. "Did I make this up? Am I am lying about what my Master told me?"

Shimon glared at her. "Since you alone seem to understand his deepest secrets, tell us what he said."

Levi stepped in. "My brother Shimon, you have always been hot-tempered. And now you are quarrelling with our sister as if she is our enemy. If Yeshua appeared to her, who are we to disbelieve her?"

The argument seemed to be settled until Magdala spoke again. "I think our brother Shimon hates women."

"Children, children." Miryam was disheartened by their bickering. "Shimon is the foundation of the church, but Yeshua sent you to witness to his brothers. And wherever the good news is proclaimed, your courage and fidelity will be remembered."

"I am not so certain," Magdala said. "I think they will only remember me as the woman who had seven demons."

There was an uneasy silence until Toma spoke. "I was absent when the Master appeared in this very room. I doubted when they told me that he had risen from the grave. I refused to believe them unless I touched his wounds myself."

Toma looked ashamed. Miryam waited for him to speak again.

"A week later, the Master came through the locked door as if it was nothing but air. He told me to touch his wounds and see for myself. When I did, he said, 'Blessed are those who do not see and yet believe.'" Toma ran his hand through his hair. "Still, I wonder how a person can walk through a locked door."

"Death could not hold him," Miryam said. "He enters places that are closed. He opens doors that we cannot open."

Magdala took her hand. "Mother, now I know why Yeshua did not appear to you. You had no need to see to believe. You believed what they told you, and that was enough."

Miryam sighed. "Still, I wish I could see his face and hear his voice again."

Yaakov stood. "Shimon, you spoke of your cowardice. I am the worst of all." He cast his eyes downward, too mortified to look at anyone. "My companions and I were pierced to the soul when Yeshua died. We hid in an abandoned tomb, knowing that the authorities were hunting us down, suspecting us of setting fire to the temple after the earthquake."

He raised his tear-filled eyes to Miryam. "I promise you: I will spend the rest of my life on my knees in repentance for my shameful deed."

She rose and went to him. "Yeshua has already forgiven you, Yaakov. You must not waste your life in mourning. He has more important things for you to do—for all of us."

47

"Today is the Feast of Shavuot," Shimon announced. "Can you believe fifty days have passed since the Pesach? The Lord freed us from physical bondage on Pesach, but he gave us the Torah on Shavuot, redeeming us spiritually. And here we are! Waiting and praying, just as the Master asked."

"Even though one of our members is missing." Yochanan dared not speak the betrayer's name.

The group grew quiet. Yeshua had told them to wait, so they waited. Miryam knew about waiting. She had waited all her life. Yet she had an extraordinary feeling that something new was about to happen.

"We must fast and pray for the Spirit to enlighten us," Shimon said. Then he looked at Miryam, "Fasting is not necessary for you."

"I will fast and I will pray," she said with firmness.

Soon the soft hum of prayer filled the room. Except for an occasional cough and shuffling of feet, there were no other sounds. Miryam's mind was heavy with memories. Now and then she wiped tears from her eyes. Time passed slowly. The room was warm, the air heavy with the smell of perspiration and foul breath. Still, no one moved.

Without warning, a driving wind blew through the open window toppling a pedestal. The house shook. They looked at one another in alarm. Another earthquake? A bright light filled the room—like tongues of fire, dancing above their heads. The power of the Spirit seized them, flooding them with peace and joy.

Miryam began to sing, not a song she knew, but words beyond understanding. The roof seemed to open above her head. With eyes closed, she saw the splendor of heaven—the Holy One seated on the throne. His penetrating gaze burned into her soul. She heard a voice, like the thunderous sound of waters. "I am the Alpha and the Omega, the first and the last, the beginning and the end. See, I am making all things new."

Near the throne was a lamb and, although slain, it was standing and speaking: "Through my death and resurrection, it has been done."

"The lamb! My son!" She opened her eyes; the vision faded. Everyone around her was in ecstasy. They were speaking all at once but in a language she did not know.

Shimon jumped up with a start and rushed down the stairs into the street. Everyone followed him. A large crowd had gathered. Having heard the wind and felt the ground shaking, they came to see what had happened. There were people from every nation—Parthians, Medes, and Elamites; citizens of Mesopotamia, Yisrael and Cappadocia, Pontus, Asia, Phrygia, Pamphylia, Egypt and the districts of Libya near Cyrene; Cretans and Arabs as well as visitors from Rome. All had come to Yerushalayim to celebrate Shavuot.

The Spirit gave Shimon words that reached every heart, the ancient prophecies of the Mashiach, now fulfilled in Yeshua.

The people were astonished and kept asking one another, "What can this mean?" Others in the crowd scoffed, saying, "They are filled with new wine."

"Listen to me." Shimon cried. "We are not drunk as you suppose, for it is only the third hour in the morning. What you hear is what the prophet Yoel foretold: 'The Spirit will be poured out upon all people. Your sons and daughters, and your servants, will prophesy. Young men will see visions and old men will dream dreams. There will be wonders in the heaven above and signs upon the earth below. And all who call upon the name of the Lord shall be saved.'"

When they heard this, the people were pierced to the heart. "What are we to do?"

"Repent and be baptized in the name of Yeshua the Mashiach so that your sins may be forgiven. Then you will receive the gift of the Spirit, your comforter, your counselor and your advocate. This is the promise he made, to you and to your children."

Miryam pondered all of this. *The blood of the cross has become the new wine of the Spirit.* She knew that the world would never again be the same.

48

"I have been away from home too long." Miryam leaned out the window, watching the reddening sky. Yochanan had built the house near Ephesos on Nightingale's Hill overlooking the Aegean Sea.

From the upper room, she could view the arched colonnades of the Harbor Road which led to the great theater. In the distance was the temple of Artemis, called *Diana* by the Romans, the goddess of the hunt. Pilgrims from all over Asia Minor came to worship the many-breasted daughter of Zeus, the twin of her brother Apollo. One man exclaimed that he had seen the hanging gardens of Babylon; the statue of Olympian Zeus; the Colossus of Rhodes; the mighty Pyramids; the Pharos Lighthouse; and the vast tomb of Mausolus. But when he saw the temple of Artemis rising to the clouds, all other wonders were put in the shade.

Though numerous religions and mystery cults flourished in Ephesos, those who followed Yeshua's teachings were growing in numbers and becoming stronger in their faith. These household churches looked upon Miryam as a wise woman, and they often invited her to share memories of her son. But she had no desire to mix with the outside world. She wanted to live out her days in solitude. Even so, people kept coming to her, telling stories of what they encountered on their travels to spread the faith. The world had opened up to her in ways she never imagined as a girl in Natzeret.

Most visitors came because she was the "Mother of the Lord," kneeling at her feet and murmuring, "O Blessed Mother," greeting her as the "refuge of sinners." Women who felt unloved and shamed asked her to pray for strength and faith. Others were widows and barren women; unwed mothers; mothers of runaway children and mothers of criminals seeking solace. She could speak to them all. She had lived as they did.

One woman surprised her by removing a knotted, silken cord that fell from her waist. "Mother, help me undo the knots of my life," she implored. Miryam took the cord in her hands, wondering what the knots meant. Were they knots of deep hurt between husband and wife, the disrespect of children, or the absence of peace in her home? Was it an illness, fear, or lack of faith? Perhaps it was some grave sin.

Without a word, Miryam untied each knot, large and small, smoothing them on her lap.

"I only had one son," she said, handing the cord back to the woman. "Now it seems that I have a multitude of children."

"And more to come, for all generations," the grateful woman replied.

Miryam's reverie was interrupted by an elderly, dark-skinned man. He bowed and kissed her hand. "Honored Lady, I have waited so long to see you."

She saw that he was almost blind. "Who are you, sir?"

"I am Balthazar, from Ethiopia." Tears formed in his cloudy eyes. "When I was in Cyrene in North Africa, I came across a man who told me that he had been pressed into helping your son carry his cross. He knew where I could find you. Now after all these years we meet again."

She took his gnarled hands in hers and held them to her face.

"Ah, you are as beautiful as I remember," he sighed. "You know, My Lady, the story of the gifts of the magi did not end in Beit Lechem."

"Is that true?"

"After Melchior offered the Holy Child the gift of gold, an angel bestowed spiritual riches upon him. And Gaspar received increased faith for his gift of incense."

"And you, dear Balthazar? What gift was given to you?"

"I was given the great treasure of truth in exchange for the gift of myrrh."

"And what is truth?"

"The truth, Honored Lady, is that your son did not die in vain. He died for all people. We three magi are proof of that."

Miryam nodded. "The cross on which my son died has become a throne for the salvation of the world."

Balthasar grew pensive. Then his wizened face broke into a smile. "You know, I searched for your house for a long time, but was unable to find it. Do you think an angel moved it here?"

"The angel left me long ago never to return," she said, forlornly.

<hr>

"My name is Loukas," the tall, slender man told the gatekeeper who answered his knock. "I have heard that a Christian community gathers in this house."

The man at the gate observed him closely, but said nothing.

"I am very thirsty from my travels," Loukas said in earnest. "My home is in Antioch in Syria and I have just arrived at Ephesos. I met some brethren who said that they were once followers of the Baptist. They were sincere, but they had a very poor understanding of the mission of the Christos."

"We call our Master 'the Mashiach,'" the man said coolly.

Loukas cleared his throat. "Yes, the anointed one, but I am Greek. I was told that I would find better teaching with one of the disciples of the Christos…the Mashiach…Yochanan by name."

"I am Yochanan." He placed his hand on the visitor's shoulder. "Forgive my caution. We recently heard disturbing news that the persecutions in Yerushalayim have worsened. The authorities decreed that no one should have any dealings with those who call themselves 'Christians.'"

"Christians," Loukas repeated, smiling. "That is a good name for the followers of the Christos."

"Come in, you are welcome," Yochanan gave Loukas the kiss of peace and ushered him into a walled courtyard.

He spoke privately to a woman who went into the house and soon returned with a basin and towel. She motioned to Loukas to sit on one of the cushions in the shade of a canvas awning.

To his surprise, the woman did not wash his feet. Instead, it was his host. Yochanan took off his outer robe, knelt before Loukas, untied his sandals, and put his dusty feet in the cool water. The woman placed a drop of attar of roses on their guest's head. After drying his feet, the woman went into the house and brought forth a tray of pomegranate juice in earthenware cups. Another woman followed, carrying a plate of fruit, soft goat cheese, and a basket of nuts and dates. Yochanan and Loukas ate while the women sat nearby.

"We are the 'Community of the Beloved Disciple,'" one of the women explained, reaching for a date.

Loukas appeared stunned. Servants, especially women, ate in separate quarters and did not engage in conversation with men at meals. "Who is the Beloved Disciple?" he asked.

"Yochanan. We call him the 'Beloved Disciple' because of the Master's special love for him," the woman told him.

"We are a community of equals—men and women," Yochanan

stressed. "We devote ourselves to prayer and work, following the teachings of Yeshua, our Master." He paused. "Tell me more about what you have been doing."

"I was brought into the faith by Paulos of Tarsus. Do you know him?"

"Yes, but we call him Shaul. He is a great missionary of the Master's teachings."

"I was privileged to accompany him on one of his journeys," Loukas said. "He traveled throughout the world bringing the Christos' message to all who would listen, often at great peril."

"Did you know that the apostle stayed in Ephesos three years—longer than any place he visited?" Yochanan asked. "He came here to win converts. Demetrius the silversmith feared that the people would stop buying the shrines of the goddess Artemis—which brought him no little business. So he riled up the people and they drove the apostle away."

Loukas' face became sad. "I knew when Paulos left for Macedonia that I would never see him again. With Nero on the throne, I fear the worst."

The two finished their meal in silence. Then Yochanan said, "His mother is here."

"Whose mother?" Loukas asked.

"Mother Miryam, the mother of our Master. She is here in Ephesos. After her son's death and resurrection it was no longer safe for her in Yerushalayim, so I brought her here."

"The city of David is no longer the city of peace." Loukas shook his head. "I heard that Stephen, one of the deacons, was stoned to death for professing his faith."

"My brother Yaakov was the first of the twelve to die for preaching the teachings of our Master. He was beheaded by King Herod Agrippa," Yochanan said. "I was told that when Yaakov was led to his execution, his accuser saw his courage and asked for forgiveness. They were both beheaded." He rose to his feet, "Perhaps you would like to meet the Master's mother?"

"Yes, I certainly would."

"She is in the garden," Yochanan said. "She likes to read in the afternoon."

Loukas looked surprised.

"Yes, she has learned to read," he said. "I like to think of Mother

Miryam as the new Chavah, the mother of all life. Her offspring has crushed the head of the serpent and she has trodden him underfoot."

When they entered the house, he instructed Loukas to wait. In a few moments, he returned.

"His mother will see you now." He pointed the way to a small enclosed garden.

When they entered, Loukas was amazed by the indescribable beauty. A soft light was streaming through white-stone arches, and a fountain bubbled in the center. Clusters of purple grapes cascaded over the stone walls. Birds found homes in the branches of a mustard tree, filling the garden with song.

Flowers bloomed in perfusion, perfuming the air—scarlet lilies, lavender anemones, and yellow, pink, and red roses. By far the loveliest flower in the garden was the slight woman who sat in the shade of an umbrella-shaped fig tree. Her white hair crowned her head with a halo of light. Her eyes were closed, her gnarled fingers intertwined as though in prayer.

"Ima." Yochanan touched her hand.

She opened her large, dark eyes. The scroll she had been reading slipped from her lap, curling to the ground.

"Ima," he said again. "I want you to meet Loukas. He is from Antioch in Syria."

"O Blessed Mother." Loukas knelt and kissed her hand.

"Come and sit beside me," she said, indicating a large cushion at her feet. "Tell me why you have come."

"My Lady, I have a wealthy patron by the name of Theophilus. He is an important Roman official, a member of the equestrian order—a convert to our faith. He urged me to write another account of your son."

"Another account?"

"Our brother Marcus has written a gospel of all that happened from the time of your son's baptism to his empty tomb."

"What is a gospel?"

"That is what Marcus called his report. It means 'good news.'"

"Good news." A smile crinkled the corners of her eyes. "That is indeed the message of my son. And who is Marcus?"

"His mother owned the garden where your son was arrested." He paused. She urged him to continue. "When Marcus heard the disturbance, he rushed to the place. The temple guards tried to take hold of him but they only tore his garments, and he ran away naked. Poor boy, he even deserted Paulos. He was so young, unprepared for the rigors of the apostle's work."

Loukas' face brightened. "But that is not the end of the story. Later, he accompanied Petros, whom you call Shimon. When he preached to the Gentiles, Petros could not speak Greek, so he needed an interpreter." He hesitated. "The last I heard, Petros was on his way to Roma. For all I know he may be dead."

Miryam was startled. "Shimon? Dead?"

"I am sorry, My Lady," Loukas said.

"Soon all those who followed my son will be gone." She sighed and then leaned forward. "But tell me: If Marcus has written a report of my son, why is another needed?"

"Some of the accounts were incomplete. I have been carefully investigating everything that was handed on by eyewitnesses. I want Theophilus, and all who read my gospel, to know the truth."

"And you want me to tell you my story."

Loukas looked relieved that she understood his intention. "I would appreciate it if you would tell me about your son—from the beginning."

Miryam was silent, lost in remembrance. Birds circled overhead in the pale-blue afternoon sky; an awning swayed in the breeze; a water wheel, turned by an ox, creaked and groaned.

"That animal keeps walking in circles without getting anywhere," Miryam said, tucking a wisp of hair behind her ear. "Like me."

"Ima," Yochanan said. "If you do not want to recall things that are too painful for you, Loukas will understand."

"No, my son, I never tire of taking out the treasures I have stored in my heart."

Loukas sat at her feet like a child eager for a story. As she spoke, he committed everything to memory. When she finished, the sun was low over the garden wall, casting golden shafts of light on her withered face.

"It has grown cold," she said with a wan smile.

"Come inside and rest, Ima," Yochanan said. He picked up a woolen cloak, the color of a dove's breast, and put it around her thin shoulders.

Loukas rose to his feet as Miryam stood. "There is something I want you to do for me," she said, holding onto the back of her chair to steady herself.

"Yes, My Lady?"

"I want you to pray."

"What is it you want me to pray for?"

"I want you to pray that this house will one day be a place where people of all faiths can come together in peace."

"I will pray," Loukas said in earnest.

"Thank you for writing about my son," she said.

"It is important to remember the past."

"Remembering the past is the promise of the future," she said, taking her leave. Then she turned to Yochanan. "Perhaps you, too, will write an account of my son."

"Ima," Yochanan grinned. "There are many things that Yeshua did. If they were all written down, the world itself could not contain the books that would be written."

Yochanan escorted Miryam to a woman who took her by the hand and led her inside. Then he walked with Loukas to the gate, bidding him farewell. The two embraced.

Yochanan scratched his beard. "Do you know that our Master called me and my brother 'Boanerges'?"

"Why did he call you that?"

"It means 'Sons of Thunder.' I suppose it was our zeal, wanting to be like Eliyahu, calling down fire from the sky on our enemies. But as I grow older, it seems there are fewer of them."

Yochanan was pensive for a moment. "My mother had the boldness to ask if we could sit beside the Master in the kingdom. Now I know. That place is reserved for someone else."

"Perhaps it is for his mother," Loukas said, as he walked away.

Yochanan watched until Loukas disappeared at the bend in the road. He then returned to the house. Crossing the garden, he noticed that the scroll Miryam had been reading was still on the ground. As he began to roll it up, his eyes fell on a verse from one of King David's songs:

> At your right hand stands the queen in gold of Ophir.
> In embroidered apparel threaded with gold she enters.
> With joy and gladness she is led to the king.

49

Magdala gazed lovingly at the old woman. Her delicate skin shone with a light she seemed to carry within.

"Is she sleeping? Is she praying?" she asked Yochanan.

"Ima," Yochanan leaned close to her ear. "A friend has come to see you."

Miryam opened her eyes and looked at Yochanan. Her wrinkled face broke into a warm smile. "Dear son, I had a most unusual dream."

"And what was your dream?"

"I dreamed that I was dancing along the shore, leading the children of Yisrael to freedom—just like Moshe's sister did so long ago. Do you know that I always wished that I could dance, but I never...."

Her voice trailed off as she noticed the woman standing next to him. "Magdala! You are here."

"Yes, dear sister, I am here. I wanted to see you before...." She faltered, unable to say the words.

"Before I die?" Her dark eyes glistened. "Yochanan promised to take me to Yerushalayim when I die and to place my body in the tomb where they buried my son." She paused for a moment. "Will you come with us?"

"No, I cannot." Her voice was tinged with sadness. "I am on a journey to Gaul. Marta and her brother Eleazar are also with us."

"And their sister? Is she going with you?"

"No, she is not strong." Magdala pushed away a strand of gray hair that had fallen across her forehead. "She is unsuited for this work. It would be too hard on her."

Yochanan frowned. "What would you do in Gaul, sister?"

"Yeshua told me to go to his brothers and tell them that he had risen. I will do as he asked and preach his message as long as I can, even to the ends of the earth."

"Do you mean to exalt yourself as an apostle?"

"Do I mean to exalt myself?" she asked, sharply. "No. I would rather be your equal."

"I only meant...."

"Are we not created in the divine image, male and female?" Magdala pressed him. "When we were together in the Upper Room, were we not *all* filled with the Spirit?"

"Magdala knows who she is," Miryam interrupted. "She is not just a follower of my son. He sent her forth as an apostle."

"And that is what I intend to do," Magdala said.

"That is what you *will* do," Miryam said, her voice clear and strong.

Yochanan stared out the window at the darkening hills of Ephesos. "Ima, Magdala has brought us sad news. Miri's son Yaakov was put to death at the time of the siege of Yerushalayim. When he refused to deny his faith, he was cast down from the terrace of the temple."

Miryam shook her head. "I am glad that his dear mother did not live to hear of this. She suffered enough when her daughters, Lysia and Lydia, died. They were such dear girls. I loved them as my own." She took a deep breath. "Have you sent word to Yaakov's brothers?"

"We told them," Magdala said. "Yaakov was a good man. Some say his knees were as hard as a camel's from kneeling in prayer so long."

They were quiet for some time as Miryam sat folding and unfolding her hands. Finally, she spoke. "Try as I might, I cannot remember that song."

"What song?" Magdala asked.

"The song I sang long ago. I cannot remember the melody."

"Why not sing another song?"

Miryam's smile was faint. "I think I have forgotten how to sing. When you are young, and there are bright days, it is easy to sing. But when you grow old and have seen dark days, it is hard…. It might even be impossible."

"Ima, the time is growing near," Yochanan interrupted. "We must take you to the boat before the Shabbat."

Magdala held Miryam's face in her hands. "Dear mother, when your days on earth are ended, you will celebrate the Shabbat in Paradise for all time to come." Kissing her tenderly, she left the room in tears.

50

The voyage to Yerushalayim was difficult. When they docked at Yafo, the ancient port-of-entry on the Mediterranean Sea, Miryam was so ill and had lost so much weight that many believed she would die. They began to prepare a grave for her, but before it was finished she recovered and felt strong enough to continue.

But the arduous trip by land was worse. With her loved ones at her side, she died reciting the words she heard in the temple long ago: "Now you can dismiss your servant in peace, for you have fulfilled your word and my eyes have seen your salvation."

Shlomit and the other women dressed her in a white linen garment. Over the shroud they placed a blue pall, as bright as the morning sky. The men bore her litter in a solemn procession down the steep slope out of Yerushalayim, then up the mount to a grotto where they laid her in the tomb as she had wished.

Miryam's nephew Shimon stood at the foot of the bier. Now in his fifties, he had been elected head of the church to replace his brother Yaakov. Tearfully, he chanted:

> *May Adonai Eloheinu be exalted.*
>   *May He be sanctified in the world.*
> *May the Holy One give life to the dead*
>   *and raise them to eternal life.*
> *May He rebuild Yerushalayim and restore His temple.*
> *May the Holy One reign in His sovereign splendor*
>   *forever and ever.*

The mourners intoned "Amen."

May the Holy One who creates peace in His celestial heights, create peace for us and for all Yisrael.

"Amen. Amen," they answered.

Yochanan bent to kiss the pall. "You are the glory of Yerushalayim; you are the great boast of Yisrael. You are the pride of our nation."

While they stood in solemn homage, the angel Gavriel, absent for so long, returned unseen. Gazing at Miryam's body, the angel lifted her gently, as one carries a sleeping child. In a nearby olive tree the plaintive song of a dove could be heard. The little bird had found its home.

First-Century Israel

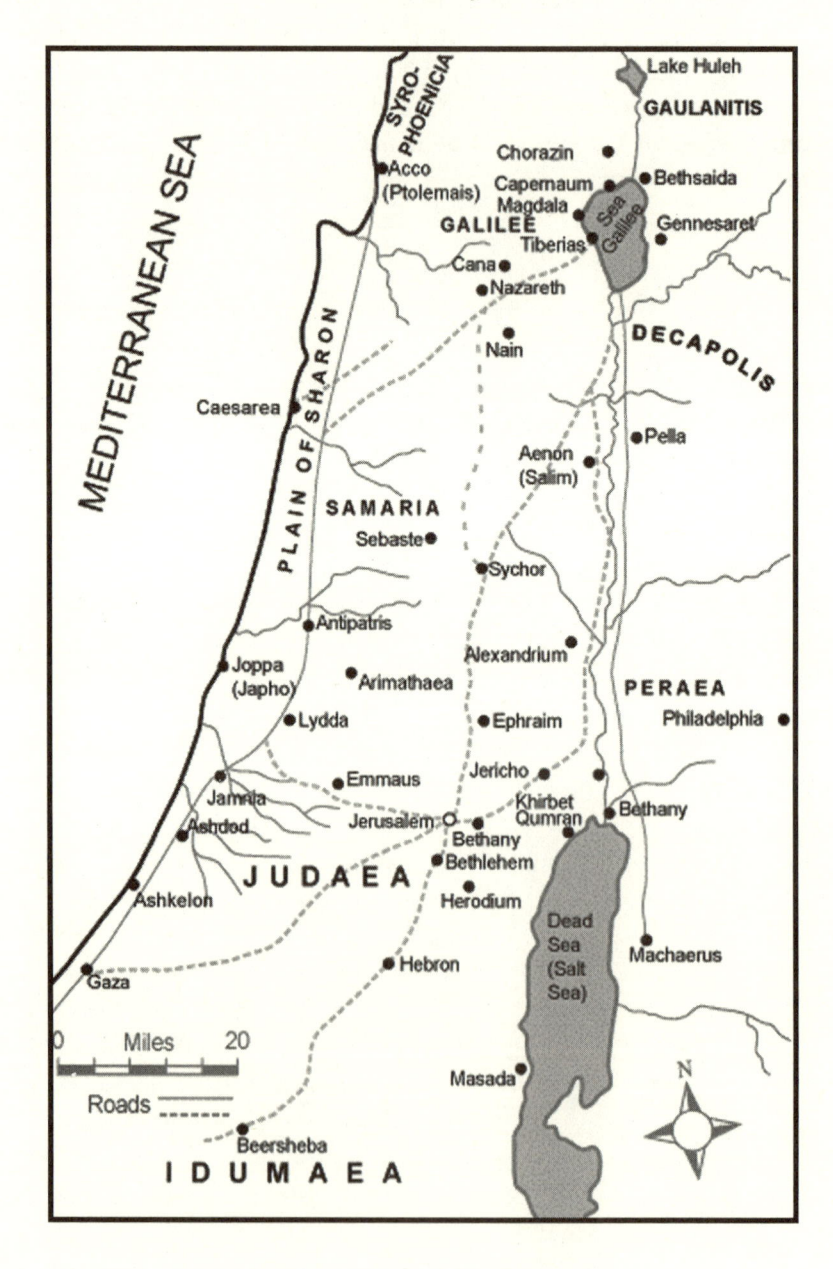

Glossary

Hebrew words for names and places are used throughout this book to honor the Jewish people of the First Covenant.

Abba—(Aramaic) Father, denotes family intimacy
Abu—(Arabic) Father
Abud—(Arabic) Bedouin bread
Adonai—Lord
Adonai Eloheinu—Lord, our God
Afikoman—a piece of matzah, hidden, and eaten at the end of the Passover meal
Aharon—Aaron, Moses' brother
Ain Karem—Ein Kerem, "House of the Vineyard," a village southwest of Jerusalem
Aleph Bet—the Hebrew alphabet
Alexandreus—(Greek) Alexandria, city in Egypt named for Alexander the Great
Alexandros—(Greek) Alexander III of Macedon, commonly known as Alexander the Great
Alláh—(Arabic) Name of God
Amen—So be it! It is true! Yes indeed!
Am—People
Am HaAretz—People of the Land, poor and illiterate
Am HaSefer—People of the Book, Jews after the Exile
Ammaus—a town about seven miles from Jerusalem
Andreas—(Greek) Andrew, apostle, brother of Simon Peter
Annas—father-in-law of Caiaphas, the High Priest
Antipas—son of Herod the Great, tetrarch of Galilee who ruled throughout Jesus' ministry
Archelaus—son of Herod the Great, ethnarch of Samaria, Judea, and Idumea
Avigal—Abigail, King David's wife
Avraham—Abraham, patriarch

Ayin Hara—an evil eye, jealousy, an arrogant spirit, a greedy soul (Al Ayn, Arabic)

Ayin Tovah—a good eye, to see the good, to look at things positively

Baal—Baal, master, lord, title for various gods

Balaam—a soothsayer hired by the king of Moab to put a curse on the Israelites

Balthazar—one of three magi

Bar—(Aramaic, Hebrew: ben) son; before a name, "son of"

Barabba—Barabbas, "son of the father"

Beit—house

Beit Ani—Bethany, "House of Poverty"

Beit HaMidrash—"House of Learning," secondary school for boys

Beit HaSefer—"House of the Book," primary school for boys

Beit Lechem—Bethlehem, "House of Bread"

Beit Pagey—Bethpage, "House of Figs"

Beit Tzaidah—Bethsaida, "House of Fishermen"

Benyamin—Benjamin, youngest son of Jacob and Rachel

Beresheet—Genesis ("In the beginning…"), the first book of the Jewish Bible

Brit—covenant, a contract

Brit Milah—covenant of circumcision

Chametz—leaven

Chanukah—Hanukkah, also known as the Festival of Lights and Feast of Dedication, the eight-day Jewish holiday commemorating the rededication of the Temple

Charoset—mixture of fruits, nuts, and wine eaten at Passover

Chavah—Eve, the first woman

Chislev—ninth month of the Jew's religious calendar

Cleopas—one of two disciples on the road to Emmaus

Daniyel—Daniel, prophet

Dayenu—("It would have been enough!") a song in gratitude for God's gifts sung at the Passover

Denarius—(plural, denarii) Roman silver coin equal to a day's wages

Devorah—Deborah, prophet and judge

Echad—one and only; alone

Eleazar—("God is my help") Lazarus, brother of Martha and Mary

Elisheva—Elizabeth

Eli, Eli, lema sabachthani—"My God, My God, why have you forsaken me?"

Eliyahu—("My God is the Lord") Elijah the Prophet

Eliysha—Elisha the Prophet, disciple of Elijah

Eloheinu—Our God

Elohim—God, Most High

El Shaddai—God Almighty

Ephesos—(Greek) Ephesus, city on west coast of Asia Minor

Essenes—monastic ascetics who flourished in the second century B.C.E., along with the Pharisees and Sadducees.

Ethnarch—the governor of a province

Exactor Mortis—(Latin, "to drive forth death") centurion in charge of soldiers who carried out a crucifixion

Ezrat Kohanim—Priests' Courtyard in the temple

Ezrat Nashim—Women's Courtyard in the temple

Ezrat Yisrael—Men's Courtyard in the temple

Galil—Galilee, Sea of Galilee, also called Tiberius for second Roman Emperor

Gaspar—Caspar, one of three magi

Gat Shemanim—Gethsemane ("oil press")

Gavriel—Angel Gabriel ("God is my strength")

Gei Hinnom—Gehenna, Valley of Hinnom

Ghareeb—(Arabic, plural Ghurabaa) stranger, foreigner

Goyim—(singular goy) Gentiles

Gulgota—Golgotha (Latin, "Calvary")

Haftarah—a selection from one of the books of the Prophets read after the Torah reading

Haggadah—"The Telling" [of the story], the text of the Exodus read at the Passover Seder

Hallel—chant of praise consisting of Psalms 113 to 118 sung during Passover and other holidays

Halleluyah—Hallelujah (Latin: "Alleluia"), "Let us praise"

Ha Kadosh—The Holy One

Halakhah—Jewish law, "the path that one walks"

Hannah—Anna, mother of the prophet Samuel, mother of Mary, Jesus' mother

HaShem—"The Holy Name," used in place of the sacred name of God (YHWH)

Hechal—The Holy Place, the sanctuary in the temple

Hoshana—Hosanna, cry of praise, an appeal for divine help—"please save" or "save now"

Idus Martii—(Latin) 15th day of March in the Roman calendar

Ima—(Aramaic) Mother

Izevel—Jezebel, evil wife of King Ahab who forced Elijah to flee for his life

Kaddish—mourners' prayer for the dead

Kaisereia—Caesarea, the name of two cities in Israel

Kanah—village of Cana

Karmel—Mount Carmel in northern Israel

Kayafa—Caiaphas, High Priest

Kefa—(Cephas) "rock" in Aramaic; the Greek equivalent is Petros, Peter

Kfar Nahum—village of Capernaum

Khamsin—(Arabic) dust-filled windstorms occurring in North Africa around the Mediterranean and the Arabian Peninsula

Kiddush—cup of sanctification at Passover

Klofah—Clopas

Kodesh HaKodashim—Holy of Holies

Kohen—priest (plural kohanim)

Kohen HaGadol—High Priest

L'Chaim—"To Life," used as a toast

Levi—(plural Leviim) son of Jacob; tribe that served in temple; another name for Matthew, disciple (See Mattityahu.)

Loukas—(Greek) Luke, evangelist

Magi—wise men from the East, astrologists and philosophers

Manna—miraculous food sent to the Israelites during their forty years in the desert

Marcus—Mark, disciple, evangelist

Marcus Antonius—Mark Antony, Roman politician and general

Maror—bitter herbs eaten at Passover

Mashiach—Messiah (Greek, Christos)

Matzah—(plural matzot) unleavened bread eaten at Passover

Mattityahu—Matthew, also called Levi, disciple

Melchior—one of three magi

Menorah—seven-branched candlestick in the temple or synagogue

Mezuzah—a case containing parchments inscribed with verses from the

Torah and placed on the doorpost of the house

Mikhah—Micah, a minor prophet

Mikveh—(plural mikvot) an immersion bath used for ritual purification

Minyan—a quorum; ten adult Jewish men required for a religious assembly

Miryam—Mary (nickname, Miri); Moses' sister; Mother of the Lord

Mitzvah—(plural mitzvot) commandment; doing a good deed

Moshe—Moses

Moshe Rabbenu—Moses, our teacher/rabbi

Naftali—Naphtali, one of the twelve tribes of Israel

Nahum—a minor prophet

Nakdimon—Nicodemus

Nathanael—disciple, also known as Bartholomew (Bar Talmai, son of Talmai)

Natzeret—Nazareth

Nissan—the first month of the Jewish Year in the spring, month of the Passover

Noach—Noah, patriarch

Olam HaBah—the world to come, the afterlife

Olam HaZeh—the present world, this age

Paulos—Paul (Hebrew name, Saul) of Tarsus, evangelist

Perush—(plural Perushim) Pharisee, the Separated Ones, one of three Jewish sects flourishing in the second century B.C.E., the others being the Sadducees and the Essenes

Pesach—Passover, one of three pilgrimage festivals along with Shavuot and Sukkot

Petros—(Greek) Peter, "rock" in Aramaic

Philippos—(Greek) Philip, apostle

Pontius Pilatus—Pontius Pilate, Roman procurator of the province of Judea

Posca—sour wine or vinegar mixed with water, a standard beverage for Roman soldiers

Procurator—title of governors appointed by Rome over Judea, later over most of Palestine

Qumran—Essene community located a mile inland from the northwestern shore of the Dead Sea

Rabbenu—"Our Teacher," a title given to Moses and all great teachers who followed

Rabboni—(Aramaic) "My Great Master"
Reuven—Reuben, one of Jacob's sons
Rivka—Rebekah, Isaac's wife
Rosh Hashanah—Head of the New Year
Ruach—breath, wind, spirit
Ruach Ha Kodesh—the Holy Spirit
Rut—Ruth, ancestress of David and Jesus
Salām—(Arabic) peace be upon you
Shabbat—Sabbath
Shalom—peace, blessing, hello, goodbye
Shalom Aleichem—"Peace be with you."
Shaul—Saul, first king of Israel; Paul, apostle
Shavuot—(Greek, Pentecost) one of three pilgrimage festivals along with Pesach and Sukkot
Shechinah—Divine Presence; the "shadow of the Almighty"
Shekel—Jewish coin, about one-half ounce
Shema—"Hear!" (Deuteronomy 6:4), centerpiece of the Jewish morning and evening prayers
Shema Yisrael. Adonai Eloheinu, Adonai, echad.—Judaism's central proclamation: "Hear, O Israel! The Lord is our God, the Lord alone!"
Sheol—Hades, Hell; the place or abode of the dead
Shimon—Simeon, one of Jacob's sons; kinsman of Jesus; a prophet in the temple; the Zealot
Shimon Kefa—Simon Peter, disciple, apostle
Shlomit—Salome
Shlomo—Solomon, David's son, king of Israel
Shmuel—Samuel, prophet and judge, means "God has heard"
Shofar—ram's horn blown on Jewish feasts of Rosh Hashanah and Yom Kippur
Shomron—Samaria
Shoshana—Hebrew name meaning "rose"
Sukkot—Feast of Booths; one of three pilgrimage festivals along with Pesach and Shavuot
Tallit—prayer shawl, an outer garment edged with fringes (tzitzit)
Tav—the 22nd, and last, letter of the Hebrew alphabet; in ancient Hebrew, shaped in an "x" or a cross

Tefutzah—the Diaspora, the dispersion of Jewish people after the Exile

Tefillin—(Greek, phylacteries) leather boxes containing scrolls inscribed with verses from the Torah, worn on the forehead and the arm by Jewish men during morning prayers

Tehillim—Book of Psalms, songs of praise

Theophilus—(Greek, "Lover of God") Luke's patron

Tekton—(Greek) a craftsman, a worker in wood or stone

Torah—teaching, the Law (in Greek, "Pentateuch," the first five books of the Law, also the entire Hebrew Scripture—the Law, the Prophets and the Writings)

Triclinium—(Latin) a formal dining room in a Roman building

Tzedakah—righteousness, the religious obligation to do what is right and just

Tzaddikim—(singular Tzadok), Sadducees, righteous man, Jewish sect flourishing in the second century along with the Pharisees and Essenes

Tzadok—Zadok, King Solomon's High Priest

Tzidon—Sidon

Tzippori—Sepphoris

Tzitzit—tassels attached to prayer shawl (tallit) as a reminder to keep God's law

Tziyon—Zion

Veronika—Veronica

Yaakov—Jacob, son of Isaac; James, kinsman of Jesus; James, disciple, apostle, brother of John

Yabok River—Jabbok River

Yafo—Joppa, a port city in Israel on the Mediterranean Sea

Yair—Jairus, synagogue leader in Capernaum

Yarden—Jordan (River, Valley)

Yechezkel—Ezekiel, prophet during the Exile ("God will strengthen"), Father of Judaism

Yehudah—Judea; Judah, Jacob's fourth son, kinsman of Jesus

Yehudah Ishkerioth—Judas [man from] Iscariot

Yehudi—Jew, Judean (plural Yehudim), a citizen of Judah

Yehudit—Jewess; Judith, heroine in the Bible

Yericho—Jericho

Yerushalayim—Jerusalem ("Foundation of Peace")

Yeshayahu—Isaiah, prophet ("God is salvation")

Yeshua—Jesus, variant of Joshua, successor to Moses

Yetzer HaRa—the inclination to do evil, by violating the will of God

Yetzer HaTov—the inclination to do good, desire to do the will of God

Yirmeyahu—Jeremiah ('God will raise up'), a prophet

Yisrael—Israel, son of Isaac whose primary name was Jacob

Yitzchak—Isaac, son of Abraham

Yizreel Valley— Jezreel Valley, also known as the "Valley of Megiddo" and the Plain of Esdraelon (Greek)

Yoachim—Joachim, Mary's father, husband of Anna

Yochanan—John, son of Zebedee and brother of James, disciples

Yochanan ben Zecharya—John the Baptist, son of Zechariah

Yoel—Joel, a minor prophet

Yom Kippur—Day of Atonement

Yonah—Jonah

Yonatan—Jonathan

Yosef—Joseph, husband of Mary (Yosi); kinsman of Jesus; son of Jacob and Rachel

Yosef Beit Ramatayim—Joseph of Arimathea

Yoshiyah—Josiah, King of Israel

Zachor—to remember the Sabbath, to observe the law

Zakkai—Zacchaeus

Zavdai—Zebedee, father of James and John, fishermen

Zecharya—Zechariah, a minor prophet; the father of John the Baptist

Zealots—members of a fanatical sect in Judea during the first century, militantly opposing the Roman domination of Palestine

A Note from the Author

My mother told me that, from the time I was a little girl, I always had a pencil in my hand, scribbling pictures or scratching out stories. Auntie Marie, my mother's sister, was an unmarried woman who lived with us in those post-Depression days. She was my role model, although I'm sure she never thought of herself that way. Although she never realized her dream to be an artist, she taught me to draw, and more importantly, how to see. "Look at that tree! What colors do you see?" she asked. "Green," I answered. "Look again, what else do you see?" I looked closer and was excited to see a myriad of colors—yellow, brown, orange, purple, and more.

When my aunt died, I wanted one of her paintings, which I remembered seeing in my bedroom as a child. It was a watercolor of Mary holding the infant Jesus in her arms, standing on a globe with a serpent under her feet. To me it was a sign that Mary would guard me from harm. But as I grew older, Mary remained on the wall, a painted figure from the dim past. Her many lofty titles—Blessed Virgin, Immaculate Conception, Queen of Angels, Queen of Heaven, Mother of God—made her seem even more remote.

I often wondered what the flesh and blood Mary of Nazareth was like. How would she speak to people today? What sort of role model would she be? Did she have the same hopes and dreams that we have?

Like her son, Mary cannot be captured by any single image. She was a daughter, a sister, a wife, a mother, and a widow. She was a poor woman, a refugee, and often homeless. Mary was a woman of joy at the nativity and a woman of sorrow at the cross.

In writing *Song of the Dove*, it was my purpose to present Mary in a way that enables contemporary believers to encounter her in their own lives. Although I have made every effort to present historical events accurately, this is a novel, not a history book. Just as good storytellers, poets and painters translate insights into verbal or visual forms that move us, my intention is to move you, the reader, to take another look at Mary's story as we know it from Scripture, Tradition, apocryphal sources, and even art.

In doing so, I have endeavored to be faithful to my Auntie Marie's artistic vision: "What do you see?" and paint her with as many colors that I have available on my palette. My hope is that the story of Mary of Nazareth will be a prism to illuminate the lives of both women and men today.

My thanks to the Writers' Club of Whittier, California, and to my readers: Janet Dovidio, Maureen Krock, and Marie Manahan. Special thanks to my husband Bob for his continuing support of my work. Finally, thanks to those at ACTA Publications, including Gregory F. Augustine Pierce, publisher; Charles Fiore, editor; Patricia A. Lynch, designer; Mary Southard, CSJ, cover artist; and Richard Fung, proofreader.